JUST HAVEN'T MET YOU YET

CATE WOODS

Quercus

First published in Great Britain in 2016 by

Quercus Editions Limited
Carmelite House
50 Victoria Embankment
London EC4Y 0DZ

An Hachette UK company

A CIP catalogue record for this book is available
from the British Library

PB ISBN 978 1 78429 374 1
EBOOK ISBN 978 1 78429 375 8

This book is a work of fiction. Names, characters,
businesses, organisations, places and events are
either the product of the author's imagination
or used fictitiously. Any resemblance to
actual persons, living or dead, events or
locales is entirely coincidental.

10 9 8 7 6 5 4 3 2 1

Typeset by Jouve (UK), Milton Keynes

Printed and bound in Great Britain by Clays Ltd, St Ives plc

Cate Woods made the most of her degree in Anglo-Saxon Literature by starting her career making tea on TV programmes including *The Big Breakfast*, *Who Wants to be a Millionaire* and *French & Saunders*. After narrowly missing out on the chance to become a Channel 5 weather girl she moved into journalism, where she interviewed every famous John, from Prescott to Bon Jovi, ghostwrote a weekly magazine column for a footballer's wife and enjoyed a brief stint as one half of *Closer* magazine's gossip-columnist duo, 'Mr & Mrs Showbiz'. Cate left the magazine world in 2009 to pursue a full-time career in ghostwriting and has since written a number of bestsellers, none of which have her name on. She lives in London with her husband (not Mr Showbiz) and two small children. *Just Haven't Met You Yet* is her first novel under her own name.

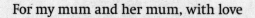

For my mum and her mum, with love

1

GET YOUR GLASTO GLAM ON!

Festival fashion essentials for all budgets

With Coachella just around the corner it's time to start planning your festival wardrobe. This summer we'll be saying no-ho to boho: the hippest chicks at Lovebox and Latitude will be rocking a Bananarama-meets-Joan-of-Arc vibe. Think plaid shirts layered with boiled-wool sweats and lurex legwarmers over distressed suede booties. Add a pop of colour with neon nails and complete the look with faux dreadlocks, tanned legs and a swipe of frosted eyeshadow.

Ooh, I love that sequinned mini-kilt. Very Kate Moss at Glastonbury circa 2005, and just gorgeous with those slouchy boots and army jacket. It's the sort of skirt you could wear all year round: with tights in the winter, flip-flops in the summer, even over a bikini if you were in, say, Monte Carlo, or *The Only Way is Essex*. Actually, when you think about it, a sequinned mini-kilt is one of those staples, like a perfectly cut white shirt or jeans, which every stylish woman needs in her wardrobe. Yes, it is a little on the pricey side, but it is an investment piece that I could pass on to my future daughter. If today goes as planned, I could buy it for myself as a congratulations present! Or as a commiserations present, although we really won't go there . . .

Either way, I badly want this skirt. I *need* it. BUT:

a) I cannot afford it (it is £620).

b) I do not have the figure for it. Unlike the model, whose legs are like perfectly knobbly Twiglets, mine are Cornetto-shaped: the cone of my lower legs steadily widening towards the ice cream bulge of my upper thighs.

c) I have never been to Monte Carlo or indeed a festival (unless you count 'Folk on the Pier 2011' in Cromer) and, at the age of thirty-one, I'm unlikely to start going to them in the future.

Lost in unrequited skirt love, it takes me a moment to realise that the train is slowing down. I glance up from my magazine: thank God, it looks like we're finally arriving in London . . . But where's the platform?

'Sorry, folks, it's your guard here again, we're just being held at another red signal outside Liverpool Street. I don't know about you, but I had no idea there were so many signals between Norfolk and London! Ha ha! Anyway, just relax and I'm sure we'll be on the move shortly.'

Relax? *Relax?* Over the past three and three-quarter hours we have been delayed by leaves on the line, sheep on the line, 'excessive heat on the tracks outside Diss' (it's April) and the onboard buffet had to close due to an unspecified incident with the hot savouries. This journey has been nothing short of Railmageddon, and as disaster has piled onto catastrophe our guard has remained as cheery and upbeat as Dick Van Dyke high-kicking his way across the rooftops in *Mary Poppins*. Well, perhaps I could be a bit more Zen about the EXTREME BLOODY LATE-NESS of this train if this were just another day, Mr Van Dyke, but this is definitely not just another day. Not by a long stretch.

Have you ever had the feeling that someone else is living your life, and the one you've ended up with wasn't meant for you at all? I, for instance, suspect that I was meant to have the life currently being lived by Gwyneth Paltrow, but at a critical moment a butterfly in the Amazon flapped its wings, my life took a radically different turn and instead of Hollywood I ended up in Norwich. Chaos Theory, I believe it's called. I'm a little hazy on the details, but I'm sure it's all on Wikipedia.

Take my name: Perseus Andromeda James. Surely that's a name that belongs in the pages of *Heat* magazine, not on an Eagle Insurance employee name badge? (Although what the badge actually says is 'Percy James', which is what everyone except my dad calls me. He saw the film *Clash of the Titans* shortly before I was born and it had a major impact on him, so much so that not only did he name me after the film's male hero, my middle name Andromeda is the girl Perseus rescues from a sea monster. I hope I won't be spoiling *Clash of the Titans* for you if I tell you that Perseus and Andromeda end up getting married, so not only is my name a bit of a mouthful, it's effectively like being called 'Becks Posh'.)

Anyway, after spending my adult years feeling like I'm in some sort of flight-holding pattern, circling around the clouds enjoying the complimentary nuts and G&Ts, it finally looks like things are about to get interesting. Fasten your seatbelts, ladies and gentlemen, make sure your tray table is stowed and your seat is in the upright position, because we're beginning our descent into Excitement Airport, Big-Time City! I have a job interview that could – and I really don't think I'm exaggerating here – change the entire course of my life. In terms of significant personal events, I imagine this is up there with marriage and motherhood. It is the FA Cup, the Oscars and Christmas all rolled into one. In short: top-level shit. And I was meant to be at this game-changer of an interview eight – *God, no* – twelve minutes ago.

In need of distraction, I rummage in my bag for the stack of post I retrieved from the mat as I ran out the door this morning – although I'm not sure a pizza menu, mobile phone bill and one other envelope can really be described as a 'stack'. I squash the menu into my empty coffee cup, return the bill to my bag unopened and turn my attention to the mystery envelope, which has 'NOT A CIRCULAR' stamped on the outside. With a slight frown, I tear it open and read its non-circular contents.

Dear Miss James,

I am writing to you on behalf of EROS Technologies, a company dedicated to the science of lifestyle enhancement.

Please forgive the unsolicited approach, but we have a very exciting opportunity that we wish to discuss with you at your earliest convenience.

Due to the highly personal nature of this matter I'm afraid I cannot provide any further information at this stage, but if you would like to call me on one of the numbers below at your convenience I will be happy to explain our unique proposition in detail.

Thank you very much for your time and I look forward to hearing from you.

Yours sincerely,

Theresa Lefevre

Account Director

EROS Technologies

Hmmm. That *is* intriguing. 'Lifestyle enhancement' sounds like it might have something to do with cosmetic surgery: a special offer on boob jobs or Botox, perhaps. I read about this amazing new treatment the other day where this machine freezes your fat, zaps it with a laser and it just simply . . . *melts* away. It sounds incredible: you can literally remould your bum into whatever shape you want – be that the Knowles, the Middleton or something rather more retro, like the Vorderman – in a matter of minutes, as if it's Play-Doh. Ooh, perhaps this company, EROS Technologies, are offering a free trial! That would definitely qualify as a 'unique proposition'. I should phone this Theresa LeFevre right away to make sure I get my name down for the J. Lo . . . On second thoughts, the reception is notoriously bad on this train line and I don't want to be cut off in the middle of hearing about the lasers. No, better to wait until I'm home. I fold up the letter and put it back in my bag.

The train *still* isn't moving, so I apply another coat of mascara. I think I must be suffering from OCD – Obsessive Cosmetic Disorder – because whenever I'm feeling jittery I reach for my make-up bag. After this nightmare of a journey my eyelashes are so clumpy that rather than the 'Billion Lashes' promised by this mascara, it looks like I have about six.

Then at last the train jolts into motion again. *Yes!* I pull out my phone to send an email.

Dear Mia,
I'm so sorry for the delay but I'm just arriving at Liverpool Street and will be with you in about 20 minutes.

I hesitate – how to sign off? Mia is the MD of hyper-cool events company Saboteur Entertainment, and potentially my new boss. 'Yours sincerely' seems way too formal. 'Kind regards'? No, too cosy. I plump for '*Ciao*'.

A couple of Tube stops and a short bus ride later I arrive in Dalston Kingsland. It's not an area of London I know well, but I can tell it is extremely trendy by the number of young men with twirly moustaches of the sort favoured by olden-days strongmen. As I follow the directions provided by Mia to Saboteur's offices I get a little thrill at the thought that this could soon be my morning commute: stopping at this charming vegan bakery for one of their 'hemp croissants', or picking up a cappuccino from this very cool coffee shop, outside which a young chap wearing a waistcoat and fob watch is smoking an actual pipe.

I *so* want this job. It's not that I'm particularly miserable at Eagle Insurance – although after ten years in the same office I am certainly ready for a different challenge, or at least a different view – it's just that I've always imagined I would end up as something a bit more exciting than PA to the CEO of Norfolk's Premier Independent Insurance Provider. So the idea of working for a company that has offices in Ibiza and Los Angeles and has organised parties for the likes of Elton John, Google and Jennifer Lopez sounds like the answer to my decade-long prayers.

I nearly missed the job advert during my weekly trawl of the employment websites, because rather than 'Office

Manager' the position was advertised as 'work/play zone director' (all lower case, a dead-cert signifier of coolness) and it was only because I recognised the name Saboteur Entertainment from the party pages of *Hello!* that I read the small print and discovered they were looking for someone 'organised' (me) and 'media savvy' (*so* me) to 'manage their bustling London office' (me me me!).

Of course, if I did get the job it would mean renting out my flat and moving to London, so I wouldn't see Adam quite as much. In my darker moments I wonder if this is madness. After all, I am in possession of what we women are led to believe is the Holy Grail: a considerate, successful boyfriend with a Clooneyesque twinkle who knows his way around a tool kit. If he were a car, Adam would be a Volvo 4 x 4: rugged, reliable, not as flashy as a Range Rover, but just as capable off-road, if you get my drift! (I'm a Fiat Punto, possibly a Golf GTI convertible if I've spent ages on my make-up and am wearing boob-to-knee Spanx.) My mother likes to joke that if John Lewis sold son-in-laws they would be exactly like Adam, and she has made it clear that if I move to London he will dump me for someone less 'flighty' and I will have no one to blame but myself. But, as I said to Adam last night, I think it might actually be good for our relationship not to live in each other's pockets the whole time – and we could still get together at weekends. I have this fantasy of waking up together in my bijou Thames-side apartment on a

Saturday morning and strolling to Borough Market to buy artisanal breads and cheeses, then stopping off at the Tate Modern. Adam would love it, I'm sure, and it would do him good to get out of his comfort zone. As wonderful as he is, he can be a bit too . . . *sensible*. For instance, when I first told him about this job his immediate response was to ask about the benefits package. Not – 'Wow, think of all the amazing parties we'll be able to go to!' No, Adam wanted to know about 'flexible pension provision' and 'group health insurance', which is obviously very prudent, but a bit of excitement wouldn't have gone amiss. So this would be a fresh start for both of us – and even the strongest relationship can benefit from the occasional kick up the arse, right?

I follow the directions down a cobbled alleyway and I end up outside a long, single-storey warehouse with metal grilles at all the windows and clumps of weeds poking out of the gutters. To those of an unimaginative, suburban mindset it might look rather grim, but I bet Elton and J. Lo just adore its gritty urban vibe. With a surge of excitement I press the intercom button and as the door buzzes open I ruffle my hair, which is thick, strawberry-blondish and the only bit of me that looks half decent in its natural state, and enter with a smile that says: 'Behold, your new work/play zone director!'

The reception area is empty except for a few hard-backed chairs and a front desk, behind which there is a girl wearing red-and-yellow stripy dungarees and a large spotty bow tie. Christ, is this what the cool kids are wearing these days? It's probably vintage Issey Miyake, but the vibe is undeniably clown-like. She's even wearing a big artificial flower on her lapel that looks exactly one of those ones that squirt – *oh*.

As water drips down my face, I rummage in my bag for a tissue. No tissue. Fab.

'I'm here for the interview,' I say, dabbing at my face with my pale-blue cashmere-mix scarf, leaving it streaked with several of my eight coats of mascara. 'Percy James. I'm sorry I'm so late.'

The receptionist pulls out one of those comedy car horns and gives it a double honk. A moment later a man appears. He is reassuringly moustachioed, but the rest of his look pretty much screams Ringmaster.

'Roll up, roll up!' he says, with a dandyish tip of his top hat. 'Are you here for the advanced clowning skills seminar?'

'Um, is this Saboteur Entertainment?'

He looks disappointed. 'This is the Hackney Circus Academy. You'll want next door.'

Mia is utterly lovely about me being so late and very sweetly doesn't ask why my hair is soaked. Perhaps it happens a lot. I was expecting Saboteur's offices to be intimidating, but actually they're very cosy: invitingly squishy sofas, vases of peonies dotted about the place and poster-sized photos from their past events decorating the pale-grey walls. And far from being some helmet-haired power bitch Mia seems completely normal, albeit extremely pretty and pixyish – like a platinum-blonde Björk with a killer manicure.

We sit in the meeting room with soya cappuccinos and Mia asks about my current job and responsibilities. She seems genuinely interested when I tell her about the new expenses system that I brought in at Eagle and laughs when I describe my attempts to persuade the more senior members of staff to start tweeting. I'm not one to blow my own trumpet – and I don't want to tempt fate here – but I honestly can't imagine how this interview could be going any better. In fact, half an hour in and I'm pretty sure I've nailed it.

'If it's okay, I'd like to ask you a few more general questions so I can get more of an idea what sort of person you are,' says Mia. 'We're a small company, so it's important we get the right fit, personality-wise. Is that okay?'

'Fire away!' I smile. I *so* want her to like me.

'Great. Well, first of all, how do you like to spend your weekends?'

Now, the truth is that I usually spend the weekend hanging out with Adam, reading the papers, watching DVDs, perhaps having Sunday lunch at the pub. But I don't think the truth is necessarily what's important here. What I think Mia is more interested in is the *essence* of who I am – which is lucky, because my essence is way more exciting than the rest of me.

'Well, I'm really into clubbing,' I say. 'I go whenever I can. I'll kick things off on a Friday night at Fabric and then move on to the Ministry. Sometimes I don't get home until Sunday evening!'

Mia seems surprised. Damn, I knew I shouldn't have worn this Boden dress. It was called 'Sassy Shift' in the catalogue, but I really thought it could pass for Whistles.

'So I'm guessing your ideal holiday would be somewhere like Ibiza?'

'Yeah, well, of course the clubs are epic, but I'm a bit of a thrill-seeker, so when I get some time off I like to do something that gets me out of my comfort zone. I'm thinking about a high-altitude trek in Tibet next year.'

'Blimey, you're quite the action woman! Any other challenges on your list?'

'Well, I've just started learning Krav Maga.'

Mia looks blank.

'It's an Israeli martial art,' I say airily. 'Lots of kicking and . . . chopping. And I've just bought a banjo.' (The bullshit gods are clearly smiling on me here, because I read a feature on 'hot new hobbies' in *Style* magazine the other weekend and updated my CV accordingly.) 'Oh, and I'm thinking about starting a pop-up restaurant in my flat. Something small and informal, you know? Probably Scandinavian-inspired. Herrings and . . . stuff. I might do a couple of nights for friends and then see where it leads.'

'Wow,' says Mia. 'Do you ever find time to sleep?'

'Rarely,' I say, with a little shrug and a rueful smile. *This is SO in the bag!*

We chat for a bit longer and then Mia walks me back to the door. I am feeling invincible, like I imagine a footballer does after scoring a hat-trick. We pass a group of people chatting by a coffee machine and I have to stop myself high-fiving each of them in turn and lifting my dress over my head.

But when Mia turns to say goodbye her expression isn't entirely reassuring.

'Percy, you seem like a lovely girl, and your skills and experience are spot on for the role, but I think it's only fair to let you know now that we won't be taking your application any further.'

My stomach lurches. 'Oh,' I manage eventually. 'Ah. I see.'

'The thing is, we're looking for someone quite . . . steady for this particular role. A safe pair of hands, you know? And what with all the clubbing and Krav Maga and kite-surfing (*kite-surfing?* Christ, of course, that was something else I put in my CV) you just seem too, well, far too cool for us. I actually think someone like you would find the position rather dull! I hope you understand.'

Inside I am screaming so loudly that I'm surprised Mia doesn't hear. The truth is I that haven't been inside a nightclub since I was twenty-three, and that was only because I thought it was Wagamamas. My last holiday was a cheese-tasting weekend in Somerset. There is barely enough room in my flat for a pop-up book, let alone a sodding restaurant! And – oh God – why did I sign that email *Ciao*?

But, of course, I say none of this. How could I, without sounding like a total nutter? So I just smile and thank Mia for her time, then walk back along the cobbles feeling like I have screwed up my last chance to make something of myself and have been sentenced to life in mediocrity, no chance of parole.

2

I make it back to Liverpool Street station as if on auto-pilot. Actually, that's not quite true; I make it back to Dalston High Street as if on autopilot and then I realise that I am very, very hungry. Despair always gives me an appetite. I stop at the vegan bakery and buy a 'sausage' roll and a slice of 'cheese' cake, which I bolt down without even tasting (probably not a bad thing) and then, replete with rehydrated textured wheat protein, I get the bus back to Liverpool Street station where the Norwich train is perversely early. It's as if Anglia Rail is taunting me: 'You don't belong in London . . . Get thee back to Norwich . . .'

The interview with Mia is playing in an endless loop in my head like a horror movie, with me as the dumb cheerleader who decides it would be a totally, like, *awesome* idea to investigate that spooky cabin in the woods. How could I have screwed things up so badly? I had the right qualifications, the interview was going brilliantly – and then at the very last minute I managed to snatch defeat from the jaws of victory. Honestly, it was a masterclass in fuckwittery. I know when I tell Adam what happened he's sure to go on about how the job wasn't right for me and that I'm on a solid career path at Eagle Insurance and a valued employee and blah blah blah, but he'll be completely missing the point! This wasn't just the chance of a new job, it was the chance – and at my age, probably the last I'll get – of a new *life*.

I buy *Grazia* and two packets of Munchies and then board the train. I usually go for a rear-facing seat, as I once read that you're more likely to survive a rail crash in that position, but right now, feeling pretty ambivalent about survival, I opt for front-facing. Fate, do your worst.

Moments later an old lady in a mackintosh, headscarf and tan tights stops at the seat opposite me, easing herself down with a gentle 'oof'. Judging by her twinkly smile and laser-like eye contact she is clearly up for a chat. Usually I enjoy talking to senior citizens on the train (it brightens their day and you often learn something useful, like how to get stubborn stains off china teacups using denture cleaner), but I suddenly feel very tired, so I return her smile and then yawn and close my eyes in the international sign for *Do Not Disturb*.

'Sorry, love, this is the Ipswich train, isn't it?'

I open my eyes. 'Yes, it is.'

'Oh good. It's just they never make it very clear, do they?'

'Don't worry, this is definitely going through Ipswich.' I close my eyes again and snuggle myself into a foetal sleeping position, just to make sure we're both on the same page.

'Goodness, isn't it a lovely day for April? Summer's come early this year! Have you been visiting London?'

'I had a job interview,' I say, sitting up. Resistance is clearly futile.

'I've just been having lunch with my granddaughter Penny. She works at one of those big banks in the City – has her own office, you know, with a lovely view of St Paul's Cathedral and all these people running around after her. She's about your age, I should think. Ooh, and you'll never guess: her secretary is a man!'

Oh cruel gods, why have you sent me a woman with an overachieving granddaughter? Why not a school dropout who works nights at Tesco Metro?

'The thing is, though,' the old lady goes on, 'and I wouldn't say this to Penny, but I don't actually think she's very happy. She has this posh flat near Harrods and goes on these fancy holidays, but I think deep down all she really wants is a nice boyfriend and a few kiddies.'

Ah, now we're talking. An overachieving, *miserable* granddaughter. Do go on, madam.

'You know, sometimes I think you youngsters have got it all wrong. You're so busy running around with your i-thingummyjigs and your man-secretaries that you forget about what's really important. As I said to Penny, a wardrobe of designer shoes isn't going to keep you warm at night!' (Not strictly true: I imagine our Penny has enough Louboutins to fashion herself some sort of 'shoe hut' – but we digress.) 'I met my dear late husband Albert when I was fifteen, married two years later and had my first baby the year after that, and every morning I woke up and felt like the luckiest girl in the world. I didn't set foot on a plane until I was sixty-eight, but I don't think my life has been any the less happy for it. When my youngest, Peter, started school, I . . .'

I wake with a jolt. The seat opposite me is empty. I have no idea how long I've been asleep, but judging by the surrounding farmland and the amount of drool on my shoulder I'd say it was quite a while. What on earth happened to my neighbour? She said she wasn't getting out until Ipswich. That's weird. Hang on a sec, did I . . . did I *dream* her . . . ? Was she – *oh my God* – was the old lady actually my subconscious, trying to tell me something . . . ?

'Shortbread finger, love?' Ah, she's back. It seems my subconscious had just nipped to the buffet car.

Penny's grandma gets off at the next stop, wishing me luck with my job search and making me promise that I'll drop round for tea if I'm ever in Ipswich. I'm quite sad to see her go: she distracted me from wallowing in self-pity/loathing/doubt. When the train is on the move again I stare gloomily out of the window, watching a tractor trundling across a field, when in that moment it suddenly hits me. *Whoa*. It's as if someone has just changed the lighting inside my head: everything is still the same, but suddenly it all looks completely different. I'm not religious, but there, a few miles outside of Ipswich, I think I might have an actual epiphany.

It goes something like this: I realise that I have spent the past thirty-one years waiting for my life to start when all the time it has been quietly slipping by without me. And for the first time I see that if I keep waiting for that cool job or for slimmer ankles or for Nick Grimshaw to become my gay best friend, then another thirty-one years will have passed and I'll wake up one morning with bad knees and *Gardeners' Question Time* on the radio and discover that I have wasted my best years just waiting. My life is happening NOW, right this very minute – and I bloody well need to start living it!

Oh my God, this is amazing! I feel magnificently and exuberantly *alive*. Colours seem brighter, sounds more vivid – in fact, I'm almost surprised when I look around the carriage and everyone else appears to be carrying on as normal. Come on folks, life is wonderful! I feel like Scrooge at the end of *A Christmas Carol*, with the old lady as Tiny Tim or the Ghost of Christmas Past or whatever. I just know I will look back at this moment in ten years' time (after I have written my bestselling self-help book *Epiphany on the 14.32 to Norwich* and moved to the Bahamas) and see it as the beginning of the rest of my life.

Right, things are going to change – starting from now. No more 'putting things out to the universe' and hoping they will happen. No more comparing my perfectly decent body to those of assorted bikini-wearing Kardashians on the *Daily Mail* website (and *definitely* no more reading the comments from angry fat blokes at the end of the article saying things like: 'Females, take note – this is what a *real* woman looks like'). No more wishing that I had Kate Moss's friends and wardrobe – or imagining life would be way better if I had either. I've been so busy searching for happiness that I didn't realise it has been right under my nose the whole time!

In a rush of excitement, I take out a pen and my diary from my handbag and write 'Gratitude List' at the top of a blank page (I read about this in *Cosmopolitan* the other day, and it sounds like just the thing to mark my epiphany). I write the following:

1. A great job with a wonderful boss.
2. Fantastic friends, two of whom like me enough to make me godmother to their offspring.
3. Family (good and bad points here t.b.h., but Mum means well, generally).
4. Good health.

5. A lovely flat with a modest mortgage.
6. A wonderful boyfriend who loves me.

Adam. I can't believe I was nitpicking about how *sensible* he is. The man is a bloody god! It suddenly feels vitally important that I tell him how much he means to me. I pull out my phone and send a text.

Dinner tonight 8pm at the Library on me? I love you so much (ps I didn't get the job but the benefit package was crap anyway) x

Almost instantly a text appears, but it is not from Adam, it is from my friend Jaye. Beautiful, screwed-up Jaye, who up until six months ago led the very definition of a charmed life. I put my epiphany on hold for a moment to read her text.

How did the interview go babe? Bikram at 5? xoxox

Ah, this is not good. Firstly because I hate Bikram yoga (although perhaps it will be more enjoyable post-enlightenment) and secondly because if Jaye is back on the Bikram it means she's had A Bad Day.

I used to wonder who bought all the size six clothes in Topshop, but now I know that it is women whose arsehole husbands have dumped them for a Texan bikini model with 30G implants and a vaginoplasty. I know – total cliché, right? Quite literally, as it happens, as the model in question is called Cliché Corvette.

Jaye and I met aged nine at an afterschool drama group. Before meeting her I'd never given much thought to the concept of attractiveness – my friends and I had faces, and I generally liked all of them – but here was a girl who was Disney's Cinderella made flesh. It was the first time I realised that in life there is a definite pecking order, looks-wise, and I was nowhere near the top of it. Nevertheless, having bonded over a shared love of Take That and guinea pigs, Jaye and I became inseparable until the age of seventeen when she landed a role on a kids' TV show, sort of *Grange Hill* meets *Hollyoaks*, alongside a young actor named Stewie Patterson. Anyway, Jaye and Stewie fell madly in love, got married in an Irish castle and then waltzed off to Hollywood. For those of us left behind in Norwich, Jaye shone like a beacon of success and glamour, brightening up our humdrum existence with tales of ketamine-snorting A-listers and twenty-something starlets getting facelifts. But while Jaye struggled to find work in LA, Stewie landed the role of dashing English brain surgeon Dr Charles Forsyth on the top daytime soap *Too Much Too Young*, and as America's womenfolk fell for Dr Forsyth, so Dr Forsyth fell for America's womenfolk – well, for Cliché Corvette. Six months ago Jaye learnt about their affair via some pap pics in *US Weekly*, packed up her things and fled back to her parents' house in Norwich, and here we are today: Bikram binges, gluten-free everything and obsessive googling of 'Stewie Patterson Cliché Corvette engagement rumours'.

Actually, I think, as the train pulls into Norwich, this could well be excellent timing: in my new enlightened state I might be able to give Jaye some perspective on her situation and help her to stop fixating on Stewie and focus instead on all the positive things in her life.

As I stroll back to my flat in the afternoon sunshine I notice as if for the first time what a wonderful city I live in. People make eye contact and smile; none of the men look like Movember rejects; the bakeries sell sausage rolls made out of actual sausages. I feel so giddy with happiness I should have little cartoon bluebirds flitting around my head and bunnies gambolling at my feet. This place feels like home – and, for the first time in a long while, that doesn't depress me.

My flat is on Pottergate in the historic area known as Norwich Lanes, a network of cobbled streets and alleyways dotted with trendy boutiques and cafes. I can only afford to live here because my res is the very opposite of des: a hobbit-sized one-bedroom flat with stained carpets and a kitchen that's considerably older than I am; but I'm very fond of it and, having paid the deposit and mortgage with my own money, rather proud. Besides, I'll let you into a secret: if you live with stained carpets for long enough you stop noticing them.

I dump my bag on the sofa and as I do so half the contents fall out, including the letter from EROS Technologies that I opened on the train. I scan through it again:

Blah blah blah 'exciting opportunity', blah blah 'highly personal', blah blah blah, 'Yours sincerely, Theresa Lefevre'.

Well bravo, Theresa Lefevre, whoever you are. No really, I applaud you. You have done your research exceedingly well. Until my epiphany I was exactly the sort of gullible gimp who would have been straight on the phone and you would have had no problem extracting money from me for your 'buy one boob implant, get the other one free' or whatever it is that you are trying to flog. But I'm afraid you are precisely sixty-two minutes too late. I have seen the light and have absolutely no need of your 'exciting opportunity', thank you very much. Now, if you don't mind I need to go and get changed for Bikram. Thank you, and good day.

3

Jaye is waiting for me outside 'Becki's Bikram'. Even with her hair scraped back and no make-up on she looks ten times more gorgeous than the rest of us, but there are dark shadows under her eyes and when we hug I can feel the bumps of her spine.

'So – how did the interview go?' she asks.

'Badly. I didn't get it.'

'Oh no, what happened? You were perfect for that job.'

'I just wasn't what they were looking for,' I mutter, unable to face explaining the full extent of my stupidity.

'You know, I met this amazing Life Coach in LA who told me that if you want to get something you need to, like, mindfully visualise what you wish to achieve and then imagine yourself . . .'

I cut her short. 'Jaye, it just wasn't meant to be. And I am very lucky that I already have a great job.'

She looks impressed. 'God, I wish I had your attitude, Perce. You're so sorted.'

Now, the old me would have jabbered on about how I'm the least sorted person *ever* and that I honestly haven't got a clue about *anything*, but the new post-epiphany me simply gives a humble smile and says: 'I'm learning to count my blessings.'

I quite like normal yoga with its happy hippy vibe, but Bikram is all sweat, mirrors and barked orders, with twenty-six positions repeated in rapid succession – pretty much how I imagine sex would be with Simon Cowell. And Becki doesn't half pack the punters into her tiny, sweltering studio. I am squashed between the back mirror and a man wearing such snug Speedos that by the third posture I have learnt that he *a)* favours a back, sac and crack wax and *b)* isn't Jewish. Unfortunately my epiphany has done nothing to improve my bendiness and I only manage about a quarter of the postures, although I think even Simon would be impressed with my 'dead body pose', to which I give 150 per cent.

After yoga – and after Speedo guy tries to get Jaye's number – we go to a nearby cafe. Jaye orders hot water with lemon; I get a cappuccino and a slice of carrot cake with two forks.

'So Stewie and that bitch have bought a dog together,' says Jaye, warily eyeing my cake as if she might absorb the calories by osmosis. 'He always told me we couldn't have a dog because he was allergic. Fucking asshole.'

'Bastard,' I mumble, my mouth crammed with cake.

'And they've called it Ludo,' says Jaye.

'Well, at least it's got a really shit name!'

Jaye's top lip wobbles. 'That was what Stewie and I had planned to call our first child.' And she starts to cry.

'Hey, I've got an idea!' I say quickly. 'Why don't we arrange a really big Friday night out? I'm sure Lou and Charlie will be up for it. We'll go out for a Chinese then find some crappy club full of twenty-year-olds and drink loads of cheap cocktails. All the blokes will try to pull you and ignore the rest of us. It'll be brilliant, just like the old days!'

Jaye sniffs and wipes her eyes. 'I appreciate the offer, thank you, babe, but I'm allergic to alcohol.'

'Since when?'

'Since, like, forever I guess, although I've only just found out. I've been reading this book I got from my Chakra healer in LA called *Your Liver, Your Temple*, and I totally fit the profile of someone with an alcohol allergy. Like, when I drink I feel absolutely terrible the next day – I get the shakes, a splitting headache, I can't get out of bed . . . Apparently I need intravenous lipid exchange therapy to heal my liver.'

'Jaye, that's called a hangover. Everyone gets them. Remember?'

'But in LA . . .'

I hold up my hand. 'Everyone gets them *who doesn't live in LA.*'

She smiles, finally.

'So are we doing this or not? You better not wimp out on us, Lou and Charlie will probably need to get babysitters . . .'

'Don't worry,' she says. 'We're on.'

'Excellent. I'll speak to the others about possible dates.' I check my phone. 'Oops, sorry, chick, I've got to go. I'm taking Adam out to dinner.'

Jaye sighs. 'You don't know how lucky you are having a boyfriend like Adam. You can tell how much he adores you. *He* would never dump you for a pair of giant plastic tits. He's just so . . . so *safe*.'

Jaye's absolutely right, I think, as I wait for the bus back to my flat to shower off Speedo guy's sweat and get changed for dinner. Adam *is* safe. I have never once had cause to doubt his love for me; he is totally reliable and trustworthy. I admit that at times I have wondered if Adam is *too* safe, but now I can see how utterly ridiculous that sounds: 'Oh poor me, my boyfriend never gets pissed and flirts with my friends. And he hates arguing and is never late. Boo hoo hoo, I'm so unlucky!' Okay, so our relationship isn't exactly swinging from a chandelier with a pair of knickers on its head, but there's a hell of a lot to be said for stability and security; I mean, look at poor Jaye. Besides, you show me a three-year relationship that is still wildly passionate and I'll show you a break-up waiting to happen.

*

Adam and I like to joke that we have an arranged marriage. I envy those couples who have great anecdotes about
how they met – you know: 'I was on this tiny Thai island
called Koh Poo Fuk and there was this really cool shack
on the beach where you could get these to-die-for banana
pancakes and one morning this guy turned up and he
asked me to pass the syrup and, you'll never believe it, it
was Gary!' – because Adam and I were set up by my mother.

Adam Lumsden moved to Norwich from his native Manchester three years ago to work as a junior associate at my
dad's firm, Titan Financial Services. Having immediately
earmarked him as potential son-in-law material (tall, own
car/teeth, non-foreign-sounding name), my mother invited
him for Sunday lunch, intending to serve up her spinster
daughter alongside the rare roast rib of beef and apple
crumble – although the first thing I knew about any of
this was when I turned up at my parents' house that lunchtime, only to be intercepted at the front door by my mother
who whisked me upstairs and tried to 'top up' my make-
up. Having been brought up to speed on her evil plan, my
immediate instinct was to march straight out of the door
but, alas, my mother is an excellent cook and I was hungry,
so I reluctantly agreed to stay for lunch while insisting
that I would have nothing to do with this Adam Lumsden
if he was *the last bloody man on earth*.

Still spiky with indignation, I strode into the living
room, where my Dad was chatting to a lanky dark-haired

bloke who jumped to his feet and offered his hand as soon as he saw me, like some gentleman caller out of *Pride and Prejudice*.

(*Him, bowing*: 'Miss Perseus, 'tis a pleasure to make your acquaintance.'

Me, haughty: 'Perhaps so, Captain Lumsden, but do not presume that our meeting will afford me any such pleasure. Now, if you will excuse me, I must to the pianoforte . . .')

As Adam shook my hand, all serious and polite, I was struck by how tall he was – well over six foot – which made me feel pleasingly Kylie-sized. He was wearing a navy V-neck jumper (I am a sucker for a navy V-neck: *très* classy) and he sounded slightly like a posh Liam Gallagher. Was it lust at first sight? No. But I warmed to him instantly, and when Adam gave me a lift home after what turned out to be a very pleasant lunch and asked for my number I thought: *why not?* Besides, by this time I'd been single for so long that I was beginning to consider 'alternative' lifestyles, such as living in a commune or becoming a Buddhist nun.

My love life had actually started out brilliantly: my first kiss was with the most popular boy in school, Doug Gray, at a New Year's Eve party, but it was all downhill from there. At university I dated a guy who referred to sex as 'lovemaking' and wrote long poems about the small of my back, then I had an eighteen-month on–off relationship with Weird Paul, a colleague at Eagle Insurance, which ended abruptly when he emigrated to Australia without telling me. And after that – *nada*. For the next five years I was stuck in a dating drought. A fella famine. A guy gap.

According to my exhaustive magazine-based research there were several likely reasons for my persistently single state: I was too fussy (nope – you should have seen Weird Paul), I was sidelining love to focus on my career (because insurance is *such* a turn-on) or I was scaring men off with psycho behaviour such as talking about baby names on a first date (come on, does anyone *really* do that?). The only other possible explanations were that I was totally unfanciable or I just hadn't met The One. My friends kindly reassured me it was the latter. And then along came Adam.

As I cross the road towards the restaurant at just after eight that evening I spot Adam waiting outside, frowning at something on his phone, but when he looks up and sees me he breaks into a big smile, and I'm hit by a huge wave of love.

'You look gorgeous,' he says, wrapping his arms round me; I still get a kick out of how dainty he makes me feel. 'Look, I'm sorry you didn't get the job, but I'm selfishly quite pleased as it means I get to keep you here. I was never convinced you'd really enjoy living in London.'

I'm about to protest, but perhaps Adam's right. I'm sure the reality of living in London would have been nowhere near as good as it is in my imagination, and I'd have ended up like one of those idiots who have a sunny week of cocktails and shagging at a full-board hotel in the Gambia and then decide it would be a really good idea to move there.

'Shall we go in?' I say, snuggling into his side. 'I'm starving.'

After we've ordered, Adam reaches across the table for my hand. 'Now that London's off the cards, I've got a proposition for you.'

'That sounds serious . . .'

'Well it is, kind of.' Adam smiles. 'How about you move in with me? I know we discussed it before and you said it was too soon, but we've been together three years now. We're round each other's place the whole time, so it seems crazy paying two mortgages.'

'Oh, you silver-tongued devil! What girl could resist such romance?'

He laughs. 'Okay, fair point . . . But I love you, Percy. You love me. We're not teenagers any more. What's stopping us?'

What *is* stopping us? My friends have all asked the same question. As have my parents. And the answer is that I don't really know, although I *am* very fond of my flat. I just can't visualise myself living in Adam's admittedly very nice three-bedroom semi with its colour-coordinated DVD collection and zero tolerance policy on clutter. And while I would in many cultures be viewed, at the age of thirty-one, as one of the tribal elders, I honestly don't yet feel grown-up enough to move in with my boyfriend.

'Tim Burton and Helena Bonham Carter are married but live in separate houses and that seems to work well for them,' I mutter, banking on the fact that Adam won't have read that they've separated.

'Come on love, we're not celebrities,' says Adam. 'We live in the real world, and in the real world couples who love each other move in together.'

And then I realise that I'm doing it again: holding myself back, living in a fantasy future, imagining things would be perfect *if only*. Why am I even thinking about this? It's a big step, so it's completely natural to feel nervous, but of course I should move in with Adam.

'Percy? What do you think?'

'I would love to move in with you,' I say. 'Let's do it.'

'Brilliant! I'm so pleased.' Adam squeezes my hand and then leans over for a kiss. 'Right, the next thing is to decide whether to rent out your flat or sell it . . .'

Later that night Adam and I are lying in my bed together, his arm snaked around my waist and leg thrown over mine; from his slow breathing and occasional snore I can tell he's out like a light. I love a bedtime cuddle as much the next person, but when it comes to the actual process of falling asleep I am extremely pro personal space. Adam, however, likes to fall asleep clutching on to me like he's Kate Winslet clinging to the life raft in *Titanic*, which is all very romantic but leads to dead arms/legs, overheating and accidental elbows in the face. Luckily Adam is usually asleep within a few minutes of snuggling, so I can simply wriggle out from under him and get comfy on the other side of the bed, but tonight, even after disentangling myself, I can't get to sleep. It feels like hours tick by – although it's probably only about twenty minutes – before I give up trying to sleep and tiptoe to the kitchen to make myself a cup of 'Sleepyhead' herbal tea (because a gentle infusion of camomile and lavender is *definitely* going to knock me out). As I wait for the kettle to boil I spot the non-circular letter with its life-changing offer that I left on the side earlier and before I can stop myself I read it again. Maybe I should just look up EROS Technologies on Google and check out who they are . . . ?

No. Percy Andromeda James, this is ridiculous. What happened to living the life you have? Whatever this character – Theresa LeFevre – is promising, you don't need it. Before I can have second thoughts, I chuck the letter in the sink and then put a match to it. A little OTT, perhaps, but at least now I won't be tempted to follow it up. The letter bursts into flame quite impressively. If this was *EastEnders* the *doof-doof-doof* would now herald the end credits, but this is not *EastEnders* and instead the smoke alarm goes off, heralding an awkward conversation with my bewildered half-asleep boyfriend who understandably can't work out why I am setting fire to things in the kitchen sink in the middle of the night.

4

According to an article I was reading in *Red* on the way to work this morning (I've vowed to stop buying magazines post-epiphany, but someone had left this on the bus so it doesn't count), the average couple have sex one and a half times a week. This has raised a couple of questions. Firstly, what are these couples doing together on the 'half' a time? And secondly, if this is true, should I be worried that Adam and I haven't had sex for nearly three weeks? We spent the whole weekend together, plus I stayed at his place last night, and in all that time we didn't have so much as a quick fumble. It just never seemed the right moment.

Anyway, the article talked about how the key to 'freshening up stale sex' is surprise, and listed the usual women's magazine suggestions for spicing things up in the bedroom: whipped cream, costumes, role-play, etcetera. Personally, I've always had serious doubts that anyone really involves foodstuffs in their 'lovemaking'. Leaving aside the practicalities (imagine the stains!) I'd have imagined that licking melted chocolate off your loved one might leave you feeling quite bloated and queasy, especially if they were on the chubby side. You'd need a Gaviscon and a lie-down before finishing the job.

Having said that, the bit about dressing-up sounds quite interesting. It's not that Adam and I have a stale sex life, but after three years together I suppose we have got a bit lazy. By now we both know what works, so rather than try something new and risk embarrassment/disappointment we stick to a tried and tested routine:

00:00: Kissing

01:10: My top comes off

01:55: More kissing

03:30: Bra off (five seconds or longer depending on the style)

03:55: Boob-centred activity

06:00: Most other clothes come off, socks too occasionally

06:20: Pants-area-centred activity (with hand or mouth, depending on enthusiasm/occasion)

09:00: Freestyle section (varies in duration)

11:00: Intercourse

14:20: FIN

Then we have a bit of a cuddle, nip to the bathroom to clean our teeth, then go to sleep. Predictable – but, as I said, it works well.

Anyway, I'm sure I remember Adam telling me that his first crush was on his school lollipop lady; I presume she was younger than average. After a quick glance round to check that nobody is standing near my desk, I type 'sexy lollipop lady costume' into Google. Hmmm . . . clearly not much of a market for sexy lollipop lady costumes . . . But surely it wouldn't be that hard to pull together? Just a yellow high-vis jacket and a matching cap. And I could easily knock up a lollipop out of cardboard. Not *obviously* sexy, I grant you, but perhaps with some stockings . . .

My phone suddenly rings with the long *brrrrrr* that denotes an internal office call. Oh God, I hope my googling hasn't triggered some anti-porn filter in Human Resources . . .

'Susannah White's office,' I say nervously. (Susannah is Eagle Insurance's CEO, and my boss.)

'Are you ready for lunch, fucker?'

Thankfully it's not HR. It's Melanie Martin from Accounts: potty-gobbed Australian and my best office buddy. Mel has been at Eagle Insurance even longer than I have after taking a temp job here during a backpacking trip from her hometown of Brisbane twelve years ago and never leaving. I'm still not sure how she managed to end up in Norwich: it's not exactly *on* the beaten track, nor does it hold many obvious attractions for the Aussie back-packer. 'Come to Norwich and see our famous . . . Mustard Museum!'

Mel and I meet in reception and walk up the cobbled street outside the office to join the lunchtime crowds swarming around the Chapelfield shopping centre, as she yaps away about a run-in she's had this morning with the company's Associate Director, Mr Hedley, over some outstanding invoices. Although I work with a generally nice bunch of people, there are a handful of weirdos and one hateful arsehole: Mr A. Hedley. No one calls him by his first name – in fact, I'm not even sure what it is – but he looks like an Aubrey. Or an Adolf. He's the sort of person who sucks all the joy out of a room just by walking into it: the office Dementor, if you will. Anyway, it sounds as if Mel gave as good as she got. She may be barely scraping five foot, but I'd back her in a fight any day. She's like a Minogue sister crossed with a Hummer.

We take a window table at Carluccio's and before the menus have even arrived Mel has ordered two glasses of Merlot and some olives from a passing waiter.

'Cheers, Perce,' says Mel, raising her glass to me. 'Here's to our Friday lunches – long may they continue. Another reason why that job in London wasn't meant to be . . . Plus, now you have plenty of time to open that pop-up herring restaurant in your flat!' She clinks her glass to mine. '*Skaal!* Or however the fuck they say "cheers" in Scandinavia . . .'

Mel was the only person at Eagle I told about the interview at Saboteur as I knew she would enjoy the full story of exactly how spectacularly I screwed it up, even if it has now provided her with ample piss-taking ammo.

'So how's your week been?' she goes on. 'I've been worried you might be a bit down about being back at work after things didn't work out in London.'

'You know, I've been completely fine. Weirdly happy.' And I mean it. It has been a week since my epiphany and those Disney bunnies are still frolicking about my feet. I've lost the anxious, niggly feeling that I'm in the wrong job and my career is going nowhere, and I've finally realised that I'm actually on to a pretty good thing at Eagle. Okay, so I'm never going to make billions from my 100 wpm shorthand and PowerPoint skills, but I have a great boss, I'm paid well for what I do and I get to drink Merlot and eat giant olives every Friday lunchtime.

'From now on,' I tell Mel, in the manner of a politician announcing some exciting new policy initiative that she knows is going to play well with voters, 'I intend to work to live, not live to work.'

'Amen to that,' she says, clinking my glass again before taking a big swig of wine. 'And you know, if you do decide you want a bit more of a challenge at work, you can always talk to Susannah about it.'

'And say what? "Hey Susannah, sorry, but I'm bored of being your PA"?'

'No, but you know how much she likes you – I'm sure she'd be open to developing your role a bit.'

'But my role's already been developed as far as it will go,' I say. 'With the best will in the world, Susannah needs me to be her PA and I can't do that if I'm busy diversifying. She's been so good to me, I don't want to rock the boat.'

I've been working for Susannah for four years now, having climbed my way up to the dizzy heights of the CEO's office from my first job on the reception desk. It's not the glittering career that I'd dreamed of when I graduated from Middlesex University with a Media Studies degree (2:1) ten years ago, but it was the best I could find at the time – and Susannah *has* been good to me. Just last month she gave me a hefty pay rise, stuck 'Executive' in front of my job title *and* put me in charge of the company's Twitter feed. Short of giving me her own job, there isn't much more she could do to pad out my role.

'Fair enough,' says Mel. 'I just don't want you getting itchy feet again the next time you get bored at work.'

I put down my glass. 'Look, there are a few people in this world who are lucky enough to have really cool, fulfilling careers, but I've realised that I'm not going to be one of them – and honestly, that's fine.'

Mel raises her eyebrows.

'It is!' Indignation has made my voice go squeaky. 'I don't need my career to fulfil me. I've got so many other great things in my life: amazing friends, a brilliant social life, a wonderful boyfriend . . .'

Mel's eyebrows shoot even higher and I instantly regret mentioning Adam. You know I said that my friends kept asking why I hadn't moved in with him? Not Mel.

'I still can't believe you're going to sell your flat for *him*,' she mutters, jabbing at an olive with a cocktail stick as if it were a tiny round green Adam. 'You don't even love the bloke.'

'That's ridiculous, of course I do!'

'You might *think* you love him, but only because you've talked yourself into it. If you were being honest you'd admit he's dull and that you've got nothing in common.'

'Oh, come on, that's hardly fair . . .' Then something occurs to me. 'Hang on, is this because you're still mad with him about your birthday?'

There was a bit of an unpleasant to-do at Mel's fortieth back in January, when Adam refused to do shots (but only because sambuca brings him out in this nasty rash) and then had to go home at 9 p.m. as he had an important client meeting the next morning. Mel, who never leaves a party unless escorted by a bouncer saying, 'I think you've had enough now,' took it rather badly; I can still see her standing by the pub door yelling after him as he scuttled to his car. In an attempt to make up for my boy-friend's early exit I stayed until the party's bitter end and woke up the next morning in Mel's bath wearing a full McDonald's uniform, complete with name badge reading 'Sheryl'.

Anyway, Mel dismisses my suggestion with a flick of her hand. 'I'm not mad about it, but it did prove to me that he's not the right bloke for you. He's just too . . . sensible. There are no fireworks. And fireworks are crucial in a relationship – or at least the *memory* of fireworks once you've gone past the rip-each-other's-clothes-off stage. You're clearly not soulmates.'

'Well, I'm sorry to burst your bubble, Cupid, but I'm afraid I don't believe there's just one special person out there for each of us. And even if there was, how would I go about finding them? It's a lovely idea in theory, but the whole soulmate concept is not workable.'

'Percy, your soulmate might be sitting in this restaurant *right this moment* and you wouldn't know it because you're so obsessed with making things work with Mr Independent Financial Adviser with his pastel knitwear and Vauxhall hatchback with that stupid dangly tree air freshener.'

Just then the waiter turns up with our food, which thankfully puts a temporary stop to the conversation.

'I can't believe you have a problem with Adam,' I mutter, as the waiter grinds pepper over pasta. 'Remember that time we got stuck in Cromer after closing time when your car wouldn't start? Adam drove for nearly an hour to come and get us in the middle of the night. Oh, and by the way, he doesn't have a dangly tree air freshener.'

'Okay, okay, so he's a nice guy, but he's not the nice guy for *you*.' Mel twirls her fork in her spaghetti and we eat in silence for a few moments. 'You know what your problem is, Perce? You don't *choose* men. You let yourself be chosen.'

I splutter a laugh into my wine. 'Yeah, because just look at all the dozens of men hanging around, oiled up and panting, just waiting for me to say, "I'll take that one."'

Mel puts down her fork. 'How old are you, Percy – thirty-one? You're just a baby. It might not feel like it right now, but you've got bloody ages to find the right bloke. I promise you, there is someone out there who is nice and kind, but who will also give you goosebumps. You mark my words, Perce, if you move in with Adam you'll be settling. Take me and Michael, for instance . . .'

Ah, now *this* is why I take Mel's advice on relationships with a handful of salt. Mel is in a committed, long-term relationship with the singer Michael Bublé – except Michael Bublé doesn't know anything about it. Mel plans her annual leave around his touring schedule, her home is a shrine to all things Bublé and she has a tattoo of a lyric from his hit 'Just Haven't Met You Yet' – 'I promise you, kid, I give so much more than I get' – in curly script across her lower back (or upper bum, however you want to look at it). For her part, Mel has given so much more than she's got from Michael, who is in fact married to someone else, that she's been single for the past five years. No, you certainly couldn't accuse Mel of 'settling'. She is whatever the opposite is of settling. Unsettling, perhaps. So while I admire her ironclad belief that Michael is her soulmate, and that if she can't have him she doesn't want anyone, it obviously makes her a less than reliable authority when it comes to matters of the heart.

'Look, I get why you think Adam is a good bet,' Mel goes on. 'I suppose he's *quite* good-looking, in an obvious kinda way, and he worships you. But you're overthinking all this. What does your heart say about him?'

'But that's the thing, Mel. For the first time ever I've *stopped* overthinking things. I'm just . . . going with it.'

Mel throws up her hands in defeat. 'All right, all right. Knock yourself out, move in with Captain Sensible. But don't say I didn't warn you when it all goes tits up.'

When I get back to my desk I already have thirty-seven new emails of varying degrees of importance. Most can be deleted without glancing at more than the subject line ('STOLEN STAPLER – still missing!!!' and 'Reminder of Company Fire Drill policy: please read'), but there is one from my friend Lou, confirming that I'm still on for babysitting her two-year-old son Alfie – my godson – tonight, and a message from Adam.

See attached links for a selection of local estate agents with competitive fees. Check them out and let's get this ball rolling! I'm going to clear out the cupboard in the spare room this weekend so you have extra space for your things. I've got a client meeting this evening that might run on a bit but will phone you later. Love you. Ax

See? I couldn't ask for a sweeter, more considerate boy-friend. In your face, Melanie! And by the way, he *does* give me goosebumps . . .

There's also one from Jaye, with the subject heading 'HA HA HA HA'. Inside she has written:

Check this out. Do you think it means they'll break up? xoxoxox

She's attached a link to a story on the *National Enquirer* website. The gist of the article is that Stewie Patterson and Cliché Corvette were overheard having a furious argument in a Hollywood nightclub last week and the journalist speculates that the 'swoonsome twosome could be on the road to Split City'. The story is based on comments from an anonymous 'onlooker' and is illustrated with a couple of blurry photos, obviously taken on a phone camera, in which you can just make out Stewie with a blonde – although the quality is so poor it's impossible to tell whether they're arguing or dancing really enthusiastically. It's such a non-story that the page has been padded out with an enormous photo of Cliché hard at work, by which I mean posing in a bikini with her mouth hanging open like there's a delicious sandwich just out of shot. I am so entranced by the cartoonish size and roundness of her boobs (how do they stay up like that? Helium?) that I am oblivious to someone coming up to my desk.

'Hard at work, Miss James?'

I spin round guiltily, fearing that it's Mr Hedley, but instead I am relieved to see Dan Dawson, who probably spends a good proportion of his time at work looking at photos like this anyway. Dan is one of Eagle's Claims Managers and his skills include doing perfect impressions of other people in the office and being really, really good-looking. It's unfortunate that he knows it, but then it would be hard for him not to with virtually every woman he meets dribbling over him. At only a couple of inches taller than me (and I'm quite short) he's not exactly male model material, but he's got this whole sexy Ryan Gosling thing going on, he's a real laugh and God, he's a charmer. When Dan first arrived at Eagle – an event that fell during my lengthy single period – I waged a highly coordinated campaign to get him to fancy me, wearing full smoky eye make-up and matching lacy lingerie to the office every day on the off-chance he might seduce me in the stairwell. Although I am obviously now happy with Adam and Dan has this on–off thing with a beauty therapist from Ipswich, we still flirt innocently – well, Dan does. My flirting is entirely non-innocent, but then even we soon-to-be-cohabiting ladies are allowed a bit of a perv every now and then.

Dan sits himself on the edge of my desk. 'So, James,' he says, leaning towards me, eyes atwinkle. 'I was wondering, are you free next Wednesday evening?'

'What's the occasion?'

'Well, we haven't had a night out for a while, I thought we could go for a few beers after work and catch up.'

If this had been a few years ago I would already have been planning my outfit and booking a pedicure and top-to-toe wax, but Dan has never given the slightest indication that he's interested in being more than friends.

'Sure,' I say. 'Good thinking. Shall I round up the troops? I know Mel will be up for it.'

Then something weird happens. For a split second Dan looks almost . . . well, disappointed. Like he doesn't want Mel or the troops to come. Like he wants – and I could well be reading too much into an admittedly very brief look here – like he wants it to be just the two of us. Bloody hell, was he asking me on a date? Obviously not a *date* date, because we're both in relationships, but perhaps he's got something he needs to say to me in private.

Before Dan can say anything, I blurt: 'Or we could just go for a quick one on our own?' Shit, that came out wrong. 'I mean go for a drink, not a "quick one". Like, you know, not sex. Ha ha ha! Obviously I just meant a quick beer.' *Shut up shut up shut up.*

As Dan sits back, arms folded, and grins his cocky grin, I realise just how deluded I have been. That look of 'disappointment' was far more likely to have been caused by my post-lunch garlic breath, or trapped wind.

'As tempting as that sounds, let's get Mel and the others out too,' he says, already getting up off my desk. 'The more the merrier, right? 5.30 at the Plough? Anyway, I'll leave you to your highly important work.' He gestures to Cliché, still panting away on my computer screen. 'See you later, James.'

After Dan has sauntered off, distributing winks and waves around the office like Tom Cruise at a premiere, I return to my inbox. At the very top of the list of emails there is one marked 'PRIVATE AND CONFIDENTIAL' from a name I don't immediately recognise but that seems vaguely familiar. I click it open:

Dear Miss James,

Apologies for contacting you via your work email, but I am writing to follow up my letter of 1st April on behalf of EROS Technologies, which I hope you have now received.

As I explained in my letter, we are very keen to speak to you regarding a potentially life-changing opportunity. I can assure you this is not a marketing campaign and will involve no financial outlay on your part.

I feel sure our proposition will be of interest, but if, once we have spoken, you would rather not pursue the matter any further then we will not contact you again. All I ask is for the opportunity to meet with you in person at our London office and provide you with more details; we will, of course, be happy to cover your travel expenses.

Thank you again for your time and I look forward to hearing from you.

Yours,

Theresa LeFevre

Account Director

EROS Technologies

Okay, this is creeping me out now. How did these people get my work email address? It all seems a bit too targeted to be some random scam. (Having said that, I had an email at work the other day from a 'Mr Wong Du' from South Korea who claimed to be a banker whose client had died leaving a $48 million trust fund and no next of kin and if I would please send over my bank details he would be happy to transfer a substantial share to me as part of some vague 'business arrangement'.) Anyway, this Theresa woman doesn't appear to be asking for anything up front, but this 'life-changing opportunity' stuff reeks of bullshit. If something sounds too good to be true, it usually is.

'Coffee, Percy?'

I look up to see Susannah sticking her head round her office door. She is in her fifties with four children and a highly pressurised job, plus runs marathons in her spare time, yet she still manages to look perfectly groomed and glamorous. You might think that Susannah is asking me, as her PA, to make her coffee, but no, she is asking if *I* want one, as she has a Nespresso machine in her office. You see? A dream of a boss.

'Cappuccino, thank you.'

'Coming up. Oh, could you please book me train tickets to London next Friday morning? I need to be in Moorgate by 10 a.m.'

'Sure thing.'

She smiles. 'Thanks, Percy.'

Before getting on the phone to sort the tickets I delete the EROS email from my inbox and then delete it from the Deleted items, just to be on the safe side; you never know if these things are carrying a virus. Then I order a yellow high-vis jacket and matching cap and set about planning how to make a cardboard lollipop.

5

At just after seven that evening I arrive at my best friend Louise's house on Cambridge Street in an area known as the Golden Triangle, which is often described as 'the Notting Hill of Norwich' by local estate agents who I suspect may not have been to the *actual* Notting Hill. Having said that, Lou's pretty terraced house with its flower-filled window boxes wouldn't look out of place in the trendier parts of West London. Lou is married to Phil, who does something well-paid in finance, and Lou herself did something well-paid in IT until Alfie came along and she decided to give full-time motherhood a whirl. I can only think she came to this decision while under the influence of dangerously potent post-birth hormones of the sort that cause people to name their children Wolf or Papaya. Or, for that matter, Perseus.

I knock on the door; moments later I hear a door slamming upstairs followed by the air-raid siren wail of a small, angry child and then Lou appears at the door, clearly mid blow-dry, with her dark hair perfectly smooth on one side and dangling damply on the other. She has pale skin that flushes easily when she's stressed; right now there are two red blotches spreading like spilt wine across her cheeks.

'I'm so sorry, Perce, I'm running late.' She gives me a hug and ushers me inside. 'Phil isn't back from work yet and Alfie won't bloody well go to bed. It's like he senses that I'm in a hurry and is just doing it to wind me up.'

'Don't worry, I was hoping to get in some playing before bedtime. So where is my gorgeous godson?'

'Oh, probably sticking forks in electrical sockets, the little shit.'

This is not said with the fond chuckle that you might expect. Lou and Charlie, my other best friend from school, both have small children and compete over the awfulness of their offspring with a vigour most mothers reserve for asserting their child's wondrousness. I know both Lou and Charlie adore their kids, but it's refreshing to get the unvarnished truth about motherhood, even if it has put me off reproducing for the foreseeable future.

We find Alfie in his mother's bedroom, investigating the make-up drawer. As Lou wet-wipes lipstick off his hands I tell her about Jaye's latest wobble and my plan to cheer her up with an old-school-style Friday night out.

'Oh hell yes, I am *totally* up for that. But can we make it a Saturday rather than Friday? I'm bound to need a long lie-in the next day and on Saturday mornings Alfie has his Little Tiddlers swimming and Phil is at football training so he can't take him, which means I have to, so no late nights on Friday.'

'Okay, I'll check dates with Charlie and get back to you with some options, but let's try for the weekend after this one.'

'Just make sure Jaye knows she's going to have to drink,' says Lou sternly. 'And tell her if she starts banging on about the evils of carbs and how we're all going to get cancer from eating cheese then I'm going straight home. No, you're a bad boy, take that out of your mouth right NOW!' This last bit is addressed to Alfie, who is licking a mascara wand. 'So,' she says, turning to me after wiping the worst of it off his tongue, 'how's the big move going?'

'Great,' I say brightly. 'I'm really excited about it.'

'Have you had much interest in your flat?'

'Well, I haven't got it on the market yet, but . . .'

'Percy, I can't believe you're stalling over this.' Lou is glaring at me with the pursed-lipped 'mum' face usually reserved for Alfie. 'You and Adam have been together for ages, it's the natural next step. What's the hold-up?'

'If you'd have let me finish I was going to say that I've brought my laptop with me tonight and once Alfie's asleep I'm going to do a bit of research and finalise my choice of estate agent.'

'Well, just make sure you do,' says Lou, then her

expression softens. 'You *are* doing the right thing, Percy. Adam's a lovely bloke. Phil and I were just saying the other day how good the two of you are together. You won't regret moving in with him, I promise.'

'Yeah, I know, it's just hard getting rid of my flat. I've been there for so long, it feels like a part of me, you know? It's like I'm putting my liver up for sale or something.'

Lou rolls her eyes. 'Ever the drama queen. Look, I know it's a big step but at the end of the day it's just a place to live, whereas you've got a whole life to look forward to with Adam. And his house is so much more practical for the two of you.' She smiles. 'Plus there's plenty of room if one day there are three of you.'

And I look down at Alfie, his curls now dusted with Bobbi Brown shimmer powder, and think: *actually, that might not be so bad.*

An hour later Lou has finished her blow-dry and de-Mummyfied herself with the help of leather leggings and what's left of her lipstick, Phil has returned from work and they have left for dinner. Alfie is tucked up in bed asleep and I am settled on the sofa with a glass of Rioja and my laptop looking through Adam's shortlist of estate agents. I'm glad he's narrowed it down a bit as they all seem pretty much the same to me. God, this is a dull way to spend a Friday night . . . Perhaps I could just have a quick glance at the *Daily Mail* online to find out what the Kardashians are up to? A lot can happen in a week in

Kardashian world: there might been a wedding, a sex change, bum implants . . . Oh sod it, I've been good for a whole week – I'm well overdue a gossip catch-up. But just as I'm about to click on the website, for some reason I think about the letter and email from the woman at EROS Technologies. There is no way I'm going to contact her, but it wouldn't hurt to see if there's any extra information I can find on the company, seeing as they seem so keen to get hold of me. Knowledge is power and all that.

I type 'EROS Technologies' into Google and at the top of the list of results is what looks like the company's website. *Bingo.* I click on the link and the screen changes to blank pale grey and, as I watch, an invisible hand writes 'EROS Tech' in a swirly white font across the middle of the screen. It looks like the website of some fabulously cool and exclusive private members' club. I wait for a while but nothing else happens, so I try clicking on the logo and a moment later the screen changes again, to a map of the world, rendered in the same classy colour scheme, and as before words gradually materialise on the screen: 'Please click on your location.' I move the cursor over the UK and do as requested. Then: 'Enter your six-digit client code.' Ah. I try a few random combinations, but no dice. There aren't any other options you can click on the page, no 'customer service' button or even a phone number. All very cryptic. I go back to the original list of search results: there is a link to a Japanese website that mentions EROS Tech, but the translation is almost as indecipherable as the original and I'm not even sure if it's *my* EROS Tech, as it seems to be about vibrators. Then there are a few rather dry business listings, which simply confirm that EROS Technologies have offices in London, but bizarrely I can't find any other information about them at all. What sort of a company has zero information about them on the Web? I'll tell you who: a bunch of crooks out to con innocents out of their hard-earned cash. I *knew* I was right to be sceptical. It is definitely a scam – albeit one employing excellent graphic designers.

Just then I hear Alfie calling from upstairs and by the time I've sung him a lullaby and got back downstairs I've remember that my favourite film of all time, *Ferris Bueller's Day Off*, is on TV tonight (ah, Matthew Broderick; how my thirteen-year-old self adored you), so I pop the M&S spaghetti carbonara Lou's left for me into the microwave and pack my laptop away. I think I'll just go for the estate agent with the nicest logo.

6

By the following Wednesday my flat is on the market and I've already had three viewings and one offer (insultingly low and rejected at once). I moved a few boxes of stuff over to Adam's at the weekend, feeling like I should offer my tatty books and albums some words of reassurance as I arranged them in the new 'modular storage system' in his spare room. Even though I've spent almost as much time in Adam's house as my own over the past few years, for some reason this weekend I felt like a stranger – but I guess it's only natural as I've never kept more than a toothbrush, tampons and knickers at his place before.

Meanwhile, the lollipop lady outfit arrived on Monday and, unsurprisingly, was totally lacking in sex appeal – but then only the most hardcore fetishist would be turned on by head-to-toe hi-vis polyester. So I cut the jacket off at mid thigh and tried it with stockings and heels and, if I do say so myself, it does look quite appealingly kinky.

Last night I made a 'lollipop' out of empty kitchen roll tubes, double-sided sticky tape and coloured paper and, although it's a scaled-down version and goes a bit floppy if you hold it too far down the stick, it certainly gives the right impression. And tonight is the night when I try it all out on Adam! Annoyingly, it's the same night as our post-work drinks at the Plough, but Adam has evening work engagements the rest of the week and at least I can have a couple of drinks for Dutch courage first. I'll stay at the pub until sevenish and then head home and get ready. Adam thinks he's just coming over for dinner, but he has no idea what's on the menu! Ha!

It's already nearing six when I leave work, having already received a gentle reminder via text from Mel – *WHERE ARE U GET YOUR FAT ARSE HERE NOW* – but the Plough is just a short stroll from our office. It's another beautiful evening so I bypass the bar and go straight out the back to the beer garden where I spot our group clustered around one of the tables. There's a good crowd: as well as Mel and Dan, there are some lads from the Broking department, a few of the Legal team, Mel's Accounts colleagues and the new girl from reception, who, with weary predictability, is huddled up to Dan with the sort of gooey-eyed expression I recognise from every other woman who comes into his orbit. Dan sees me arrive and immediately shakes off his new fan and nudges his way through the group to meet me. He looks pleased to see me and briefly I feel flattered.

'Thank God you're here, James, that girl keeps asking me about my star sign.' He glances at the new receptionist, who does her best sex-face at him. Dan turns back to me, rolling his eyes. 'So can I buy you a drink? Or would you' – he lowers his voice – 'prefer a quick one?'

Ah, he obviously hasn't forgotten my faux pas last week. Great.

'Thank you, but I think I should probably get a round in,' I say tartly.

'Well, why don't I give you a hand at the bar, then?'

'Okay,' I shrug. 'Thanks.'

But when we join the group to get everyone's orders it turns out that Jan from Legal has just appeared with ice buckets full of bottles of beer so Dan and I don't need to go to the bar after all, and then Mel, who judging by her volume has already had several pints, corners me to settle an argument between her and Craig, one of the Broking technicians and a devout born-again Christian, as to whether Jesus was Australian.

The evening is warm and the beer is delightfully cold and it feels like I've only been there ten minutes when I glance at my mobile and see it's already quarter past seven and I need to go home to prepare for my sexathon. I'm bound to get a bollocking from Mel if I leave early, so I wait until she's engrossed in a beer-mat-flipping match and head for the exit, but just as I'm making my escape I hear someone call my name and look round to see Dan jogging up to me.

'You leaving already, James?'

'Yeah, sorry.' I glance over to Mel, but she's still distracted. 'I've got plans back home.'

'Oh come on, stay for another. I've barely had a chance to talk to you.'

'I can't, really. Adam's coming over for dinner. Have fun.'

I turn to leave, but Dan grabs my arm. 'Percy, please don't go yet. I need to talk to you about something.'

Okay, this time I am definitely not imagining it. Dan is looking very serious, like a man with a bombshell to drop, but before I can find out what it is Mel appears.

'All right, fuckers,' she says. 'What's going on here, then?'

Dan and I glance at each other, then suddenly he reaches for me and gently pulls me towards him until we're close enough to kiss. 'Percy, I love you,' he says softly. 'I have always loved you. Please don't move in with Adam. I can't live without you.'

Okay, so that last bit didn't happen.

What actually happens is that as soon as Mel turns up Dan drops my arm like it's a poisonous snake and rearranges his face into his usual yes-I-know-I'm-gorgeous grin. 'Oh, just trying to persuade the boring married lady here to stay for another,' he drawls, 'but she's not having any of it.'

I give a nervous little laugh, still totally unnerved by what just happened (um, what *did* just happen?), but play along. 'Well, the old man expects dinner on the table by eight o'clock sharp and if I don't go now there'll be hell to pay. See you tomorrow, folks.' And before Mel can stop me, I head swiftly for the exit.

Well, that was very weird. Dan clearly had something pretty important to tell me, and from the way he acted when Mel appeared it was obviously private. If I didn't know better, I'd have thought he was about to ask me on a date. No, that's ridiculous – he's never given even a hint of an indication that he's interested. Unless . . . Perhaps, now I'm moving in with Adam, I'm giving off 'taken' vibes that are proving irresistible to other men. I read about that once, how blokes are suddenly attracted to women the moment they know they can't have them. Well, if Dan *is* planning to ask me out then quite frankly he's about three years too late! I walk on with a spring in my step, enjoying the last of the evening sunshine.

By the time I get home my mind is firmly on the fun to come. I whizz round the flat tidying up, uncork a bottle of red wine and, after draping a red scarf over the bedside lamp to give a pleasingly slutty glow in my tiny bedroom, I focus on turning myself into a LLILF (Lollipop Lady I'd Like To . . . well, you know the rest). I thought I'd be a bit nervous, but once I've put on all the kit, complete with red lipstick, lacy lingerie and heels, I look in the mirror and feel properly, powerfully sexy. I am Beyoncé, Rihanna and Madonna, all packed into one fierce, hi-vis raunch-bomb. *Raaaahh!*

At 8 a.m. on the dot I hear Adam's key in the lock and a moment later:

'Percy?'

'In the bedroom,' I call. 'I've got a surprise for yooooo-hoooo . . .'

I position myself as far from the door as possible, on the opposite side of the bed, and as the door opens I hold out one hand in a halt signal and brandish the lollipop in the other. It's show time!

'It's very busy on the roads today,' I say huskily, when Adam's head pokes round the door. 'You're just going to have to wait there, young man, and I'll tell you when to . . . *come*.'

When I play out this scenario in my head, as I have done many times, Adam gives a confused yet delighted grin and joins in enthusiastically, but this doesn't happen. Well, the confused part does, although he's not grinning and he actually looks more alarmed than delighted. Perhaps he can't see my costume clearly – with that scarf over the light it *is* quite dark in here.

'I'm your school lollipop lady,' I say loudly, hitching the high-vis jacket up a little on one side to reveal the hold-ups underneath. The jacket rustles off-puttingly; damn, I should have put on some music. 'You've been a very naughty boy, crossing the road before I tell you to,' I go on, sliding my hand up and down the lollipop stick in a suggestive fashion. 'I think you need to be taught a lesson.'

But Adam is still hovering by the door. The seconds tick by. He glances behind him, as if considering whether to leave, and then clears his throat noisily. 'Um, do we have a fancy dress party coming up?'

What? No, we don't have a bloody fancy dress party! Clearly I'm going have to kick things up a gear.

'Okay, your turn to cross,' I purr, fixing him with my best seductive look. It is taking every ounce of my rapidly dwindling self-confidence to keep this up. Why didn't I have a couple of shots at the pub? 'Get that gorgeous butt over here, young man. *Now.*'

Adam reluctantly comes and sits on the bed, still looking a bit scared, but I've gone too far to throw in the towel and so I straddle him and start to kiss him. Okay, this is more like it . . . But as I grind up against him the Velcro fastenings on my hi-vis jacket get snagged on his jumper and when I try to pull away there's a horrible tearing noise.

'Shit,' I mutter, looking down. The front of his pristine wool V-neck is now all bobbled. 'Oh God, I'm so sorry. I think I've got one of those lint brushes in the drawer, I can go and get it?'

Adam rubs ineffectually at the front of his jumper; he is very particular about his knitwear. 'No, no, it's fine . . .'

No it's not, it's *awful*.

I start to kiss him again, but I can tell his heart isn't in it and after a moment I stop and pull back to look at him.

'Is everything okay?'

'Of course it is.' But he can't even meet my eyes. 'It's just, I don't . . . what's with the outfit, love?'

'I thought it might be fun,' I say, throwing off the cap and sitting on edge of the bed. I hug the jacket around me like a shield, trying to cover up the stockings and lacy lingerie that I can now see look totally ridiculous. So much for my big seduction: what a disaster. I will never, ever be able to do anything except missionary position with my bra on and the lights off ever again.

'But why a lollipop lady, Percy?'

'Because you once told me about that crush you had on your school lollipop lady.'

He looks blank.

'You said she had really sexy legs, remember? And that you used to go bright red every time she waved her lollipop at you to cross the road . . . ?'

And then in a horrible, sickening rush it hits me. It wasn't Adam who told me that. It was Weird Paul from Eagle. Of course it was. *Shit.*

I have no idea how I'm going to get out of this, so I do the only sensible thing: I provoke a massive argument.

'What the hell's wrong with you?' I jump up from the bed. 'I'm just trying to inject a bit of fun into our relationship and you can't even be bothered to play along. Most blokes would love it if their girlfriend went to this sort of effort to get them into bed, but all you've done is sit there giving me the third degree! I spent ages getting this all ready for you!' And then the killer blow: 'Don't you fancy me any more, is that it?'

Adam gawps at me. 'Of course I fancy you . . .'

'Ha! That is exactly what people say when they *don't* fancy someone.'

'Percy, I love you, I can't wait to live together, you just caught me unawares, that's all . . .'

'That was the whole bloody point! It was meant to be a surprise.' I sit back down on the bed, put my head in my hands and try to squeeze out some tears. Adam puts his hand on my leg, but I brush it away. 'I think you should leave,' I say in a small, tight voice.

Oh God, now *he* looks like he's going to cry. 'You want me to go?'

'Well, you clearly don't find me attractive any more.'

After a moment I feel him slowly get up from the bed.

'Percy, I really am sorry, I just didn't get the whole . . . lollipop lady thing. If it had been, I don't know, a sexy policewoman, or a nurse, I would have got it straight away, but a lollipop lady is just quite . . . out there . . .'

'Just GO!'

I don't really want him to leave – more than anything I'd like a hug – but shame and embarrassment have made me bolshie, and a moment later Adam picks up his jacket, mutters, 'I'm so sorry, Percy. I do love you,' and then I hear the front door close.

I feel angry, fleetingly, and then start to cry.

7

I check the clock on my computer screen; it's ten to eleven, eight minutes since the last time I looked, during which time I've been shutting each of my eyes in turn while staring at the fire drill sign on the opposite wall of the office to check which one sees better (FYI the left one, marginally). That's . . . um . . . 480 seconds of my life I'll never get back again.

Susannah is in London for the whole day and I've dealt with the mail, updated the company's Twitter feed with a link to some tedious car insurance survey, checked Facebook multiple times and now have nothing else to do.

I should really take this opportunity to do something useful, like learning a language. I've listed 'conversational Italian' under Skills on my CV, and now would be the perfect time to make a start. There must be a free course online somewhere . . .

My phone starts to ring and I jump on it.

'Susannah White's office.'

'What time are we doing lunch?' It's Mel.

'Oh God, I'm so sorry, but I just don't think I'm going to be able to get away from my desk. Susannah's in London and I'm completely snowed under. Can we reschedule for early next week? Tuesday?'

'You're no fun any more,' huffs Mel. 'But I suppose we could do it on Tuesday instead – *just this once*, mind. I'll come and see you for a coffee later. That is if you're not too busy with your highly important filing.'

I hate lying to Mel, but she's bound to ask me about Adam again and I can't face another grilling about the state of our relationship. Try as I might, I can't block out the vision of me in hi-vis polyester and an M&S balconette bra giving a hand-job to a *Blue Peter* craft project. I just know that somehow Mel will manage to get all the details of the whole sorry episode out of me – and two days on I'm nowhere near ready to see the funny side.

I actually made up with Adam the morning after it happened. He phoned me at 7 a.m., when he knows my alarm usually goes off, and begged me to forgive him for his 'insensitive behaviour', even though I was the one who should have been apologising for picking a fight then throwing him out. I really don't deserve such a considerate boyfriend. I mean, Adam wasn't to know that I'd had such a terrible night's sleep, stressing over what had happened, that in the early hours I'd reset my alarm for 8 a.m. so I could have a bit of a lie-in. And okay, so he did overanalyse things a wee bit, and I could really have done without discussing how 'the incident' made us feel (him: 'confused', 'regretful', 'mildly aroused'; me: mortified), but isn't that better than just sweeping it under the carpet like most blokes would do? Anyway, we're going out for dinner tonight and then hopefully we'll go back to his house, have a shag and the whole LLILF disaster will be forgotten. So why do I still feel so *flat*?

Just then an email pops into my inbox from one of the Claims team, the same department that Dan works in. I've been quite surprised that I haven't heard anything from him since the drinks at the Plough on Wednesday. The poor bloke is obviously struggling to pluck up the courage to talk to me; in the circumstances, wouldn't the kind thing to do be to reach out to him, to let him know that his words will fall on sympathetic ears? I bash out an email and hit Send.

Hey Dan, just wondered if anything interesting happened after I left the Plough on Wednesday. Did you manage to shake off the new receptionist?! Hope it was a fun night and apologies again for the early exit.

A reply appears almost immediately. Wow, he *is* keen.

I am out of the office on annual leave until Monday 3rd May and will respond to your email on my return. If it is urgent, please contact . . .

Bugger.

11.03.

God, this day is going sooooo slooooowly.

Definitely time for a coffee. Yes, that would perk me up.

I'm strolling back to my desk, thinking how amazing it will be when I can order a cappuccino in Italian, when Kerry, who is PA to one of the senior directors, shouts across the office to me.

'Phone call for you, Perce. Shall I put it through to your desk?'

'Thanks, Kerry.' Or rather – *grazie!* I make it back to my chair just as my phone starts to ring.

'Susannah White's office.'

'Good morning. Could I please speak to Perseus James?'

The voice is clipped and confident, with a hint of a European accent.

'This is Percy James.'

'Ah, Miss James, good morning. I've been trying to contact you regarding a personal matter of some importance. My name is Theresa LeFevre . . .'

I'm so surprised that for a moment I can't speak. The cheek of the woman, calling me in the office!

'. . . and I work for a company called EROS Technologies . . .'

'I know who you are,' I interrupt, with as much indignation as I can muster. 'And I've not replied to either your letter or email because I'm not interested in whatever it is you're trying to sell me. Now if you'll excuse me, I have work to do. And please, do not contact me again or I shall have to notify *Watchdog*.'

'Miss James, as I said in my letter, if you would just take a few moments to meet with me I feel sure you will be interested in my proposal.'

'Well, why don't you tell me what your proposal is right now and then I can let you know whether I am interested or not.'

Way to go, Percy! I sound like the sort of woman who doesn't take any crap; this LeFevre chick probably thinks I'm some kick-ass executive type.

'I'm sorry,' she says (sounding anything but), 'the matter is highly confidential and I would need to speak to you about it in person.'

'Well, I'm afraid that's just not going to happen. There is no way I'm wasting my time and yours trekking down to London to hear your sales pitch.'

'But you wouldn't need to come to our London office.'

'Well, to wherever you are, then.' Honestly, this woman is relentless!

'I'm outside your office.'

'You're . . . what?'

'I'm outside Eagle Insurance. I had business to attend to in the area so I thought I would make a detour to Norwich on the off-chance you had time for a very quick coffee. Miss James, I really wouldn't persist in trying to set up a meeting with you if this wasn't important.'

Oh my God, this woman is actually stalking me. I need to hang up, right now, and then report her to the police. Actually, perhaps I should first go and check what she looks like, just in case I need to provide a full description to the detective in charge of the case.

'Would you excuse me a moment, please,' I say, as calmly as possible. 'My assistant tells me I have an important call waiting on the other line.'

I put her on hold and dash into Susannah's office; we are on the fifth floor, so her window gives a clear view of the street outside. The only people I can see are an old man walking a Jack Russell, a couple snogging and a woman who looks like Angelina Jolie en route to give a keynote address on child poverty at the United Nations, except she's just been delayed by an irritating call to her mobile. The woman is the approximate height and weight of a supermodel and is wearing a white shirt, a navy pencil-skirt suit and the sort of heels that I would last five minutes in, tops. She certainly doesn't look like a stalker; in fact, she looks way more like a kick-ass executive type than I do.

I walk back to my desk trying to get a handle on the situation. On one hand I'm furious with this Theresa LeFevre for turning up at my office unannounced and assuming that I'll just drop everything and see her, especially after I've pointedly ignored all her other messages.

On the other I am furious with myself that part of me – quite a large part, if I'm honest – is desperate to find out what it is she has to say. I can't imagine what's so important that she'd come all the way to Norwich to speak to me in person. Maybe I've won something; ooh, perhaps it's the Lottery! I haven't bought a ticket for a while – well, years actually – but you do hear about millions of pounds'-worth of prizes going unclaimed because people don't realise their numbers have come up. As the image of me waving aloft a giant cheque for £72 million flashes into my mind, I take the call off hold.

'Sorry about that, Ms LeFevre, Fridays are particularly busy for me. How long did you say this meeting would take?'

'No more than ten minutes. And, as I said, if you're not interested then you will never hear from me again.'

Well, it's not like I've got anything better to do . . . Right, I will go and hear what she has to say, but I will not sign anything or give her any money, whatever it is she's offering.

'Okay, I'll come down,' I say. 'But only for ten minutes.'

'Of course, Miss James, and thank you.'

I grab my jacket and bag and head for the lift, dabbing on some lip gloss as I go. 'Kerry, I'm just popping out for a few minutes.'

'Okay, Perce. Grab us a Twix on the way back, there's a love.'

Moments later I walk up to where the sleek Ms LeFevre is standing, feeling dumpy and shabby and wishing I was wearing heels.

'Hi, I'm Percy James.'

She smiles smoothly and offers me a slender hand. 'Miss James, it's a pleasure to meet you. And thank you again for agreeing to hear me out. Is there somewhere nearby we can talk . . . ?'

I nod towards the Costa at the end of the road and we start walking.

'I'm sorry for the cloak-and-dagger nature of my correspondence to date,' she says. Every bloke we pass checks her out, but she appears oblivious. 'Once I've explained the situation I'm sure you'll understand why I couldn't be more candid in my original letter.'

'Well, we'll see,' I say. 'But I won't hesitate in reporting you to Trading Standards if this is all a con.'

'Of course.'

Moments later we arrive at Costa and I grab a table while Ms LeFevre orders the coffee. She returns with Jason, one of the baristas, trailing behind her with our drinks on a tray. Jason has served me virtually every day for the past few years and he has never once offered to carry my coffee to the table.

'So, Norwich seems like a very . . . interesting city,' she says to me, ignoring Jason who is still hovering by our table like a hungry, hopeful dog. 'Have you lived here long?'

'Most of my life,' I say. 'Although I was at university in London. Anyway, could we please get to the point?'

'Of course,' she says, smoothing a non-existent crease out of her skirt. 'To put it in the simplest possible terms, Miss James, EROS Tech specialises in the business of love and relationships, and I've been trying to contact you because you have been selected as the perfect match for one of our clients.'

'So you're from a dating agency?'

Is that it? What a bloody anticlimax! Even Mr Wong Du's offer was more appealing than this. 'Well, I'm afraid I'm already in a relationship, so you've had a wasted journey.'

I pick up my bag and begin to put on my jacket.

'Please, just hear me out,' says Ms LeFevre, with enough bite to make me hesitate. 'EROS Tech is not a conventional dating agency, not by any stretch of the imagination. Our technicians have developed unique compatibility algorithms that have made it possible to match an individual to the one person in the world who is the most suited to them. To put it very simply, we have developed a truly revolutionary system that allows us to find a person's soulmate, wherever they are in the world.'

'Yeah, and so says all the other dating websites out there,' I mutter.

'Compared to our technology, Miss James, the matching algorithms used by other dating websites are still in the

Stone Age. Just because two individuals are non-smokers and like jazz, does that mean they will make a great couple? No, it most certainly does not. At Eros we have made an unprecedented leap forward with our technology.'

'Okay, whatever, you've got really amazing algorithms, but it doesn't change the fact that you've been hassling the wrong person because *I've never signed up to any dating websites.*'

'But that's the point,' she says with a patient smile. 'You don't have to sign up, because everyone in the world is in our pool of potential dates.'

This makes no sense to me at all, a fact that clearly translates to my face because Theresa LeFevre now reaches into her bag and draws out a leaflet.

'I'm sure this will answer your questions,' she says, still smiling as if she's in possession of some fabulous secret.

The booklet is made out of thick card, like a very posh wedding invitation, and is in the same grey-and-white colour scheme as the company's website.

'Please, take a moment to have a look through,' says Ms LeFevre, sitting back, crossing her freakishly perfect legs and scooting them to one side, like she's posing for *Vogue*.

Reluctantly, I start to read.

8

Welcome to the Future of Love

There are seven billion of us in the world. Somewhere out there is your soulmate: your perfect match, ideal partner and ultimate true love. The One.

If you could somehow find them, your life would be complete and happiness forever guaranteed, but the chance that you will ever bump into this magical someone – the 'other you' – is infinitesimal. A NASA scientist recently calculated that even if your soulmate is similar to you in age (five years older or younger), there will still be half a billion people in that demographic – and most of us won't meet more than 50,000 within that age range in a lifetime. So instead you settle for a pale imitation of true love and set yourself up for a lifetime of heart-ache, disappointment and unfulfilled relationships.

But what if it didn't have to be like that? What if there was a way to track down that one in seven billion, to decode the mysteries of love . . . ?

Well, now there is.

Here at EROS Tech we have created SoulDate, a revolutionary

matchmaking system that is set to transform the future of relationships. Thanks to our cutting-edge technology, we are now able to give destiny a helping hand and find your other half wherever they are in the world, be they a lawyer in Chicago, a Masai warrior in Kenya or a student in Saudi Arabia.

Unlike conventional internet dating websites and introduction agencies that can only pair you up with a limited pool of members, our 'Date-a-base' includes everyone in the world who owns a mobile phone or has access to a computer. That's a staggering six and a half billion people – and growing fast.

Forget the usual indicators of compatibility, such as whether you share the same tastes in movies or music, or filling out endless pointless questionnaires: the SoulDate system analyses the vast amount of highly detailed personal data available on every individual and, with the help of our exclusive matchmaking algorithms developed over years of research, we will find your UCM or Ultimate Compatibility Match – the one person in the world who is the most compatible with YOU.

Within weeks of receiving your SoulDate application we will pinpoint the name and location of your UCM and – if you would like to proceed – we will make the initial contact with them on your behalf. And the rest . . . ? Well, that's up to you and your soulmate.

So stop wishing on falling stars and waiting for Prince or Princess Charming to whisk you off your feet. Take the first step to securing your own Happy Ever After and contact EROS today.

Welcome to the Future of Love. Welcome to SoulDate.

'I'm sorry,' I say, looking up at Ms LeFevre. 'But this sounds like science fiction.'

She bobs her head slightly, as if having dealt with similar reactions in the past. 'I'm sure you know that every time you go online you broadcast personal details about yourself,' she says. 'Not just the obvious, such as your bank details or facts that you share freely on social media, but browsing logs and search queries can be processed to disclose far more revealing details about an individual, such as political and religious views, sexual preferences, levels of intelligence – your whole personality. You could answer endless questions about yourself, but when you're online what you *do* is far more revealing than what you *say*. Our SoulDate system collates all the information available on individuals through different sources: not just material facts such as your demographic, income, hobbies and medical history, but the vast amounts of non-verbalised information implicit in your online browsing habits and activities. All of this creates an extremely accurate and detailed profile of every individual.'

I have probably understood less than half of what she has just told me, but the bits I have got sound worryingly Big Brother-ish.

'Is this even legal?' I ask.

'Of course!' Ms LeFevre gives a photogenic little laugh, showing her perfect Tic Tac teeth. 'Your activities online are not private, Miss James. We give away huge amounts of information about ourselves through our browsing habits and activities. On a very basic level, that's why you get those targeted adverts on your Facebook page.'

I think back to the last time I went on Facebook; there were links to ads for miracle celebrity diets, a Topshop dress I've been eyeing up online and beauty products – I actually clicked on one and bought a really excellent mascara.

'So you're telling me that you've got my soulmate' – I make sarcastic quote marks in the air – 'waiting to meet me?'

'I prefer the term "Ultimate Compatibility Match", but yes.'

I take a sip of coffee to buy some thinking time. This sounds so far-fetched it has to be bollocks. Besides, even if I believed in soulmates – which I don't, not really – then surely I'm already with mine?

As if reading my mind, Ms LeFevre goes on: 'Believe me, Miss James, the system works. We haven't been in active operation for many months, but already every couple we have matched have been astonished at their levels of compatibility. Quite frankly, it's been incredible.' She leans towards me, her dark eyes fixed on mine. 'I have no doubt that our system will revolutionise the way the human race conducts relationships.'

I glance at the leaflet again. As well as London, EROS Tech apparently has offices in Paris, Milan, New York, LA,

Tokyo and Beijing: it sounds like a huge operation. Then I remember my furtive googling session at Lou's house and how my search for information on the company brought up a big fat zero.

'If your system is so revolutionary,' I ask, 'why haven't I heard anything about it?'

But Ms LeFevre is unfazed. 'As I said, it's still very early days. We have been developing the system for well over a decade, but have only just launched. We're keeping it private at the moment, promoting only in very exclusive circles, before rolling it out worldwide in the next few months. To date our clients have been high-net-worth individuals as the service is currently extremely expensive to use, but we plan to make it more accessible in the future.'

'You mean your current clients are all loaded?'

Ms LeFevre laughs prettily again. 'Well yes, they do tend to be quite wealthy.'

A vision flashes into my mind of a suited Bradley Cooper lookalike standing beside a helicopter that is filled with red – no, white – roses. Bradley's doppelgänger holds up a little box that looks like it might contain a large diamond . . .

'You'll appreciate I can't tell you any more about your particular match at this stage, to protect their privacy,' Ms LeFevre goes on. 'If you decide to proceed we will arrange a meeting and you can find out as much as you wish in person. We work within a ten-year age range to find a match, but that's all I can share at this point.' She smiles conspiratorially. 'Although having met this particular individual on several occasions, I can tell you that they are *very* charming.'

I feel a sudden rush of protective love for Adam. 'But I've got a boyfriend,' I say. 'We're about to move in together.'

She nods. 'We are aware of that. As you can imagine, it's not unusual to find that our matches are already in a relationship or even married, given the unique way our system operates. If the first match on our list is not interested in taking things further then we look to the second, third or even fourth match. The system provides the top ten most compatible matches for an individual, as even the tenth will be infinitely more compatible than someone you would meet at random. In your case, however, you are the UCM for this individual – the first on their list.'

I feel disorientated and queasy, the way I used to feel when I'd endlessly spin round and round for fun when I was a kid. 'I've just put my flat on the market,' I say weakly.

'And the last thing we would wish to do is break up a happy relationship,' says Ms LeFevre, with a slight softening of her highly polished manner. 'But in some instances, deep down, people know that when it comes to relationships they have made choices that, while completely understandable, have not been entirely prudent. For various reasons, when it comes to love people often find themselves in . . . imperfect situations. All we're saying at Eros Tech is that you don't have to compromise. You *can* have the perfect relationship.'

'Can I get you anything else, ladies?' It's Jason, back again. Ms LeFevre ignores him.

'I know this must be a lot to take in,' she continues to me, 'and of course you must give yourself some time to think about it. But if you did decide to meet with your UCM there would be no pressure to take things any further. I'll leave you my details and if I don't hear from you by the end of next week I'll assume you're not interested, remove you from the system and you won't hear from me again.'

She slides a pale-grey business card across the table and then stands up, fastening the single button on her jacket.

'Goodbye, Miss James, it's been a pleasure to meet you.' She holds out her hand and I shake it robotically. 'If you have any questions, please don't hesitate to get in touch. I very much hope to hear from you before next Friday.'

And then she strides towards the exit, with both Jason and me staring after her. I keep my eyes fixed on her as she opens the glass door and pauses for a moment outside, her long dark hair billowing across her face, then she strides across the road and disappears amongst the traffic.

It takes me a moment to realise that Jason is talking to me.

'Sorry, what was that?' I say.

'I was just asking if she's a mate of yours?'

I shake my head, still staring out of the window. 'No, she's a . . . a saleswoman.'

Jason gives a low whistle. 'Well, whatever it is she's selling, I'm definitely buying. Is that her card?'

Before he can reach for it I tear my eyes away from the street and scoop up Ms LeFevre's business card, which is still lying between our barely touched cups of coffee. In the now-familiar font it reads, 'Theresa LeFevre, Account Director, EROS Technology', above a direct line, mobile number and email address. I turn it over in my hands, wondering how many other people have been left holding this card and feeling, like me, utterly shell-shocked.

All of a sudden, anger surges up inside me: how dare this woman just waltz into my life and assume she knows everything about me and my relationship? What was it she said? 'People often find themselves in imperfect situations.' What a cow! I glance down at her card again; I need to throw this away, now. It's not a business card, it's a ticking bomb . . .

'Uh, Percy?'

It's Jason again, looking at me with squinty eyes as if I'm not quite all there.

'What?'

'Your mobile. It's ringing.'

'Oh right, thanks.' I dive into my bag for it and hit answer. 'Hello?'

'Morning, love, I had a quiet moment between meetings so I thought I'd check in.'

Oh God, it's Adam. The last person I want to talk to right now. I'm instantly swamped with guilt, even though I haven't done anything wrong . . . or have I? It's not as if I told Ms LeFevre that I wasn't interested in her crazy proposal. I very noticeably failed to do that, plus I am still holding her business card. Shit, I need to say something to Adam.

'Hello!' I blurt out, far too cheerily. 'What a nice surprise! It's so lovely to hear from you.'

'Are you busy?'

'No, I'm not. I mean yes, very busy indeed. Manic.' (So, along with Mel, that's two people I've lied to today, although in my defence I really need to get my head straight before I can have a normal conversation with Adam.) 'I'm just grabbing a coffee at Costa then rushing back to work. It's go go go! How are you doing?'

'Well, it looks like the Miller deal is finally going through. I had a meeting with Mr Miller this morning and although he and his sons had some reservations about our terms . . .'

As Adam talks, my attention is dragged back to the car crash inside my head. If I'm feeling this guilty, does it mean that my subconscious is actually thinking about meeting up with this man? And (I'm playing devil's advocate here, obviously) would it be so wrong if I *did* meet up with him? Er, hello – of course it bloody would. For a woman who is about to move in with her boyfriend it would effectively be cheating. Post-epiphany and in the spirit of living the life I've been given, I really shouldn't be giving this 'opportunity' a moment's consideration.

. . . But then again, how many people get the chance to meet the one person in the world most compatible with them? I mean, wouldn't it be a little narrow-minded not at least to go and say hi? Just to see what my soulmate looks like (how weird would it be if it actually *was* Bradley Cooper!) and then obviously take it no further and forget all about it. That wouldn't be cheating, that would be *research*. God, I really need to talk about this with someone, to get some perspective. Then I remember the girls' night tomorrow with my three closest friends, all with differing viewpoints and strong opinions, all with my best interests at heart. Perfect. They're bound to be able to help me decide what I should to do. Then I realise Adam has stopped talking.

'Sorry, hon,' I say, 'the phone cut out there for a moment. What were you saying?'

'I said have you got any thoughts about where we should go tonight?'

Oh bugger, I forgot about dinner. There is no way I can sit opposite Adam and chat to him like a normal, non-evil girlfriend. I need some time to think about Theresa LeFevre's proposal. Or do I? Why the hell am I not just tearing up her card right now and forgetting about the whole thing?

'Percy? Is everything okay?'

'Yes, of course! Why wouldn't everything be okay? Everything is terrific. Except . . . I've got really bad period pains.'

Lie number three. Whoever this person is that Theresa LeFevre has lined up for me is bound to be a serial fibber.

'Ah, right,' says Adam; he's rather squeamish around 'women's issues'. 'Poor you. Do you want to give dinner a miss? Perhaps you should get an early night.'

'Do you mind? Sorry, I know we usually keep Friday nights for ourselves and I was so looking forward to seeing you.'

'Don't worry, love, you get some rest. I should probably work late anyway. I know you're out with the girls tomorrow night, but how about we get together for lunch on Sunday?'

'Yes, that would be lovely.' Perfect – by then I'll have got my head straight and put all this craziness behind me. 'We could drive out to the country and find a little pub, I've heard really good things about this place on the way to Bungay . . .'

'Well, actually, your mum popped into the office this morning and asked if we would like to go theirs for lunch on Sunday, and I told her we'd love to. I hope that's okay? We haven't been round there for a while.'

And that, right there, is why you should never go out with someone who works for your father. I make a non-committal grunt, which roughly translates as: 'No, it's not okay, but you've told her we'll go now so we're going to have to, aren't we?'

'Righty-ho, I'll let you get on,' says Adam cheerily. He's never been very good at deciphering my grunts. 'Hope you feel better soon, love. I'll phone to check on you later.'

'Adam?'

'Yes?'

'Do you believe in soulmates?' Why did I ask that? *Why why why?*

'Oh Percy, you really mustn't worry about moving in together,' he says gently. 'I know it's a big step, but I promise you that I love you and will take care of you. And yes, of course I believe in soulmates, because I'm talking to mine right now. Okay, beautiful?'

I mutter goodbye and put the phone down before my head literally explodes with guilt.

9

It has been decreed in the spirit of Old-School Girls' Nights Out that we should all get ready together on Saturday evening. As Lou and Charlie have husbands and children, both wholly contrary to the spirit of the occasion, and Jaye is staying with her parents, the plan is to meet at my flat at 7 p.m., so it has fallen to me to arrange OSGNO-appropriate drinks and music, which means Britney and Blue and a large jug of Archers Peach Schnapps with vodka and lemonade, our beverage of choice circa 2002. I can't believe we used to drink this stuff; I get a sugar rush purely from the fumes. No wonder we used to be able to keep going until 6 a.m.

Jaye is the first to arrive, looking like she's taken the wrong turn off a red carpet; I half expect the paparazzi to jump out from behind the wheely bins. Beneath her camel cashmere coat she is wearing a crop top and matching pencil skirt, showing off an expanse of tummy so sculpted it looks like it's been airbrushed. I am in skinny jeans and a 'fancy' top with a blazer (my default going-out outfit) and next to Jaye I look like – well, somebody going on a girl's night out in Norwich a few years after they could justly be described as a girl. But I'm well used to being outshone by her and besides, tonight's not about me, it's about getting Jaye's mojo back – and she is mojoed to the max in that outfit.

'You look incredible,' I say. 'Norwich will have a melt-down.'

'Aw, you're lovely but this skirt does nothing for my hips, and I'm really not sure if I'm too old for a bra top . . .'

'Jaye, listen to me.' I grab her by the shoulders. 'You are stunning. Just say thank you.'

She smiles. 'Thank you, babe. And thank you for organising tonight, I'm really looking forward to it. I brought snacks,' she adds, holding up a carrier bag as we go up the stairs to my flat.

'There better not be any raw carrot sticks in there,' I say. 'That would *not* be an era-appropriate snack for the occasion. Hummus didn't reach East Anglia until 2004.'

'Don't worry, everything in here contains processed carbs, salt and saturated fat, okay?'

Charlie turns up a few minutes later with a bottle of Prosecco and a box of Ferrero Rocher that's already missing a couple. I have known her and Lou since the first year of primary school when the three of us formed a tight gang that weathered the storms of puberty, boys, university and careers, and survives to this day pretty much unscathed. There have been periods when we've not seen much of each other, but even after months apart, when we meet up it's as if we only saw each other the previous evening at netball practice. Along with Jaye, I know the two of them will always be in my life.

Charlie is one of those girls who everyone always remembers, even years after a brief meeting: 'Oh yes, of course, *that* Charlie.' She is six foot, as lithe as a ballerina and her face, with its distinctive nose and strong chin, looks like it should be carved out of marble in a Roman temple. Even when at work (she's a primary school teacher) she wears her long brown hair in complicated plaited buns on the top of her head, pinned with silk flowers, and favours vintage prom dresses from Oxfam; I don't think I've ever seen her in jeans. The dreamy boho vibe is deceptive, though: up until they got married Charlie and her husband Jake lived in a shared loft in Shoreditch and they still go clubbing in London whenever they can, which admittedly hasn't been very often since the arrival of their twin girls, Florence and Plum (my god-daughter). The family now live in an old farmworker's cottage just outside Norwich and although Charlie has thrown herself with her usual gusto into vegetable-growing and jam-making, a set of mixing decks sits in their kitchen alongside the Aga. She is Mary Berry crossed with Fatboy Slim.

'All right my lovers?' Charlie kisses us both on the mouth, leaving tangerine lipstick tattoos. 'Jesus Christ, Jaye, you look hot. Ladies, I am so up for tonight I can't tell you. Well done Percy, for getting it sorted.'

She slumps next to us on the living-room floor and scrolls through my iPod. 'Ooh, "Reach for the Stars"! We've got to have that one on . . . What are we drinking?'

'Perhaps mineral water to start off?' Jaye looks at me hopefully.

'Sorry, there's only one option,' I say, nipping to the kitchen to fetch the jug of Archers, which I have garnished with paper umbrellas and slices of orange. *'Ta-dah!'*

Jaye takes the teeniest sip; from the look on her face you'd think it was petrol. 'Jesus, what is this stuff?' she splutters. 'It's revolting.'

'I quite like it,' says Charlie, draining her glass. 'Gis a top-up, Perce.'

As the Spice Girls sing about really really really wanting to zigazig-ah, Jaye empties her make-up bag on the coffee table and Charlie and I fall upon the pots, palettes and tiny bottles from Los Angeles promising 'mesmerising radiance' and 'dewy plumpness'.

'So, you'll never guess,' says Jaye, as she expertly wields an eyeliner, 'I read in *US Weekly* that my ex and that bitch are thinking of adopting a baby from Africa. Apparently their "pal Madonna" has been encouraging them to visit her orphanage in Malawi.'

'Fucking hell, I didn't know Stewie was friends with Madonna,' says Charlie, impressed.

'Well, of course he isn't, it's all bullshit,' snaps Jaye. 'Old Plastic Tits is such a publicity whore she probably made it all up. Honestly, I . . .'

'Jaye, this is all very interesting, but aren't you forgetting the first rule of tonight?' I interrupt. 'No discussing your ex. For the purposes of this evening, he doesn't exist.'

She pouts sulkily. 'But I was just going to say . . .'

'Zip it.'

Silence. We turn our attention back to the make-up. I try out a lip-plumping gloss that gives my mouth pins and needles.

'Ooh, Flo said her first proper word today,' says Charlie, swiping purple eyeshadow across her eyelids. 'It sounded a lot like "fuck".'

I hold up a warning hand. 'That's lovely, Chaz, but no parenting talk tonight either.'

Charlie rolls her eyes at Jaye.

Lou doesn't turn up until just before eight, by which time I'm feeling nicely buzzy and the pain in my lips has just about died down.

'I'm so sorry I'm late, girls,' says Lou, who is barely managing to walk in a pair of slingbacks. 'Alfie wouldn't go to sleep, he's got a tooth coming through and . . .'

Charlie cuts in. 'You better watch it, Lou, mein Führer over there has banned any kiddy chit-chat tonight.'

Lou glares at me.

'Oh come on,' I say pleadingly, 'it's a girls' night out, not a mothers' meeting! We're meant to be talking about . . . I don't know, boys and make-up. Look, just have a drink . . .'

At 8.30, half an hour later than scheduled, we arrive at the Chinese restaurant that was always our first port of call on our nights out. I haven't been here for years but nothing has changed, from the paper tablecloths to the same surly waiter. Without looking at the menus we order Set Meal B with extra prawn crackers and a round of vodka and tonics. 'And a large bottle of mineral water, no ice,' murmurs Jaye as the waiter hurries off.

Nostalgia (and drinking on an empty stomach) have worked their magic and as I look around the table at my friends I feel a giddy surge of love for all of them. This is fun, my three best girls all out together! We should *definitely* do this more often. I wonder if I should bring up the subject of Theresa LeFevre's bombshell, but now isn't the right time. That's definitely an end-of-night conversation.

Moments later the hors d'oeuvre platter arrives: spring rolls, seaweed, prawn toasts and spare ribs, decorated, as ever, with an elaborately carved radish.

'Lou, do you remember when you went on a date here

with that bloke and he actually *ate* the radish?' says Charlie. 'And you were too polite to tell him it was just the garnish?'

'God, yeah,' laughs Lou. 'And then he dipped his spring roll in the finger bowl! What a loser. God knows why I married him . . .'

'Do you use monosodium glutamate in the food?' I overhear Jaye asking the waiter. 'I'm sensitive to MSG.'

'MSG in everything,' he snaps.

'Jaye, just eat it,' says Lou, chewing a spare rib. 'I'm not having a lecture on nutrition tonight.'

'Fine, but I'm telling you now, MSG really doesn't agree with me. And while we're on the subject, you should really educate yourself on the effects of eating red meat. I did a month-long detox retreat in Palm Springs where we had colonic irrigation and you should have seen the stuff that came out that tube . . .'

'JAYE!'

She holds up her hands. 'It's okay, I've said my piece. But I'll be sticking to the seaweed, thank you very much. Did you know seaweed is one of the only foods containing iodine? It also helps regulate hormone levels.'

'I believe this is actually deep-fried cabbage,' muses Charlie. 'And not seaweed at all. Still bloody delicious though.'

Jaye looks in panic at her plate. 'Is that right? Percy, is this really cabbage?'

'Of course not!' I say, desperate to keep the peace. 'Well, I suppose it might be, but cabbage is still healthy, right? Lots of . . . antioxidants?'

It is nearly half ten by the time we get to Tombland, the area that makes up the epicentre of Norwich's student nightlife. Everything has changed since we were last here so we join the queue outside the biggest and glitziest of the places on the main drag, which is called Club Xtreeem.

'Isn't this fun? Just like old times!' I say, as we stand shivering in the line of underdressed teens and twenty-somethings. Do the youth of today not own coats? 'Hey, do you remember that New Year's Eve when we were *still* queuing up outside the club when it struck midnight and, Charlie, you ended up snogging that bouncer just so he would let us in?'

Jaye wraps her coat tightly around her and looks warily at the crowd ahead of us. 'Is there a VIP guest list?'

Lou slips off one of her shoes and rubs her foot. 'I really hope there is somewhere to sit down. Couldn't we go to that other place we passed on the way here? It looked much quieter.'

'No,' I say firmly. 'We are going here, and we are going to dance.'

After a half-hour wait we make it into the club. Inside it is enormous: the ceiling soars way above the huge central dance floor and there are mezzanine levels rising to each side, all packed with people. It is dark and stuffy and the music is so loud it's impossible to make out what it is, but as the thump of the bass pulses through me I force myself to ignore the voice inside my head that, like Lou, is wondering where all the chairs are, and vow to throw myself into the experience.

We make our way to the bar, although it's slow going because Jaye gets hit on approximately eighty-two times as we push through the crowds. When we finally get there Jaye offers to get the drinks in; she is served immediately and the very fit (and very young) barman gives her the round for free. I'm pleased to see her flirt back and catch a glimpse of the carefree, confident Jaye of old, which makes my achy feet and the prospect of tomorrow's hangover far less painful. Surely tonight must be doing her some good?

Two cocktails later I drag us all to the dance floor, but while my mind is willing my body is weak. I'm not sure what has happened in the years since I last went to a nightclub, but I seem to have forgotten how to dance. I find myself stepping from one foot to another in time with the music, like my mother at a wedding, and even start doing finger-clicks. Perhaps this song is too fast, or maybe I'm not drunk enough? I notice a girl in a pair of very small shorts (possibly knickers) and try to copy her Beyoncé-style moves, but my hips stubbornly refuse to do what hers are doing and, besides, at my age I should probably not be twerking.

A couple of songs in, though, and I'm past caring what I look like. The music and cocktails have combined to create that wonderful flying sensation when you forget your inhibitions, stop thinking and just move. I feel like I could dance all night. Jaye catches my eye and it's clear she's in the same place; we grin at each other and she mouths: 'We should do this more often!' A couple of blokes with footballers' haircuts are dancing around her, clearly out to impress, but Jaye is oblivious, closing her eyes and raising her arms above her head as the music soars. Nearby Charlie is dropping some serious moves while even Lou, who is draped in a pink feather boa courtesy of a group of hens, looks like she's enjoying herself. This is amazing. We should go clubbing every weekend!

Then out of the corner of my eye I notice Jaye pause for a second to rummage in her handbag. At that moment she is caught in a strobe light and I clearly see her taking a plastic pouch containing a few small pills out of her bag, a couple of which she then palms into her mouth and washes down with a swig of her drink. I'm about to say something to her when a bald man in a leather jacket and headset with the thickest neck I've ever seen appears at her side.

'Okay, you're out,' he says, jerking his thumb towards the exit.

Jaye looks confused. 'Why? What have I done?'

'Don't play the innocent with me, I saw what you were

up to. Read the signs: this establishment operates a zero-tolerance policy on drugs.'

'What, these?' Jaye holds up the little plastic bag of pills. 'These aren't drugs, they're milk thistle tablets.'

The bouncer folds his arms with an expression that suggests he's heard it all before.

'It's a herbal supplement,' Jaye persists, shouting to be heard above the music. 'To support liver detoxification function.'

'You think I was born yesterday, love?' He shakes his head wearily. 'Look at the state of you: wide eyes, pale, sweaty – believe me, I've seen enough people off their nuts to know the signs.'

'That's the monosodium glutamate!' Jaye swings round to look at me, beaming triumphantly. 'See, I *told* you I was allergic to MSG!' She turns back to the bouncer. 'We've just been for a Chinese! I've got an allergy to MSG!'

I try to intervene. 'Honestly, sir, she wouldn't touch drugs. She won't even take paracetamol.'

But the bouncer is still looming over her. 'Listen, lady, I don't care if you're on MSG, MDMA or whatever else is doing the rounds these days – you're out. And if you don't go now and take your friends with you I'm calling the police.'

'What's going on?' Charlie has come twirling over.

'Jaye's just been busted for popping milk thistle tablets,' I say, trying not to snigger. 'This gentleman has asked us to leave.'

'Are we going?' Lou appears. 'Thank God, I've got to take off these shoes.'

The bouncer is looking between us, his meaty brow furrowed in confusion; clearly we're not his average clients. 'Listen, are you lot going or am I calling the police?'

'We're going, we're going,' I say, and we start heading towards the exit. But as we shoulder our way through the crowd, a sweaty, skinny bloke grabs Jaye and furtively shoves a handful of banknotes at her.

'How much for those pills?'

She looks about her and hands the little plastic bag over. 'You can have them for free,' she says. 'But be careful, they're MENTAL.'

We manage to make it outside before collapsing onto each other in drunken hysterics.

'Sorry about that,' snorts Jaye, wiping her eyes.

'Why the hell did you put the milk thistle tablets in that little bag?' gasps Charlie. 'It couldn't have looked dodgier. You should have left them in the original packaging.'

'Ah, but then I wouldn't have had room for the rest of these,' says Jaye, and she opens her clutch to show an assortment of identical plastic bags, each containing pills of all different colours and sizes. 'This is wild burdock root, this one's a probiotic, these are dandelion root, these are psyllium husk, this is high-potency vitamin C and this one' – she holds up a bag with a single tablet and examines it – 'you know, I think this might actually *be* Ecstasy. I found it in my old bedroom hidden down the back of the chest of drawers in an envelope on which I'd written *JAYE'S ASPIRIN – DON'T TOUCH* in large letters.'

This sets us all off again.

'Okay, where to now?' I ask, when we've finally calmed down. 'How about that cocktail bar just down the street – I bet they do espresso Martinis.'

The other three look sheepishly at each other.

'Well, the thing is . . .' begins Jaye.

'I mean, I'd hate to be a killjoy, but . . .' says Lou.

'It *is* quite late,' agrees Charlie.

Ten minutes later we arrive back at my flat.

'Okay, what are we drinking?' I ask. 'Vodka? More Archers?'

Silence.

I sigh. 'Tea?'

'Ooh, yes, that would be lovely.'

'Decaf if possible, Perce.'

'Do you have anything herbal . . . ?'

After I've made tea and toast and we're all slumped in the living room I realise that now is the moment for The Chat.

'Right,' I say, putting my mug on the coffee table and sitting forward in the armchair. 'There's something very important I need to talk to you all about.'

'I knew it, you're pregnant!' Lou is triumphant. 'Charlie,

didn't I say to you the other day that I thought Percy looked like she was pregnant?'

'You did! Oh, this is amazing! Congratulations, my darling. Are your boobs sore?' Charlie pauses for a second, frowning. 'Percy, a woman in your condition really shouldn't be drinking that much, you know . . .'

'Whoa, hang on there, I'm not bloody pregnant! Although, Lou, nice to know I look it.' She mouths 'sorry' to me. 'Okay, this is very complicated so I need your complete and undivided attention. Nobody speak until I say you can talk.'

So I start from the very beginning and explain about the letter and email from Theresa LeFevre and how she ambushed me at work. I tell them all about EROS Tech and their revolutionary matchmaking system and their claim that I'm some mystery man's soulmate. I mention my Bradley Cooper theory. I explain how confused I am. Then I sit back and wait for my friends to sort it all out for me.

There is a stunned silence.

'Okay, you can talk now,' I say.

Lou jumps straight in. 'Percy, you're not actually thinking about meeting up with this man, are you?'

'Of course she isn't!' cries Jaye, turning to me with Bambi eyes. 'You're not, are you, Percy? You wouldn't do that to Adam, surely?'

'Well, I honestly have no idea what to do; that's why I wanted to talk to you about it.'

'Percy, you need to steer well clear of this,' says Lou sternly. 'It all sounds *highly* dodgy. You don't actually know anything about this woman or her company. It might be a scam or a cult or . . . or a front for a human trafficking operation. You should just forget about the whole thing.'

Jaye is nodding vigorously. 'Absolutely.'

Then Charlie, who has been polishing off the last piece of toast, speaks up. 'Well, I think she should meet up with him.'

Jaye and Lou round on her. '*What?*'

'Why not? What's wrong with having an innocent drink with someone?'

'But it wouldn't be innocent, would it? It would be a date,' snaps Lou.

'No, it would be a . . . a reconnaissance.' Charlie licks the jam off her fingers. 'If Percy agreed to go out with him a second time, *then* it would be a date.'

I nod enthusiastically; that's exactly how I see it.

'I think we're all missing the point here,' says Lou. 'Which is that Percy has already met her soulmate, has been happy with him for over three years and is *about to move in with him.*'

I take a deep breath. 'But how do I know for sure that Adam really is my soulmate?'

Jaye looks very much like she might cry. 'Percy, you are lucky enough to be with Adam, the sweetest, most considerate boyfriend you could ever hope for, and the fact you're even thinking about . . . That you could even consider . . .' Then she does start to cry.

Lou gives me a hard stare. 'Now look what you've done,' she says.

'Oh God, Jaye, please don't get upset.' I go over and sit next to her on the sofa, wrapping my arms around her tiny frame. 'I'd never cheat on Adam, you know that.'

'But you don't know what it's like,' she whimpers, 'finding out the person you love and think you're going to be with forever is seeing someone else behind your back . . .'

And she breaks into more sobs.

'Shhh, it's okay,' I say, rubbing her back. I feel terrible. 'Would you like another cup of camomile tea? Or I think I've got some mineral water somewhere . . . ? I'm so sorry I've upset you, please don't cry – we've had such a lovely evening.'

Lou is sitting back, arms folded, looking at me with a 'this is all your fault' expression. 'Percy,' she says, 'how would you feel if Adam did this to you?'

'I'd . . . well, I'd be upset,' I admit reluctantly, but I need to be honest if I'm going to work out what to do about this. 'And I'd feel betrayed.'

She throws her hands up in the air in triumph. 'Well, there you go. You've just solved your own dilemma. You need to forget about this whole thing and get on with your life – *with Adam*. And Charlie, you should be ashamed of yourself. Percy is in cloud cuckoo land at the best of times—'

'*What?* I am not!'

'—but I expected better of you,' finishes Lou tartly.

'Christ, keep your effing wig on,' says Charlie. 'I'm not saying Percy should split up with Adam – far from it. If she meets up with this bloke odds are he'll be totally wrong for her and then she can move in with Adam happy in the knowledge that he is The One. But if she doesn't, then she'll always be wondering "what if"? I know I would.'

Lou scoffs. 'What, so if this woman contacted you out of the blue and said you were someone's soulmate you'd go and meet with them, even though you're married?'

Charlie shrugs. 'Yeah, probably.'

'Bollocks.' Lou shakes her head. She looks furious.

'No, I think I would. I'd be dying to know what they were like. Maybe it *is* all bullshit, but I'd want the facts. And, as Percy pointed out, it might turn out to be Bradley Cooper, and I'd kick myself for not at least getting a photo with him. I'd tell Jake beforehand though. It's a bit of a unique opportunity, and I'm sure he'd understand in the circumstances.'

This hadn't occurred to me. 'Do you think I should say something to Adam?'

Charlie looks at me in horror. 'What? No of course you bloody shouldn't; are you mental?'

'But you just said you'd tell Jake.'

'That's different, we're married and Jake's the sort of bloke who would understand.'

'And Adam isn't?'

'He's just a bit less . . .' She fumbles for the word. 'Liberal.'

We sit in silence, each engrossed in our own thoughts. Jaye's tears have finally stopped and her breathing slowed; I think she might have fallen asleep. Charlie has started on the Ferrero Rocher again. Lou is still looking livid.

'This is a can of worms, Perseus, mark my words,' she says darkly. 'What if this person turns out to be a loony? They might be a rapist or murderer. What if they start stalking you? What if Adam finds out?'

And my head finishes off the one thing Lou doesn't say: what if you meet this person and fall madly in love?

10

'Hello, darling.' My mother kisses me briskly on both cheeks, ladies-who-lunch style, before pulling back to look at me. I await the inevitable comment on my weight, hair, make-up or outfit.

'Look at those freckles!' She taps me lightly on the nose. 'I think someone's been forgetting their high-factor sun-screen again . . .'

Well, that's a new one at least.

My mother is tall and willowy; in her late teens she actually worked for a while as a model (or 'fashion man-nequin', as she puts it, possibly concerned that otherwise people would assume she got her bits out for *Penthouse*). I, on the other hand, have inherited the sturdier physique and low centre of gravity of the women on my father's side of the family, and while I know Mum loves me I often get the feeling that her only child's lack of svelteness and poise is a disappointment to her. I'm quite sure that one of the reasons she's so keen on Adam is the fact he's over six foot and has a speedy metabolism so will rebalance the family gene pool.

'Ooh, and the gorgeous Adam,' she gushes. 'Looking as handsome as ever.'

'Hello Anthea, lovely to see you. What a beautiful dress, is it new?'

'Goodness no, I've had it for ages, but bless you!'

We are ushered into what my mother refers to as 'the blue drawing room', as if we had a whole load of different-coloured drawing rooms hidden somewhere, where I'm thrilled to see that we have someone else joining us for lunch.

'Maggie!' I say, rushing over to give her a hug.

Maggie is my granny, although she wouldn't thank me for calling her that. She had an epiphany of her own when my grandfather died five years back, declaring that she was now going to live life *her* way, and in the process has transformed from a cosy gran to a bob-haired, orange-lipsticked, Doc-Martens-wearing hipster who works part-time in Gap, has more followers on Twitter than I do and has just got engaged to a forty-eight-year-old semi-pro darts player called Derek. I don't know what my mother is more angry about: the fact that her new stepfather will be three years younger than she is, or that he is known as 'Dead-eye Del' and has a tattoo of Kim Wilde on his right bicep. Having just been voted Lady Captain of her golf club, she may suspect neither fact will play out particularly well at the clubhouse.

As ever, Mum has prepared the most wonderful lunch; I keep telling her she should apply for *Masterchef*, but she insists that would be 'common'. The conversation, however, is not quite as palatable, as Mum wastes no time getting onto her favourite topic: getting Adam and me down the aisle. She's not even subtle about it any more.

'I bought the most gorgeous new hat the other day in Jarrold's,' she begins, passing around a tray of roast potatoes. 'It's almost identical to one I saw Carole Middleton wearing at Cheltenham Ladies Day. Now all I need is a special occasion to wear it.' She simpers forcefully in Adam's direction. 'A wedding, perhaps . . . ?'

I glance at my poor boyfriend, who suddenly finds something very interesting to examine on his plate. Thankfully, Maggie comes to our rescue.

'Well, that's perfect timing, Anthea, because Derek and I have just set the date. We're going for the 26th June, just after the European Darts Championship has finished. You could give your new hat an outing then.'

I catch Maggie's eye and she gives me the ghost of a wink.

My mother's eyes widen in alarm. 'It isn't really a registry office sort of hat, Mum.'

'We're not getting married in a registry office.'

'You're not honestly thinking of having the ceremony in church?' Mum's voice disappears in a shocked squeak.

'No, we're getting married in woodland just outside

Norwich. Derek and I both enjoy walking, so it made sense to have the ceremony outdoors.'

'That's a lovely idea,' I say.

'And we were hoping to have the reception at the golf club. What do you think, Anthea? Perhaps you could put in a good word for us?'

It's obvious she's joking, but my mother looks like she might combust.

'Oh, well, the club gets terribly booked up around that time,' she stammers. 'I could ask the Secretary, of course, but I'm really not sure they would be able to accommodate a party of that size at such short notice . . .'

'She's pulling your leg, love,' my dad says gently.

Mum recovers herself and gives a nervous laugh. 'Of course. Silly me.'

'So what *are* you going to do for the reception, Maggie?' I ask.

'We've found a lovely little pub where we're going to have fish and chips, then a disco and a live band.'

'Sounds perfect,' says Adam. 'I do love weddings that have a personal touch.'

'Yes, but the elegance of a traditional church wedding is wonderful too, don't you think, Adam . . . ?' says Mum, desperation creeping into her voice.

There's an awkward silence.

'Adam, did I tell you about this vintage car rally in Lowestoft next month?' This time it's Dad who saves the day. 'I was thinking of taking the MG and wondered if you'd like to tag along . . .'

After lunch Dad takes Adam to look at his beloved 1963 MG Midget, which he's been tinkering with on the driveway, Mum disappears off to do golf club paperwork and I relax in the garden with Maggie. We sit in silence for a while, reading the papers and enjoying the spring sunshine, then it occurs to me that if anyone I know is well placed to give advice on matters of the heart it's my very cool granny.

'Maggie,' I ask her. 'Do you believe in soulmates?'

'Oh yes,' she says, putting down the paper. 'In fact, I think we can have many soulmates during our time. Your grandfather, now he was definitely my soulmate. We had such a wonderful connection. Even in the rough times, I always felt it was the two of us against the world. The passion gradually died down, of course, but it was replaced by something else, something deeper and more intense – I just knew I couldn't have *not* been with him. To me, that's a soulmate. And before your grandfather there was this very handsome sailor called George. The most gorgeous arms, he had, so big and muscly . . .' She sighs, staring mistily off towards the bottom of the garden, then turns and gives me a very naughty look. 'Actually, on second thoughts I don't think George was my soulmate, but goodness, we did have some fun together . . . And now, of course, I have found Derek, and I have no doubt that the pair of us are soulmates too.'

'But isn't the whole point of soulmates that you're supposed to have just the one?'

'Oh God no,' Maggie chuckles. 'It's a long life, Percy, and believe me, things can get boring. People change. And if you can change together then wonderful, but if not – well, you'll always find another soulmate out there somewhere.'

I think about Adam and try to picture us together in ten, twenty, thirty years' time, but that just makes me feel panicky. He's undoubtedly a lovely guy, so what's the problem? The only conclusion I can come to is that the issue lies with me: I'm crap at relationships.

'How do you know if someone's your soulmate?' I ask.

She thinks for a long time. 'I think it comes down to the amount of chatter in your head. When a relationship is right – really right – you don't need to talk yourself into it. There's no question or debate, it just . . . *is*. The way I see it, if someone's your soulmate there's this feeling of inevitability, sort of like – "Oh, there you are, I've been waiting for you", and that's the end of that.'

As I think over what Maggie has just said a little voice inside me pipes up and says: *You've never felt that way about anyone, have you, Percy?*

Of course I have, I reply. *That is* exactly *how I feel about Adam.*

Bollocks, the little voice goes on. *In fact, you currently have a debate raging 24/7 inside your head over whether Adam is the right man for you. I should know, I bloody well have to listen to it . . .*

'Why all the questions about soulmates, lovey?' asks Maggie, thankfully putting a stop to the squabble in my head. 'Is everything all right with Adam?'

I take a deep breath. 'Well, the thing is, I've been contacted by this woman from a company called . . .'

But then I hear Dad laughing and glance around to see him and Adam walking towards us with a jug of Pimms and some glasses. I turn back to Maggie.

'I'll tell you about it another time,' I say quickly.

'Make sure you do,' she says, reaching over and giving my hand a squeeze.

Sometimes, you wish hard enough for a sign and out of the blue you get one. That night when we get back to his house Adam and I have amazing sex. Really lovely, loving sex, that ends in the most incredible orgasm. The thing is, more often than not I end up faking it. Yes, I know that runs contrary to every single piece of advice in magazines, but is it really so bad? The way I see it it's just good manners. Men tend to assume that unless they give you an orgasm they haven't been doing their job properly – and I'd hate Adam to think I don't enjoy myself when we have sex, because I really do, regardless of whether or not I come. The way I see it, an orgasm is just the cherry on the top of what is still a very delicious cake.

But this time – wow! We're going through our usual routine when Adam suddenly veers off course. *Hello*, I think, with a very pleasant jolt of surprise, *what's going on here then?* I'm not exactly sure what it is that he's doing differently – perhaps he's moving his fingers in a new way or touches a spot he doesn't usually reach – but after a while I realise that I'm going to come and the lovely buzzy feeling of anticipation builds into an intense burst of light and heat and it's so magical and unexpected that as we collapse together in a tangle of limbs – because by some amazing sexual alchemy Adam comes at the same time – I actually laugh out loud.

A few moments later, once our breathing has steadied a little, Adam props himself up on his elbow and looks at me. Christ only knows why, but he looks worried. 'Is everything okay?' he asks.

I nod, still grinning. 'Okay? That was incredible.'

'But did you come?'

'Uh – *yeah*,' I say. 'Wasn't it obvious?'

'It's just you don't usually laugh when you come.'

'Well, it was just particularly amazing.' I reach up to kiss him, making a mental note to include occasional laughter in future performances. '*You* were particularly amazing.'

That seems to reassure him, and as we lie together, our breath perfectly in sync, the warmth and smell of his skin works like a drug, soothing away my worries and making me feel like all is absolutely right with the world. That night, for the first time I can ever remember, I fall asleep still in Adam's arms. If ever there was the universe telling me *not* to meet up with this SoulDate person this is it.

Arriving at work the next morning I am in a fantastic mood, which is given a further boost by Susannah asking if I'd like to be on the organisation committee for the company's annual conference, a weekend-long jolly masquerading as a serious team-building exercise that takes place in a country house hotel each summer. I've always thought that I have something of a flair for events organising (your loss, Saboteur!) and even the news that Mr Arsehole Hedley, the office Dementor, will also be on the committee does little to dent my enthusiasm.

On Tuesday Mel and I go out for the lunch we missed last week. At her insistence we order a bottle of wine to share and after two goldfish-bowl glassfuls I decide to tell her about EROS Tech, giving the whole tale a jokey 'you won't believe this crazy shit!' spin so even Mel, who is *obsessed* with the idea of soulmates, can't help but think it would be better for me to steer clear. To be fair, it's not hard to convince her it's a scam: from Theresa LeFevre's stalkerish behaviour to her ludicrous explanation about the way SoulDate works and, probably most conclusively, the fact that there is absolutely nothing on the internet about this supposedly 'revolutionary' matchmaking system, the whole thing sounds comically far-fetched. Mel still manages to get in a few digs about Adam – 'you're condemning yourself to a lifetime of ironing his Y-fronts' – but even she seems to be coming round to the idea that I'm moving in with him. We roll back into work at 3.30 p.m.; thankfully Susannah is in a meeting all afternoon so isn't around to witness me falling drunkenly over my chair and ripping my skirt.

On Wednesday, in between research into suitable hotel venues for the company conference, I scan recipe websites in order to plan a special dinner for Adam on Friday night, hoping that it will lead to a repeat performance of the sexual fireworks of last weekend. That evening a girl comes over to view my flat and seems very taken with it; sure enough, moments after her visit the estate agent calls to say that she's thinking about putting in an offer. Whoopee!

But then Thursday arrives – Thursday bloody Thursday, as U2 should have sung – and I get another sign, a whole series of signs in fact, only this time the universe appears to have changed its mind about what I should do. Fickle bloody bastard.

My morning starts at 5 a.m. when I'm awoken by the sound of foxes outside the window either making sweet love or viciously ripping each other apart – it's difficult to tell the difference with foxes. I can't get back to sleep so go to the kitchen to make coffee and as I reach up into the top cupboard for a mug it slips from my sleepy fingers, tumbles into the sink and breaks. Worse, it is the photo mug that Adam gave me to celebrate our first anniversary, and the picture of the two of us, sitting on a beach in Majorca on our first holiday together, all squinty smiles and Sangria, has cracked cleanly down the middle. It's a good job I'm not superstitious.

Later that morning I'm at my desk when Charlie calls my mobile.

'Hey, can you talk?' she says.

'Yup, what's up?'

'I've been thinking about what we discussed the other night,' she says. 'About this whole SoulDate business.'

'And?'

'And you've got to go for it, Perce.'

'Well, I've been thinking about it too and I've decided not to take it any further. What would be the point? The whole thing is clearly bollocks, Chaz, and besides, I'm happy with Adam.'

There's a pause at the other end of the line. 'I didn't want to say this in front of the girls the other night, what with Jaye being so fragile at the moment, but are you? We all know he's a nice guy and everything, but you've never seemed sure. *Really* sure, I mean.'

This throws me; I want to reassure Charlie that I am absolutely sure, that we came at the same time the other night and that *must* mean we're perfect together, but I can't seem to find the words.

'And I may be wrong,' she goes on, 'but you really don't seem that excited about moving in with him – quite the opposite, in fact. Percy, this is a serious business. You're thinking about selling your flat. You've really got to be sure this is right for you.'

'Don't you think I realise that?' I snap, cringing at the defensive note in my voice. 'This isn't some spur-of-the-moment decision. I've been thinking about moving in with Adam for ages.'

'Yes, and until very recently you've been pretty reluctant to go through with it,' persists Charlie. 'Just go and meet this SoulDate guy. What harm can it do?'

After Charlie's call I sit at my desk staring out of the window, chewing my thumbnail. Why, why, why did she have to go and plant a seed of doubt when I had been so sure of my decision?

Moments later, as if summoned by the conversation I've just had with Charlie, Adam phones me.

'Percy, did I leave my golf shoes at yours? They're black and white with studs on the bottom.'

'Um, no, I don't think so.'

'Hmmm, I wonder where they can be, then? I need to find them for this weekend with the boys.'

'What weekend with the boys?'

'The golfing trip this weekend? With Lyle, my old mate from Manchester, and some of his friends, remember?'

'You didn't mention it to me.'

'Yes, I did.'

'No, you didn't.'

There is a pause. 'Well, I must have forgotten to, sorry.'

'You never forget anything,' I say.

'Percy, I'm really sorry if I didn't tell you about this—'

'You didn't,' I say again, more emphatically.

'—but it's not like I was trying to keep it from you. I'm under a lot of pressure at work at the moment, which is why it must have slipped my mind. Anyway, I'm going up to Manchester tomorrow afternoon and then we're playing golf on Saturday and I'm coming home on Sunday. Okay?'

Of course it's okay – I'm always encouraging him to spend more time with his mates – but Adam is usually so reliable, and this 'memory lapse' is so out of character, I can't help but feel suspicious. I do know he's stressed at work because he's had so many late nights at the office recently, unless . . . A terrible thought suddenly strikes me. What if he hasn't been working late at all, but having an affair? And – oh God – that would explain his snazzy new sex technique: he learnt it from *her*!

Percy, you are being utterly ridiculous. You couldn't get a more trustworthy, loyal boyfriend than Adam; stop being childish. It was clearly just a straightforward misunderstanding.

Yet I'm left feeling unsettled and a little bit cross, and not just because of the fifty quid I blew on ingredients for the fancy lamb dish and chocolate and raspberry roulade that I was going to cook for our romantic Friday night in.

Then later that afternoon Mel appears by my desk. The first thing I notice is that she looks weirdly excited in a kid-at-Christmas type way. The second is that she is wearing earrings with little dangly Michael Bublé faces hanging off them.

'Here, take a look at this,' she says, throwing a copy of *Grazia* on my desk. 'You are not going to *believe* it.'

The magazine is open at an article entitled 'The New Dating Revolution'. I skim through; it seems to be a round-up of dating apps, singles nights and supper clubs.

I look up at Mel's expectant face. 'So . . . ?' I say, unsure about why she's showing this to me. 'Nice earrings, by the way. Did you make them yourself?'

'No, shithead, this bit!' she says, jabbing her finger at a column running down the side of the page, making the mini Michaels do a jolly little jig. The headline, written in caps, screams: 'THE FUTURE OF LOVE . . . ?' Reluctantly, I read on.

Imagine how much easier dating would be if there was a guaranteed way to meet the one person in the world who is most compatible with you.

Heartache, humiliation and painful break-ups would be a thing of the past, and happy endings would be routine.

It might sound like the stuff of Hollywood movies, but rumours persist of a revolutionary new dating system that claims to be able to match individuals up with their 'soulmate', wherever they are in the world.

According to a source, a Russian company called EROS Technologies has been secretly developing the system – believed to be called SoulDate – over the past decade, and has spent millions perfecting the groundbreaking matchmaking technology.

Our spy in the white coat reveals: 'SoulDate looks set to revolutionise the way in which the human race conducts relationships.

'The system claims to be able to locate your soulmate wherever they are in the world, whether they're a cattle farmer in Australia or a brain surgeon in Sweden.'

Details on how the system actually works are sketchy, but the company has reportedly already started matching couples and the results have been described as 'astonishing.'

The source adds: 'No longer will you need to question whether someone is right for you – with SoulDate you'll know for sure. This is a genuine game-changer.'

We can't wait to hear more . . .

Mel is standing over me, hands on hips, eyebrows raised, awaiting my reaction. How I dearly wish I hadn't mentioned anything to her about SoulDate.

'This doesn't prove anything,' I begin, with far more confidence than I'm feeling. 'It just says there are "rumours" about it. It could still be a load of bollocks.'

'Don't be so fucking dim!' The Michaels jiggle manically. 'If it's in the press it means this SoulDate business isn't a scam – it's *real*. And if they've found your soulmate you HAVE to meet them, Perce!'

I shrug, as if to suggest that the article is really no big deal, but my insides are churning with dread and excitement. Now that EROS Tech has been mentioned in a magazine – and not just any magazine, in *Grazia*, my pre-epiphany bible – it instantly gives it an appealing sheen of credibility. I had all but convinced myself it was a scam, but now . . .

Mel is still staring at me, waiting for some sort of reaction.

'I really don't think this changes anything,' I say in a small voice.

'Argh, Percy, you are so bloody infuriating!' She growls in frustration. 'Right, I'm not wasting my time on this any more. You can make up your own mind. But let me just say you are *mental* if you don't at least agree to meet with this bloke.'

You know those times when you wake up in the middle of the night, when the world outside is still and quiet, and something that has been vaguely on your mind suddenly assumes the proportions of an immediate and absolute crisis? And, as you lie there in the darkness, rigid with fear, you can't believe you haven't seen things this way before. In that terrible moment it's like you're teetering on a knife-edge: unthinkable things are about to happen right now if you don't take decisive action – and, blind fool that you are, you've been blithely carrying on with your life like everything is completely fine!

But then sleep gets the better of you and when you wake the next morning everything seems rosy again, and you merrily dismiss your fears as night panic and go on with your life as normal.

Well, that happened to me last night. I woke at 2.42 a.m. and a thought struck me as clearly and emphatically as if someone was saying it out loud. In that moment I knew for sure, without a doubt, that I had to meet this SoulDate person – HAD TO – and that if I didn't I'd be making the biggest mistake of my life. It was such an urgent, indisputable feeling that I had to stop myself from phoning Theresa LeFevre that very minute.

Sure enough, when my alarm woke me this morning I remembered how I felt and was all set to dismiss my fears as night-time jitters – but then something else occurred to me. Suppose those 2 a.m. panics are the one time in your life that you're actually seeing things clearly? What if that early-hours revelation is the one moment you grasp the absolute truth of the matter, and the rest of the time you're in denial?

I sit up in bed and rub my forehead with my fingertips, as if trying physically to arrange my thoughts into order. Adam doesn't have to know, I tell myself. I can go and meet this person, discover that they're totally wrong for me – because they're bound to be – and then move in with Adam reassured by the knowledge that I'm already with my soulmate.

Before I can have second thoughts I reach over to get my handbag, dig out Theresa LeFevre's card (which somehow I never got round to throwing away) and dial her mobile. I'm intending to leave a message, as it's only 7 a.m. and she's the type of woman who's bound to be on a treadmill or juicing kale, but she answers immediately.

'Oh, hi, Theresa, it's Percy – Perseus – James here . . .'

'Perseus! How lovely to hear from you. How are you?'

'Fine, thank you. I'm fine. Anyway, I've been thinking about your offer and I've decided that I am prepared to meet this person – my, er, UCM – on the understanding that it's just a quick drink, with absolutely no strings attached.'

'Of course, that's all the first encounter ever is. Just a straightforward meet-and-greet.'

'And it'll have to be this weekend,' I say. *While my boyfriend is out of town*, my subconscious adds. (Hey there, Guilt! Nice to see you again!)

'Leave it with me,' says Theresa LeFevre.

Moments later she calls back, as briskly efficient as ever.

'How does Saturday at 5 p.m. in the American Bar of the Savoy Hotel in London suit?'

'Great,' I say. I've never been there, but a hotel sounds like a good idea; it'll be large and impersonal and I'm highly unlikely to run into anyone I know. 'How will I know who I'm meeting?'

'We instruct our clients to carry their SoulDate folder so you can identify each other. It's very discreet, just plain grey with a small logo. I'll courier one round to your office today. It will contain all the information you need.'

'Great. And what happens afterwards?'

'That's up to you.'

'If I'm not interested, then . . . ?'

'Then you tell me and I will let the other party know and that's the end of that. We're not in the arranged-marriage business, Perseus, we just make the introductions and then you take it from there.'

'Of course,' I say. 'So, um, that's it?'

'Yes, you're all set. I look forward to hearing how the meeting goes.'

As I press the button to end the call my breath comes out in a huge *whoosh* and I realise I've barely been breathing for the whole conversation. Still sitting in bed, my eyes fall on the framed picture on the opposite wall: it is a photo of me and Adam at Charlie and Jake's wedding, shortly after we started dating. We're sitting together, Adam with his arm cuddled around my shoulders, me looking up into his eyes and laughing. Neither of us is aware of the photographer; we are in our own little world and look so perfectly happy and in love that I have to choke back a sudden sob.

Oh God, what have I done?

11

As I struggle to get through the revolving doors of the Savoy – I don't push hard enough, leading to an awkward 'you go first – no, please, after you' exchange with an elderly gentleman who's trying to get out – I begin to wish that I hadn't agreed to have the meeting here. Everything about this place is so unnervingly posh, from the top-hatted doorman to the display cases of diamond necklaces in the foyer, that I feel desperately out of place, as if I have a flashing neon sign on my head that says: *COUNTRY BUMPKIN*. In fact, I'm beginning to wish that I hadn't agreed to this meeting full stop.

I spent nearly an hour this morning deciding what to wear, although in my defence it is pretty tricky trying to choose an outfit when you have no idea who you're going to be meeting. I decided on my usual jeans and blazer – not overtly sexy, but stylish in a laid-back Gwyneth-slash-Cameron type way – and left my hair loose, as men generally like hair. Not that I'm trying to impress anyone, obviously, but I want to make a good first impression; this guy believes he's meeting his soulmate and I'd hate for him to feel short-changed.

On the train ride into London, most of which I spend staring out of the window with my chin resting in my palm until the fields give way to concrete and my hand goes numb, it occurs to me that the last time I made this journey was for the interview at Saboteur – and look at how well *that* turned out. Am I just repeating the same old mistakes: chasing rainbows when I should be focusing on all the good things I already have? Have I learnt nothing from my epiphany? I'm meant to be making the most of the life I've got, not taking some mad gamble on trying to create a whole new one.

This is just research, I remind myself firmly, a straightforward fact-finding mission. I'm the dating equivalent of one of those United Nations teams going to evaluate the situation on the ground in Syria, but with more alcohol and less conflict (hopefully).

Adam phones me as I arrive at Liverpool Street; he's about to tee off at the seventh hole. I tell him that I've come up to London for the day to go shopping, making sure I pop into Topshop on the way to the Savoy to ensure that this is not technically a lie.

As befits an establishment as swanky as the Savoy, there are no signs telling you where anything is, so I have to ask the concierge how to get to the toilets, then ask the toilet attendant how to get to the American Bar, but when I eventually find it I'm pleasantly surprised to discover that the vibe is relaxed, almost cosy. It feels like the sort of place you see in old movies: there are velvet banquettes with little round mirrored tables, framed black-and-white photos on the walls, and the soft background piano music is punctuated by the maraca of a cocktail shaker wielded by a white-jacketed barman.

The bar is quiet, but then it is still quite early. I hover at the entrance pretending to look for someone I know so that I can subtly check out the other customers. There is a couple cooing over each other, hands entwined, surrounded by designer shopping bags; near to them is a smartly dressed woman talking on her phone in what sounds like German. She is drinking champagne and her relaxed body language suggests she is far more at ease in this place than I am. Across the other side of the room there is a man sitting alone. Could this be him? He is reading something on his phone, which gives me a chance to get a good look at him. First impressions: suited, balding, a little on the chubby side, i.e. not exactly my type. But I can't see a SoulDate folder, so that counts him out, hopefully. Phew.

I sit at a table near the entrance and try to distract myself from my growing jitters by focusing on the menu, which is the size of a telephone directory. The only cocktail I recognise is a Negroni, which is priced at £80. Is that a typo? Surely that can't be £80 for one glass? Perhaps you get a pitcher for that price – although this doesn't look the sort of place that would serve pitchers . . .

'Good afternoon, madam, what can I get you to drink?'

A waiter has appeared by my table; he places down a small silver tray containing a few perfectly symmetrical crisps, a selection of nuts and three shiny green olives, plus a folded linen napkin. Toto, I've got a feeling we're not in TGI Friday's anymore.

'Just a gin and tonic, thank you.'

'And do you have a preference as to the gin?'

Whatever's cheapest, I reply in my head. 'Gordon's, please,' I say, the first brand I think of.

He nods, smiles and says, 'Of course,' as if I'm hugely clever to have made such an excellent choice, then disappears.

Then out of the corner of my eye I spot someone coming into the bar and risk a glance. The new arrival is male, mid thirties at a guess, and looks like the model in the M&S pants advert; he's clearly quite wealthy too, as even I can tell that suit is beautifully tailored. He notices me looking at him and smiles quizzically, and I get a sudden stab of panic as I catch a glimpse of a grey folder. Oh sweet Jesus, this man is *way* out of my league . . . But it's too late to back out now. With shaking hands, I reach for my own

SoulDate folder and place it on the little round table in front of me, but when I look up I find that Mr Cheekbones has joined the chubby man I'd clocked earlier, and what I thought was a folder is in fact his iPad. I can't say I'm disappointed; I'm not sure how I'd feel about dating someone prettier than me.

Just then the waiter reappears with my drink and I take a couple of large swigs to calm my nerves. Mmmm, that is a really excellent G&T – although I'd say it was considerably more G than T. I have another sip, enjoying the tingle from the near-neat booze, then try one of the crisps. OMG. That is literally the most divine crisp I have ever eaten. Total snack-crack. Even if I'm stood up by my date, it will have been worth coming here just for that crisp . . .

'Snap,' comes a voice.

I look up to see the woman who I had spotted earlier talking German on her mobile. She is now standing in front of my table, an expectant smile on her face.

'I'm sorry . . . ?' I say, confused, my hand frozen over the crisps.

'I said, snap.'

And everything seems to move in slow motion as she holds up a pale-grey folder, identical to the one that is sitting on the table in front of me.

12

It takes my brain a good few seconds to process what is happening. This woman is clearly carrying a SoulDate folder; therefore this woman – this unmistakably female lady-person of a woman – is my date; which means my soulmate is . . . *a woman?* Surely not, Theresa LeFevre would definitely have mentioned it, and I clearly remember her referring to my date as 'he' and 'him'. I'm absolutely positive I remember that; I mean, I would have *definitely* noticed if she'd described her as a 'she'. Perhaps there is more than one SoulDate couple meeting here today, although that seems unlikely – but then so does the fact that I've been a lesbian all these years and haven't known about it.

'I'm Flora,' says the woman. She has a soft Scottish accent – not German at all, then. 'May I . . . ?'

I realise she is expecting to sit down. Well, of course she is, that's what people do on dates, isn't it? So I smile and nod to the chair opposite while frantically trying to work out how I can GET THE HELL OUT OF HERE without being rude.

'I'm Perseus,' I tell her. 'Well, Percy.'

'*Clash of the Titans*?' Flora beams at me.

Despite the turmoil going on inside my head, I return her smile. 'Yes, how did you know?'

'It was a big part of my childhood. In fact, that film is probably the reason I studied Classics at university.' She nods towards my almost empty glass. 'Can I get you another drink, Percy?'

Of course, the sensible thing to do now would be to explain that there's been a mix-up and that we're actually on fairly different pages, sex-wise. Entirely different books, in fact. But I just can't bring myself to say the words: 'I'm not gay.' It just sounds so narrow-minded. So instead I say: 'That would be lovely, thank you.'

As Flora turns to signal to the waiter I take the opportunity to have a better look at the woman who is supposed to be the love of my life. The most striking thing about her is her hair: long, thick and reddish-brown like a conker. She has wide-set eyes and is wearing a dress that looks a bit sack-like but is probably from one of those pricey Scandinavian designers who do artily-cut clothes in shades of fog and drizzle. Her excellent skin and shoes suggest she's spent a lot of money on both, although I'm sure I spotted that crystal necklace she's wearing in Zara last week. If she were a car Flora would be something luxurious yet sporty: we're talking calfskin leather and walnut interiors but with four-wheel drive and a roof rack. Do Bentley make jeeps . . . ? There's something very appealing about her – she has a nice aura, as Jaye would say, and she is certainly attractive – but my soulmate? *Really?*

As I suspected when I first spotted her, Flora is clearly at home in places like this. She orders champagne and doesn't say 'house is fine' as I would, but instead asks for 'two glasses of the Ruinart Blanc de Blanc' with a proper French accent without even needing to look at the menu.

When the waiter's gone Flora sits back and smiles at me. I'd put her at fortyish, but she has a cute gap in between her two front teeth that makes her seem much younger.

'So – this is rather weird, isn't it?' she says.

You don't know the half of it, love. But then . . . perhaps Flora was expecting to meet a man too? Maybe that's what she means by this being 'weird'? I need clarification, pronto.

'Yes, totally weird!' I say. 'So . . . first impressions? Am I your usual, um, type?'

Flora puts her head on one side and looks at me, like she's sizing up a painting in a gallery. 'Well, you've got beautiful hair. An ex-girlfriend of mine was strawberry blonde, too.'

So that clears that up. Of all the various cans of worms

I feared I might be opening today, outing myself as a lesbian was not one of them.

I need to come clean and explain to Flora that there's been a mix-up – or else say that I've received an urgent text and have to leave immediately. I know, I'll tell her that a friend's car has broken down, she's stuck on the hard shoulder of the M25 with a screaming baby and she needs me to go and pick her up right away. No, I'll say that my mum is in hospital and has suddenly taken a turn for the worse; that's far more convincing, nobody would lie about something like that. I just need to think of a condition that isn't necessarily life-threatening but is serious enough to require a bedside vigil . . .

'So, Percy, what do you do?'

Men, I think miserably. *I do men.*

'Christ, what a boring question, sorry,' laughs Flora, misinterpreting my expression. 'It's just . . . I haven't done this before – used a dating agency, I mean. Although I suppose Eros Tech isn't really your average dating agency!'

'No, I suppose not,' I say sullenly.

There is a brief, not unawkward silence and I think we're both relieved when the waiter reappears with our champagne and another silver dish of the Holy Crisps of Bliss. When he's gone Flora raises her drink to me and says, 'To new friends and new adventures,' and as I clink my glass with hers, taking care not to make too much eye contact, I notice a small tattoo on her wrist. Well, that's a surprise: Flora really doesn't look like the tattoo type. I'm just trying to work out what it is (it looks like a little red sports car, which seems an odd choice) when I notice with surprise that her hand is shaking slightly. Surely she isn't nervous? She seems so poised and confident that it hadn't even crossed my mind that she might feel uneasy – but then, why wouldn't she? The poor woman was hoping to meet her soulmate and I've been sitting here with a face like a grounded sixteen-year-old on the night of the school prom. The least I can do is put a smile on my face and enjoy a glass of champagne with this perfectly nice woman. Theresa LeFevre can sort things out afterwards; this whole mess is her fault, after all.

'Cheers!' I say brightly, vowing to pull myself together. 'So, Flora, you asked me what I did for a living? I should warn you, it's pretty dull.'

'Well, that's at least one thing we have in common, because that's exactly how I feel about my job.' She flashes a relieved smile. 'You first.'

So I tell her about Eagle Insurance and try to make my role sound as fascinating as possible by playing down the Post-it ordering, and because Flora turns out to be a really good listener who asks lots of interesting questions I find myself talking about my frustrated ambitions to make something more of my life and even tell her about the Saboteur balls-up, which makes us both laugh. She is also totally on board with my 'work to live, not live to work' philosophy – although to be fair both her working and her living sound far more interesting than mine. Flora is the chief legal officer at a large technology company, she lives between London and Boston and, despite having a job that requires her to jet around the world doing high-flying things, she still finds time to have hobbies – and not just reading, shopping and going to the cinema, like normal people. No, Flora's hobbies include heli-skiing, tennis and – get this – Krav Maga. I *know*! And I don't even think she's lying, because she knows way more about it than I do, plus she has upper arms like Madonna.

The conversation flows as effortlessly as the bubbles in the champagne and I realise I'm actually really enjoying myself – and thinking that we do indeed seem to have a connection – so when Flora suggests another drink I happily accept. And *that's* when things start to go wrong.

'It's great to finally get the chance to talk to you,' Flora is saying, 'because I really didn't know what to expect. Theresa LeFevre wouldn't tell me a single thing about you before we met.'

'Me neither!' I'm feeling a bit drunk. 'I didn't even know that you were' – FEMALE – 'a fellow Brit!'

'Yes, it was all unbelievably cloak-and-dagger . . .' Flora takes a sip of champagne and crosses her legs. (Objectively speaking, I can say she has very good legs. Toned and cankle-free.) 'Percy, I hope you don't mind me asking, and I hate to bring up the "R" word at this stage, but Theresa did warn me that often the people they pinpoint as matches are already in relationships. What I'm trying to say is that I would completely understand if you were . . . attached. I mean, if I was in your shoes and Theresa had contacted me to say I was potentially someone's soulmate then even if I had a partner I'd probably want to come along, just to check them out!'

Okay, so here is the perfect opportunity for me to straighten things out with Flora. I'll tell her that yes, I'm afraid I *am* in a relationship – with a man, funnily enough! – but it's been lovely to meet her and I hope we can be friends. Great. That's *exactly* what I'll tell her. But then Flora starts talking again before I can get the words out.

'I've been single for about eighteen months now,' she says. 'I lived with Sara – that's the ex I mentioned earlier – for nearly seven years, but for the last year I think we both knew the relationship had run its course. And since then . . .' She gives a shrug. 'I work such long hours that it's hard to meet new people.'

'Mm-hmm,' I say, befuddled with booze and trying to remember how I was going to phrase my excuse.

'. . . And now I'm getting to the age when I want something serious, maybe even marriage and kids, with the right person.' Flora gives a slight grimace. 'Sorry, Percy, I hope that doesn't scare you, but I have got to the point when I feel it's far better to be honest about my priorities up front, so everyone knows where they stand. There's nothing worse than meeting someone with whom you think you have a connection only to discover that they want totally different things from the relationship . . .'

I jump up with such force that everything on the table wobbles.

Flora looks at me uncertainly. 'Percy? Is everything okay?'

'I'm so sorry, I just need to nip out to make a quick call.' I grab my bag, narrowly avoiding knocking over our glasses in the process. 'It's my mother, she's in hospital. She's got . . . malaria.'

Flora's eyes widen in concern. 'Oh Percy, that's terrible. You should have said! A good friend of mine had malaria last year, she was in hospital for weeks. What treatment is your mother having?'

'Oh, you know, the usual. All the drugs. Drips. Lots of . . . fluids.'

'Which strain does she have?'

Shit. 'Um, the one Cheryl Cole had.' I can feel my face flushing. 'Sorry, Flora, I'd better . . .' I wave my phone at her.

'Oh God, yes, of course, please – go. I've been sitting here giving you the third degree and you must be worried sick! Take your time.'

I scuttle out of the bar, nauseous with guilt, and find a quiet spot next to a display case of diamond-encrusted watches where I make a call, just in case Flora comes out to check up on me.

'*Welcome to the EE voicemail service. You have no new messages . . .*'

'Good afternoon, could I speak to the doctor dealing with Mrs Anthea James, please? Yes, I'll hold.'

'. . . *Main menu. To review your deleted messages, press one . . .*'

'Ah yes, hello, Doctor. I'm calling to check on my mother's condition.'

'. . . *To change your personal greeting, press three . . .*'

'Mmm, I see. So she's been asking for me again?'

'. . . *To hear these options again, press five . . .*'

'And you think it would be advisable if I come straight away?'

'. . . *For help, press zero . . .*'

'Of course, no problem at all. I'll be there as quickly as I can. Thank you, Doctor, and goodbye.'

I walk back into the bar, convinced that Flora must have rumbled me, but no, she looks genuinely worried, which makes me feel even more wretched.

'How is she?' she asks, her face so full of kindness that I have to stare at my feet to stop myself blurting out that actually my mother is not in hospital after all but is perfectly healthy and probably at home stuffing a pork tenderloin as we speak.

'She's stable, but I think I better go and see her, just in case,' I mutter at my shoes, cheeks burning.

'Of course. Can I do anything to help? I'll give you a lift to the station.' Flora starts gathering up her things.

'No! No, really, I'm fine, I'll just hop on the Tube – probably be quicker than driving at this time of the day. Thank you anyway. Let me give you some money for the bill.'

'Absolutely not, this is on me.'

'Are you sure?' I wish she would stop being so nice. 'That's really lovely of you. Thank you.'

Then Flora stands up and when she leans over to kiss me on the cheek I assume that because she's the sort of person who speaks French and looks like she flies business class she's going to do one on each side, and when she doesn't there's a bit of an awkward moment when I go back for a second kiss and it misses completely, ending up near her ear. Anyway, the point is that up close she smells properly amazing – sort of spicy, smoky and mysterious, like a Moroccan souk – and I have to stop myself grabbing her and taking a really big whiff.

'Well, it was lovely to meet you, Percy,' says Flora, smiling her gap-toothed smile.

'You too,' I say. And maybe it's because I'm drunk or perhaps it's that perfume, but I'm suddenly hit by a wave of regret that I'll never see Flora again, and even though I know it's for the best as there's obviously no future for us love-wise, before I can stop myself I say, 'Perhaps we should do this again some time.'

'Well, we are soulmates after all,' says Flora, raising an eyebrow. 'We wouldn't want to disappoint destiny.'

'Or Theresa LeFevre. She terrifies me.'

Flora laughs. 'What's your number?'

We swap details and I reassure myself that if she does get in touch I can just make my excuses over text.

'Take care, Percy, I do hope your mum makes a quick recovery.'

After the hushed marble-floored luxury of the Savoy it's a shock to step out onto the Strand, which is rammed with early-evening shoppers, drinkers and theatre-goers. The pavement is so busy that I end up walking along in the gutter; *where I belong*, I think gloomily as I make my way to the Tube. As a bus roars up behind me I hop onto the kerb and as it passes I catch sight of a dumpy, miserable-looking woman in the window; it takes a split second for me to realise that it's my own reflection. I feel terrible about all the lies, worse for not having the guts to be straight (quite literally) with Flora and, if I'm honest, a teeny bit disappointed about not meeting Bradley Cooper, but the irony is that if Flora had been a bloke I'd be feeling pretty chuffed right now. Funny, kind, successful, attractive and delicious-smelling: what more could I ask for in a soulmate? In the circumstances it seems almost churlish to quibble over the fact that she's missing a Y chromosome. But the fact is that I'm not a lesbian. I'm really not. You don't just decide you're going to fancy the ladies one day and – *ta-dah!* – you're gay. Surely there has to be a flicker of something . . . downstairs? Okay, so I did once have a drunken snog with my university roommate, Kerry, but that was just to make this bloke whose name I've forgotten fancy me – and he ended up going out with Kerry instead, so that worked out well. And yes, I do find Flora attractive, but only in the way that I can look at Jaye, Lou or Charlie and appreciate their hotness. That doesn't mean I want to jump into bed with them, does it . . . *Does* it?

It's past ten in the evening by the time I get back to Norwich and the buzz of the alcohol has worn off, leaving me feeling a bit sick and very hungry. I'm too tired to cook anything and the only ready-to-eat option I can find in the kitchen is a bag of crisps, but they are such an inferior offering next to the Savoy's that I end up chucking them in the bin. I sit on the sofa and look around me, taking in the peeling paint and the damp patch on the ceiling; my flat suddenly feels as small and shabby as my life does next to Flora's. I'm not sure how long I sit there but I must have dropped off because the next thing I know I'm jolted awake by my home phone. After a few moments the answerphone kicks in.

'Hi love, just calling to check in.' It's Adam. 'Golf was great, I went round in 112, my best yet, but I'm really missing you.' I hear blokeish jeering in the background. 'Okay lads, calm down, I'll just be a moment . . . Sorry about that, love, Lyle and Darren are doing shots, I better go and make sure things don't get out of hand! Love you, beautiful.'

And that's another thing, I think sulkily, jabbing at the Delete button, the whole reason I agreed to this date in the first place was to clear up my feelings about Adam, but if anything it's raised more questions than it's answered. Rather than appreciating how lucky I am to have such a loyal, reliable boyfriend, I'm feeling weirdly angry towards him for being so loyal and reliable. Forget heliskiing, Adam's idea of adventure is wearing a cardigan instead of a V-neck. But then isn't my boyfriend, with his lint-free knitwear and golfing weekends, a better match for me than the glamorous, globetrotting Flora? Quite apart from the sexuality issue, Flora and I can't possibly be soulmates because she is way out of my league. She's a high-flying businesswoman, and I'm the lying coward who goes on dates behind her boyfriend's back. If I were Flora, I think to myself, as I put on my pyjamas and climb into bed, I'd be asking Theresa LeFevre for a refund.

13

I wake up late on Sunday morning to discover, like rapper Jay-Z, that I have ninety-nine problems. They are as follows:

1) My head is throbbing.

2) It is also spinning.

3) I feel sick.

4) I'm so hungry that I have to get the crisps out of the bin. (I know, shameful.)

5) I slept in my make-up and now have a large spot on my chin.

6) I have a voicemail from Adam wondering where I am and asking – jokily, I think – if I'm in bed with another man. Ha ha ha.

7) I have a voicemail from my mother asking why I haven't sold my flat yet and reminding me once again how lucky I am to have a wonderful, tolerant boyfriend like Adam.

8–98) Yesterday afternoon. *Oh God.*

99) Flora has sent me a text message.

I stare at the little green icon of her unopened text with uneasiness bubbling in the pit of my stomach (or maybe that's the bin crisps). I really wasn't expecting to hear from her this quickly, but perhaps there's none of that game-playing crap – you know, wait three days *minimum* before making contact or you'll scare them off – when you're dating women, which would be refreshing.

I'm still holding my phone, working up the courage to open Flora's message, when it starts to ring. Ah, now this will be interesting. I can see from the caller ID that it is Theresa LeFevre – a.k.a. the world's worst matchmaker – who is no doubt keen to know how things went yesterday. Well, it just so happens that I'm very keen to tell her.

'Theresa,' I say brightly. 'How are you?'

'Good morning, Perseus, very well, thank you. How was the date?'

'It was . . . surprising. I enjoyed meeting Flora, she's a lovely woman, but . . .'

'Isn't she just? I told you she was charming – and such flair.'

'. . . but she's a *woman*. Theresa, I'm not gay. I thought you knew that?'

'Well, I knew that you have been in a relationship with a man,' she says breezily, 'but that's hardly relevant.'

I gape at the phone. 'What are you talking about? Of course it is! I've never been out with a woman – never even thought about it. How on earth can that not be relevant?'

'Perseus, you have to remember that a woman's sexuality is extremely fluid,' says Theresa, as if explaining table manners to a toddler. 'Which is why you often find women who've been in heterosexual marriages for years suddenly finding themselves attracted to another woman. Have they been in denial about their sexuality? Perhaps. Or maybe they've discovered that when it comes to sexual attraction, gender is far less relevant than society would have us believe.'

'I'm sorry – are you saying that I'm actually a lesbian but am in denial?'

'What I'm saying is that superficially you might be attracted to a deep voice and broad shoulders, but that may well be a consequence of social conditioning. To put it simply: you expect to be with a man, so that's what you've been looking for. But what if you've been wrong in this assumption? When it comes to potential mates, I advise my clients not to think in terms of 'men' and 'women', but 'human beings'. Gender is just a label, after all.'

'I think it's a bit more than that, Theresa.' I don't want to have to say 'vagina', but I will do if pushed.

'This is not your fault, Perseus,' she says, soothingly. 'The problem lies with society itself. Girls are raised to believe in a Cinderella fantasy, to dream of being rescued by a handsome prince, but the truth is that we women are infinitely more complex, fascinating creatures. Sometimes we are attracted to the prince, sometimes the fairy godmother.'

'The . . . fairy godmother?'

'Indeed. Were you not drawn to her character as a child?'

'Well, yes, but only because she could turn pumpkins into glass coaches and had sparkly wings and a wand.'

'There you go, then.' Her tone strongly suggests that this is the end of the matter.

'Theresa, I don't see what any of this has to do with the fact that *I'm not gay!*'

'There you go again with the labels!' She gives an elegant little huff of exasperation. 'Putting aside all preconceptions, as a *human being* do you find yourself drawn to Flora?'

Oh, this is ridiculous. Ridiculous and confusing. I wish Theresa would stop talking so I could get my hung-over thoughts in order.

'Perseus? Do please try to answer the question, it's important.'

'Flora *is* attractive,' I begin, 'and I have no doubt that she'd make a wonderful partner, but . . .'

'You see?'

'Theresa,' I say, as patiently as possible. 'I'm. Not. Gay.'

Another long-suffering sigh. 'You know, Perseus, when I met you I was very struck by your energy. I sensed that you were . . . searching for something. That you feel like a piece is missing in your life. Am I right?'

I keep quiet; she's a bit close to the bone with this.

'Perhaps, deep down, you have never been truly happy in a relationship with a man,' she goes on. 'And while you might not ever have thought of yourself falling in love with a woman, it is this very *thought* that could well have been stopping you.'

'Isn't it more likely that your computer has just screwed things up?'

'These are exciting times, Perseus,' says Theresa, ignoring me. 'Thanks to the SoulDate system we can now match people by their very essence, by their *soul*. We're on the brink of a genuine revolution in the field of relationships – and YOU are leading the way! You're a pioneer, blazing a trail for future generations of women! In the circumstances don't you owe it to yourself, and to society as a whole, to leave aside your prejudices and meet up with Flora one more time?'

I'm about to say that I'm very much *not* prejudiced, I just would rather have sex with men, when something occurs to me.

'Have you spoken to Flora since our date?'

'I tried her before phoning you, but she's terribly difficult to get hold of so I left a message. *Such* a busy woman.'

'Well then, it doesn't actually matter what I want, because I think you'll find that I'm not Flora's type.'

'Ah, but you most definitely are,' she says. 'According to our system you are Flora's Ultimate Compatibility Match, and our system is the most highly developed match-making tool in the world. You can't argue with science.'

Nor, I'm realising, with Theresa LeFevre.

'I appreciate Flora was not quite what you were expecting,' she says, 'and perhaps I should have briefed you a little more thoroughly prior to your meeting, but my concern was that you would have refused to have gone through with the date – and that would have been a great shame.'

'Theresa, I—'

'You should also remember that Flora has invested a great deal of money in this process and it would be very disappointing for her personally if the whole exercise had been in vain. Would it be so hard to meet with her once more?'

Well, that's hardly fair, I didn't ask to be involved in any of this – but then again she has got a point about Flora. 'I'll think about it,' I say eventually.

'Don't think too much – that's half the problem!' She gives a melodic giggle. 'Goodbye, Perseus, I look forward to hearing about your next date.'

'But I really don't know if . . .' But she's already gone.

Bloody Theresa LeFevre. That woman has an annoying knack of twisting things around to make you feel like you're the one who's being unreasonable. I'm not sure how she's done it, but she's planted a seed of doubt in my mind and a tiny part of me wonders if perhaps she does have a point. I'd always assumed that my sense that there was something missing in my life was because I was in the wrong career, but what if it was down to being in the wrong sexuality? No, that's ridiculous . . . Yet I can't deny that in the brief window between my shock at meeting Flora and my mother's medical emergency I definitely enjoyed her company. I don't fancy her, but I can't deny I'm drawn to her, and while I'm absolutely sure there's nothing sexual about it, would it hurt me to see her again?

With a mixture of nerves and anticipation, I click open Flora's text.

Hi Percy, how's your mum? I'm having a party next weekend and wondered if you would like to come. Bring a friend if you'd like. Saturday from seven – I'll send over the details if you can make it. Take care, Flora.

No 'x' at the end: that's weird. I put kisses on virtually all my texts, even to the old bloke who came to give me a quote for fixing my shower, which is possibly why he kept asking where 'Mr James' was. In fact, thinking about it, the absence of kisses is so strange that it must be a *deliberate* omission, to make some sort of statement. Perhaps it's Flora's way of saying that she just wants to be friends?

Yes, that would make sense . . . That must be why she's asking me to a party, rather than dinner: she must have realised she can do far better than me as a girlfriend, but, being polite, wants to let me down gently. And she says to 'bring a friend' – well, that's basically asking me to come with a date, isn't it? Oh, this is perfect! I can *totally* imagine being friends with Flora, she's such a fascinating woman, plus if I put in an appearance at her party I can get Theresa LeFevre off my back once and for all. I'll go on my own though, it'll be far too complicated to take anyone with me. My head suddenly feels *so* much clearer! Relief flooding through me, I reply:

That would be great, thanks Flora. Look forward to it. PS. Mum's on the mend, thankfully.

I don't put a kiss at the end either.

14

'Morning shithead, how was your weekend?'

I look up from my computer to find Mel waiting expectantly by my desk holding a Michael Bublé mug and a plate of toast.

'Great!' I say brightly. (And with the benefit of hindsight, I can see that it *was* a great weekend. I made a new friend who's invited me to a super-fun party where I'll drink champagne and mingle with high-flying techie folk like the guy who invented Facebook. Flora sent over the details yesterday and it sounds like it's going to be quite an occasion: black-tie cocktails in a City penthouse. There are bound to be canapés – and I am a total sucker for a canapé. Give me a mini burger or a tiny pavlova and I'm as happy as a pigeon on a chip. And now that this whole SoulDate nonsense is behind me, I can focus on my relationship with Adam. Okay, he might not be perfect, but what about me? I'm not exactly Miss Universe, am I? And I mustn't forget the mind-blowing sex we had last time we were together, which surely confirms how great we are as a couple. Yes, the events of this weekend have given me the green light to sell my flat, move in with Adam and start the next exciting chapter of our lives together. Not that I'm going to share any of this with Mel, obviously.)

'It was a quiet one, didn't really do much,' I say. 'How was yours?'

Pulling up a chair to the opposite side of my desk, Mel lays out her breakfast on top of a pile of paperwork I've yet to file.

'Messy. I went to a rave in Hunstanton.' She crams a quarter of a slice of toast into her mouth whole and chews thoughtfully for a while. 'You ever had magic mush-rooms, Perce?'

'Nope.'

'Me neither, so I bought some from a bloke in a jester's hat and they had no bloody effect at all.' She takes another bite of toast. 'I went back to him and said, 'I want my money back. These are fucking shiitake.'

'Did he give it to you?'

'Nah.' She takes another bite. 'They were nice in a stir-fry though.'

'Never buy anything from a bloke in a jester's hat, Mel,' I say. 'That's just basic common sense.'

'You're not wrong there.' She nods sagely. 'So anyway, I was thinking about you and this soulmate business. Are you going to meet up with this fella or not?'

Uh-oh. 'I thought you weren't going to bring that up again?'

Mel licks Vegemite off her fingers. 'Percy, you're a good mate, and the way I see it is that as your friend I have a duty to tell you that if you don't meet up with this bloke then you're f—'

'Good morning, Melanie.' With impeccable timing, Susannah sticks her head out of her office door. 'Sorry to interrupt your breakfast, but could I borrow Percy for a moment?'

'No worries, I've just finished,' says Mel, picking up her mug and plate. 'See you later, Perce.' But then, as Susannah disappears back into her office, she shoots me a meaningful look and mutters: 'This conversation is NOT over.'

After spending twenty minutes with Susannah going through her diary and hearing about her eldest son's rugby triumphs at the weekend I only have enough time to grab a cappuccino from the ancient machine in the kitchen (which delivers flimsy paper cups of lava-hot coffee topped with pond scum) before heading downstairs for my eleven o'clock meeting with the conference organising committee. I'm just waiting for the lift, flicking through my notes on the various venue options I've been researching, when my mobile starts to ring.

'Hello?'

'Patsy, hi. Roger Robshaw here.'

'Hello, Roger. It's, um, *Percy*.'

Roger is the estate agent who's handling my flat sale. His company might have had the nicest logo, but he's rubbish with names.

'Good moment to touch base re your flat?'

'If it's quick, I'm just heading into a meeting,' I say.

'Okay, well how does this sound: Cash offer. Asking price. No chain. *Boom!*'

'It sounds . . . good?'

'Good? Chuffing GREAT is how it sounds! The girl who viewed your flat last week loves – and I mean *loves* – your place. She is looking for an exchange date ASAP. We're talking major-league keenness.'

'Wow, that's, um, totes amazeballs,' I say, cringing. Roger's patter tends to rub off.

'You can say that again! So what I need you to do now is have a chatterama with your solicitor and get the ball rolling. I'll email over the deets.'

'Okay great, thanks Roger, I'll get onto that right away.'

'Today if you can, yeah? We don't want to lose this buyer, Patsy, it's a real sweet dealio.'

So I've got a buyer for my flat. Asking price, too! You couldn't ask for any more than that, could you? Adam will be thrilled; we're going to the cinema after work tonight so I'll be able to tell him the good news in person. I must get myself a solicitor (I'm sure Adam will be able to recommend one) and, as Roger says, get the ball rolling. Yes, this is very exciting news indeed.

Hmmm. I feel a bit shaky and dizzy. Must be the excitement. God, it's stuffy in here, and hot – is the heating on too high? My forehead feels all clammy. Actually . . . um, I feel a little faint . . .

I duck into the ladies' loos and pat cold water on my face and then hold my hands under the dryer, letting the roar drown out the rushing sound in my ears. Once I'm feeling a bit steadier I lean on the sink, looking at my pale, frowning face in the mirror, and take a few deep breaths. And then in the silence I hear it again: the little voice that seems determined to get me to screw up my life.

You don't want to get the ball rolling, do you, Percy? it says, in that annoying know-it-all tone. *The ball already feels like it's out of control, like that bit at the start of* Raiders of the Lost Ark *when Indiana Jones nearly gets crushed by a giant boulder. You're starting to think you should have just left the bloody ball alone in the first place, aren't you?*

You stop that right now, I say firmly. (I need to give this voice a name; it sounds like a Brenda.) Moving in with Adam is the right thing to do. He is a wonderful man and living with him is the natural next step. Nerves are to be expected, as with all the important changes in life such as marriage, children . . .

Well, if you move in with Adam then that's what'll be on the cards, says Brenda. *If you sell your flat you're as good as saying 'I do.' You mark my words.*

Bloody hell, Brenda, what is this – the 1950s? Can't I live with a man without marrying him? Besides, what's the alternative? I can sell my flat and look forward to a secure future with a man who loves me, or stay where I am, buy a cat and grow old on my own. Case closed.

Suit yourself, tuts Brenda. *Perhaps you are a lesbian after all.*

I get to the conference room five minutes after the meeting is due to start and hope to sneak in unnoticed but discover that they've been waiting for me. Mr Hedley is sitting at the head of the table, having appointed himself unofficial chairman and secretary of our supposedly informal committee. He looks like Mr Burns from *The Simpsons*, right down to the yellow face and demonic eyebrows, and is radiating ill-will. I once asked Susannah how he's managed to hold onto his job for so long: apparently he has an encyclopaedic knowledge of employment law, which has meant that every attempt to get rid of him has collapsed in a storm of legal letters. I choose a seat as far away from him as possible, next to a woman called Jane Townsend who works in Claims and is a terrible gossip. (Actually she's brilliant at it, but you know what I mean.)

'All right, Perce?' she says. 'You're looking a bit peaky, love, everything okay?'

'Fine, thank you,' I reply, plastering on a smile. Knowing Jane it'll be all round the office by the end of the day that I'm suffering from morning sickness.

Mr Hedley raps on the table. 'Now that everyone is here' – pointed glower in my direction – 'I'll bring the meeting to order. I trust you've all read through the agenda that was emailed to you on Friday? So we'll start with a progress report from Susan Myerson, who has been collating the list of conference attendees. And remember' – a sweep of the table with his laser-like glare – 'any remarks must be addressed through the Chair.'

As Susan drones through the list of potential conference attendees (i.e. pretty much everyone in the company) my thoughts drift back to the subject of my imminent move. On the paper that Mr Hedley has provided for note-taking I write PHONE SOLICITOR in large letters, then put a circle round it and add three exclamation marks. Underneath that I write BUY STORAGE BOXES (IKEA?) and BOOK VAN FOR MOVE. I shudder to think about the amount of crap I've accumulated over the past few years; Lord knows how it's all going to fit into Adam's house. I suppose I'll have to chuck a lot of it away.

I glance at Jane, who is texting under the table, and it occurs to me that Jane's desk is next to Dan's, which reminds me of that mysterious conversation I had with him at the pub. I wonder if he's back from his holiday yet? And then, as if she's progressed from reading other people's emails to reading their minds, Jane leans over and whispers: 'You're mates with Dan Dawson, aren't you, Percy?'

I nod, keeping an eye on Mr Hedley who is busy taking minutes; I don't want to get told off for talking in class.

'Did you hear what happened with that beautician he was seeing? Apparently she dumped him!'

'Really?'

She nods, clearly thrilled to be the bearer of bad news. 'Yes, poor Dan. I bet he'll get a lot of offers of shoulders to cry on! Apparently he's heartbroken. That's why he's gone on holiday – to get some space to deal with it.'

From what I know of their relationship I very much doubt this is true – Dan once told me they were 'friends with benefits' – but still, it's never nice to be dumped. Perhaps that was what he wanted to talk to me about. I'll have to ask him out for a drink as soon as he gets back to cheer him up: that's what a mate would do, isn't it? I write DAN – DRINK? on my pad and underline it twice.

It's only been a week since I last saw Adam, but so much has happened since then – I've been a lesbian, changed my mind about moving in with him at least eight times and (nearly) sold my flat – that it feels much longer. Prompt as ever, he's already waiting in the bar of Cinema City when I arrive, still in his suit with that pale-blue tie

I love, engrossed in some work papers with a pint of beer (his) and a glass of red wine (mine) on the table in front of him. I imagine seeing Adam through a stranger's eyes: successful, responsible and handsome – perfect boyfriend material. Whoever he's waiting for is a lucky girl, you might think. As I make my way across the bar towards him, I remind myself that lucky girl is *me*.

As I approach Adam looks up from his work, breaking into a broad smile. 'Beautiful girl,' he says, pulling me in for a kiss. 'How was your day?'

'Oh, you know, typical Monday. We had a meeting about this conference weekend – you remember Susannah asked me to be on the organisation committee?'

As we chat about work I think about when to tell Adam about my flat sale and I get a lovely shiver of anticipation as I imagine breaking the news to him and how excited he'll be. Perhaps I'll leave it until after we've seen the film, make it more of a surprise . . .

'So I was thinking about our summer holiday,' Adam is saying. 'And I was wondering if we should get something booked up?'

'Excellent idea!' I love planning holidays. 'Where do you fancy going?'

'Well, I was thinking about Tuscany . . .'

'I've always wanted to go there! All that lovely wine and pasta.'

'But then I had a better idea,' he says, eyes a-twinkle.

Now this sounds exciting. Wherever could he have in mind? Ooh, maybe Thailand! Adam knows I've always wanted to go to Koh Tao. He's never seemed very keen (he doesn't like long-haul flights or large buzzing insects), but perhaps he's had a change of heart?

'Tell me more, Mr Lumsden,' I say with a smile, my head swimming with visions of palm trees and turquoise seas.

'Well,' he grins, 'I was remembering what a nice time we had in Bergerac last summer and I suddenly thought, why don't we go back to the same place? The hotel was great, and we already know where the best restaurants are, so we wouldn't have to risk a bad meal. Plus I've got the golf course nearby and you can sunbathe by that lovely pool. What do you think? Makes sense, right?'

My heart plummets all the way into my shoes. What I think is: why on earth would we want to go back to the same place as last year, especially when it wasn't that much fun the first time round? It was nice enough, but hardly very exciting for anyone below retirement age. Adam played golf most days with an accountant called Stephen we met in the hotel restaurant, meaning I had to hang out with his wife Debbie, who'd brought PG Tips and Rich Tea biscuits in her suitcase and fretted about 'the water'. It was *constant*. 'Has this lettuce been washed in tap water?' 'Is this water from a bottle?' 'Is the ice made of tap water?' And she didn't speak any French, so she used that REALLY SLOOOOOOW LOUD voice that English people use to communicate with Johnny Foreigner. So no, it makes no sense to me at all to go back to Bergerac.

'It *was* lovely,' I say carefully, because I don't want to offend him, 'but wouldn't it be fun to go somewhere different? We might find a place we like even more than Bergerac!'

'But you loved that bistro where we had dinner on the last night,' he says. 'You said it was the best chicken you've ever had.'

'Yes, that's true, it was delicious, but . . .' How to put this tactfully? 'There are loads of bits of Europe we haven't seen. I was reading about Ibiza the other day, it sounds beautiful.'

Adam pulls a face. 'Not sure about that, love – all those nightclubs.'

'No, I mean the quiet side of the island, away from the touristy bits. The countryside looks stunning and apparently there are some gorgeous little beaches off the beaten track. We could hire a car and go exploring . . .'

'But that's exactly why I thought it would be a good idea to go back to Bergerac! We know where everything is already, so we wouldn't have to waste any of our precious holiday stuck in the car. We know we'll have a nice time.'

Nice. Ugh. Not to be overdramatic, but the word feels like a dagger in my heart. For some reason I think of Flora.

She wouldn't want a 'nice' holiday; she would be canoeing down the Amazon or climbing icebergs in Alaska. That panicky feeling of suffocation starts to creep over me again. Is this what life with Adam is going to be like? Golf for him, Rich Tea biscuits for me and then a quiet meal and off to bed with our Kindles? A life of . . . *nice*?

'Adam,' I say, trying to stay calm. 'I would really rather go somewhere different this summer if it's okay with you.'

'But I've already emailed the hotel in Bergerac and asked them to hold a room for us,' he says, an injured look on his face. 'I assumed you'd feel the same way as I do.'

He clearly thinks I'm being awkward and something inside me snaps.

'For God's sake, there's a whole world out there! Why can't you live a little? Jesus, Adam, sometimes you can be so' – *don't say it, Percy* – 'so boring.'

Too late.

Adam looks hurt. I know I should apologise, but I'm wound up. I almost wish he'd have a go at me, call me a cow, it would be easier to deal with than this self-righteous silence.

Then – 'Percy,' he says quietly, 'is everything okay?'

'Yes, everything is fine, thank you, I just don't want to go back to bloody Bergerac.'

'I mean, is everything okay with *us*? You've seemed really distant lately and I thought it might be down to worry over that job interview you had, but if anything it's been getting worse since then.'

'How exactly have I been distant? Name one time!' I'm being unfair, because I'm quite sure that I *have* been distant. Guilt does that to you.

'Just . . . not as loving,' he says. 'Snappy. And you take ages to return my calls.'

'Maybe I'm just busy.'

Adam rubs his chin; he looks worried. 'You know,' he says, 'I was talking to your mum about this the other day . . .'

'Oh God . . .'

'Just hear me out, love. I was talking to your mum, and she said that she thinks you might have commitment issues.'

'*Really*, Adam? Are we really going to have this conversation?'

'She blames herself, she thinks it's because you were an only child, but what I'm trying to say is that I *understand*.' He reaches for my hand and as he gives it a squeeze I feel myself tensing up further. 'I know that moving in together is a big deal. You're an independent lady and that's one of the things I love about you, but . . .'

'I do NOT have commitment issues.'

'. . . but what I was thinking was that perhaps it would

be helpful to go and see someone, just to talk through any . . . concerns you might have? A counsellor, perhaps? It might help you feel happier about letting go of your flat.'

I cannot believe what I'm hearing. 'Right, I was going to tell you this after the film, but I accepted an offer on my place today. Asking price, and they want to move in as soon as possible.'

Adam's face instantly lights up. 'Really? Oh Percy, that's fantastic!'

'And I was going to ask you if you could recommend a solicitor to get things moving, but if you'd rather recommend a fucking counsellor then that's just FINE.' I know I'm being childish, but the thought of Adam discussing me with my mother makes me livid. 'In fact, maybe you don't want me to move in with you any more,' I say. 'Maybe *you're* the one with commitment issues.'

'I'm so sorry, my darling, I was just worried because you never seemed that excited about living together. You know how much I love you.'

'Commitment issues,' I mutter, shaking my head, still furious. 'As *if.*'

'Please don't be mad at me, Percy,' begs Adam. 'Will you forgive me?'

I glare at him, but the fight is ebbing out of me; it's difficult to be cross with someone when they've got a face like a kicked puppy.

'Let me make it up to you, please,' he goes on. 'After all, you've sold your flat – we should be celebrating! I think this calls for champagne, don't you?'

A pause, then I nod sulkily.

'Great.' He pulls my hands to his lips and kisses them. 'Just wait there!'

As Adam dives up to the bar I try to fight the gloom that's replaced my anger of moments ago. *Do* I have commitment issues? I can't see why else I'm struggling to come to terms with selling my flat. Perhaps my mother is right after all . . . Just then my phone beeps and I glance at the screen to see Adam has sent me a business card. I shoot a quizzical look to him at the bar and he mouths, 'My solicitor's details,' giving me a grin and a thumbs-up. He looks so happy, despite my stroppiness. This guy is a saint to put up with my crap, I think. I should really be thanking my lucky stars that *anyone* wants to live with me.

Just then Adam reappears with the champagne, hands me a glass and raises his in a toast. 'To our future together,' he says, and as we drink I think about the toast Flora made last weekend. What was it again? 'To new adventures.' The vision of that perfect Thai beach fleetingly appears in my mind, but I replace it with a picture of a charming French town. Bergerac wasn't so bad, was it? And Adam's right, that chicken *was* delicious . . .

'We should probably set up a joint account to use for

things like groceries and household bills,' he is saying. 'I can talk to my bank – that is, if you're happy for me to do that, darling?'

'Yes, great,' I say. That makes sense, doesn't it? I'm lucky that Adam is so organised: the yin to my shambolic yang.

'Give the solicitor a call first thing in the morning, won't you? Tell him you're my other half. He's a good bloke, helped me when I bought my place.'

'Absolutely,' I say.

And I absolutely will, but maybe not in the morning, as it's always manic first thing, but I'll call him at some point tomorrow. Or if I don't have time then I'll definitely speak to him on Wednesday. *Definitely.*

15

'Okay, my little beauty bunnies, now you need to paint a line down either side of your nose in a shade at least two tones darker than your usual foundation to make it look smaller and more defined . . .'

In readiness for Flora's party tonight I'm attempting contouring make-up with the help of a YouTube tutorial. It's my first time, but I'm in the expert hands of a perky American called Ashlee who keeps saying stuff like 'glam-dorable' and 'fantast-chic', which gets a bit annoying when you're struggling to locate the hollows beneath your cheekbones (I *am* sucking my cheeks in, Ashlee), but she used to be Khloé Kardashian's deputy make-up artist so she must know her onions. My face is a patchwork of white triangles and brick-coloured streaks, but Ashlee reassures me that once it's all blended together I'll look 'bad-ass', which obviously is exactly the look I'm aiming for tonight.

I can't remember the last time I went to a bad-ass black-tie event (university, probably) and so my wardrobe is not exactly bursting with outfit options. The best I can come up with is a green shift dress that's seen better days (again, university), but I can cover that stain on my left boob with a brooch and besides, it's not like I'm trying to impress anyone, is it? I'll just pop in and say hello to Flora, hit up the canapés and then get the 22.14 back to Norwich so I'm tucked up in bed by midnight. And at least my feet will look 'fantast-chic': I've had a gel pedicure and am wearing a pair of strappy snakeskin heels which, despite being as old as the dress, look immaculate because I've only ever managed to wear them for half an hour before switching to emergency flip-flops.

Ashley's contouring lesson is eight minutes, but I have to keep pausing it to copy what she's doing, so it takes me nearly an hour just to finish and the end result is, well, stripy. More badger than bad-ass. But it's too late now, the party starts in a couple of hours and I don't have time to take it all off and start over as I need to catch my train. Hopefully the room will be quite dark.

On the journey to London I feel increasingly nervy. Not about seeing Flora – now that the pressure is off relationship-wise I'm actually looking forward to that – but going to a party where I don't know anyone. If the other guests are anything like Flora then my small talk is going to be seriously inadequate.

ME: And what do you do?

MAN IN GLASSES: Charitable work these days, mainly.

ME: Oh, that's nice. I don't think enough people give back, do you? We had a cake sale at work a few months ago in aid of a local hospice and it was really gratifying to know that we were helping the community – plus there were some seriously good brownies! Ha ha ha!! I'm Percy James, by the way *(holds out hand)*.

MAN IN GLASSES: *(reluctantly shakes hand)* Bill Gates.

Hmmm. Hopefully I'll speak to Flora early on and she'll be able to introduce me to a few people; anyway, I'm sure I'll be feeling chattier after a couple of drinks. *Only* a couple though, because I've got to be at Adam's house first thing in the morning: we've invited Lou and her family for Sunday lunch and I'm in charge of the vegetables and apple crumble, and I find cooking enough of a challenge without being hung-over. Actually, it would probably be better if I *did* turn up to Adam's with a hangover, as he thinks I'm going out tonight with Mel, Queen of Shots, and I've never got home from a night out with her sober. I know, another lie – but what else could I tell him? 'So, Adam, I'm going to a party thrown by this woman who I met for a date the other weekend (when you thought I was shopping!), believing she was actually going to be my soulmate. Oh, and by the way, she thinks I'm gay and that Mum has malaria.' No,

I'm afraid a little white lie was my only option. Besides, after tonight I'll be able to put the SoulDate debacle behind me and move forward with life together with Adam. (That reminds me: I *must* call the solicitor about my flat on Monday. It was a crazy week at work and I didn't have time, but first thing next week, definitely.)

I don't know this part of London at all, but according to Google Maps the party is a twenty-minute walk from Liverpool Street station. Three blisters later I arrive at the address to find one of those Manhattan-style glass skyscrapers that looks like it's been designed by a male architect with an inferiority complex, and probably has some tongue-in-cheek nickname like the Gherkin. Craning my head back to look at its 'thrusting' peak, I decide this one should be called the Dildo. The main foyer seems to be deserted, but then I notice a group of people in evening wear heading around the side of the building and follow them to find another entrance. Ah, this must be it. People are waiting in front of a black-clad man with a clipboard and as I join the queue I get another jolt of nerves as I realise that all the other guests seem to know each other, plus they all look like they run multinational corporations, and none of them look like badgers. But I'm here now; it would be lame to back out.

It turns out the entrance is actually the door to a glass-walled lift that shoots straight up the outside of the Dildo, and as we glide up fifty-two floors to the penthouse I get a glimpse of the most gorgeous view of London in the early evening sunshine, then all too quickly the lift slows and the doors slide open.

There is another man in the same black uniform waiting to greet us with a tray of drinks. I take two: champagne and something pink in a Martini glass. 'One for my friend,' I tell the waiter conspiratorially, then take a deep breath and make my way into the penthouse.

Wow. This is a seriously posh affair. There must be over a hundred guests here already and it's still quite early. The room is spectacular, with floor-to-ceiling windows, panoramic views and lampshades that look like alien eggs. There's a man playing a white grand piano and waiters carrying trays of tiny canapés so beautiful they could be jewellery. I skirt around the edge of the crowd looking for Flora but can't see her, so I position myself by a six-foot flower arrangement and down my champagne in three gulps, then get my phone out of my bag and pretend to be engrossed in something important so that it doesn't look like I'm just standing here on my own with no one to talk to. (Seriously, what did people do before mobile phones?) I sip at the pink cocktail, reminding myself that I'm supposed to be stopping at two drinks, but it is sweet and tangy and moreish, like Haribo Fangtastics, and doesn't taste at all alcoholic. I'm sure it would be fine if I had another one of these.

'Parfait of langoustine with a foie gras soil and bilberry foam?'

I look up from my game of Candy Crush to see one of the canapé waiters.

'Ah, lovely, thank you,' I say, popping it in whole. Man oh man – that is *amazing*. 'For my friends,' I say, taking another two.

I'm just scanning the room for the next canapé opportunity when a beam of light from the setting sun is reflected across the room and suddenly I spot Flora lit up in its glow. She is wearing a black halter-neck jumpsuit with a chunky gold cuff on her wrist and has her hair tied back, and – speaking simply as a woman admiring another woman's style – I can honestly say she looks fantastic, like a rock star. I really should go over and say hello, but she is deep in conversation with a very tall bearded man and I suddenly feel shy and awkward. I take a sip of my Haribo drink for Dutch courage but discover that my glass is empty, so I make my way over to the bar; I'm sure party etiquette would deem it impolite to greet the host empty-handed.

'Could I have one of those pink cocktails, please?'

'Sure.' The barman does his show-offy bit with the shaker and then pushes the drink across the bar to me.

'Thank you,' I say. 'How much will that be?'

He looks at me witheringly. 'It's a free bar, madam.'

'Oh, right. Sorry.'

I start back across the room, trying to find Flora again, but by the time I get to the other side I haven't seen her and my drink has been drunk (Martini glasses *are* quite small). Just then a waiter walks by with a tray of drinks and I take a glass of champagne, reassuring myself that as those pink cocktails contain so little alcohol this is really only my second drink. Yet despite weaving my way across the room a few more times, striding purposefully through the babble of chatter as if I've just spotted a dear old friend who I simply *must* go and talk to, I can't see Flora anywhere, and so I return to my flower arrangement and skulk amongst the fronds.

Oh, this is pathetic. I really ought to be better at mingling now I'm in my thirties, but there isn't much opportunity to practise cocktail party small talk in Norwich. Why don't I just join that group over there? They look nice and approachable. I'll be totally honest and say: 'Hello, I'm Percy, I don't know anyone here, could I please join you?' No, that sounds too needy. Maybe I could break the ice by asking the time, which I could follow up with a comment along the lines of, 'Gosh, ten past eight and still light out? Summer must be on the way! Do you have any holiday plans this year?' But then who doesn't have a mobile with a clock these days? I know, I'll say my phone has run out of juice . . .

'Sirloin sashimi with a spinach brittle and bone-marrow jelly?'

But by the time I and my greedy imaginary friends have enjoyed our canapés my target group has moved on and besides, I've just noticed that there's a giant clock hanging over the bar, so I'd need to think of a new opening line anyway. Then nearby I spot a woman about the same age as me standing on her own, staring out of the window. Maybe she doesn't know anyone else either? I glance at her every now and then, just to make sure that she's not waiting for someone, and after a few minutes when nobody else has joined her I go over to stand next to her.

'Quite a view, isn't it?'

She seems transfixed and I assume she either hasn't heard me or is ignoring me, but then after a few moments she says, ' "London – that great cesspool into which all the loungers and idlers of the Empire are irresistibly drained." '

'I'm sorry?'

'Arthur Conan Doyle. *Sherlock Holmes*.'

Her voice is a little slurry; clearly she's been getting stuck into the free bar too.

'Ah, right. That's a great quote. I'm Percy, by the way, nice to meet you.'

'Sara,' she says, eyes still fixed on the horizon. 'So how do you know Flora?'

'Oh, we go way back. We've known each other for ages.'

'Really?' She turns to look at me for the first time, frowning. 'I wonder why we haven't met before?'

'I've been overseas,' I say quickly. 'How about you?'

'I lived with her for seven years.'

Shit. I should have recognised the name – and the hair colour. But who invites their ex-girlfriend to their party?

'We were together for eight and a half years in total,' Sara goes on. 'That's longer than some marriages. Then just like that' – she makes a dismissive flicking gesture – 'it's over.'

'Well, it's nice that you and Flora are still friends,' I say, trying to move the conversation on. 'Did you catch the TV series of *Sherlock Holmes*?'

But Sara is warming to her theme. '*Friends.* I don't want to be fucking *friends* with her.' She downs what's left of her drink and stares miserably at the empty glass. 'Have you ever had your heart broken?'

'Um . . .'

'Eighteen months on and I still miss her every day. *Every. Single. Day.* I thought we'd always be together.' To my horror she looks like she's about to cry, but instead, even worse, she starts to sing, her voice wobbly with emotion and vodka. '*Islands in the Stream, that is what we are, no one in between, how can we be wrong . . .*'

Ah, now I understand why she was standing on her own. I drain my glass in a single gulp and wave it at her. 'I just need to go to the bar, Sara. Can I get you another . . . ?'

But she is lost in her song and doesn't even appear to register that I've gone, so I head straight for the ladies' loo where I can legitimately kill a bit more time.

As I reapply my lip gloss, wondering if Sara noticed that I had spinach brittle stuck in my teeth, I debate whether it would be rude to make my excuses and head home. I've been here over an hour, after all, I've mingled and exceeded my two-drink limit – and the idea of sitting on the train, shoes off, with a magazine and one of those gin and tonics in a tin seems very appealing. I really should say hi and bye to Flora first though – or would it be naughty to just . . . slip out? She's bound to be busy talking to her real friends, and there are so many people here she probably hasn't even remembered that she's invited me. If I left now I could probably make the 20.33 train . . . But just as I'm putting my make-up away the door swings open and who should walk in but Flora.

'Percy!' She rushes over and throws her arms around me. 'Lovely to see you. How long have you been here?'

'Oh, not long at all,' I say, a little taken aback by the warmth of her welcome. 'Thank you so much for inviting me.'

'Well, I'm just glad you could make it. How's your mum?'

'Much better, thank you,' I say quickly, kicking myself again for the lie. 'In fact, she's improved so much it's almost as if she never even had malaria at all.'

'Thank goodness, you must have been so worried.' Flora smiles and the red of her lipstick make her teeth look ultra-white under the bright lights in the bathroom. Her make-up is so perfect, all flicky black eyeliner and identically arched eyebrows, I suddenly feel extremely self-conscious about my 'contouring'. Thankfully, however, Flora doesn't seem to have noticed that I look like an extra from *The Wind in the Willows*.

'Are you here on your own?' she asks.

'Yes, but I've been mingling. It's an amazing party – what's the occasion?'

'There isn't one really,' she shrugs. 'I just wanted to get some interesting people together. And I suppose I got a bit tired of going to all these fabulous engagement parties and weddings when that wasn't yet on the cards for me, so I decided to have a celebration of my own.'

'What, like an "I'm not getting married" party? You should have gone the whole hog and had a gift list at John Lewis.'

She laughs. 'I would have, but I've got all the fish knives and hand towels I need. Hang on a sec, will you, Percy, I've just got to nip to the loo and then I'll introduce you to some people, okay?'

As we head back into the party Flora stops a waiter and gets us each a pink cocktail. 'Have you tried one of these?' she asks, handing me the glass. 'I created the recipe myself. I call it the "Flora Sour".'

'Ooh, yes, it's delicious. What's in it?'

'Vodka, mainly, plus peach schnapps and a bit of lime juice and grenadine.'

'Quite potent, then.' Now I come to think about it, I *am* feeling rather tipsy. Better stick to water after this.

'Ah, here she is, the woman of the hour!' A man wearing a kilt, standing in a group of particularly glamorous types, kisses Flora on the lips. 'Wonderful party, Flo, really terrific. Now, if you only had a decent drink on offer it would be perfect.'

'I thought you usually brought your own, Declan,' says Flora. 'Surely you've got a hip flask hidden under there somewhere.'

'Ah, you know me too well,' he laughs.

Flora puts her arm around my shoulders. 'Everyone, this is Percy; Percy – everyone. I'd tell you their names, but if you're anything like me you'd instantly forget!'

I'm surprised at how nice Flora is being: she barely knows me, but she makes sure I'm included in the conversation and when she moves on to the next group she takes me with her. I suppose she feels obliged to look after me because I'm here on my own. Watching her work the room is like a masterclass in socialising: she asks interesting questions, compliments effortlessly and you can see she has this knack of making people feel special. And the weird thing is, as I tag along, some of Flora's magic starts to rub off on me. When I'm with Adam I can feel tense – worried about doing something stupid or saying the wrong thing – but right now I feel like a strong, interesting woman: still me, just more so. Of course, being a bit tipsy (okay, *a lot* tipsy) does help, but I swear it's not just the booze. It feels like hanging out with Flora has unlocked a part of me that's usually hidden away. At one point a woman asks how we know each other and Flora turns to me with a playful look. 'How *do* we know each other, Percy?'

'Now that's a good question,' I say. 'I guess you could say an algorithm brought us together.'

The woman nods politely. 'So you work in technology too, then, Percy? Are you a programmer?'

'Something like that,' I say.

And then Flora smiles at me and it feels as if we're sharing a wonderful secret, and I get this surprising little burst of happiness.

An hour later and I'm starting to feel guilty about hogging the party host.

'I should really let you get on and talk to your other guests,' I say to Flora, as we stand by the bar.

'No, I'd like to talk to you, Percy,' she says, squeezing my arm. I really like the way she says my name with that rolling Scottish 'R'. 'I reckon I've done my bit and spoken to everyone else.'

'Even Sara . . . ?'

'Ah, so you met her, then.'

'I did. She seemed a little . . . emotional.'

Flora laughs. 'She's an actress. Never knowingly under-performed.'

'She's clearly still not over you.'

'Sara just loves the drama,' she sighs. 'I think it's more about that than actual heartache. And she'd be the first to admit we weren't right together, although God knows we tried to make it work . . .' She takes a sip of her drink. 'Have you ever had one of those relationships that look perfect on paper, but in reality something doesn't feel right, and you have no idea what that something is?'

Yes, I think to myself, I know that only too well.

'I spent so much time talking myself into that relationship,' continues Flora, 'trying to convince myself that things would be great *if only*, that I lost sight of the fact that Sara and I were just fundamentally wrong for each other. I suppose that's what appealed about SoulDate: the promise of finding someone perfectly compatible.' She picks at a bowl of rice crackers on the bar. 'So anyway, how about you, Percy? You never gave me the low-down on your love life.'

'It's . . . complicated,' I say carefully. I don't want to lie again, but at the same time I worry that if I tell Flora the truth it will ruin our budding friendship. 'I've been in a longish relationship, but it sounds a lot like you and Sara. I suppose you could say things have run their course.'

This slips out of my mouth so easily that I suddenly wonder if somewhere deep down I actually feel this is true, then instantly feel guilty for betraying Adam.

Flora is nodding, but she's looking at me quizzically, as if she's trying to make a decision, and then after a moment she says: 'Come with me, Percy, I want to show you something.'

I follow her through a door in the entrance foyer marked 'PRIVATE', then up two flights of stairs and through another door from which we emerge onto a roof terrace – although calling it that is like describing Buckingham Palace as a detached house. We are at the very top of the Dildo, standing on an open-air platform with just a waist-high glass wall separating us from fifty-something floors of London air. Flora takes my hand, as naturally as if we are old friends or lovers, and together we cross over to the railing and look out across the city, the lights from cars and building windows decorating the city like garlands of fairy lights. It's a breathtaking view, but it's a good job I don't suffer from vertigo because right now I would be lying flat on the floor, nails digging into the concrete, weeping.

'Isn't it beautiful?' says Flora. 'It's so quiet up here. You can barely hear the traffic.'

'It feels just like you're flying,' I say, leaning over as far as I dare, feeling the breeze blowing my hair. 'That would definitely be my superpower. How amazing would it be to just soar away . . . ?'

Looking out over the city I feel like an overexcited child: there's the Tower of London, over there is the Shard and – ooh, look, Big Ben! We watch as a boat, lit up like a carnival float, glides down the inky blackness of the Thames towards the London Eye.

Flora gives a happy little sigh. 'Life moves pretty fast,' she says, almost to herself. 'If you don't stop and look around once in a while, you could miss it.'

'I know that quote! *Ferris Bueller's Day Off*. My favourite film of all time.'

'Really? Snap!' Then she holds out her wrist and moves her gold cuff out of the way to show me the tiny tattoo of the red sports car that I'd first noticed at the Savoy. 'It's the 1961 Ferrari 250GT California from the movie,' she says. 'I had it done when I was young and stupid, but I actually rather love it now.'

'That's brilliant!' I put on my best American accent: ' "Ferris, he never drives it, he just rubs it with a diaper." ' God, I had such a crush on Matthew Broderick in that film . . .' I suddenly stop myself, remembering that I'm supposed to be a lesbian, but Flora is nodding. 'Oh, me too,' she says. 'I still do, really.'

Then I remember what Theresa LeFevre said to me about a women's sexuality being fluid. I thought it was ridiculous at the time, but right now it makes perfect sense.

'You know, I meant what I said earlier,' says Flora. 'I'm

really glad you could come tonight. I've been thinking about you a lot since that drink at the Savoy. I admit I was sceptical about SoulDate and I only really signed up because my friends were nagging me to start dating again, but there's something about you, Percy. I really like spending time with you.'

'Me too,' I say. She might be a high-flying lawyer in her forties, but she's got this infectious fearlessness and enthusiasm for life that's almost childlike, and I wish I could be more like her. 'I'm really glad we met each other,' I say – and I mean it.

There's a spark between us, I know. It's been there since we bumped into each other in the ladies' and has gradually been getting more and more intense, but for some crazy reason it doesn't worry me. I now realise that I was wrong when I assumed that Flora just wanted to be friends: the way she has been with me tonight – it's not how you are with friends. As for me, I'm completely confused about my feelings: do I want her, or do I just want to *be* her? Either way, we're heading towards dangerous territory and I know I should go home, but it's almost like I'm daring myself to stay here, just to see what happens.

I'm jittery with excitement, but also feeling weirdly Zen-like: the future doesn't seem important; right now I'm just buzzing off this view and whatever this is between me and Flora. So when I turn to look at her and she smiles, still holding my gaze, I don't feel at all surprised or scared that she starts moving towards me, and as she gets nearer my eyes drift shut and I feel the warmth of her breath and her hand in my hair gently pulling me towards her, and then the touch of her lips on mine, and I get another waft of that heady, addictive perfume, and I'm lost.

16

Enveloped in Flora's softness and scent, my head spinning from the alcohol, I have no idea how long we kiss for but it's probably only a few seconds until the conscious part of my brain (which admittedly is working far more slowly than usual due to multiple Flora Sours) registers the fact that I am kissing someone who is not my boyfriend and that this is therefore WRONGWRONGWRONG and I immediately pull away.

'I've got to go,' I stammer. 'My train . . .'

'I understand,' says Flora gently, letting go of me. 'It's okay.'

I hesitate. 'I had a lovely evening, I'm just . . .'

'Percy, it's fine.' She gives me a reassuring smile. 'You get going. I'm going to stay out here and enjoy the view for a while longer.'

I nod, then turn and walk back down the stairs, still in a daze, but as soon as I emerge through the door the noise of the party suddenly jolts me back to reality and a wave of panic washes away whatever strange spell had been over me. What have I done? I've got to get out of here *right now*. I repeatedly jab at the button for the lift until it arrives and I collapse into it, grateful to be its only occupant, and lean against the glass wall trying to steady my breathing, which is so fast and shallow it reminds me of the time I briefly took up running. How did I let things go so far? What the hell was I thinking . . . ? I can't even *begin* to deal with what just happened back there; right now I need to focus on getting back to the station and getting home, then I can sort out this mess when I'm sober. Yes, that's what I'll do.

Once outside I set off in the direction of Liverpool Street station. If I'm quick I should be able to make the 22.14 train; I might even have time to get that gin-in-a-tin if I'm lucky. Christ, these shoes are agony . . . One foot in front of the other, Percy, stay focused, you can do it . . . Then – shit! I've barely made it to the end of the street when I trip on an uneven bit of paving, my heel slips out of my sandal and I leave it stranded behind me, like Cinderella fleeing the ball at the stroke of midnight, except instead of a princess turning back into a pauper I'm a lesbian turning back into a heterosexual. *Sometimes we're attracted to the prince, sometimes the fairy godmother* . . . Oh for God's sake, this is all so bloody confusing . . . I hop back to where my shoe is lying and am leaning down to put it back on when something slams into me with such force that I fall to the ground with a yelp, and when I look up I see the back of someone running off – and I realise that the someone is holding my bag.

I try to shout, but I'm winded or in shock or both, so can only manage a feeble moan. I cannot believe that just happened. I've been mugged. I am the victim of a mugging! I was struggling to keep myself together before this happened, but now – well, game over. Still sprawled on the pavement, I start to cry.

'Are you okay?'

I look up to see one of the Three Musketeers bending over with his hand outstretched towards me, cape thrown over one shoulder. I must be suffering from concussion. I close my eyes, rub my face and then open them again, but he's still there: plumed hat, striped tunic, knee-high boots and rapier – Le Full Works.

'I was just getting out of a taxi and saw what happened, but I'm afraid that arsehole was long gone before I could run after him. Are you hurt?'

Hmmm, he sounds quite posh; I thought the Musketeers were French? But then again, I don't think the Musketeers carried Nike rucksacks either. I let him pull me to my feet – at least I don't seem to have injured anything – then instinctively I reach for my phone and the full horror of the situation hits me. My bag had everything in it: not just my mobile, but house keys, purse, train tickets, my whole *life*. How the hell am I going to get back to Norwich?

'I'm . . . I'm fine, thank you,' I say, struggling to keep myself together in the face of this fresh catastrophe. 'Just a bit winded.'

The Musketeer is looking at me with concern. He has a black moustache and pointy goatee, but they're clearly fake because the hair peeping out from beneath his hat is a sandy colour. 'Come and sit down here for a moment,' he says, steering me towards a low wall. 'You're in shock.'

'Thank you, I just . . . My bag, it had everything in it. I need to get the train – I live in Norwich. I can't . . . I don't . . .'

'It's okay, calm down,' he says soothingly. 'We'll sort it out, don't worry.'

As we're in the financial district and it's the weekend there's nobody else around and it suddenly occurs to me that I'm in a rather vulnerable situation here – on my own in a dark street with a man who could potentially be a mass murderer – but then it actually crosses my mind that it's okay, I'll be safe with him because he's a Musketeer. *That's* how screwed up I am right now.

He offers me a bottle of Evian. 'I've just opened it, so you won't have to share my spit,' he grins. 'I'm Milo, by the way. Milo Turnbull.'

'I'm Percy James. Thank you for being so kind.'

'Would you like to use my phone to contact someone?'

Yes, that's a good idea. I'll call Adam – he'll know exactly what to do. *But Adam thinks you're at the pub with Mel in Norwich.* Shit. How am I going to explain to him that I'm actually in London on my own? Oh, this is bad. This is very, very bad. Maggie has got a spare set of my flat keys, but she always stays at Derek's on Saturday night and I don't know his number. I know, I'll call one of my friends, ask them to book me a train ticket to Norwich, then I'll stay at theirs for the night and sort things out in the morning. Yes, that would work! I just need to remember one of their numbers. Charlie's is 0777 something . . . Think, Percy, think! 07775 maybe? Why the hell have I never committed it to memory in case of emergency? Or I should have written it on a bit of paper and kept it in my purse – but that would have been no good because YOUR PURSE HAS BEEN STOLEN! Okay, calm down . . . I can definitely remember my parents' phone number because it's been the same my whole life; I'll try calling them. I'll get the third degree from Mum, but that's preferable to having to explain things to Adam.

With a little leap of hope, I dial their number on Milo's phone (he's got a cool photo of someone canoeing down rapids as his wallpaper – I wonder if that's him?) but there's no answer, which is not that surprising because my parents have a better social life than I do. No, my only option is Adam. *I am doomed.*

He answers after just a couple of rings.

'Adam Lumsden.'

'Adam, it's me.'

'Percy! What number are you calling from?'

'My bag's been stolen.'

'Oh my God, are you okay?'

'Yes, I'm fine, a man is helping me – that's whose phone this is.'

'Right, where are you? I'm leaving now, darling, I'll be there as quick as I can.'

'No, I'm . . . You can't . . . I'm not in Norwich, Adam. I'm in London.'

There's a brief silence. 'I thought you were at the pub with Mel?'

'Last minute change of plan. I'll explain when I see you, but I didn't go out with Mel after all.' I glance at Milo, but he seems occupied with something in his rucksack, clearly well mannered enough at least to *pretend* not to be listening. 'I'm so sorry about this, but would you mind booking me a train ticket from Liverpool Street? And then I'll walk to yours from the station – if that's okay.' I just hope I'll be able to come up with a decent explanation on the journey home.

We sort out the logistics and say goodbye, but there's an edge to Adam's voice, which is hardly surprising in the circumstances. I had a feeling all those lies would catch up with me at some point – and here we are.

'Thank you so much for your help,' I say to Milo, handing back his phone.

'All sorted?'

'Yes, my boyfriend is booking me a train ticket,' I say. My kind, trusting boyfriend whom I've just lied to and cheated on. Struck by a wave of self-loathing, I burst into tears.

'You mustn't let me keep you any longer,' I wail. 'Honestly, I'm fine.' Snivel. 'Really. *Waaaaaaah.*'

'You should report this to the police,' says Milo. 'Let me walk you to the police station, at least.'

'But if I miss the last train I'll be stuck h-h-heeeeere.' Sniff. Sob. 'I'll r-r-r-report it tomorrow.'

He holds out a tissue, unfazed by my hysteria. 'Fair enough, but I'm going with you to get you on the train. You've had a nasty shock, you shouldn't be on your own.'

I'm about to insist that it's quite all right, I'll be fine, but actually, what option do I have? Without Google Maps to guide me I'm not entirely sure how to get back to Liverpool Street. I'm drunk and I'm scared. I have no money. Right now I need all the help I can get.

'Are you sure you don't mind?' I ask in a small voice, wiping my nose.

'No problem at all.'

'But don't you have plans?'

Milo shrugs. 'I was on my way to a birthday thing but I'm late already; it doesn't matter if I'm later. I'm not that fussed about going anyway. Are you okay to walk?'

And so we set off towards the station together, the sound of Milo the Musketeer's boots echoing around the quiet side street. Distracted from my emotional turmoil by the fresh pain in my blisters, I begin to calm down.

'So,' I ask after a few moments, 'is this party you're going to fancy dress?'

'What, this?' He looks down at his outfit. 'No, I've been at my Am-Op group. We're doing *The Three Musketeers*. I'm Porthos.'

'Am-Op . . . ?'

'Amateur opera.' We've reached a main road now but he suddenly stops and breaks into song, as loudly as if he was trying to reach the cheap seats, unfazed by the looks he's getting from passers-by. His voice is surprisingly good and at the end I give him a little round of applause and he bows, sweeping off his plumed hat to reveal a shaggy head of hair that's more surfer dude than Three Tenors.

'That was brilliant! You've got real talent.'

'Oh, it's just a hobby,' he says, but looks pleased. 'I've never had any training – unless you count singing in the shower.'

'Well, I'm impressed. I get stage fright even when I'm doing karaoke.'

'In my non-expert opinion, the trick is to not give a toss what other people think,' says Milo. 'That's the key to singing – the key to life, in fact. That, and a really good beard.'

'Ah, *that's* where I've been going wrong,' I say with a smile.

When we get to the station I still have half an hour before my train and Milo suggests going to a cafe so I can have a hot, sweet drink 'for the shock'. He's doing such a good job of taking my mind off the car crash that my life has become that I gratefully agree. We chat about Norwich and Milo tells me more about his Am-Op group; I'm relieved he doesn't ask anything personal, but he's probably realised that things are a bit delicate in that area and it would be wise to steer clear.

Just then his phone starts to vibrate and he checks the screen: 'My girlfriend Luiza,' he tells me, then answers the call: '*Hola, querida.*'

Even above the din of the busy station cafe I can hear a woman's voice at the end of the line. She doesn't sound happy; in fact, I'd describe her tone as 'ranting'.

Milo listens patiently. 'I know, sweetheart,' he says, 'but I—'

More shouting at the other end.

'Okay, but just let me—'

'Lu, I—'

'But I couldn't—'

It seems to go silent at the other end and after a moment Milo takes the phone from his ear and looks at it. 'Ah,' he says sheepishly. 'She hung up.'

'I hope she isn't mad because you're not at the party?'

'Oh no, Luiza's always mad. It's her default setting.' He shows me a photo on his phone of a girl who looks like a member of the Brazilian beach volleyball team who models for *Vogue* in her spare time.

'She's beautiful,' I say, glancing up at Milo with renewed curiosity. It's difficult to see exactly what he looks like under the hat and false tache, but – being admittedly totally superficial here – he must be quite attractive to have a girlfriend who looks like *that*. (Either that or – even more superficially – really rich.)

'I have a type,' he explains. 'And that type is crazy Brazilians. Or sometimes I mix it up and date crazy Spaniards . . . Oh, I don't know, I'm probably being unfair. Perhaps they're sane and I'm the one who's crazy.'

For the first time since we met, he seems a little downcast and I feel a pang of sympathy: it looks like I'm not the only one with relationship issues. If only SoulDate could deliver what it promised and *really* find your soulmate then the world would be saved from endless bullshit, Theresa LeFevre would be a gazillionaire and EROS Tech would win the Nobel Peace Prize.

'Well, you might well be mad,' I say to Milo, 'but you've been an absolute hero tonight and I can't thank you enough. I don't know what I'd have done if you hadn't come along.' I glance at the clock. 'I better get going, my train leaves in ten minutes.'

Milo reaches in his pocket and holds out some money. 'Here, take this.'

'Thank you, but really, I couldn't, you've been so kind already.'

'Please, just in case of an emergency. What if the train breaks down? What if none of the other Musketeers are on board? Do you *really* want to take that risk, Percy?'

I smile – he's got such a nice way about him. Perhaps that's how he pulls stunners like the Brazilian super-model. 'Okay, but at least give me your contact details so I can repay you.'

We swap emails and I promise to be in touch, then Milo walks me over to the platform.

'Well, thank you again – for everything,' I say.

'My pleasure. Nice meeting you, Percy.'

And with that he turns and walks away, swagger fully restored, leaving me to face my fate.

17

I arrive back at Adam's house just before 2 a.m. and find the door key under a pot of pink Japanese anemones, just as he said it would be. For some reason the fact that he was so particular about the exact type of flower breaks my heart: how could I be so awful to the sort of man who knows what a pink Japanese anemone looks like?

Back on familiar territory with the beginnings of a Class A hangover, the events of the past evening feel as distant and far-fetched as a dream. If only I had dreamt them, I think unhappily as I tiptoe up the stairs, dreading the conversation that's to come with Adam. At least he doesn't stir when I get into bed, so I've got until the morning to come up with a reasonable explanation as to why I was in London on my own when I was supposed to be in Norwich with Mel. I don't want to lie to him again, but having wrestled with this the whole way home I have decided that in this instance honesty would probably not be the best policy. If I told Adam the truth it would devastate him; besides, it's not like it's ever going to happen again, is it? Kissing Flora was a crazy, drunken one-off, a moment of madness. I certainly didn't go to her party with the intention of cheating – if, indeed, what I did even counts as cheating. Some blokes might actually quite *like* the idea of their girlfriend kissing another woman, although I strongly doubt Adam would subscribe to this 'sexy adultery' school of thought.

I don't expect any sympathy, but I have an awful night. I can't get to sleep as thoughts are whirling around my head like a hamster on a wheel – perpetual motion with zero progress – and I'm desperate for a drink of water but don't want to get up in case I disturb Adam. Just before 4.30 a.m. I look at the clock again and decide that I might as well give up on trying to sleep as it's clearly not happening, so I lie on my back wondering why the designer of Adam's very modern new-build house decided to decorate the ceilings like badly iced Christmas cakes, then a few minutes later I roll over and check the time again and realise that I must have fallen asleep after all, as those few minutes were in fact six hours and it's now 11 a.m., Adam's side of the bed is empty and Lou and her family will be here in two hours. Bollocks.

Okay, I can't put this off any longer: I need to talk to Adam and smooth things over before lunch. I have come up with a way of explaining where I was last night that's

90 per cent truth, 5 per cent misrepresentation and 5 per cent blatant barefaced lie, which is about the best I can do in the circumstances, but Adam's not in the bathroom, and when I go downstairs to the kitchen I find piles of peeled potatoes and carrots, trimmed green beans and an apple crumble waiting to join the lamb in the oven, but no Adam. He's clearly taken care of my designated jobs while I was sleeping off my hangover; great – I'm not exactly redeeming myself here. Then I see a note propped up by the kettle: 'Gone to get mint sauce and wine. Back shortly.' No kiss; not even a smiley face. He's clearly furious with me.

:(

I've just got out of the shower when the doorbell rings – it must be Adam with his hands full of bags. I rush downstairs wrapped in a towel, but when I open the door it's not Adam.

'Auntiiieeee Perceeee!'

Alfie bursts in and throws himself at me, closely followed by Phil and then Lou, who raises an eyebrow at my near-nakedness.

'All right for some people having a lie-in,' she says briskly. 'Didn't you get my message about us coming round early?'

'Um, no,' I say. 'I've . . . lost my phone.'

'Well, I texted to say that Alfie's been up since 5 a.m.

and will need a nap soon, so we thought we'd head over and put him down here. Not a problem, is it?'

'Oh, not at all,' I say, wrestling with Alfie who is yelling, 'Make a tent, Auntie Perceee! Make a tent!' while yanking at my towel. 'Come on in, Adam's just popped to the shops. No, please don't do that Alfie, sweetheart . . . Just give me a minute to get dressed, okay?'

'Is there anything we can do to help, Perce?' asks Phil. Bless him, he's such a sweet guy, and so laid-back – which is lucky because as much as I love Lou she can be a little 'challenging' at times.

'No, it's all under control, thanks. Just go through to the living room and I'll be with you in a sec.'

Thankfully I've left a pair of jeans and a sweatshirt here for emergencies (God knows how I would've explained why I'm wearing a satin shift dress for Sunday lunch) then just as I'm coming back downstairs the front door opens and in walks Adam. Our eyes meet and he looks away again almost instantly, but it's enough for me to see how upset he is. My heart lurches horribly; God only knows what he's imagining I got up to last night. I need to talk to him as soon as I can and make things right between us.

'You're awake then,' he says without enthusiasm, closing the door behind him. 'I didn't want to wake you. I thought you might need the sleep after . . . what happened.'

'Thank you, that was really kind of you.' I hover awkwardly at the bottom of the stairs, wondering whether I should try for a hug despite Adam radiating 'DON'T HUG ME' vibes. 'Listen,' I begin, 'about last night, I can explain—'

'Hello there, Mr Lumsden!' Lou sticks her head around the living-room door. 'We came early, I hope that's okay?'

Adam instantly rearranges his frown into a smile – 'Of course it is, lovely to see you!' – and follows her into the living room without a second glance at me. 'Hello, Alfie!' he says, giving him a hug. 'Phil – how are you, mate? Let me sort out some drinks. Is it too early for wine, do you think?'

'Ooh no, that would be great,' beams Lou.

Phil looks at her. 'I thought you were going to drive?'

'I am, but I can have one glass. I'm not that much of a lightweight! Just a small one, thanks, Adam.'

'A *very* small one,' mutters Phil.

Lou laughs, but the thing is, I'm pretty sure he's not joking. He's scowling at his wife in a very un-Phil-like fashion, while Lou's manic smile seems to say: 'Nothing to see here! Move along, folks!'

Hmmm. Perhaps they had an argument on the way here?

'And an apple juice for Alfie?' asks Adam, heading for the door.

'Thanks, but he's tired, I think he should probably go for a sleep,' says Lou. 'Is it okay if I put him to bed upstairs?'

'Well he seems all right to me,' says Phil, watching his

son play with his Lego. 'Better to keep him up now and let him sleep in the car on the way home.'

'He might seem fine now,' replies Lou, 'but he's going to be overtired if he doesn't have a nap. Adam, can I tuck him up in your bedroom?'

'Um, yes, of course,' says Adam, clearly wary of getting involved in a marital tiff.

Phil looks thunderous. 'Lou, it's hardly bloody surprising that he keeps waking up at five in the morning if you insist on giving him these long naps.'

But she ignores him. 'Won't be a minute!' she trills, carrying Alfie out of the room, leaving Phil shaking his head in irritation.

There's an uneasy silence for a few moments. 'Well, I'll just go and get those drinks,' says Adam.

'I'll help you,' I say, jumping up and following him to the kitchen. Right, here's my chance to sort things out.

'Thank you so much for rescuing me last night,' I say. 'You've probably been wondering what on earth I was doing in London!'

Busying himself with the drinks, Adam just shrugs.

'I can explain everything,' I say. 'It'll only take a minute, it's all very simple really.'

'Not now, Percy.'

'But I want to clear the air,' I persist, wincing at the whininess in my voice. 'I feel so bad about what happened, if you could just let me—'

'We'll talk later.' And he stalks out of the room carrying the tray of drinks.

Oh, this is bad. Adam has never given me the cold shoulder before – although it's no less than I deserve, obviously. But I don't want to cause a scene with Lou and Phil here; I'll just have to put on a brave face until they go home and we can sit down and sort this mess out, tough as that will be with the events of last night looming over us like a big, black, question-mark-shaped thundercloud. So I plaster on a smile and walk back into the living room, humming breezily to show that everything is absolutely A-okay.

As it turns out, though, I needn't have worried about our problems spoiling lunch. Things might be frosty between Adam and me, but Phil and Lou seem to have plunged headlong into the Ice Age. Thanks to their constant bickering what should be a pleasant pre-lunch chat becomes a battlefield, with Adam and me as the UN peacekeepers running for cover amongst the rubble, and even the most innocent of comments triggering a brutal new skirmish.

For example: 'Have you seen that new Ryan Gosling thriller?' I ask at one point.

'Ooh, no, but I'd watch any old crap if he was in it,' says Lou. 'Especially if he had his shirt off.'

Phil snorts loudly and mockingly.

'And what's that supposed to mean?' snaps Lou.

'It means that if I made that comment about, say, Mila Kunis, you'd have something to say about it.'

'That's because Mila Kunis looks like a gnome.'

Phil smirks. 'Jealous, are we . . . ?'

'No, I just thought I'd married someone with taste,' says Lou. 'Clearly I was wrong.'

You see? It's exhausting. Clearly something is very wrong between them. Phil is so mild-mannered that usually he'd just laugh off Lou's stroppiness, whereas today he's being even more vicious than she is. I know Alfie isn't sleeping well at the moment, but surely it can't just be sleep deprivation? I'm beginning to worry that something terrible has happened, so I try to get Lou on her own to find out what it is.

'Hey, why don't you come and help me make the custard?' I ask her in the chirpy, over-bright tone I've adopted today to offset all the venom. 'We can leave the boys in here to chat about sport and beer! Ha ha!'

But Adam screws up my plan. 'I've already made it,' he says, pointedly. 'While you were asleep.'

So I sit down again, none the wiser about what's going on between Lou and Phil and desperately wishing I could talk to Adam about last night, because I'm quite sure if he gave me a chance to explain I could smooth things over in a matter of minutes. Just keep smiling, I remind myself, and in another hour or so the pair of us can sit down together and sort everything out. It will all be fine; in fact, we'll be laughing about this by the end of the day.

Probably.

Thanks to Alfie's nap it's nearly two by the time we sit down for lunch and, after a few glasses of wine, Lou and Phil's sniping is getting even worse.

'Please don't do that,' Lou says to Alfie, who is banging his spoon on the table. *Bang bang bang.* 'Sweetie, Mummy has asked you to stop it.' *Bang bang bang.* 'No – nasty noise. No, Alfie.' She grabs the spoon off him. 'I said *no.*'

'There's no need to snap at him,' says Phil, 'he's just having a bit of fun. Aren't you, buddy?' Phil tickles his son and he collapses into giggles.

'Don't do that, please, Phil, you'll get him overexcited.' Lou is smiling, but her voice has an edge. 'And I wasn't snapping, I was asking.'

'That's the problem, there's not much difference these days,' he mutters.

'Well, one of us needs to teach him how to behave,' says Lou.

'Meaning what?' says Phil angrily, but Lou ignores him, turning back to Alfie who is now dipping his finger in gravy and drawing circles on the table.

'Don't do that,' she tuts, wiping his hands with a napkin, but he does it again. 'No, Alfie, bad boy!'

'For God's sake, he's just playing!' Phil huffs.

Desperate to avoid an argument, I jump in. 'Really, it doesn't matter about the table!'

But they ignore me. 'Phil, I spend my week trying to teach him table manners and then you undermine me,' says Lou. 'It's not fair.'

'Well, in case you've forgotten,' Phil bites back, 'I have to spend my week stuck in an office to keep a roof over our heads. I don't think that's very fair either.'

Alfie has started to grizzle, picking up on the hostility between his parents.

Phil rolls his eyes. 'Great, now we're going to have a full-blown tantrum.'

'And that's my fault, is it? For not allowing him have his way the whole time?'

'Oh, come on,' spits Phil. 'It's a bit rich you trying to play the perfect mother after . . .' He stops himself, but you can't miss the venomous look he gives her.

'Why don't I get the apple crumble?' I say, in a last-ditch attempt to lighten the atmosphere. 'You'll be pleased to hear that Adam made it, rather than me! Ha ha! So what do we think – custard or cream? Or both? What would you like, Alfie? I think we might have some ice-cream too . . .'

But he's now screaming, while Phil just looks furious.

'I'm so sorry,' says Lou, her voice quivering with emotion. 'I think it might be better if we went home.'

'Yes, of course, whatever you think best,' says Adam, as Alfie kicks things up another gear.

'Do you want me to take him for a walk in his push-chair while you finish lunch?' I shout, struggling to make myself heard above the wailing. 'It might calm him down a bit.'

But Phil is already collecting up their things. 'No, that's kind of you to offer, Percy, but we better get going.'

'Shall I wrap up some crumble for you to take home?' offers Adam.

'No, really, thank you.' Lou looks like she's about to cry. Things must be bad – I can't ever remember seeing her close to tears. 'Lunch was delicious,' she says. 'I'm just so sorry about . . . everything.'

'Shhh, don't worry, really, it's fine,' I say. 'I'll see you out.'

After they've left I go into the kitchen where Adam is stacking plates in the dishwasher, rinsing each one clean before loading it, as is his habit. Usually I tease him about this (what's the point in washing plates before they go in the dishwasher? I mean, surely the clue is in the name?) but today it doesn't feel right.

'Well that was a nice relaxed lunch, wasn't it?' I say, trying to lighten the atmosphere before I tackle The Chat. 'I wonder what on earth had got into them? I'll call Lou later and find out if they're okay.'

Adam, who is now methodically rinsing and stacking the glasses, ignores me.

I try again. 'Thank you so much for taking care of lunch, it was delicious. That lamb was amazing – really tender.'

Still nothing. His silence is unnerving; it would be easier if he shouted and threw things, at least then I'd have something to work with. I cross over to where he's standing at the sink.

'So what can I do to help?' I say brightly. 'Shall I get started on the pans?'

Finally, he stops what he's doing and turns to look at me. 'Percy,' he says. 'Are you having an affair?'

'*What*?' For some reason this knocks me sideways – although it's hardly surprising he should come to that conclusion. 'Because of what happened last night?'

'No, not just because of last night – although that would seem the obvious explanation for why you lied about where you were. You've been distant for weeks.'

'Of course I'm not having an affair!' I go to touch his arm, but he pulls away. 'Please, come and sit down so we can talk properly.'

Reluctantly he wipes his hands on a tea towel and follows me to the kitchen table, looking suspicious and tired and miserable, and I curse myself for causing this kind man so much grief.

'I'm not seeing anyone else, okay?' I tell him. 'I wouldn't do that to you – deep down you must know that, surely?'

'I don't know what to think any more,' he says quietly.

'Look, just let me explain what happened last night, please.' He gives the tiniest of nods. 'Okay, first of all I better give you a bit of background.' I take a deep breath and launch into my carefully prepared account. 'Remember I went shopping in London last weekend when you were in Manchester? Well, while I was there I met this woman. Flora. She's a lawyer – works for a big technology company. Really nice. She's a lesbian.' Adam instantly looks suspicious. Shit, I should have left the lesbian bit out. 'Anyway, we got talking and hit it off and she invited me to a party, which was last night. It was like an "I'm not getting married" party – isn't that funny? Anyway – and this is going to sound really silly – it was quite a small party so I couldn't bring a guest, but I really wanted to go because it was this fancy black-tie thing, so I stupidly didn't tell you about it because I didn't want you to be upset that I couldn't take you, which in hindsight was really dumb because of course you'd have understood.'

'Wait – she's a lesbian?'

'Yes. Her name's Flora,' I say, trying to move the conversation on from the 'L' bomb. 'She's great: successful, funny, dynamic – you'd love her.'

'And it was her party you were at last night?'

I nod enthusiastically. 'And it was in London, so that's why I was there. In London, I mean. Last night. And I was just leaving when that bastard stole my bag.'

Adam is looking at me like I'm speaking Urdu. 'Percy, are you telling me that you're gay?'

'What? *No!* No, no, that's not it at all. The fact that she's a lesbian isn't relevant – I don't even know why I brought it up.' I shrug hopelessly. 'I was just . . . giving you the full picture, I suppose. Filling you in.'

'But why wouldn't you tell me about the party? I wouldn't have minded in the slightest. I thought we had the sort of relationship where we could tell each other anything. I thought we *trusted* each other.' He leans towards me, an earnest look on his face. 'Trust is essential in a relationship, Percy. It's the bedrock that love is built on.'

Oh, I know that he's right, but I do have to stop myself rolling my eyes. Adam has this knack of making me feel like a naughty schoolgirl – and not in a good way. I feel a flicker of annoyance and firmly remind myself that I'm very much the one who's at fault here, although in my defence it can be quite tiring being with someone who never puts a foot wrong.

'I do know that,' I tell him, 'I was just . . . Look, it was really stupid of me and I'm so sorry that I wasn't honest with you. Really, the last thing I wanted to do was hurt you. Will you forgive me?'

But Adam is still deep in thought, a little crease between his brows; he is clearly struggling to process my explanation. I stupidly assumed that he'd hear what I had to say and everything would be hunky-dory, but I didn't count on Adam's Poirot-esque powers of logic and deduction.

'How did you meet this woman again?' he asks. 'You said you bumped into her when you were in London last weekend?'

'Yes, I met her in a shop.'

'And you just . . . started talking to her?'

He's looking sceptical, but surely that's not so hard to believe, is it? Women chat to each other in shops all the time. (Okay, not *all* the time, but Adam's not to know that.)

'Well, she was trying on this pair of shoes and I said something like "Hey, great shoes, they look comfy", and she said, "Yes, they are very comfy" and we got chatting and then we went for a drink together and, um, that was it.'

'She wasn't trying to chat you up, then?'

Argh, why did I have to mention the fact that she's a lesbian? WHY?

'Oh no, she's . . . in a really serious relationship.'

He frowns. 'But earlier you said she was having an "I'm not getting married" party?'

'Yes, well, it *is* a serious relationship, but . . .'

I tail off with a shrug, desperately hoping that will be the end of it – but no.

'Percy, I'm at a loss to know what to think,' says Adam.

'You've been behaving so strangely recently. First there was that lollipop lady incident—'

'I've told you, that was just supposed to be a bit of fun!'

'And now you're running around with a bunch of lesbians.'

'I went to a party! It's hardly running around!'

But Adam ignores me. 'The point is, Percy, that you've clearly got some issues you need to work through. I really do think a course of therapy might help – it certainly can't do any harm, can it?'

At his mention of therapy again I feel such a surge of anger that I'm about to lose it, but then a thought pops into my head with such force that it brings me up short, cutting through all the bullshit with laser-sharp clarity.

This is not how a relationship should be.

And as that sinks in, I suddenly remember what Maggie said the other day about soulmates, about how you know a relationship is right when you don't need to talk yourself into it. She made it sound so simple. But when I think back over the past few weeks – all the lies, deceit, doubt and agonising – I realise that things between Adam and me have been the opposite of simple.

'Percy?' I look up to find him frowning at me. 'Are you listening to me? Because I'm sure it would benefit both you and our relationship if you went to talk to a professional.'

This is not how a relationship should be.

I take a long, hard look at Adam: his dark hair, the navy V-neck, that mole just below his left eye; all the bits of him that I have loved for the past three years. I know him so intimately I could almost draw the constellations of freckles on his forearms from memory. Isn't it crazy how some guy from Manchester who grew up two hundred miles away from me has become as familiar to me as my own face? The randomness of fate is mind-blowing. And with that thought it dawns on me how many other blokes there must be out there who grew up two hundred miles away (or more) whom I could just as easily be sitting opposite right now, and I find myself wondering if perhaps – just possibly – one of *those* blokes might be a little better suited to me than Adam is? Maybe there's someone out there who wouldn't think I need therapy, because they would love me in spite of my 'issues'. Perhaps I wouldn't have had to tie myself in knots coming up with an excuse for where I was last night because I'd have wanted to spend last night with them. Maybe he's out there . . . but I just haven't met him yet?

And with that my thoughts fall into place, one after the other, like the pieces in my favourite childhood board game Mouse Trap. Adam might well be perfect, but he's perfect for somebody else, not for me, and that doesn't mean that I'm a bad person who will never be happy, it just means that I'm in the wrong relationship. Clunk, boing, kerplunk. *I'm in the wrong relationship.*

Wow. It suddenly seems obvious; how had I never realised this before? It's like the way in which the colour red suits some people, but on others it brings out the ruddiness of their complexion and makes their hair colour look cheap (thanks, Mum) and no matter how hard they try to make it work by wearing a cool scarf or different lipstick, the bottom line is that red will never, ever suit them. It's not their fault – they just look better in blue. So I can keep chucking cool scarves and different lipsticks at this relationship, but it will never work because Adam isn't right *for me*. Despite my emotional turmoil, I feel borderline euphoric: I'm not an unlovable commitment-phobic freak after all! It's not me, it's not him – it's *us*.

And just as when you're in a plane and you're coming into land there's that moment when you dip beneath the clouds and you suddenly see all the hills and roads and buildings that were always there but had been hidden, so I finally see our relationship the way it is – the way it has always been under the cloud – and I realise with a mixture of wretchedness and terror that Adam and I are coming to the end of our flight.

I fear the final descent may be a little bumpy.

18

I need to do this. I've been a coward, but it's the right thing to do. I take a deep breath, willing myself not to burst into tears.

'Adam, I've handled everything so badly. I've been a terrible girlfriend. But I've been having doubts. About us.'

'I'm not daft,' he says flatly. 'I know you have.'

'And I've been trying to tell myself that it's okay, that I'm just having a silly panic about moving in together, but I think there's a bit more to it than just that.'

I've been staring at my hands while I get the words out, but now I steal a glance at Adam. I can't believe I'm about to break up with him, it feels completely surreal.

'Percy,' he says, narrowing his eyes. 'What are you trying to say?'

'I'm saying that I don't think we should move in together. And I'm also saying . . . That I think . . . What I'm trying to say is . . .' Oh, for God's sake, woman, just spit it out! 'That I don't think we should go out with each other any more.'

The words linger in the air like a particularly stinky fart and for a moment Adam just stares at me in disbelief. Then – 'I knew it!' he cries, slapping the table. 'I thought, "There's something going on with her, she's not happy," but you *kept* telling me you were. You kept on insisting everything was fine.' He reaches for my hands, his eyes filled with anguish. 'Why didn't you talk to me about this before, Percy? Why didn't you tell me you were having doubts?'

'I know I should have, but you're such a wonderful boyfriend that I assumed the problems were all in my head. I couldn't work out why I wasn't more excited about moving in together – I mean, it's not like there's anything really wrong with our relationship, is there? So I figured I had commitment issues, or whatever it was Mum said about me . . .'

'But we can do something about that!' Adam squeezes my hands. 'That's why I suggested you see a therapist – they can help you deal with it! They can fix you!'

I shake my head hopelessly. 'It's not just that, Adam. There's something else. Something a therapist can't fix.'

'Which is?'

I have to force the words out. 'That I don't think we're right for each other.'

I'll spare you the gory details, but suffice it to say the next hour and a half is horrible – just horrible. There is arguing, pleading and so many tears that the table is soon covered in sodden piles of snot-soaked kitchen roll. Sticking to my guns takes every ounce of my conviction, because I can't quite explain why, as Adam keeps asking with increasing desperation, I'm throwing away a perfectly good relationship for no real reason. It's just not a clear-cut case of 'I don't fancy you any more' or 'I've met someone else' and my whole red/blue theory, which had been so convincing in my head, sounds insane when I try to explain it to Adam.

'So let me get this straight,' he almost shouts, 'you're destroying everything we have and our future happiness together because *red doesn't suit you?*'

By five o'clock we've used up all of the kitchen roll, my voice is hoarse from crying and Adam has gone from tearful denial to angry acceptance.

'I think you should leave now,' he says, still sitting at the kitchen table.

I hesitate, desperate to ask if we can still be friends, as after all that time together the prospect of not having Adam in my life at all seems unbearable, but I can imagine what he'd say to me – and I'd deserve it. Isn't it mental how fragile relationships are? You can spend three years loving someone, sharing everything, being closer than to anyone else in the world, but all that can be destroyed by just a few words.

I can't bring myself to ask Adam for the spare set of keys to my flat and he doesn't offer, so I get a taxi to Maggie's using the money Milo gave me, praying that she'll be home – and in an undeserved piece of luck, she is. She answers the door wearing a baggy T-shirt that says 'WILL WORK FOR COFFEE' and her usual orange lipstick.

'Hello love, this is a nice surprise.' Then she takes in my red, puffy face and stricken expression. 'Percy, whatever's wrong?'

'I've just broken up with Adam. Have I just made a huge mistake? I have, haven't I?'

'Oh darling, come on in.'

'And my bag's been stolen so I've lost my keys, phone and purse. Everything.' I start to cry again, harder than ever. 'Maggie, I've lost everything.'

'Shhh, it's okay, we'll sort it out, don't worry.' She herds me inside and hugs me tightly. Her smell is so familiar and comforting, my sobs gradually subside into sniffles.

'Can I stay here tonight?'

'Of course you can. You stay for as long as you need, I'd love to have you here.'

To my relief Maggie immediately takes charge, as I'm not in a fit state to make a cup of tea, let alone deal with the fallout from a stolen bag and a buggered love life. While I get stuck into a medicinal brandy, which at least takes the edge off the pain a little, Maggie contacts the police to get a crime number, cancels my credit card and somehow manages to arrange a replacement mobile *and* an upgrade. Then she brings me a bowl of treacle sponge and sits with me while I shovel it down, trying to smother the horrible ache inside me with sugar and carbs.

'Maggie,' I ask between mouthfuls, 'did *you* think Adam wasn't right for me?'

I'm desperate for her to tell me I've done the right thing, to reassure me that I had no choice, because at the moment I'm seriously concerned that I have made a hideous mistake.

'Well, you can never know what goes on in other people's relationships, even when you're as close as you and me,' she says. 'More cream?' I nod and she sloshes it on. 'I've always thought Adam is a wonderful man—'

'He is!' I sob. 'Oh, he really is!' Adam didn't deserve to be treated like this. The man is a god. A *god*. I'm never going to find anyone who is as sweet and kind and generous to me as he was. I am going to be alone forever and it's my own fault. 'Maggie,' I stammer, tears streaming down my face, 'what the *fuck* have I done?'

'Shhhh, let me finish,' she says soothingly. 'What I was going to say is that Adam is a wonderful man, but I was never completely sure you two were a good match. He's a methodical, controlled sort of person, whereas you're more of a free spirit. When you were with him I got the impression that you squashed the dreamy, flighty bit of you to fit in with Adam – and that was a shame, because that's one of my favourite bits of you.'

I know Maggie's just trying to be nice, but to be quite honest the dreamy, flighty bit of me can go fuck itself. If it wasn't for my sodding free spirit I'd still have a boyfriend, rather than being single. Oh Christ, I'm *single*! Detached. Deserted. Lonely. ALONE. My future stretches out in front of me like one of those endless roads that criss-cross America with nothing but red dirt and the occasional cactus as far as the eye can see. Adam has been part of my identity for so long that without him I have no idea who I am. If I don't have an 'other half', am I just a half? I really don't think there's enough of me to be on my own.

I have another large brandy and as a woozy numbness starts to creep over me and my eyelids droop Maggie tucks me up in the spare-room bed beneath the black-and-white poster of Joni Mitchell sitting cross-legged with her guitar, and, thanks to the lethal combination of a hangover, heartache and Hennessy, I am out like a light in moments.

Man, that was a brilliant sleep, I feel like I've been flat out for twelve hours! Mmmm, nothing like starting the day with a nice, big stretch . . . right down to my toes . . . Right, what time is it? I better check my mobile. Uh, where's my mobile? Hang on a sec, why am I at Maggie's house . . . ?

Oh . . . shit.

The part of my brain containing yesterday's horrors flickers into life and as my good mood vanishes beneath the memory of Adam's anguished face I bury myself in the pillow with a sob, willing myself to get back to sleep.

*

Percy.

PERCY!

Great, Brenda's back. My inner agony aunt – with the emphasis firmly on the agony.

That's a bit rude. I'm only trying to help.

I'm sorry, Brenda, but I want to be left alone. I'm wallowing.

Oh, pull yourself together, for the love of God. You think you're the first woman to have man trouble?

Please, let me sleep. I feel terrible . . .

You think you've got it bad? Well, look at poor Joni Mitchell up there. She had a godawful life: polio, teenage pregnancy, a crap marriage, tragically limp hair. Did she stay in bed and cry? No, she did not! She broke out the volumising mousse and headlined at the Isle of Wight Festival. The woman's an inspiration. There's even a saying: WWJD. 'What would Joni Do?'

I think WWJD actually stands for 'What Would Jesus Do?'

Really? Well, he wasn't one for malingering in bed either. So get up.

So I do. I need to call the office anyway, as I can't face going into work, and I speak to Susannah who is very concerned and sweetly tells me to take as much time off as I need – which obviously makes me cry all over again. (How can I have any tears left? Seriously, I'm beginning to worry that I might be at risk of dehydration.) Maggie cooks me bacon and eggs and then, as much as I want to

crawl back into her spare-room bed, Joni Mitchell's knowing half-smile persuades me to get in the shower, borrow
my spare keys from Maggie and head back to my flat – via
the phone shop to pick up my new mobile – to start my
life again.

So much has happened since I was last home that even
though it was only the day before yesterday it feels like
months ago. I half expect everything to be covered in dust
and cobwebs, Miss Havisham-style. The last time I walked
through my front door I had a boyfriend, but now there's
a huge chasm that's opened up in my life like that sink-
hole that appeared in the middle of a housing estate the
other day, only rather than lamp posts and letter boxes it's
my happiness that's been swallowed up inside it.

I can't describe how much I miss Adam right now. I
miss his friendship, I miss the feeling of his arms around
me and I miss his stability – which ironically is one of the
very things I dumped him for in the first place; I'd laugh
if it wasn't so bloody tragic. I immediately take down the
photo of the two of us at Charlie's wedding, but it leaves a
faint outline on the wall and somehow that's more painful to look at than the photo, so I put it back up again. My
insides ache like really bad period pains. No, it's worse
than that: like *childbirth* – the mention of which brings
up a whole other issue that I haven't dared think about yet,
i.e. that I am now a Single Woman in her Thirties, which

means according to popular opinion (a.k.a. the *Daily Mail*) I have less than four years until my ovaries shrivel up like the squashed currants in a garibaldi biscuit – except there'll always be a demand for garibaldi biscuits, whereas soon nobody will want me. I've never really been that bothered about having children, but right now I WANT A BAYBEEEEEEEE!

I stand at the door to my bedroom, the vision of Adam's dark head against my white pillow seared in my mind, and feel panic crawling over me like ants. What have I done? I have chucked away a good relationship with a wonderful man because . . . because . . . Oh Christ, now I can't even remember *why* I finished it! I throw myself on the bed and give in to the tears, crying so hard that the duvet is soon pooling with rivulets of tears and snot and my downstairs neighbour Mrs Bagshawe bangs on the ceiling. I must be making a hell of a racket because she's deaf.

Just then a phone starts to ring and, because of the unfamiliar new ringtone, it takes me a second to realise that it's mine. I frantically scrabble to find it, desperately hoping it's Adam, but it's not: it's Flora. Seeing her name on the screen I feel such a screaming rush of rage that I have to stop myself chucking the phone at the wall. *Bloody Flora.* If it weren't for her filling my head with talk of Ferris Bueller and flying then I'd probably still be with Adam. It was *her* that planted doubts in my mind and made me think that my wonderful boyfriend was somehow wrong for me. If only I'd never met her then everything would be fine . . .

Oh God, what am I talking about? Of course Flora's not to blame! Like me, she's just an innocent victim of the real villain here: Theresa Le-Fucking-Fevre. Christ, I should have listened to my instincts and never had anything to do with that woman. I'll never have a baby and it's ALL HER FAULT! And what about poor Flora? She spent God knows how much money to meet her soulmate and out of all the people in the world they couldn't even find her someone with the same sexual preference! It's ridiculous. No, it's worse than that – it's criminal. Poor Flora . . . Actually, Flora's such a fantastic listener perhaps it *would* be good to talk to her about what's happened with Adam . . . but I can't bloody do that, can I, because she thinks I'm a lesbian – and anyway, now it's gone to voice-mail. *Waaaaaah!*

I throw the phone on the bed and then cry some more, shuffling over to a different bit of the duvet so I'm not lying in the wet patch – the only wet patch this bed will see for some time, I think miserably, probably *ever.* I've forgotten all the reasons I had for finishing with Adam and all that remains is a deep longing for his arms and three simple thoughts:

I'm a spinster.

I want a baby.

My life is a complete mess.

19

Dearest Adam,

I'm so so sorry to keep bombarding you with emails and I completely understand why I haven't heard anything from you, but I'm hoping that if you are reading my messages then perhaps you'll begin to understand my reasons for what I did on Sunday. I know I have absolutely no right to ask this, but if there's any way you could bring yourself to send me a brief reply, maybe just a line or two to tell me how you're feeling, I'd be so grateful. I hate myself for causing you pain and just hope that one day you'll forgive me. I think about you constantly and endlessly wonder if I've done the right thing—

'Hey Perce, check this out.'

I look up from the email I've been struggling to write for the past half an hour to see Mel standing in front of my desk holding up a flyer.

'What's "Speed-Plating"?' I say.

'It's a cross between speed-dating and speed-eating.'

'Speed-eating?' I make a face. 'Like how many dough-nuts can you eat in five minutes?'

'That's it,' nods Mel excitedly. 'It's an event run by an Aussie mate of mine. He used to do a speed-dating night, but there were never enough blokes, so he came up with the genius idea of combining speed-dating with competitive eating to pull in more men. Worked a treat, apparently. Go on, have a look.'

Reluctantly, I take the flyer from her.

SPEED-PLATING – PUTTING THE GORGE INTO GORGEOUS
20 girls, 20 guys and all the burgers you can eat!!!
Meet hot babes and impress your mates!!!
Cash prize for the night's biggest burger-eater.

I look back to Mel with a sinking feeling. 'And you're showing me this why, exactly?'

She swiftly pulls up a chair. 'Percy, when you fall off the horse, what do you do?'

'Swap your horse for a nice safe car?'

'Get back on the fucking horse!' She grabs the flyer and waves it at me. 'And this would be the perfect opportunity!'

'Mel, I'm not sure I want to date the sort of man who thinks competitive burger-eating is a good night out.'

'Oh, come on, it'll be a laugh. I'll go with you – for moral support only, obviously.'

'Obviously, because you wouldn't want to cheat on Michael.'

'Too right.' She nods emphatically, ignoring the sarcasm in my voice.

'Look, I appreciate you trying to help, but it's way too soon. I only split up with Adam three days ago. Maybe in a month or two, okay?'

Thankfully, Mel doesn't argue: she's being gentle with me because yesterday when I told her I'd broken up with Adam and she said she was relieved I'd 'finally seen sense', I burst into tears. At least Charlie and Jaye were more sympathetic when I phoned to tell them the news on Monday (I couldn't face seeing anyone in person), although it clearly came as a bit of a shock – especially to poor Jaye whose emotions are still raw post-Cliché. I called Lou as well, of course, but it went straight to voicemail and although I left her a tearful message telling her about Adam and asking if everything was okay with her and Phil she still hasn't phoned me back. I'm trying not to worry about why that might be.

In one way it was a relief to talk to Charlie and Jaye about Adam, as they loyally insisted that I'd done the right thing and right now I need all the reassurance I can get, but I was on edge throughout our conversations because one of the first things both of them asked was if my decision to split up with Adam was anything to do with SoulDate.

'You didn't go on a date with that guy, did you, Percy?'

Jaye asked, her voice quavering. 'I mean, you wouldn't have done that behind Adam's back, would you . . . ?'

I had a choice of two possible answers:

Option 1: 'Please don't think badly of me, but I did go on the date and the crazy thing is that it wasn't a guy after all, it was a woman. I know – mental, right? Anyway – long story short – I went to this woman's party in London on Saturday night and we ended up on a roof terrace, kissing, and now I'm not sure if I like her or *like* her, if you get my drift. But honestly this has absolutely nothing to do with splitting up with Adam. *Honest*.'

Option 2: 'No.'

I'm afraid I took the coward's way out and went with Option 2, although in my defence I was in such a state over the split that I couldn't bring myself to throw a lesbian kiss into the mix as well. (Besides, it's true: meeting Flora is a totally separate issue from the split with Adam. A casual observer might assume that the two events are connected, but with all due respect that casual observer would be off his/her rocker.) Anyway, since then Charlie, Jaye and I have been texting and now I'm back in the land of the living we've arranged to meet up at the Wig and Pen after work tonight for an emergency summit. I have no idea whether Lou will be there or not.

When Mel has gone back to her desk, leaving me the flyer in case I change my mind, I finish the email to Adam and then check my inbox, hoping he might have replied to one of the previous six emails I've sent him in a feeble attempt to explain/apologise, but there's still nothing. At least I know he's okay, because Dad told me he came into work yesterday. I grilled him for more details, but even Oprah would struggle to get my father to open up. 'He seems fine,' is all I manage to get out of him. (My mother, however, is not fine. She has gone on a three-day spa break to recover from the news of our break-up.)

But while Adam is studiously evading my inbox, it turns out that Milo the Musketeer is not. As much as I didn't want to revisit the events of Saturday night I was feeling guilty about the thirty pounds he gave me, so I emailed to ask his address so that I could send a cheque, and now here he is. I click open his email.

Percy, you're alive! Terrific news. I was wondering if you made it back home in one piece. Now, how's this for a coincidence: having never once set foot in Norwich during my thirty-three years I will be passing through your fine city on Saturday. As you seem to be insisting on repaying me (really not necessary), would you like to do so in person? It'll save you the price of a stamp at least.
Best,
Milo

Well, that *is* a coincidence. I wonder what he'll be doing in Norwich? After a moment's thought I reply with my mobile number, telling him to get in touch when he arrives. It'll be nice to see him again – and I admit I'm curious to discover what he looks like under the fake beard. I barely know the guy, but for some strange reason I find myself wanting to tell Milo about what's happened with Adam. Perhaps going through a trauma with some-one fast-tracks the friendship process? Probably best if I don't mention it now, though, as losing a bag *and* a boy-friend in less than twenty-four hours looks a little sloppy.

Thinking about Milo and that fateful evening brings me right back to Flora again. She left me a voicemail on Sunday, saying how much she enjoyed seeing me at her party, and asking if I wanted to meet up for lunch, and after much deliberation I've concluded that the best course of action is to be decisive and proactive – so I have decided to proactively ignore her message.

The thought of seeing her again sends conflicting feel-ings ricocheting around my insides like emotional pinball: I find her fascinating, yet I'm embarrassed about the kiss; I'm attracted to her but at the same time a bit scared of her (well, her sexuality); I want to get to know her, but how can I when I've lied to her about who I really am? The momentousness of splitting up with Adam has rather overshadowed everything, but in any other cir-cumstances what happened between us on Saturday night would be all I could think about. Yes, Katy Perry, I too kissed a girl and I liked it. *Did* I like it? Well, it was . . . interesting. Less prickly, obviously. I didn't get those groin-trembling fireworks that I've had during previous first kisses, although from what I remember there was this soft, melting sensation that was rather lovely. But it's not like I wanted to rip Flora's clothes off; I'm not even sure I fancy her. The fact remains, however, that The Kiss did happen, which surely means that we're no longer just friends – and if we're no longer just friends, what are we? I'm so confused about where we go from here that for now it seems safer just to ignore her voicemail and focus on getting over Adam.

One emotional trauma at a time.

As soon as I walk into the Wig and Pen, a little pub just outside the city centre, I spot Charlie at a table in the far corner – and not just because she's waving furiously.

'Hello,' I say. 'Your hair is blue.'

'You like?' She tilts her chin and turns her head from side to side, as if modelling. 'It's not a bit . . . Smurf?'

'It's a lot Smurf. But it suits you.'

She looks pleased. 'Oh goody. So – are you all right?'

'Not really,' I say in a very small voice, because I fear that if I say it any louder I'll cry again.

'Aw, come here, love.' She pulls me to her and hugs me tightly. 'It was the right thing to do, Percy, but I know it must have been a tough call. I'm proud of you.'

'Hank ooo,' I mumble into her shoulder.

We sit down and Charlie pours me a glass of Prosecco from the bottle already on the table, then she leans towards me in the manner of Jeremy Paxman grilling the shadow chancellor.

'Right, before the others get here I need to talk to you about this SoulDate business. I know it's going to take you a long time to get over Adam, but now you're single perhaps you should meet up with this bloke? Just so you've explored all avenues?'

I hesitate, wondering whether I should come clean to her about Flora, as the burden of keeping her a secret is weighing on me. It would be such a relief to talk to someone about it – and Charlie would definitely be the least judgmental of my available someones – but the matter is taken out of my hands, because I look up to see Jaye approaching our table.

'Oh babe, I'm so sorry, you must be devastated! How are you doing? Here, I've brought you my healing rose quartz, it's meant to cleanse and detoxify your emotions.' Looking close to tears herself, she presses a crystal into my hands. 'It's really helped me through my break-up with that shitting fuckwit arsehole.'

'Not sure the emotional detoxification worked,' mutters Charlie.

Jaye shoots her a dark look then turns back to me, her Barbie-blue eyes wide and glittering. 'You know that I loved Adam, but if you felt your energies were, like, misaligned then you've definitely made the right decision. *Definitely*.' Bless her, she's trying her hardest, but I'm sure she thinks I'm insane. 'I'm totally here for you, babe,' she finishes with a brave smile.

'Thank you, my love, that means a great deal. And thank you for the crystal. Is Lou on her way?'

I notice Charlie and Jaye exchange glances.

'What? Is something wrong?'

'She'll be here in a minute,' says Jaye carefully, 'but I should warn you that she thinks you're a bit . . . well, she doesn't quite understand *why* you split up with Adam. And it's not that she doesn't support your decision, but you know Lou can be a little . . . inflexible. I'm sure when she hears your reasons for ending things she'll totally get it, but it was quite a bolt from the blue and because there was nothing obviously *wrong* with your relationship – well, nothing any of us were really aware of . . .'

'It's okay,' I reassure her, 'I understand.'

'Well, I don't,' says Charlie fiercely. 'You're our best friend, so whatever you decide, we should be there for you. Lou's being a div.' She glances at the door. 'Ah, speak of the devil. Or rather the divil. Ha ha.'

Lou makes her way over to our table, a frown fixed on her face, and pulls up a chair next to me, oozing disapproval. 'What on earth were you thinking, Percy?' she asks, shunning any greeting. 'You seemed fine when we saw you for lunch on Sunday.'

Only because you and Phil were too busy sniping at each other to notice, I think to myself.

'Lou, don't start,' Charlie says warningly.

'Well, pardon me for trying to stop Percy screwing up her life.' Lou turns to me again. 'Are you absolutely sure you've made the right decision?'

Charlie rolls her eyes. 'Of course she's bloody sure. Aren't you, Percy?'

'Yes, I suppose I am. Well, sort of.' I look at my friends uncertainly. 'Um, not really.'

'Well, you should be,' says Charlie fervently. 'Adam's a nice guy, but as you've already explained' – she glares at Lou – 'he's not right for you. And if you hadn't ended things now, you would have moved in with him and probably got married and then ended up a few years down the line having an affair, by which time there would be children involved and it would all be horribly messy. Am I right?'

Jaye nods tearfully. Worryingly, Lou looks like she might be sick.

'Are you okay?' I ask her. 'You're really pale.'

'Of course I'm okay,' she snaps, taking a large gulp of Prosecco. 'Hang on a sec, you suddenly dumping Adam isn't anything to do with that SoulDate rubbish, is it?'

Thankfully, Jaye jumps in before I have a chance to answer. 'Of course it's not,' she says indignantly. 'She wouldn't have done that to Adam.'

'Then why the rush, Percy?' Lou shakes her head despairingly. 'Why not have a trial separation? Really, I just don't understand you at all.'

'Look, I know it might seem sudden,' I say, 'but Charlie's right, I've been having doubts about our relationship for a while and then things came to a head after lunch on Sunday. I realised we were wrong for each other, so the fairest thing to do seemed to be to end it.'

'What does that even mean – "wrong for each other"?' asks Lou incredulously, pouring herself another glass of Prosecco. Wow, she's really gunning through it. 'You've thrown away a perfectly good relationship for some . . . chick-lit cliché! You need to start living in the real world, Percy. Adam is a lovely guy – and I don't think you realise how few of them there are out there. You could do a hell of a lot worse, I'm telling you.'

Charlie rounds on her. 'What, so she should have stayed with him even if she was unsure it was right because it's better than being on her own?'

Lou shrugs. 'We're not getting any younger.'

'For Christ's sake, Lou . . .' Charlie glares at her, while Jaye looks between the two of them like a panic-stricken child watching her parents fight.

'Shhhh, it's okay,' I say, desperate to keep the peace. 'Lou, I know you think I'm mad, but . . .'

But I don't get the chance to finish because just then Lou's phone beeps and she holds up a hand to me, checking

the screen. 'Shit, it's the babysitter, Alfie has got a tem-
perature.' She drains her glass and gathers up her things.
'I've got to go, sorry. But think about what I said, Percy,
I've got your best interests at heart. And I can't give you
my blessing if I think you're making the biggest mistake
of your life.'

20

Bloody hell, I'm unfit. I've climbed three flights of stairs at a moderate pace – somewhere between 'chillaxed' and 'FIRE!' – and I'm already out of breath. I'm sure all the comfort eating I've been doing isn't helping, which of course is the reason I'm taking the stairs rather than the lift to our fifth-floor office in the first place. If I do this twice a day I reckon I'll be justified in adding an extra portion to my RDCA (Recommended Daily Cake Allowance).

I stop for a few seconds to catch my breath and at that moment a door swings open a couple of stairs above where I'm bent over wheezing away like a forty-a-dayer. As I quickly straighten up so that whoever it is doesn't panic at the sight of me and call an ambulance, I come face to face with Dan, clearly back from his holiday. A bit of sun makes everyone look better and, as Dan was already a solid eight out of ten, Dan with a Tan is nudging a nine point five.

'James,' he says, with a surprised smile.

'Daniel,' I reply, mainly because I don't think I have enough breath left to say anything else.

'How are you?' he asks.

'Great.' I'm glad that I bumped into him at the start of the day when my make-up hasn't yet had a chance to wear off, although I fear I may be looking a bit ruddy post-stairs. 'Have you been away?' I ask innocently. I don't want him to think I've been stalking him.

'Spain,' he nods. 'Got back yesterday.'

'Good weather?'

'Amazing. Me and my mates were out surfing most days.' The image of Dan in a wetsuit, running out of the waves, flashes across my mind. 'Drop by my desk some-time this week,' he continues. 'I bought a giant Toblerone at the airport and there's a triangle with your name on it.'

'Will do,' I say. 'Cheers.'

I assume that we're done, but Dan seems in no hurry to move, and it suddenly occurs to me that perhaps he's going to talk to me about whatever it was that had seemed so important at the pub the other week, but instead he says: 'So I hear it's all been happening while I've been away.'

I look at him blankly. 'What has?'

'Apparently you've split up with your boyfriend. Well, that's the rumour, anyway.'

Now, *that* I wasn't expecting. It's just not a very blokeish thing to say, is it? I'd expect it from a girl, but surely a guy would only mention something like that if he had a particular . . . *interest* in the situation? Anyway, I give a sort of rueful shrug/nod, as if to convey that yes, it's true and it's a shame, but hey, no biggie, plenty more fish, etcetera, and instantly feel terrible about underplaying my feelings for Adam.

'On that subject,' I say quickly, 'I was sorry to hear about you and . . .' I suddenly realise that I don't know the beauty therapist from Ipswich's name.

Dan doesn't look like he does either.

I try again. 'I heard you'd split up with . . . ?'

'Oh, you mean Lexie?' he says after a few moments. 'Yes, we did – not that we were really together in the first place. But that was ages ago.'

'Well – sorry to hear that anyway. It's always tough.'

'Not really.' He gives that lazy half-smile. 'She was just using me for sex.'

'Oh, you poor lamb. Well, it might take a few years, but I'm sure you'll meet someone else eventually.'

Dan folds his arms, still smiling at me. 'Perhaps I already have.' And then – I *swear* I'm not imagining this – he gives me this look. You know the saying 'undressing someone with your eyes'? Well, Dan's eyes are not just undressing me, they're doing things that are probably illegal in forty-eight of the fifty American states. Honest to God, if looks could talk then this one would be done for gross indecency. I'm suddenly aware that we're very alone here and he's standing very close to me, and I feel my already red face flush several shades deeper. I need to say something to fill this silence, which seems to be stretching on for an embarrassingly long time, but in my flustered state I start to speak at the same time as swallowing and what comes out is a sort of 'Fnuuurgh' noise. Cringing, I clear my throat and try again.

'Well, I'd better get on,' I croak, starting up the stairs. 'Lots to do!'

'Of course.' Dan steps to one side to let me pass. 'Always busy on the fifth floor, right? Good to see you, James.'

'You too,' I say over my shoulder.

'Oh, Percy?'

I turn round to see Dan on the landing below, looking up at me, which for some reason makes me think of the balcony scene in *Romeo and Juliet* – although instead of 'Percy, Percy, wherefore art thou Percy?' Dan says, rather less romantically, 'Are you going to the annual piss-up weekend this year?'

'Yeah – I'm on the conference organising committee.'

'Great,' he says. 'Cos it'll be a lot more fun with you there. See you later.'

As he turns and continues his leisurely way down I dash up the last two flights, tumble through the door to the fifth floor and then lean back against it, trying to catch my breath – although this time it's more to do with embarrassment than exertion. What was all that about?

As I make my way to my desk I replay our conversation

in my head. That comment about the conference being more fun with me there could be totally innocent – we are mates, after all – but that look he gave me certainly wasn't. I know Dan's naturally flirty, but seriously, that was off the scale! And what did he mean when he said that perhaps he's already met someone else? Surely he wasn't suggesting that someone was *me*? Yet combined with that look it's a fairly reasonable conclusion . . . As this sinks in I start to feel quite perky. I've been pretty down on myself since the split – when I look in the mirror all I see are wrinkles and cellulite – but I can't be completely unfanciable if Dan's interested, can I? As I turn on my computer I glimpse my reflection in the screen and give my hair a ruffle, allowing myself a small, hopeful smile. Still got it, Perce! Unless . . . what if it was a pity flirt? Oh God, that *must* be it. In Dan's eyes I'm a pre-menopausal spinster who's just a few years away from beige slacks and bingo, so he had a harmless little flirt to brighten up my otherwise dull, sexless existence, like throwing a stray dog a bone. Here you go, buddy – but just this once, don't get used to it! My sunny mood of a few moments ago abruptly darkens. I am never going to have sex ever again. I am going to die without ever joining the Mile High Club or trying more than five of *Cosmopolitan*'s top forty (forty!!) sexual positions. Dear God, I can't go to my grave knowing the most adventurous thing I did in bed was to dress up as a lollipop lady!

Percy – breathe. You're being silly. Things aren't that bad yet, surely? I still get wolf-whistled on the odd occasion, even if it's only by builders working very, very high up. So let's be glass-half-full about this and assume that Dan *is* interested: what now?

By this time my computer is up and running and as usual the first thing I do is to check my inbox, hoping Adam might have emailed, but although it's been over a week he's still not replied to any of my messages. I wish he would get in touch, even if it was just to tell me to eff off, because I'm finding the lack of daily contact – the sweet texts, the phone calls 'just to see how you are' and chatty emails – almost the hardest part of our split. If anything happens, good or bad, it's Adam I want to tell first. Yet as I scroll through my other emails I find my mind drifting back to the image of Dan in a wetsuit and find myself wondering if he has a six-pack and whether his chest is hairy and what it would be like to unzip that wetsuit and find out. I bet Dan's tried at least half of *Cosmo*'s top forty . . . Right now it feels like cheating on Adam even to consider it, but perhaps a little fling might be a good way to move on? I am single now, and Dan would be undeniably excellent rebound material – or perhaps . . . perhaps he could be more than that? We get on brilliantly after all, and we've had this low-key flirty thing going on for years; if we actually ended up falling in love it would be super-romantic, like something out of a movie. *Sleepless in Norwich* starring Perseus James-Dawson and Daniel Dawson: 'They were workmates – who discovered they were soulmates.' I've never really thought of Dan as potential boyfriend material before, but wouldn't it be crazy if my perfect match has been under my nose this whole time?

Whoa there. Before I get carried away planning our wedding I need to look at this logically. Is Dan *really* the right man for me? I know I fancy him, but does he measure up in other ways too? I really don't want to make the same mistakes I have with men in the past. I have a quick look to check nobody's hanging around my desk, then I start typing a list of the qualities I'm looking for in a potential boyfriend: a 'soulmate shopping list', if you will.

1) funny
2) good listener
3) sense of adventure
4) open-minded
5) kind/considerate
6) takes an interest in their appearance but not gym-obsessed
7) good kisser etc. (!!!)
8) minimal facial hair
9) stylish without being a fashion victim
10) shares same interests/views

Well, despite Dan being a bit of a gym bunny and own-
ing a pair of skinny jeans I'd say he scores pretty highly,
although number 7 is obviously still an unknown quan-
tity. But then it occurs to me that there's someone who
ticks even more of the boxes on this list – and that's Flora.

Hmmm. I can't say I'm thrilled at this realisation. Life
would be far easier if my ideal man was not a woman. I
haven't got back to Flora since she left that voicemail
about meeting for lunch and I've been hoping that with
time I'd move on and forget about her, but that hasn't
happened. While my feelings for Dan are simple – (I fancy
him. End of.) – the way I feel about Flora is an infinitely
more mysterious, complex beast. It's like the difference
between a chocolate cake and a chocolate soufflé. You
know where you are with the cake, but the soufflé brings
with it a multitude of questions. For example: isn't soufflé just eggy chocolate air? Won't I miss the icing? Will it
satisfy me? I know I like cake, so shouldn't I just stick
with that?

But I can't ignore the fact that according to SoulDate
Flora and I are the most compatible people in the world –
the entire WORLD. If you're looking for a reason to see
someone again, you can't get much better than that. I'd
all but written off SoulDate, but what if their algorithms
actually work? What if we really are soulmates? I've tried
to imagine what it would be like to date Flora: to get
dressed up for her on a Friday night, to walk down the

street holding her hand, to lie in bed with her reading the Sunday papers, to introduce her as my girlfriend . . . If she were a man I wouldn't have a single doubt, but do I really think I can fall in love with a woman?

I lean back in my chair, deep in thought. I need to see Flora again: that much is clear. I have no idea what our relationship actually is – and, more importantly, what it might become – but I suppose you'll never know exactly how you feel about soufflé until you try the soufflé.

I glance around the mainly deserted office floor: now seems as good a time as any. Before I can change my mind I bring up her number and hit Dial. She answers after three rings.

'Flora MacDonald,' she says, and I realise with a start that I didn't know her surname.

'Oh Flora, hi, it's Percy.'

'Percy! Well this *is* a nice surprise,' she says, a smile in her voice. 'How are you?'

'Really great, thank you. I'm so sorry it's taken me a while to return your call; things have been a bit, you know, manic.'

'No problem at all. I've actually been in Zurich for the last week, so your timing is excellent.'

We chat for a while. I'm relieved she doesn't mention the kiss or ask me about my love life (from what I remember of the night of the party, I told her that I was in the middle of breaking up with my long-term partner – so not a total lie), but she's as funny and sweet as ever and I'm glad I called. And then, a few minutes into our conversation, it's suddenly decision time.

'So,' says Flora, 'how about we meet up for that lunch?'

I hesitate, scared where things might go, but just then a saying pops into my head: 'Feel the fear and do it anyway.' *Try the soufflé, Percy.* 'That would be lovely,' I say.

'How about this weekend? Saturday?'

'Great.' And then I remember I'm meant to be meeting Milo. 'Actually, could we make it Sunday?'

'Yes, of course. I'll have a think about where we can meet.'

I end the call, my heart pounding with a mixture of nerves and anticipation, but then almost instantly my phone starts to ring again. It's a Norwich landline number that I don't immediately recognise.

'Hello?'

'Percy love, sorry to bother you, it's Sandra here, Jaye's mum.'

'Hi, Sandra, how are you?'

'Oh, I'm fine, thank you, but I'm afraid Jaye isn't.'

'What's happened?'

'That bastard husband of hers – well, his bastard solicitor, he didn't even have the decency to speak to her himself – has sent her a letter asking for a divorce. Percy, she's devastated. I've never seen her so upset.'

'Oh God, I'm sorry.' Poor Jaye, she must be in bits.

'The letter arrived first thing this morning and she's been crying ever since. I've tried to talk to her, but everything I say just seems to make it worse. I was wondering if you might be able to pop round on your way home? I know she'd listen to you.'

'Of course I can. I'll come straight round after work.'

'Oh, thank you,' says Sandra, relief flooding her voice. 'Thank you. I know you'll be able to cheer her up. See you later, love.'

21

Jaye's parents live in a chalet-style brick house that sits on a gravel drive lined by rhododendron bushes. I've spent so much time here over the years – almost more than at my own parents' house – that everything about the place is instantly familiar: there's the old apple tree we used to swing on, that's the window we broke during a game of rounders and there's the ornamental urn I threw up in after Jaye's big brother Olly (whom I had a massive crush on) spiked our drinks.

As I walk down the drive Sandra opens the front door holding the family's dog Yoda – they have obviously been keeping an eye out for me. Sandra is strikingly similar to her daughter, with the same delicate features and Scandinavian colouring, but on a far more ample scale. Yoda is a smooth-coated chihuahua with enormous pointy ears like, well, Yoda.

'Percy love, thank you so much for coming round.' She hugs me to her, crushing a squirming Yoda, and when she pulls back I can see how worried she is. 'Jaye's in her bedroom, go on up. I'll bring you a cup of tea.'

The staircase wall is lined with framed cuttings from Jaye's showbiz days, including a photo of her and Stewie's wedding from *OK!* magazine. As one of the bridesmaids I even made it into print, although I was cut out of most of the pictures in favour of a *Hollyoaks* actress they'd had to rope in to fulfil the celebrity guest quota. I pause by the photo of Jaye and Stewie emerging from the church into a cloud of confetti: Stewie is grinning like he can't believe his luck, while in her silver slip dress and pearl crown Jaye looks like a foxy elf princess from *The Lord of the Rings*, her beautiful face radiating joy. Surely it can't be healthy for her to see this every time she goes downstairs? I make a mental note to ask Sandra to take it down.

I knock softly on her bedroom door. 'Jaye, it's Perce, can I come in?'

I can hear the sound of the TV from inside her room, but there's no reply. Yoda has trotted up the stairs and has joined me in front of the door, head cocked to one side and skinny tail wagging, waiting to be let in. 'You and me both, Yoda,' I mutter.

I knock again. 'Jaye? I'd really like to talk to you. Please, I think I might be able to help.'

Still nothing. Yoda looks up at me expectantly and after a moment I nod to him in agreement.

'Right,' I say to the door. 'I'm going to come in now, okay hon?'

I find Jaye sitting on her bed, her arms wrapped around her legs and chin resting on her knees, staring at the TV. Her blotchy face attests to a mammoth cry-athon. On the screen is Stewie in his role as Dr Charles Forsyth in *Too Much Too Young*, his chiselled features arranged into a grave expression as he talks to a young female patient (who is wearing a surprisingly skimpy outfit for someone about to undergo brain surgery). Next to Jaye on the bed sits a family-sized tub of marshmallow Flumps, a packet of Oreos and a scattering of empty Monster Munch packets.

'He wants a divorce,' she murmurs, eyes still fixed on the TV screen, her fingers obsessively twisting the large diamond on her ring finger. 'I thought he'd get sick of that walking boob job and come back to me, but he wants a divorce.'

'Oh love, I'm so sorry.' I cross over and sit next to her on the bed; after a couple of attempts Yoda manages to jump up too. 'The man is a complete and utter arsehole, he was never good enough for you. In fact you'll soon realise that you've had a lucky escape.'

But she's shaking her head. 'I still love him, Percy. Despite everything, I'd take him back in a heartbeat. I just miss him so much . . .' And she starts to cry.

'Shhh, it's okay,' I say, hugging her to me. 'I know you must be hurting now, but it'll get better, I promise.'

'No, it won't,' she says, reaching for a handful of Flumps and cramming them into her mouth. 'I'm fat and ugly and old and nobody's ever going to love me ever again.'

We cuddle up together on the bed and while Jaye sobs furiously I rock her like a baby, making soothing noises, but rather than calming her down it seems to be making her cry even harder. Hmmm, I'm not sure sympathy is the right way to go here – I think a tough love approach might be more effective. I disentangle myself from Jaye's arms, remove Yoda's muzzle from a crisp packet and then place my hands firmly on her shoulders.

'Right, look at me,' I order, waiting until she reluctantly glances up through wet lashes. 'Your marriage is over, okay? It's done. Finished. History.'

She starts to wail again. 'I thought you were supposed to be making me feel better!'

'Jaye, just listen to what I've got to say. Yes, this is shit, and yes, it's going to hurt, but look at it this way: at least now you know where you are. You've been in this awful limbo for ages, but now you can move on with your life! Let's try and see this as something positive – as an *opportunity*. Besides, would you really want that arsehole back after what he did to you?'

'Yes,' she says instantly.

'Well, bollocks to that! You're young, you're talented, you've got friends who adore you and a whole future ahead of you just waiting to be filled with adventures.

Now that you're not tied down, you can do anything you want. If you sold that rock on your finger you'd have enough money to travel around the world for a year! As for being fat and ugly – do you really have no idea how gorgeous you are? You were nominated for Most Fanciable Female at the Smash Hits Poll Winners Party in 2002, for God's sake!'

'Yeah, but Holly Valance actually won it . . .'

I ignore her. 'And Vernon Kaye described you as "Norwich's hottest export since mustard", remember? So when you are ready to start dating again, you'll be able to do far better than that . . . that' – I gesture to the screen, where Dr Forsyth is now examining an X-ray, assisted by a scantily clad nurse – 'that D-list wanker. Jesus, will you look at him! Look at those ludicrous fake white teeth! Look at his orange tan! And is he losing his hair? Seriously, do you really want to be married to a man who wears guyliner?' I'm relieved to see Jaye's mouth twitch into a smile. 'I guarantee, my darling, that in a year or so Dr Charles Forsyth will have been replaced by a younger, hotter medic, Stewie Patterson will be unemployed and suffering from some nasty sexual disease and you'll have an excellent divorce settlement and be living the high life.' I hand her a tissue. 'What goes around comes around.'

'What, like karma?' She dabs at her eyes. 'We learned about that in my Buddhist prayer circle in LA.'

'Exactly! Just like karma. Stewie Patterson is going to

be reincarnated as a cockroach, while you, my gorgeous girl, will be reincarnated as an . . . um . . .'

'An Oscar-winning actress?' suggests Jaye hopefully, rubbing Yoda's tummy.

'That's right! You can't change what's happened, but you can change *you*. So forget your tosser ex-husband – in fact, forget men altogether – and let's concentrate on making your life as fabulous as it can possibly be. You don't need to be in a relationship to be happy, do you?'

She looks unconvinced. 'I don't know, Percy . . .'

'Well, you don't,' I say smartly. 'We need to start by finding you a new focus, because sitting around here all day moping isn't going to make you feel any better. Have you considered going back to work?'

Jaye furrows her brow; clearly the last of her LA Botox has now worn off. 'I suppose it might be quite nice to start working again . . .'

'There you go!'

'But I'm so old, Percy! Seriously, once you hit thirty in showbiz you're basically over the hill.'

'Um – hello? Davina McCall? Tess Daly?'

'Well, I guess I could always get in touch with my old agent, see what she thinks . . .'

'That would be an excellent idea.' I rub her back and give her an encouraging smile. 'I promise you, Jaye, soon you'll look back on your marriage to that loser and realise that it was just a part of your journey that you had to experience so that you could grow and become stronger, wiser and, ultimately, happier.' (I'm not sure where this is coming from – possibly I've absorbed it via osmosis through years of reading women's magazines – but Jaye is looking a bit brighter, so it seems to be doing the trick.) 'And once you're happy and secure in yourself and living life to the full then the right man will come along, and you'll realise that he's just the cherry rather than the cake itself. A wonderful bonus, but not the be-all and end-all.'

It's only when I get home later that evening and I find myself moping around, missing Adam, while simultaneously getting lost in a daydream about Dan proposing to me wearing a wetsuit on a tropical beach, that it occurs to me that while I might be able to give out advice, I'm not quite so good at taking it myself.

I'm woken up at around 6 a.m. on Saturday morning by the arrival of a WhatsApp. After a few fruitless minutes spent trying to get back to sleep to continue the very pleasant dream I was having about Tom Hanks (not your usual lust object, I grant you, but I'll certainly be looking at him in a whole new light after *that* dream. Tom Hanks? Tom Hunks, more like!!!) I eventually roll over to check my phone, cursing myself for forgetting to set it to silent before bed, and am not displeased to discover that my early-bird correspondent is Milo.

Morning! I'll be in Norwich around 10 a.m. Coffee?

I ping back details of where we can meet and then get up to make myself a cup of tea. While I wait for the kettle to boil I look out of the kitchen window at the early-morning sun shining on the rooftops and for the first time since I split up with Adam I realise that I'm feeling, if not quite happy, then hopeful. Like perhaps things aren't quite as bleak as they've seemed for the past few weeks.

Milo and I have arranged to rendezvous in a square near the shopping centre, a short walk from the station, but when I arrive there's no sign of him – although as I'm not sure exactly what he looks like without the Musket-eer costume he could be dancing a jig in front of me and I might not realise it. I sit on a bench and subtly scan male passers-by of approximately the right age and build to check for recognisable signs. No, that one's too short . . . That one's got the wrong-coloured hair . . . Wait a minute, could this be him . . . ? A sandy-haired bloke is coming out of Paperchase, but he's got his arm around a girl who is definitely not the crazy Brazilian supermodel, so that counts him out.

Just then a seven-foot chicken with yellow feathers and giant red feet strolls around the corner, probably handing out flyers for some restaurant, and I watch as a group of teenagers crowd around it to take selfies. As the chicken flaps its wings and pretends to peck them with its enormous plastic beak, making the teenagers shriek with laughter, I cringe in sympathy. Poor sod, what a way to earn a living . . . Oh God, now the chicken is heading towards my bench. I hope it's not going to want to 'inter-act' with me, I'm still mildly scarred by a childhood encounter with an overenthusiastic Goofy at Euro Dis-ney . . . But then I notice that it is carrying a rucksack that I vaguely recognise and as it raises a fluffy wing in greeting a muffled yet familiar voice says: 'Percy! Sorry I'm late.'

'Milo . . . ?'

The chicken lifts up its beak and there he is. Well, I think it's him. It's quite hard to see with all the feathers.

'Hello!' he says cheerfully. 'I have to say, I do like Norwich – what I've seen of it, anyway. Everyone's very friendly. How are you?'

'Fine, thank you,' I say, still a bit taken aback by his appearance. 'Um, you?'

'Eggs-cellent! I've been waiting to crack – ha ha! – that joke.'

'Really?' I smile. 'Cos you look a bit beaky. *Beaky*. Geddit?'

'Ah, very good, Percy. One all.'

'So what's with the . . . ?' I wave a hand over his costume.

'Yes, sorry about this, I'm en route to a stag weekend in Great Yarmouth and this is so bulky it just seemed easier to wear it rather than carry it. I hope you don't mind hanging out with a chicken for a while?'

'Not at all,' I say. 'Let's get coffee.'

It's a beautiful morning, so we get takeaway cappuccinos and croissants and sit in Chapelfield Gardens, enjoying the sunshine. Well, I am, at least; Milo isn't exactly dressed for tanning. It's weird: although I hardly know the guy – I don't even know where he lives or what he does for a living – I feel relaxed in his company, perhaps because he seems so comfortable in his own skin. Or feathers.

'Before I forget, here's your money,' I say. 'Thanks again for all your help. I don't know what I'd have done if you hadn't come along that night.'

'Really, it was my pleasure,' he says. 'I bet your boyfriend was relieved when you got home, wasn't he?'

'Mm-hmm,' I say, vaguely.

'The poor guy must have been worried sick. How long have the two of you been together?'

'Three years.' But although I intend that to be the end of that particular conversation, I'm left with a feeling of vague uneasiness: there have been far too many lies in my life of late. So I say: 'Actually, we've just split up.'

'Oh Percy, I'm sorry. What happened?'

'We had an argument – well, more of a discussion, Adam wasn't one for arguing – the day after I met you, and I realised that we weren't right together so I broke up with him. Christ, that sounds lame, doesn't it? But I had been having doubts for a while, although I'd assumed that *I* was the one with the problem, rather than the relationship itself . . .' I tail off, aware I'm oversharing. 'Sorry, this is probably very dull.'

'Not at all,' says Milo, shaking his head so vigorously the foot-high red comb on his head waggles. 'Were you living together?'

'No, but I was about to sell my flat and move in with him. I think that's one of the reasons things came to a head when they did . . . I'm sure it was for the best, but sometimes I do wonder if I made the right decision.'

'After three years together I very much doubt you'd have ended things on a whim, you really don't strike me as the flighty type. And if you had been having doubts, and you couldn't see a way to make things work, then it was the right thing to do.' Milo lifts his beak to take a sip of his coffee. 'You know, I admire you, Percy. Far too many people end up in mediocre relationships because they're terrified of being alone.'

I nod and smile, trying to cover up the fact that I'm terrified of being alone too, but Milo is clearly rather more perceptive than the average bloke.

'So is there someone else?' he asks after a moment.

'Oh no,' I say. 'Well, maybe. There's this bloke at work . . .'

'Ah, I see.' He grins at me, raising his eyebrows. 'Your eyes met across a crowded photocopier, that kind of thing?'

'Something like that . . .' I hesitate, wondering whether to go any further, but there's something about Milo that invites confidences; besides, if I don't talk to someone about Flora soon I might burst. 'The thing is, there's not only a man, there's also a woman.'

'That you're attracted to?'

I give a nervous nod.

'And this is . . . new territory for you?' It's disconcerting not to be able to see Milo's face clearly, but he doesn't sound too shocked, at least.

'Very much so,' I reply. 'She's wonderful and we've got loads in common, but I've never dated a woman before. Never even considered it.'

We're both silent for a moment as we share the last piece of croissant. 'At the risk of sounding pervy,' asks Milo, 'how far have things gone between the two of you?'

'Just a quick kiss, but I've been thinking about her a lot.'

'So what's stopping you taking things further?'

I shrug, unsure of how to put the overwhelming mass of doubt and confusion into words. 'I've just always thought of myself as straight,' I say eventually.

'Well, I say go for it,' says Milo, firmly. 'Love doesn't always look like you think it's going to – unless of course you're me, in which case it always has long dark hair, a Brazilian accent and a hormone imbalance.'

I laugh. 'Going well with Luiza, is it?'

'Define "well".' He gives a weary sigh. 'We fight. We make up. We fight. We make up. And so on.'

'Doesn't that get tiring?'

'Yes, it does, very much so, but at the risk of getting Freudian I think I must get a kick from all the drama. I'm a bit of an adrenalin junkie, you see. I write about extreme sports for a living.'

Interesting. 'What sort of stuff?'

'Jumping off high things, climbing steep things, sitting in fast things – basically anything a teenage boy would consider "sick",' he says. 'When I was little I was obsessed with the idea of being able to fly and I never really grew out of it. I used to give my poor mother heart attacks by dressing up as Superman and jumping off trees and buildings. Now I give her heart attacks by jumping off mountains and out of planes.'

'Still dressed as Superman?'

'Occasionally,' he laughs. 'So what about you, Percy, any daredevil tendencies?'

I open my mouth to tell him about all the ker-azy times I've had kite-surfing and hang-gliding, but again decide to come clean. 'I've never even been skiing. There isn't much opportunity for extreme sports in Norwich. But I'd like to try one day.'

'Well, just say the word and I'd be happy to steer you in the right direction,' says Milo, and I feel pleased that he wants to keep in touch. 'Right, I better get going; I'm supposed to be meeting a cow and two pigs at the station in ten minutes. It's been great seeing you again, Percy,' he says, standing up and brushing crumbs from his feathers.

'You too, have fun in Great Yarmouth,' I say as we hug goodbye.

'Do I get a peck on the cheek as well?' asks Milo. 'A *peck*. Ha! Game, set and match to me . . .'

After Milo has flapped off I wander back to my flat, thinking how nice it is to have a male friend – because I'm sure that's what Milo is becoming – without sex buggering everything up like it usually does. I suppose, in different circumstances, that I might be attracted to him, as I enjoy his company and (from the little I've seen) he's quite pleasant-looking, but it makes things refreshingly straightforward to know that *a)* I'm categorically not his type, *b)* he has a girlfriend and *c)* he thinks I'm gay. Perhaps, if things work out with Flora, this is what all men will become to me now: just friends. It's a very strange thought.

22

My lunch date with Flora – and I'm using the word 'date' deliberately to get myself into the right frame of mind – is at a restaurant in London's Mayfair which, according to its website, specialises in 'De-formalised Fine Dining' and 'Contemporary, Ingredient-Focused Cuisine'. What it doesn't specialise in, I'm now realising, is a warm welcome. In fact, having been determinedly ignored by the woman at the front desk for a good ten minutes, I'd go as far as to say that they offer an unparalleled standard of service with a scowl. When I first arrived the receptionist gave my skater dress and L.K. Bennett espadrille wedges a disdainful once-over and said, 'Your table is just being prepared,' although the clear subtext was, 'I may be a receptionist, but I am younger, thinner and hotter than you are, so you will wait here until I decide otherwise.' We're talking five-star inhospitality here.

To pass the time – and to distract myself from my jitters at seeing Flora again – I look through the menu, a leather-bound copy of which is presented reverentially on a stand next to the front desk like it's the Bible. Each dish on the menu is listed by breaking it down into its component ingredients, as appears to be the fashion in up-their-own-arse restaurants these days. For instance, a Big Mac and Fries would be described: 'Beef. Bread. Gherkin. Chipped potatoes' while trifle would appear as: 'Cake. Jelly. Custard. Sprinkles.' You get the idea. Anyway, as I'm still being doggedly ignored by the woman at the front desk (Hair. Eyelashes. Scowl. Wonderbra), I retrieve my phone from my bag and pretend to be reading an email while cunningly checking my mascara for smudges using the camera. I've gone for the 'no-make-up' look today, which, as any woman knows, takes three times as long as the '*Corrie* barmaid' look. Blokes, of course, have no idea about the thirty-two beauty products it takes to give the impression that you've just awoken, dewy of skin and winsomely flushed of cheek, from a ten-hour sleep, although as Flora is not a bloke she'll be well aware just how much effort goes into effortless.

Hopefully, at the very least, she'll appreciate all my hard work. I guess I'm about to find out as here she is now, totally nailing the 'what – this old thing?' look in a white shirt and jeans, her gorgeous hair loose and artfully messy.

'Percy!' She holds out her arms, looking genuinely thrilled to see me. 'I'm so glad we could get together again.' She kisses me on the cheek: just the one side, like she did at the Savoy. Somehow it's far more intimate than the usual double kiss.

Flora obviously looks much cooler than I do, because Miss Congeniality at the front desk is suddenly all smiles and seats us immediately, then launches into a long-winded description of the 'menu concept'. It's pretentious bollocks, like she's explaining the workings of the Large Hadron Collider, but when I glance at Flora, assuming she'll be finding it equally funny, I'm surprised (and a bit disappointed) to see that she seems to be taking it all very seriously. But then when the receptionist finally finishes Flora smiles sweetly and says: 'So what you're basically saying is that if we're hungry we should order lots of food, and if we're less hungry then not so much food?' And I'm so relieved that she's just as immature as I am after all.

After receptionist leaves, urging us to 'enjoy our dining experience,' Flora turns to me, rolling her eyes. 'I thought she'd never finish! When she started going about the "chef's philosophy of nourishment" I could barely keep a straight face.'

'Perhaps we should have gone to Pizza Hut,' I say. 'No menu concept *and* they have an all-you-can-eat salad bar.'

We both giggle and I love the feeling of complicity, like it's us against the world – or at least against snooty receptionists everywhere. My nerves begin to fade and by the time we've got our starters the only thing I'm worrying about is how I can impress Flora and make her laugh. She's like that older girl at school who always seemed so much cooler and more together than you could ever hope to be – except that rather than blanking me in the corridor, Flora actually seems to want to spend time with me. And then just as I start to relax and let my guard down – *bam!* She drops a chat-bomb.

'So, what's happening with your partner?' asks Flora. She's concentrating on de-shelling a langoustine, but I think we're both well aware that this is an Important Conversation.

'We split up. It's been tough, but I think it was probably for the best.'

'I'm so sorry to hear that, Percy.' She looks up at me, smiling kindly. 'I don't think you ever told me her name?'

I've given a lot of thought to how to handle this and have concluded that now is not the right time to tell Flora that my ex is a him, not a her. I will definitely tell her the truth at some point – *definitely* – but today, for the purposes of our date, I want to fully commit to the idea of a same-sex relationship. Today needs to be the opening night, not the dress rehearsal.

So I say: 'Amy. Her name's Amy.'

Flora nods her head slightly, as if acknowledging Amy. 'I know it must be hard right now, but selfishly I'm quite pleased that you're now single because I—'

'Percy, it *is* you!'

With a start I turn towards this new voice and the roof promptly collapses in on my head. Not literally, of course, but I am up to metaphorical neck in rubble. Standing by our table, a vision in Country Casuals and a 'jazzy' necklace, is my Auntie Iris. She's not my real auntie, just a very old friend of my mum's – a very old friend of my mum's who knows everything about me and to whom gossip is like oxygen. Oh, this is bad. We really should have gone to Pizza Hut.

'I knew it was you!' Iris says gleefully. 'I was sitting with your Uncle Roger over there' – she gestures to the far corner of the restaurant, where I can see him waving – 'and I said, "Look, there's Percy," and he said, "Don't be silly, Iris, that's not Percy," but I said, "I know Percy when I see her" – and here you are!'

'Yes, here I am!' Here I am in serious shit. 'Um, what are you doing here?'

'We came up to John Lewis to buy your Uncle Roger some new golfing trousers and he's treating me to lunch. Not that we've been very impressed with the food here, I must say. I ordered the lamb and sweetbreads for my main – I wasn't sure what they were, but sweetbreads sound nice, don't they? Well, it turns out that they are neither bread nor are they sweet.' She drops her voice to a traumatised whisper. 'Percy, sweetbreads are an animal's *glands.*'

She mouths the word 'glands' with utter disgust, like she's saying 'anus'. Or 'Asda'.

'Really?' I ask, desperately trying to think of a way to get rid of her.

'Oh yes.' She nods emphatically. 'Imagine that, spoiling a lovely bit of lamb fillet by serving it with a *pancreas*? I sent the whole plate back, of course. Your Uncle Roger told me I should try it, but I said to him, "The day I start eating pancreas is the day *you* start ironing your own shirts!"' She gives a little tinkly laugh, and then looks over at Flora with an expectant smile.

'Oh, I'm sorry,' I say, 'this is my friend Flora. Flora MacDonald – Iris Proctor.'

Flora stands up and leans over to shake her hand. 'It's a pleasure to meet you,' she says.

'You too,' simpers Auntie Iris. 'I'm best friends with Percy's mother, Anthea. We've known each other for – ooooh – must be getting on for twenty-five years now!'

'And how is she?' asks Flora, as alarm bells ring inside my head. 'Has she made a full recovery?'

'She's absolutely fine, fighting fit!' I shrill, praying Flora doesn't mention the malaria. 'Iris, how are Amanda and the kids? I haven't seen them in ages.'

I'm well aware that the subject of Amanda, Iris and Roger's youngest daughter, is her favourite topic of conversation, and to my relief she launches into a rambling anecdote about how Amanda and her banker husband have just bought a house in the same village as Mary Berry – 'and Amanda has already bumped into her in Waitrose! Apparently she had a ready-made Battenberg in her trolley, would you believe it?' But just as I'm beginning to think I might get away with this after all – *disaster*.

'We were so sorry to hear about Adam, Percy.' Auntie Iris is shaking her head sadly, but her eyes are sparkling with the promise of gossip. 'Your mother was *devastated*. We all thought he was a keeper.'

'Well, you know – life goes on,' I say quickly, panic shooting through me. 'We mustn't keep you from your lunch, Uncle Roger will be missing you.'

But she isn't going to be fobbed off that easily. 'I don't know if I should tell you this,' she stage-whispers, 'but I saw Adam at your father's office the other day and I thought he was looking *very thin*.'

'Oh, I'm sure he's fine, really,' I say, praying for the roof to *really* fall in this time (although without causing any injuries, obviously. Well, perhaps something minor to that woman on the front desk). 'Iris, that's a fabulous necklace, where's it from?'

'Phase Eight. I do hope Adam's eating properly, it can't be easy for him, can it? It was all so sudden . . .'

And then – a glorious miracle! The gods must be smiling on me, because at that moment a waiter magically appears with our main courses; I don't think I've ever been so pleased to see a plate of pork belly with rhubarb confit in my life. Auntie Iris hovers by our table for a moment, clearly in the grip of an internal debate over whether it would be rude to linger, but thankfully etiquette triumphs over nosiness.

'Well, I'd better let you get on,' she says, reluctantly. 'Lovely to meet you, Flora. See you soon, Percy darling.'

I watch her making her way back to her table, amazed that I've managed to swerve the bullet. 'Well, I'm glad I didn't order the lamb now!' I say to Flora.

I'm not out of the woods yet, however.

'So, who's Adam?' she asks. She's looking curious rather than suspicious, although I'm sure I must be radiating guilt like a fan heater.

'Now that's an interesting story,' I say. 'Adam is . . . is . . . a dog. A husky–Alsatian cross. Beautiful animal. My parents got him from a rescue shelter when he was a puppy, but as he got older he just became too big and boisterous for Mum to cope with, so Dad persuaded her to give him away to . . . a work colleague of his. Which obviously is why Iris saw him at the office. I think Mum knows it's for the best, but she's taken it really hard. She loved that dog so much.' I sigh, playing for time. 'They become like family, don't they? And Adam's probably finding it tough too, because he was so attached to Mum, which is perhaps why he's not, um, eating.'

Flora is nodding, but she seems a little dubious. Understandably so.

'I have this theory,' I plough on, aware that I'm babbling, but desperate to keep talking so Flora can't ask anything else about Adam, 'that being an animal lover always skips a generation. I mean, I like dogs well enough, but I'm not *crazy* about them because my Mum is such a dog fanatic. It's sort of . . . put me off, I suppose. So what about you, Flora – are you a dog person? Or do you,' I finish with a flustered shrug, 'prefer cats?'

Flora is looking at me through slightly narrowed eyes. *What bollocks*, she is clearly thinking. *This woman is a liar and a nutcase and the sooner I get out of here the better.* Except – perhaps she isn't, because after a moment's thought she says: 'Neither. I'm all about the guinea pig.'

'No way!' I break into a delighted grin, giddy with relief. 'I'll have you know that I am a founder member of the Norwich Guinea Pig and Gary Barlow Club.'

'Impressive,' smiles Flora. 'At the risk of sounding foolish, what does being a member of the Norwich Guinea Pig and Gary Barlow Club involve?'

'We meet on a weekly basis to share grooming and feeding tips, and learn the dance routine to "Relight My Fire".'

'Well, I'm a member of Soho House, but that sounds much more fun,' says Flora. 'Can I join if I like guinea pigs but *not* Gary Barlow? I'm more of a Robbie fan myself.'

'I'd have to put that to a vote at the next meeting. But seeing as the only other member is my friend Jaye, and the NGPGBC hasn't met since, ooh, 1993, I'm sure it won't be a problem.'

One thing leads to another and I end up telling Flora all about Jaye, and then Charlie and Lou as well. It's the first time I've really spoken to Flora about my friends and I can't help thinking how well they would all get on.

'I'd love you to meet Jaye and Charlie one day,' I say. (Lou – not so much. I haven't heard from her since she told me leaving Adam was the biggest mistake of my life.)

'I'd like that. Here's an idea, why don't we . . .'

But she doesn't get a chance to finish, because at that moment I get a telltale waft of Rive Gauche and look round to see Auntie Iris zeroing in our table again like a scandal-seeking missile, this time with Uncle Roger and armfuls of John Lewis bags in tow. Of all the restaurants in London, why did they have to come here? WHY?

'We're off now, darling, so we just thought we'd come and say goodbye,' she says, as Uncle Roger gives me a hug. 'Flora, this is my husband Roger.'

'Enchanted,' he says, kissing her hand. 'So how do you know Percy? I don't think that's a Norwich accent I can hear!'

'No, I'm from Perthshire,' says Flora with a polite smile. 'Percy and I met through friends.'

'Well, we must let you get on with your lunch,' says Uncle Roger. 'Iris, shall we . . . ?'

'Yes, I'm just coming, but before we go, Percy, I wanted to say one more thing to you about Adam.'

Oh God, this is it. The missile is locked on its target. I hold my breath, bracing myself for impact.

'For Christ's sake, woman,' booms Uncle Roger, 'I'm sure Percy doesn't want to talk about that now.' And to my astonished relief he starts to steer Auntie Iris away. 'You must come round for lunch one weekend, my dear,' he calls over his shoulder. 'We'll let you know next time Amanda is at home, I know she'd love to see you.'

Praise be for Uncle Roger! I will never complain about having to sit through his stroke-by-stroke analysis of Ian Woosnam winning the 1991 Masters ever again! I wave goodbye as he corrals her, gently protesting, towards the door, and then they have gone. Iris has left the building.

'Sorry about that,' I say, turning back to Flora, while every particle of my body screams: *thank FUCK for that.*

'Please don't worry, it was nice to meet them.'

Her smile seems a little tense; oh God, perhaps she still has her doubts over Adam? We eat in silence for a while and I'm just wondering how I can rescue the conversation when Flora pushes her empty plate to the side and rests her forearms on the table, clearly meaning business.

'So, Percy,' she says, 'we were talking, earlier, about how you're now single.'

'We were.'

'And I was saying to you that I'm actually quite pleased

about that.' She looks down at her hands, distractedly rubbing her tattoo with her thumb. 'I really like you, Percy. I enjoy spending time with you and I hope we can see each other again. In fact, I'd like to start seeing you more regularly. If you want to as well, that is?'

I feel a fluttering of excitement mingled with nerves. Far more of the latter, to be honest. I was pretty sure this moment would come, but now it has I have no idea how to react. As much as I love being with Flora, as soon as there's a prospect of intimacy I go to pieces – and not in a sexy way. I might be single now, but the thought of going to bed with her still terrifies me. The only things I know about lesbian sex come from *Sex and the City* and *Orange is the New Black*, and neither are particularly encouraging role models. But perhaps fears are to be expected, as with any new experience? I can't deny that I've got a serious girl-crush on her – and we are, supposedly, soulmates, after all. I'm sure things will just . . . fall into place.

'Flora, I think you're an amazing woman,' I begin. 'I've been thinking about you a lot and I do want to see you again, but I'm still quite messed up after the split with Amy. Could we take things slowly?'

'I wasn't suggesting we get married, Percy,' she says with a wry smile. 'I'm going to Boston tomorrow for a couple of weeks. How about we meet up when I get back? For dinner, this time?'

'I'd like that,' I say – and I mean it. Because perhaps, in

the end, it doesn't really matter exactly *why* or *how* I'm attracted to her; surely the most important thing here is that I *am* attracted to her.

Then she leans over the table towards me and as I realise what's on her mind I tilt forward to meet her and she kisses me briefly, gently, on the lips. Her perfume works the same magic as it did before and her lips are amazingly soft and suddenly for the first time – *yes!* – I feel it: that addictive glow and tingle you get when you fancy someone like mad and you can't believe you're getting to kiss them. And as we sit back down, smiling stupidly at each other, I think that perhaps this might work after all.

23

The events organiser at Riverview Court Hotel, a cheery woman called Steph with spiky black hair and large hoop earrings, is talking me through the audio-visual equipment in the hotel's wood-panelled conference suite. I have to admit to glazing over slightly with all the talk of 'digital visualisers' and 'induction loop amplifiers', but even a techno-numpty such as myself can see that Steph's facilities really are top-notch. I'm not sure if we actually *need* any of this stuff for our annual conference – I was kind of assuming that the guest speakers would just stand up and, well, speak, which would surely only involve a microphone, perhaps two at a push – but I suppose it's good to have the option just in case we do require any induction loops, um, amplifying.

We've got less than a month to go until the conference, and this week is proving to be the busiest I've ever had in all my years working at Eagle. This is because – drum roll please – you are looking at the new chairman of the conference organising committee! What happened was this: a few weeks ago the conference organising committee (or COC as we refer to it in emails, leading to ledge bants about 'COC-ups', etc.) staged a dramatic coup to oust Mr Hedley, who had been relentlessly vetoing any proposal that might add a bit of fun to the proceedings. The last straw was when he attempted to ban alcohol from the entire event. 'We must not forget that this is a *work* conference,' he droned, 'the purpose of which is to promote and consolidate interdepartmental relationships and offer opportunities for knowledge-sharing, NOT to facilitate juvenile high jinks and debauchery, such as that shameful incident in the swimming pool at last year's event.' And yes, with hindsight, that pool incident probably *was* regrettable, but the cow was absolutely fine in the end, and besides, how can you have an annual booze-up without booze?

Anyway, needless to say I was amazed (and rather touched) when the rest of the committee members voted unanimously for me to take over the chair, and since then I have been busier than Kim Kardashian's Spanx. I have arranged the venue, booked the keynote speaker, organised dinner for Saturday night and planned hangover-friendly team-building games for the Sunday. From his new position as COC's unofficial tea-boy Adolf Hedley is still trying to thwart our plans at every turn – for instance last week he objected to the inclusion of inflatable sumo wrestling in the team games on the grounds of 'cultural insensitivity' – but he's been consistently outvoted and now sits in the meetings silently fuming, no doubt planning his occupation of the Rhineland.

I have to say, I really do feel I've found my niche with event-planning. I get into the office early, buzzing at the prospect of work, I never find myself staring at the clock or boredom-eating HobNobs – and as an added bonus it's distracted me from wondering whether Dan fancies me (or just feels sorry for me) and endlessly speculating whether I'm bisexual, straight, bi-curious or just terminally indecisive. I'm trying not to think about what will happen when the conference is over and I have to go back to ordering envelopes, booking train tickets and obsessing over my love life, because it's just too depressing.

'Well, I think that's everything,' Steph is saying, as I drag my attention back to all matters audio-visual. 'We will of course supply pens, notebooks, water and complimentary branded mints for all the delegates. You just need to let me know how many hand-held wireless voting units you'll require.'

'Of course,' I say, making a mental note to google what these are. 'Probably just a couple.'

Steph looks puzzled. 'You don't think you'll need enough to supply all the delegates?'

'It's still being decided,' I say quickly. 'I'll check with my IT team and let you know.'

'Super,' she beams. 'Would you like to look at the bar area now, Percy?'

'Lead the way,' I say happily. Now *this* is more like my area of expertise.

'I assume that you'd like to sample the wines we'll be serving with dinner?'

'I think that would be prudent,' I say, trying my best to suppress a gigantic goofy grin at the prospect of mid-morning drinking. Come on, Percy, this is important research: you are an events-planning professional, simply performing your job with the appropriate diligence and thoroughness.

Ha! Bring on the breakfast wine!

Holding a glass of Prosecco – 'Mmmm, a touch of apple sweetness and a lively finish,' I pronounce to Steph, after swishing it around my mouth like Listerine – we walk out onto the sunny terrace overlooking the lawn, which is perfectly green and invitingly rollable.

'Our gardens will of course be open to your guests and delegates for the duration of the weekend,' says Steph, as we take a seat at one of the tables on the terrace. 'It's such a beautiful morning, why don't we go through the paper-work out here?'

Seriously, I can't believe people get to do this for a living. If *only* I'd got that job at Saboteur. Organising Elton

John's birthday party isn't that different from organising an insurance conference, after all, and I bet Elton wouldn't complain about a cow in the swimming pool. I reckon his parties have cows in the pool as a matter of routine. He probably pays extra for them.

If I'm honest, the thing that first attracted me to Riverview Court as a potential venue, aside from its proximity to Norwich, was the star-studded list of previous guests featured on the hotel's website – Kate Garraway! Spandau Ballet! Alan Titchmarsh! – but these gardens are a major plus. If it's a warm evening I can see everyone coming outside after dinner, sitting on that wall and enjoying their drinks before hitting the dance floor. An image appears in my mind of Dan and me walking together in the moonlight and stopping by that fountain over there, where he finally plucks up the courage to tell me what he's wanted to for so long, and then he takes my hands, gazes into my eyes and slowly tilts his head towards mine . . .

'There are toilets just next to the bar area,' Steph is saying. 'Our toilet facilities were awarded a TripAdvisor Certificate of Excellence last year, you know.'

'Impressive,' I say. Complimentary branded mints *and* prize-winning lavs: this place just keeps getting better! Then something occurs to me. 'Do you have a pool?'

'No, I'm afraid not.'

Well, that's one less thing to worry about, at least.

*

After my early-morning vino I'm feeling quite frisky, so instead of heading straight back to the office I make a quick diversion to Topshop, as I saw a dress on their website that might be good for Maggie and Derek's wedding. What with all my extra work and emotional crises I hadn't really registered quite how soon it is now – the weekend after the conference – and I want to look my best for Maggie's big day. The wedding invitation says, 'Dress for Dancing and Darts' and this sparkly Topshop dress looks like it would be perfect – well, for dancing, anyway. I'm not exactly sure what you wear for darts. Perhaps I should get a temporary tattoo?

More of a concern, however, is the bit of the invitation that says 'Percy plus guest', which has been niggling at me since I received it. I'd like to take someone with me because it would be much more fun, plus it would stop my mother trying to sell me off to the highest bidder, but the question is who? I can't imagine taking Flora, as there would be a whole heap of lies that would need to be explained to her first, but then again the wedding is over a month away – and a lot can happen in a month. And if I turned up with Flora on my arm at least it would distract my mother from her horror at having the reception in a pub . . .

I get back to the office just before lunchtime (the dress was a bit on the short side in the end, so the search continues) to find Dan perched on the edge of my desk, apparently charming the M&S knickers off Kerry, another of the senior PAs, who has three grown-up children and breeds Yorkshire terriers. As I get nearer I notice with a jolt of surprise that there is a bunch of flowers sitting next to him on my desk. It's not a huge bouquet, but what it lacks in size it makes up for in sophistication. These are properly stylish flowers – exotic blooms with tufts of grey-green foliage, tied together with raffia. I feel a twinge of discomfort. Dan's bought me flowers? What's he planning to do – ask me out, in front of everyone? Jesus, this could be embarrassing . . . I'm just thinking about whether I should hide in the toilets until he's gone when he looks over and sees me.

'Ah, hello, James. Kerry and I were just discussing the sleeping arrangements for the annual conference.'

'Oooh, you're so naughty!' Kerry gives him a playful shove. 'Right-ho, I better get on. I can't waste my day talking to you, Dan Dawson.'

'Don't forget I've got first dibs if you need a roommate!' he calls after her, and a delighted Kerry turns and sticks out her tongue, shaking her head in mock exasperation as she returns to her desk, her day clearly made.

I wait for Dan to say something about the flowers, but he's just sitting there smiling at me like he owns my desk.

'So – what's up?' I ask.

Then he nods to the bouquet. 'You got a secret admirer, James?'

Ah, so they're not from him after all. I don't know whether to be relieved or disappointed. (Actually, I do: perversely disappointed – but I quickly squash it.)

'What are you doing up here?' I ask, ignoring the question.

'Seeing as you haven't been down to see me, I've brought up your share of the Toblerone,' he says, holding out a foil-wrapped package. 'I hope you enjoy it. I had to fight off most of the Claims department for that.'

'Thank you,' I say, pleased that he's thought of me and grateful to have something to take the edge off the post-wine munchies. 'Fancy going halves?'

Dan clearly isn't in any rush to leave, so while I sort through Susannah's post I tell him about my morning at Riverview Court – leaving out the part where I fantasised about kissing him, obviously – and give him the low-down on the conference.

'Top work, James, it sounds like it's going to be even better than last year.' Then he glances over at the flowers again. 'Well, go on, don't you want to know who they're from?'

I'd far rather wait to open the card until I'm on my own, but then something occurs to me. Perhaps the flowers *are* from Dan after all? That might be why he's so keen for me to look at the card: there's a message asking me out and he wants to wait to hear my answer. Christ, what shall I say? Bracing myself, I open the envelope and pull out the card.

'We've seen the whole city, we went to a museum, we saw priceless works of art, we ate pancreas!'

Let's do the museum and the priceless works of art another time.

Fx

I break into a delighted smile. I recognise the quote instantly, of course: it's from *Ferris Bueller's Day Off*. Brilliant, funny Flora. I don't mind *that* much that they're not from Dan, because it means we don't have to have an awkward conversation, plus how lucky am I to have an amazing person like Flora sending me flowers? I feel a wave of happiness and a sudden urge to see her, but she's in Boston until the end of next week – which inevitably makes me want to see her even more.

'So?' Dan is looking at me with interest.

'They're from a friend,' I say. He raises his eyebrows. 'A *female* friend,' I quickly clarify.

Am I imagining it, or does he look relieved?

'Morning, Percy, hello Dan.' Susannah has just appeared, back from her morning meeting, and Dan immediately gets up off my desk, like he's been caught slacking in class. 'Beautiful flowers, Percy,' she says. 'Who are they from?'

'Just a girlfriend I met for lunch the other day.'

'Well, she's got excellent taste,' she says, as I hand over her pile of post with the envelopes slit open, contents reviewed and Post-its stuck on the bits that need her attention. After years of working together we've got the system down to a fine art. 'Thanks, Percy. Could we go through the diary together in my office in twenty minutes or so?'

'Of course.'

With a smile she disappears into her office, closing the door behind her.

'Well, I better get on,' I say to Dan. 'Thanks again for the Toblerone.'

'My pleasure.' He hovers by my desk, but then after a moment he gives a sort of half-smile and says, 'Don't work too hard, James,' and heads off to the lifts, whistling to himself, leaving me wishing for the umpteenth time that he'd make his intentions a bit clearer. Life would be a hell of a lot simpler if you were legally obliged to state whether you fancy someone up front. Imagine how much more productive society would be without all those hours spent speculating whether a smile was simply good manners or rampant horniness?

Before I get back to work, I text Flora to thank her for

the flowers, and although it must still be early in the morning in Boston a reply arrives back moments later.

> You're very welcome. I'm out for breakfast trying to decide between egg-white omelette or blueberry pancakes w/ bacon. Thoughts? x

I hesitate, trying to compose a response that's cute and witty but not too try-hard, as you do when you're trying to impress a new someone. After a moment's thought I write:

> Pancakes, obviously. All major food groups covered: protein, carbs, one of your five a day – plus maple syrup is full of anti-oxidants (probably). No-brainer. Px

A few seconds later she replies:

> Pancakes it is. Thank you for the excellent advice. Wish you were here to issue it in person. x

I'm about to ping back another cute and witty response when I remember that texting America will probably be quite expensive, so reluctantly I put down my phone and turn my attention to my email inbox. I skim through the long list of messages – boring . . . important . . . ooh, 20 per cent off at Warehouse . . . boring . . . boring – until I come to an email from Theresa LeFevre. She's phoned a few times since we last spoke, but I haven't picked up. I wonder what she wants?

> Dear Perseus,
>
> I have spoken to Flora and she tells me that you had a very enjoyable lunch date and plan to meet again soon. Wonderful news – and just what I would expect from two such compatible individuals, despite your initial reservations!
>
> I'm thrilled that things are working out so well for you. Do let me know if you'd consider being interviewed about your SoulDate success story for use in our marketing material.
>
> With all best wishes,
>
> Theresa

Ha, I like her dig about my 'initial reservations'. *So* unreasonable of me to have been a little bit unsure about dating another woman, no? As for an interview – I don't think so, buddy. *Delete.*

Ah, now this is much more promising: an email from Milo, with the subject heading 'Your Feathered Friend'. With a leap of cheerfulness at seeing his name, I open the message.

> Percy, how are you?
>
> I survived Great Yarmouth, although sadly I can't say the same for the chicken. She became fatally waterlogged after a dip in the

sea and I had to abandon her on the pier. Ah well, such is the circle of life.

I enjoyed our chat the other day. Have you come to a decision regarding your tangled love life? Will it be Arthur or Martha?

Yours on tenterhooks,

Milo

Although I really should be prioritising the more pressing emails, I immediately write a reply. The wine has made me bold.

Sad news about the chicken. I'd like to say she's gone to a better place, although I'm not sure Great Yarmouth Pier fits that particular bill.

I met up with 'Martha' for lunch the other day and as it happens we had a great time – and she just sent me flowers! I think I'm going to go for it. More as it happens.

Percy

Right, I *really* must get started on the work emails now; I've got that meeting with Susannah in a few minutes. But hang on, here's an email from Dan, sent just a few moments ago. I wonder what he wants?

New haircut, James? Looking good.

See? What does that even *mean*? Well, obviously it means that he likes my haircut (and bonus points for noticing, as it was just a trim) but what's the *subtext*? The government really should consider introducing some sort of 'attraction monitoring' body, like MI5 but with emoticons, whereby the fancied gets an automatic text notifying them of their fancier. Now *that* would be a policy I could see myself getting behind. Then again, where there's uncertainty at least there's still hope: it would be pretty crushing if you knew for a fact that you were totally undesirable – or only fancied by, say, Mr Hedley.

'Are you ready, Percy?' It's Susannah, leaning out of her office door.

'Yep, just coming.'

I have a quick squirt of breath freshener to disguise any lingering wine fumes and follow her inside, shutting the door behind us.

After going through the diary I tell Susannah about my morning at Riverview Court and give her a status report on the conference weekend, noting her look of approval with pride.

'I have to say, Percy, I've been extremely impressed at your handling of all this. You're doing an amazing job.'

'Thank you. I'm really enjoying it.'

We chat for a while longer, Susannah telling me about the preparations for her latest triathlon, and then I'm just tidying my papers away when she adds, casually, 'So what did Dan want earlier?'

'Oh, he was just bringing me up some of his duty-free Toblerone. I was supposed to have been down to collect it, but what with the conference and everything . . .'

She nods. 'He's a nice guy.'

'Yeah, I guess so.'

Susannah hesitates for a moment. 'Percy, this is obviously none of my business,' she says, 'but you do know what Dan's like, don't you? That he can be a bit of a player?'

'Of course I do,' I say, more tetchily than I meant to, but then I'm taken aback – and probably rather defensive too. I know Susannah has my best interests at heart, but does she really think I'm so naïve that I'd just be swept off my feet by a cute grin and some free Toblerone? 'We're just mates, you know,' I add in a friendlier tone.

'That's what I thought,' smiles Susannah, and I feel bad for snapping at her. 'I just wanted to mention it because I've noticed that he's been hanging around quite a bit recently, and after the split with Adam . . . I know Dan can be very charming.'

'Don't you worry about me,' I say, with a confident smile. 'I've got Dan Dawson's number.'

But as I walk back to my desk I feel sure that Susannah is wrong about Dan. I know him far better than she does, after all, and although he can be very flirty I really wouldn't say he was the 'hump 'em and dump 'em' type; I can't ever remember him having a fling with anyone at work, for instance. No, if Dan really *is* interested in me then I'd wager his intentions are almost entirely honourable. The perfect blend of honourable and dishonourable, at least. Thankfully, when I get back to my computer there's a response from Milo to my email to distract me from the endless analysing.

Excellent news re Martha. Keep trusting your instincts – and keep me posted. In the meantime, when we met up the last time you expressed an interest in my job. A PR has offered me a session on an indoor ice-climbing wall and I wondered if you would like to join me? I asked Luiza but she 'doesn't do cold'. Being a Norfolk girl, however, I imagine you would be made of sturdier stuff. If you're free, that is?

My first thought on reading this (after a flicker of indignation at his use of the term 'sturdier stuff', for which I obviously read 'fat thighs') is that I am very much up for going ice-climbing. I mean, I have no idea what it involves, beyond ice and climbing, but I'd definitely love to give it a whirl. They say that everyone has a sport for which they have a natural talent – perhaps ice-climbing will be mine? I get a vision of myself nimbly sprinting up a wall of ice with Milo and the instructor watching me from below, marvelling at my goat-like agility. 'Are you quite sure she's never tried this before?' asks the instructor, who looks a lot like Bear Grylls. 'No, it's her first time,' says Milo, admiringly. 'She clearly has the thighs for it. My girlfriend, Luiza, has legs like a baby giraffe, so I brought sturdy Percy instead.'

Then it occurs to me that Milo is the *only* person I've told about Flora. If there is a possibility that our relationship could go somewhere – and, as I glance at her flowers, I realise that it's certainly looking that way – then I need to tell my friends what's going on. They know me better than anyone, after all; they've been there through all my previous hook-ups and break-ups. I need their advice; more importantly, I need their blessing. After a moment's deliberation, I send an email to the three of them asking them to dinner at my flat on Friday night. God only knows how they'll react when I tell them. Actually, I have a pretty good idea: once the shock has subsided Charlie will be enthusiastic, Jaye will be concerned-slash-confused and Lou – well, Lou will probably try to have me sectioned.

24

I am not a good cook. Adam was always the one who took care of the catering, so I'm out of practice, plus I'm a big fan of hummus so left to my own devices I've always had a last-minute meal solution that involves little more than opening a tub. I have no time for those faux-modest types who say, 'Oh, I'm a terrible cook, I can only do roast chicken.' Um, hello – Nigella? Roast chicken is *advanced*. The only time I attempted a roast it turned out medium rare (great for steak, not so much for chicken, apparently), although my gravy was perfect – if you prefer a bit of 'texture' to your gravy, that is. Hummus Surprise: now *that's* the signature dish of the genuinely terrible cook.

Now that I'm single, however, I'm going to make a real effort to improve, which is why I'm attempting a Jamie Oliver fish tagine for dinner tonight. Perhaps my friends will be so shocked by my new-found capability in the kitchen that it will lessen the impact of the evening's other major revelation. Certainly, with only a few minutes to go until they are due to arrive, my culinary efforts look set to cause quite a stir – although not for the reasons I was hoping. In my defence, as a novice cook I didn't realise that pan-frying salmon in a small flat with inadequate ventilation would cause such a strong smell. And surely Jamie should have mentioned something in the recipe about the smoke?

I have opened all the windows and am fanning the fishy fumes with a copy of *Closer* when the doorbell rings and I stick my head out of the window to see one blue head and one blonde waiting on the doorstep.

'Give me a sec, I'll be straight down!' I yell.

Jaye and Charlie look up and wave.

Lou is not coming tonight. She sent a very brief reply to my invitation, saying she wouldn't be able to make it, but didn't offer any explanation beyond saying she had plans. I can't believe this coldness towards me is just because she thinks I've made a mistake with Adam; surely there must be something else going on? I emailed Phil to ask if she was okay, but while he sent me a very sweet reply the gist of it was that I should speak to Lou directly – and Lou obviously doesn't want to speak to me. I'm trying not to feel hurt, but as she's one of my best friends it's hard not to take it personally.

'Looks like someone's been busy,' says Charlie, eyeing the chaos in the kitchen as she tries to find a space to put down the bottle of wine she has brought. For a supposedly simple recipe there were a lot of ingredients involved – although fortunately I already had quite a few of the herbs and spices required lurking in my cupboard. And those 'use-by' dates are just meant as a sort of . . . loose guideline, aren't they?

'I hope you haven't gone to too much trouble,' says Jaye, discreetly covering her nose.

'Oh, it's just a simple Moroccan fish thing,' I say. 'Salmon, fennel, preserved lemons – a casual kitchen supper, you know? Anyway, my timing was a bit off and it's ready now, so let's eat!' I usher them to the table and start sloshing wine into glasses. 'Come on, tuck in! It's not going to get any better after sitting around!'

Charlie grabs a plate and serves herself a large portion. 'Well, it smells delicious,' she says, ever the optimist. 'Like we're actually *in* Morocco.'

'By a large bonfire,' mutters Jaye, with a cough.

Actually, the tagine isn't too bad. It isn't the 'zingy taste sensation' that Jamie promised, but then five-year-old cumin seeds probably don't have much zing left to them. I feel very proud for producing something edible, like a proper grown-up adult, which, for a thirty-one-year-old, is a way I feel remarkably infrequently. I have this theory that the number of years you've been on the planet has little to do with your actual age and instead, we each have a 'default age' that we remain at for our whole lives. Mine, for instance, is twenty-four (clearly

I'm talking mentally here, not physically). Flora is also twenty-four, Adam is forty-six and Charlie, who is at this moment attempting to persuade us to do red wine 'shots', will still be seventeen even when she's drawing her pension.

With the cooking hurdle safely cleared, I am starting to relax and it's only now that I notice how incredible Jaye is looking. She's always gorgeous, of course, but tonight she is literally glowing – and it's all the more striking because the last time I saw her she was in the pits of despair over the divorce. Her face has lost that pinched, worried look that's been lurking since she got back from Los Angeles and she even seems to have put on a bit of much-needed weight. Best of all, she is looking smilier than I've seen her in ages: a genuine, full-on, sunny beam. It is the blissed-out smile of someone who has either *a)* found God or *b)* is having lots of sex with a new partner. After a little investigation, however, it turns out to be neither of these; instead it is *c)* the smile of someone who has just got a screen test for a presenting job on a TV shopping channel.

'So I phoned my old agent, like you suggested, Percy, and she was really happy that I got in touch and suggested we meet for lunch,' explains Jaye, her eyes shining. 'So I went down to see her in London yesterday and she took me to this Japanese place – oh my God, the sashimi was to die for – anyway, we discussed my options and she said that she sees me moving into presenting, rather than acting, which I *totally* get, and then she phoned me today and said she'd got me a screen test to be a presenter on the Shoptabulous TV channel!'

'That's amazing!'

'Isn't it?' Jaye looks so excited. 'Apparently Shoptabulous gets a larger audience share than *EastEnders*! And my agent says they loved my showreel – I mean, it's a bit out of date, but I'm sure that won't be a problem – so the screen test is basically just a formality.'

'That's fantastic, I'm so pleased for you,' I say. 'And, you know, if you don't get this job, there's bound to be others . . .'

But Jaye ignores my well-meaning attempt to moderate her expectations. 'Check it out, I've been practising,' she says, slipping off her engagement ring (which I'm happy to notice she's now wearing on her right hand) and holding it up to an invisible camera. 'And welcome back to Shoptabulous! We're expecting an instant sell-out for our next item, this stunning three-carat diamonique platinum-style ring. Created by master craftsmen, this is perfect for both day and evening wear and would be the ideal gift for your lucky fiancée if you're planning on dumping her for a *Playboy* reject with a plastic vadge.'

We all laugh; even Jaye, who usually can't even refer to Stewie and Cliché without convulsing into tearful fury.

'You're a natural,' I tell her. 'The job is in the bag.'

'I'll drink to that,' says Charlie, raising her glass, and I'm flooded with gratitude for my lovely friends – which then brings me to the absent ones, specifically Lou. She's barely been mentioned tonight and I wonder if Charlie or Jaye know more than they're letting on.

'It's a shame Lou couldn't make it this evening,' I say, testing the waters.

'Yeah, what the fuck is up with her?' says Charlie. 'She's not returning my calls.'

'Mine neither,' says Jaye.

So it's not just me, then. But the realisation that this is an equal-opportunity blanking doesn't make me feel any better, as it means there must be a serious problem. If that's the case, though, why isn't she talking to any of us about it?

While Jaye entertains Charlie with more of her shopping channel chat, I get out the pudding. I have something of a signature dessert, as it happens, known as Ice Cream Surprise, which is basically a tub of vanilla ice cream with a couple of bananas and crumbled-up Flakes mashed into it (the 'Surprise' part) and then refrozen. Give it a whirl; it's really tasty. Anyway, after we've finished dinner and put the world to rights I realise, with a degree of alarm, that the time has now come to share my news. I'm sure that Jaye and Charlie will be sympathetic, but still – it *is* quite a bombshell.

So when there's a lull in the conversation I say, 'Right, ladies, I have something to tell you. It might come as a bit of a surprise, so try not to be too shocked.'

'You're a lesbian!' quips Charlie. But then she sees my reaction, which I imagine is a heady brew of shock, bewilderment and discomfort, and her grin segues into narrow-eyed confusion.

'Percy?' she says, uncertainly. 'You're a . . . lesbian?'

I consider backing out, laughing it off as a joke; it would certainly be far easier. But no, I need to do this, so I take a deep breath to help force the words out. 'I've met someone,' I say. 'A woman.'

Charlie's mouth drops open slightly, while Jaye's eyes grow so wide that I can see white all around the irises. Nobody says a word for five minutes. (Okay, it's probably nearer five seconds, but it certainly *feels* far longer.)

Charlie breaks the silence. 'What do you mean, "met"?'

'Just that. We've been out a couple of times. She's gay and I . . . have feelings for her. She's – ' I shrug, struggling to find the right word – 'amazing. I can't explain it, but I really like her.'

Charlie is still frowning, clearly trying to process this information, but then I glance at Jaye, concerned she may have stopped breathing, and to my astonishment she's nodding in apparent understanding.

'Well, I for one can totally relate to this,' she says.

Charlie gawps at her. 'You can?'

'Oh yeah, *totally*. There was this woman I became friendly with in LA. We met at my SoulCycle class. Oh my gosh, she was beautiful, and she had such a special aura, you know? Anyway, one day we went for lunch at this little vegan place on Venice and we'd just finished our appetisers when she gave me this look and I just *knew*. We didn't need to speak – it was like an understanding just flowed between us. We were somewhere beyond words, like we were communicating on a higher plane. Anyway, if I hadn't been married I'd have seriously considered taking things further.'

Charlie and I are both staring at her.

'What?' asks Jaye. 'Why is that so surprising?'

'You've just always struck me as . . . solidly heterosexual,' says Charlie.

'I'm not saying I'm not attracted to men,' she explains. 'But it was like I was drawn to her spirit, and the fact she was female didn't matter.'

I nod enthusiastically. 'That's exactly the way I feel about Flora!'

'Well, this *is* turning out to be an enlightening evening,' says Charlie, topping up our glasses. 'So, Percy, tell us about this amazing Flora.'

And so I start from the very beginning, with SoulDate and our first meeting, and then move on to everything that has happened since, including all the embarrassing bits, and for the first time I can see why people go to confession (the religious element aside) as it is such huge relief to get everything off my chest.

'You don't think this is just a reaction to things not working out with Adam?' asks Charlie. 'You do hear about women getting disillusioned with men.'

'No, definitely not. It's not like I went out consciously looking to meet a woman. In fact if the perfect man came along it would be a lot more straightforward.'

Jaye is looking thoughtful. 'You know, if you and Flora are *genuinely* soulmates and have that deep compatibility like EROS say, then perhaps gender just ceases to be an issue.'

Charlie pulls a sceptical face.

'Maybe,' I say. 'I don't know. Oh, it's just so confusing. I'm attracted to her, but I don't want to rip her clothes off. The way I feel about Flora is totally different from how I feel about that bloke I fancy at work, for instance.'

'The Ryan Gosling one?'

'Yup. Dan.'

'Didn't I meet him that one time when we were outside your office?' asks Jaye. 'He was hot.'

'That's him,' I say. 'Now Dan I could – and frequently do – consider having sex with.'

'Well, you're straight then,' says Charlie. 'If the lust is missing, you're not gay or bisexual. Case closed.'

'I know, but whatever it is between Flora and me – it's not just friendship, I'm sure.'

'What is it, then?'

I think for a moment, trying to put the emotional turmoil into words. 'It's a sort of . . . possessiveness,' I say eventually. 'I want Flora to like me more than she does anyone else. I want *exclusivity*. And she completely intrigues me. Every time I see her I unwrap another layer of who she is and discover something incredible . . .'

'Like Pass the Parcel?' asks Charlie, straight-faced.

I bash her on the arm. 'Seriously, we have so much in common,' I continue. 'And I'm desperate to get to know her better. But I don't think I want to sleep with her. Does that make any sense at all?'

'Babe, emotions don't make sense,' says Jaye earnestly. 'They are messy and irrational and you just have to go with them.'

Charlie takes another large swig of wine. 'I hate to be the fun police here, but have you considered that you might only feel this way about Flora because you *think* she's your soulmate?' She makes finger quotes around the word 'soulmate'. 'I mean, it's a pretty intoxicating idea, isn't it, that this is the most compatible person for you in the whole entire world. That's got to make you more intrigued than you would be if she was just another . . . random someone.'

Hmmm. I hadn't looked at it like that before. 'I suppose there might be an element of that,' I say, uncertainly.

'I just know if it was me in your position I'd be looking

out for little things to prove how compatible we were,' she goes on. 'You know, like: "Whoa, so you love chocolate too? We have SO much in common!" Perhaps it could be that you're finding the *idea* of being soulmates more attractive than Flora herself?'

Jaye pouts at her. 'That's a little cynical.'

'Maybe,' shrugs Charlie. 'I'm just trying to help Percy work out her feelings.'

Lost in thought, I swirl my finger around the empty ice cream bowl then lick it, mulling over what Charlie has said. Have I been so swept away by the romance of meeting my (alleged) soulmate that I've effectively talked myself into liking Flora? In fact, could the same apply to Flora's feelings for me? She is a pretty incredible woman, after all: in terms of what each of us brings to the table, I'm definitely punching above my weight. If we'd just met in a bar, without any of the expectations fed to us by EROS, would we still feel as attracted to each other? It's an interesting-slash-disturbing thought.

'You may well have a point, Chaz,' I eventually concede. 'But I'm pretty sure there's more to it than that. I genuinely love spending time with her.'

'Well, okay then,' says Charlie. 'See Flora again and hopefully things will become clear.'

'Absolutely,' agrees Jaye. 'But you have to be honest with her, Percy. Right away. About *everything*.'

'I know, I know.'

'You can't pretend to be something you're not. It's not fair on Flora.'

'Why don't you send her an email explaining everything?' says Charlie.

Jaye rounds on her. 'What? No way! That's a terrible idea. You should call her.'

'I can't face telling her over the phone,' I say.

'Well, tell her in person then,' says Jaye, firmly. 'But Percy, you've got to do it soon.'

25

Milo and I had arranged to meet in a cafe in Covent Garden before our ice-climbing session, but my train from Norwich is running late – *quelle surprise!* – so we agree to rendezvous at the ice wall itself, which, to my surprise, is located inside an outdoor clothing store, within a sealed chamber just along from the thermal long johns and camping stoves. I can't see my climbing buddy when I arrive, so I'm browsing a display of heavily discounted snowboards and wondering whether if I bought one it would actually encourage me to learn how to snowboard (and, if it didn't, whether the board might work as an unusual coffee table) when I hear the rustle of Gore-Tex and look round to see Milo, already togged up in full ice-climbing gear, his sandy hair sticking up like he's just come in from a gale-force blizzard.

'No, I don't see you as a boarder, Percy,' he says, shaking his head.

'You've got far more style than that. You're definitely a skier.'

For a moment I am lost for words. I open my mouth to speak and then shut it again, cod-like. This is the first time I've seen Milo's face unobscured by beard or beak and, I have to say, I can totally see how he hooked a stunner like Luiza. 'Rugged' is the word that immediately comes to mind, quickly followed by 'square-jawed' and then '*phwoar*'.

'Perhaps,' I reply, still shaken. 'But it would be far trickier to make a coffee table out of skis, don't you think?'

He looks at me quizzically and I'm about to explain, but I can feel a blush creeping over my face, so instead I just stare at my feet and stammer, 'Doesn't matter.'

Oh, this is not good. I hate to say it, but the discovery that Milo is bona fide fit has unsettled me. Since we last met up we've been emailing quite regularly and I've been enjoying getting to know him via his chatty, funny messages. I have learnt, for instance, that he currently lives in south London, where he is renting a room from the editor of one of the extreme sports magazine he writes for (who is also a mate), but is hoping to buy his own place next year, ideally somewhere by the sea. His favourite food is anchovies. He is terrified of wasps, but seems quite blasé about scuba-diving with sharks. In short, I feel like we're becoming good mates – but that was jokey, chicken-wearing Milo, not this new, unnervingly handsome Milo.

Shit, this is going to ruin everything, isn't it? I'm going to become all silly and girly and he'll think I fancy him and that will be it, friendship over. Nice work, Percy. Really excellent.

But then Milo reaches for a hideous rainbow-coloured snowboarding hat, plonks it on his head and turns to me, wobbling his head to make the bells jingle, and – hallelujah! – I get a timely reminder that he's still the same Milo, just with an extra helping of manly hotness. Phew. Crisis averted.

'Here, there's one for you too,' he says, chucking me a matching hat. 'Do you think they'll let us wear them to go ice-climbing?'

Unfortunately Kris, who will be our instructor for the afternoon, explains that it very much *won't* be possible for us to wear our rad new headgear to go ice-climbing – no, not even over the top of our helmets. Our health and safety are his paramount concerns, he says, with the weary air of a man who has, over the years, given too many safety briefings to too many jester-hatted twats.

Disappointingly, Kris, while perfectly nice, looks nothing at all like Bear Grylls. Paddington Bear, perhaps, but not a six-packed action man who drinks his own urine and wrestles badgers. Still, I imagine that a bit of extra padding around the middle is a positive advantage in icy conditions, and he's certainly very knowledgeable about ropes and knots, which is obviously far more useful when you're attempting to scale a vertical wall of ice rather than the ability to fashion a bivouac from a deer carcass. Kris helps us into our boots and crampons and then secures our harnesses, which fit snugly around the groin area to create an attractive camel-toe effect at the front and a bum hammock (bummock?) at the back, and by the time I'm fully kitted up, complete with a bright-orange helmet, the impression isn't so much sexy Alpine Bond Girl as dumpy sixth-former on an Outward Bound for the Duke of Edinburgh Award (Bronze). But hey, I'm not here to impress anyone.

The ice wall itself is, to be honest, a bit of an anticlimax. I've had a vision in my mind of the Great Wall in *Game of Thrones* – a soaring expanse of sheer ice, stretching into the clouds, besieged by giants and fur-clad tribes – but this is more like the inside of a freezer that's got all frosted up. Kris is taking us through the comprehensive safety briefing, but all I can hear is my mother's voice: 'You'll never be able to shut the door properly with all those lumps of ice. You need to take everything out and give it a thorough defrosting or that casserole will spoil.'

Still, it *is* eight metres of vertical ice, with no apparent hand- or footholds, and the idea that I might manage to climb this – me, the girl whose upper-body strength has been finely honed by years of sitting at a desk not doing press-ups – seems unlikely.

It gets worse. Kris now demonstrates how we will use ice axes (more like long knives than actual axes) to scale the wall like Spiderman. I thought there would be, well, railings or something to hold on to, but no, we will be suspended by nothing but a couple of glorified tooth-picks, which at any moment might give way, sending us plunging into the crevasse below. And yes, we will be safely roped up, and no, there isn't a crevasse, but still: definitely daunting. I glance nervously at Milo and he gives me a cheery thumbs-up, which I weakly return.

'You okay?' he asks, as Kris gives our ropes a final check.

'Absolutely,' I say emphatically, although I can tell Milo's not convinced. 'Well, a bit nervous,' I admit.

He puts a reassuring hand on my shoulder. 'There's this quote: "Always do what you're afraid to do." It's some-thing of a personal motto of mine, actually.'

'Who said that?'

'Ralph Waldo Emerson. It always gets me through the moment before I throw myself off a mountain.'

I nod, thinking it over. 'Always do what you're afraid to do . . . Well, I better get up this wall, then. See you at the top.'

Milo grins and gives me a squeeze. 'Atta girl, Percy.'

Back to Kris and his demonstration. 'When planting your axe use a firm, direct movement from the elbow,' he explains, driving his axe effortlessly into the ice. 'If the motion comes from the shoulder you could unbalance yourself. All clear?' We nod obediently. 'Right, you first, Percy. Why don't you show your boyfriend how it's done?'

I give a hysterical shriek of laughter. 'OH MY GOD, he is *not* my boyfriend!' I screech.

Kris flinches like I've just taken a swing at him with my toothpick, while Milo looks almost as startled. I suppose I did sound a bit unhinged, but after my gooey-eyed moment earlier I just wanted to make it crystal clear to Milo that I definitely don't fancy him. No way, absolutely not.

'We're just mates,' I add in a more reasonable tone. 'Milo's girlfriend is a Brazilian supermodel and doesn't like the cold, which is why I came with him today.'

'Luiza's not a model, Percy,' laughs Milo, with a puzzled expression.

'Ah. Right. Well, she should be.' I turn to Kris again. 'She's beautiful, you know. Absolutely stunning. Not that I fancy her though,' I say, swivelling my head back to Milo. 'I'm not trying to steal your bird. Ha ha! She's not my type. And she's a bit, well, mental, isn't she, Milo?'

Jesus, will you just shut up, Percy . . .

'Well, let's get this show on the road!' I say briskly. 'I just sort of flick my wrist, then, do I, Kris?'

'That's right. A nice, smooth motion.' He gives another demonstration.

'Okay. Well, here I go . . .'

I shove one of my axes at the wall, causing a shower of ice splinters to rain down on my face, but to my surprise the axe appears to be stuck firm. Well, that was easier than I thought it would be. I try again with the next one, give it a wiggle, and that seems secure too.

'Excellent work,' says Kris, once he's double-checked. 'Now, give a good firm kick to drive your toe into the ice. That's it . . . Now, move the other foot up. Push your hips right into the ice, Percy . . . Great. You're doing really well . . .'

By now I am a few feet off the ground, suspended by my axes with only some knife-tipped boots for support, and yet my nerves have vanished in a puff of euphoria. I can do this! I continue upwards and to my surprise it turns out that I'm actually rather good at ice-climbing; I was convinced I'd be crap, but I'm soon halfway up the wall and have left Milo in the dust. Perhaps I have a natural affinity with winter sports? In that case I should *definitely* get a snowboard. I'm mentally amending my CV to include ice-climbing and, potentially, snowboarding in the Hobbies section (I could stick ice-skating in there too – Charlie had her twelfth birthday party at a rink in Hunstanton and I remember being quite good) when I hear Milo's voice from below.

'How's it going up there?'

'Brilliant!' I shout over my shoulder. 'This is amazing!'

'Sure you don't need my help?' he says, a teasing note to his voice. 'I could tell you where you're going wrong, if you like?'

I hear a sudden scrabbling, the clang of an axe hitting the floor and a muttered 'bugger'.

'Everything all right back there?' I ask.

'Yup, all fine!' calls Milo, as I glance down to see Kris coming to his aid. 'Just . . . trying out an advanced climbing move I learnt in the Himalayas. *Veeery* tricky.'

I smile to myself and, as I wrench my axe free ready to plant it higher, I think again how very lucky I am to have found a friend like Milo, especially after meeting in such shitty circumstances. Isn't fate bonkers? 'Of all the muggings, in all the towns, in all the world, he walks into mine . . .' I assumed that by the grand old age of thirty-one I'd have made all the really close friends I was going to have, but I have a feeling that's just what Milo will become. Not only do we share the same daft sense of humour, he's got this fizzing energy and adventurous spirit that I find really appealing. Actually, in that respect he reminds me a lot of Flora; I reckon the two of them would get on brilliantly. Perhaps, if everything goes well with our dinner date next weekend, I could have a party at my flat to introduce Flora to my friends, both old and new . . .

At the end of our session Kris helps us take off our harnesses. 'You're a natural, Percy,' he says, as he unbuckles me.

I grin, still on a high. 'Thank you! It's been brilliant.'

'We have an ice-climbing club if you're interested?

There are social evenings, group holidays – the details are all on our website.'

'Okay, I'll check it out.'

'Make sure you do,' he says, hovering for a moment. 'Well, I'll leave you to get changed. Great to meet you both.'

Once Kris has gone, Milo turns to me with a smile. 'Looks like someone has got the hots for Percy,' he teases. 'I'm surprised the ice wasn't melting.'

'What are you talking about?'

'Our friend Kris,' says Milo, with a suggestive waggle of his eyebrows. (He has very nice brows, now I come to look at them more closely: perfectly even, yet manly . . . Percy – you're staring. Stop it.)

'As if!' I scoff. 'You're just bitter because he didn't ask *you* to join his gang. Anyway, he's really not my type.'

'Yes, on that subject, what's going on with "Martha"?'

For a moment I think about telling Milo Flora's real name, but I quite like the chumminess of our secret code, so I don't bother. 'Well, it's still early days but we're meeting for dinner next weekend,' I say – then decide it might be wise to lay it on a bit thicker, just in case Milo has any lingering doubts about my intentions towards him. 'But it feels right, you know? Like we're meant to be together. In fact, I think I might be finished with men for good!'

His smile flickers uncertainly; maybe that *was* a bit extreme.

'Just in terms of sex, I mean,' I add. 'I'll still be keeping a select few on for friendship purposes . . . So on that note, what are you up to now? Fancy getting a drink?'

'Ah, no, that would've been great, but I've got plans.'

'Of course.' There's a slightly awkward silence. 'Well, thank you again for letting me tag along today,' I say brightly.

'No problem. I'm glad you enjoyed it.'

Am I imagining it or has Milo's manner changed? He suddenly seems tense. Oh, shit, don't say he somehow picked up on my moment of lust earlier and assumed I was asking him for a *date* drink . . . ? No, I'm being paranoid – I couldn't have been more enthusiastic about how brilliantly things are going with Flora. It's probably just because his pride's a bit dented at being outmanoeuvred by a girl on the ice wall.

'Let me know if you need a wing-man for any other extreme sports,' I say, as we stand outside the shop. 'I imagine I'll be better than you at most of them.'

Thankfully, he breaks into a smile. 'Is that a challenge?' he asks. 'Well then, I'll be in touch.'

He gives me a mock salute – no kiss this time – and heads off into the crowds of shoppers. As I watch him go, I find myself hoping that he'll turn round and look at me. *Just look back*, I instruct him mentally, via Jedi-style mind vibes. *Turn around and look at me.* And I am utterly convinced that he will do so, right up to the moment that he turns a corner and his sandy head disappears from view without a single glance in my direction.

26

The next week flies by so quickly it's as if it never happened. All I do is I work, sleep and eat, and quite often work gets in the way of the other two. I miss so many meals that I begin to feel quite virtuous and smug, like I'm on some kind of trendy fasting regime. 'Oh yes, I've been doing the 5:2 diet,' I imagine telling impressed colleagues. 'On my fast days all I eat is two KitKats and a Müller Corner.'

For the third week in a row I have to cancel my regular Friday lunch with Mel, and I get an arsey email from her, all in caps, asking why I'm being SUCH A FUCKING TOSSER and threatening to UNFRIEND ME ON FACEBOOK AND IN REAL LIFE. Feeling guilty, I meet up with her for a coffee and go some way towards redeeming myself by helping with her entry to a Michael Bublé superfan competition, the prize of which is to spend a day with the man himself. To say that Mel wants to win is putting it mildly; if she applied just a fraction of her determination to a different challenge – swimming the Channel, for instance – she would beat all known records. She seems convinced that if she can just hang out with Michael for a few hours he will realise that they are indeed soulmates and drop to his knee to ask for her hand in marriage.

'You have to write a poem about your feelings for Michael,' she explains of the competition, 'but I can't think of any good rhymes for "Bublé".'

I think for a moment. 'How about – "I love you Michael Bublé, you make my heart rise like a soufflé."'

Mel beams delightedly. 'Fuck yeah, that's awesome! Great job, Perce. If I win you can be our maid of honour.' I give her a look, which she completely misinterprets. 'Well, you're too old to be a bridesmaid, sorry, mate.'

As Saturday night approaches I get messages from Charlie and Jaye, wishing me luck for my date with Flora and, in the case of Charlie, threatening to gatecrash our dinner so she can check out my 'new girlfriend'. Yes, Flora and I are going to be meeting in Norwich. It might seem insane to have our date where the chances of bumping into someone I know are so high, but Flora sounded desperate to see my hometown and I couldn't come up with a convincing reason why she shouldn't, so Norwich it is. At first I assumed that Flora was intending to stay at my flat, which sent me into such a flurry of anxiety that I googled 'What do lesbians do in bed' so that I wouldn't come across as a complete novice, but my search yielded little in the way of practical advice; in fact, judging by the results I got the distinct impression that most people who search for this on Google aren't necessarily doing so for self-improvement purposes. In a follow-up email, however, Flora sent the details of the hotel she's booked into for Saturday night, so the pressure is off. We've been talking or emailing every day while she's been in Boston and I've been looking forward to hearing from her with the same feverish anticipation as I would a potential new boyfriend, so all the signs are good for Saturday.

On the morning of our date I whizz round my flat making sure there is no visible evidence of my relationship with Adam, just in case Flora does end up coming back to mine for a nightcap, and it is only now it really hits me that tonight's the night I'm going to have to tell her the truth about Adam – about everything, in fact. I freeze, mid tidy-up, paralysed by nerves. Christ, that is going to be a *very* difficult conversation. What if she chucks a drink over me and then storms out? No, she's not that kind of woman. Flora will understand, I'm sure of it, and it will be a huge relief to get everything off my chest. We can start afresh, with all our cards on the table, and perhaps, once I've come clean, everything will fall into place and we'll reach a new level of trust and understanding. At least, that's what I'm hoping.

I spend the best part of an hour trying to decide what to wear for dinner. By this stage in previous relationships I'd be erring on the side of slutty, as I'd be confident sex would be on the agenda, but in this instance that feels wrong. The way I feel about Flora is a far purer, more elevated thing than lust. Put it this way: you don't need to get your tits out for your soulmate. So I forgo the low-cut tops and short skirts and instead decide on a patterned wrap dress and mid-height heels, the sort of thing you might wear to the christening of a friend's child where you're the godparent (which is in fact exactly where I last wore this outfit). Smart, but not vicar-scaringly sexy. I also wear my best matching lingerie, however, because it's sensible to be prepared for every eventuality – and in my experience people are more grateful for mediocre presents if they're nicely wrapped.

As it's another fine evening I decide to walk to the restaurant that I've booked for our date tonight – a bijou fine-dining place that often tops the 'Best of Norwich' lists – which gives me an opportunity to rehearse how I'm going to explain my lies to Flora. I consider the merits of a humorous approach – 'You'll never guess what: I'm straight! No, really!' – compared to a more remorseful one: 'Flora, I'm so sorry, I've been an idiot, I hope you can forgive me . . .' But either way I can't imagine saying the words out loud to her, and as I get nearer to the restaurant I start to wonder if perhaps tonight isn't the right time to come clean after all. I know Jaye and Charlie thought I should do it sooner rather than later, but it's still very early days in our relationship, isn't it? Flora doesn't need to know *every last thing* about me at this stage; it's probably more alluring to keep a bit of mystery for now. Besides, it's not like I've lied about anything really awful, like saying I'm single when I'm actually in a relationship: I just haven't told her every little detail about my past. Yes, on second thoughts I really do think it would be a mistake to be quite so *forthright* when we're still in the honeymoon of the honeymoon stage. I'll tell her soon, definitely, just not tonight. Decision made, I instantly feel lighter and walk on with as much of a spring in my step as my mid-height heels will allow.

By coincidence, Flora is getting out of a taxi just as I walk down the road towards the restaurant and when I call out to her she looks up and breaks into her wonderful smile.

'I made it!' she beams. 'Ah, Percy, it's so good to see you again.'

'You too,' I say, as we hug. But although it *is* good to see her, that's not what I'm thinking. What I'm thinking is: *Man, this feels weird.* Up until this point Flora has existed in a completely separate place from my everyday life, but now here she is standing on a street I've walked down countless times over the years, her coral-coloured dress clashing fabulously with her russet hair, and I'm struggling to get her to fit into this world – into *my* world. It's like seeing a unicorn down your local Sainsbury's. And although when we were in London anything seemed possible, here on Upper St Giles Street, just along from my opticians and across the road from the dry-cleaners, the idea that we might be lovers seems as likely a proposition as me winning an Olympic gold in ice-climbing. It's a fantastic idea in principle, but come on – get real. I know it's just nerves and once I have a drink I'll relax and it will be fine, but still: definitely weird.

'Well, shall we go in?' I ask brightly, vowing to pull myself together. 'I hope you're hungry. The last time I came here was for my dad's birthday and the food was amazing.'

Flora's eyes sparkle; I love that's she's as greedy as I am. 'I'm starving! I've been saving myself for this all day.'

'They do an eight-course tasting menu if you think you're up to it?'

'Is that a challenge?' She gives me a wicked grin. 'This waistband is elasticated, lady. I'm game if you are.'

'Let's do it,' I say, returning her smile.

As the waiter shows us to our table I find myself scanning the other diners to check if I know any of them and am relieved when none of the faces look familiar. It's not that I'm embarrassed at being seen with Flora – far from it – but I really don't want a repeat of the Auntie Iris fiasco. I don't think my nerves could stand it.

Once we have ordered food and our drinks have arrived Flora rummages in the bag by her feet and pulls out a parcel, which she hands across the table to me.

'I've brought you a present from Boston.'

'Thank you so much, you really shouldn't have,' I say, embarrassed. First the flowers and now this – should I have brought something for her? 'Dinner is definitely on me.'

Flora waves her hand dismissively. 'Don't get too excited, it's just a little something. Go on, open it . . .'

Inside the package is a Boston Red Sox baseball cap. 'I love it!' I say, putting it on. 'That's so kind of you, thank you.'

Flora cocks her head to one side, checking me out, and then flashes a flirty grin. 'Very sexy,' she says, her eyes locked on mine.

My own smile fades a little. If a bloke had said this to me I'd be fizzing with excitement (He fancies me! He thinks I'm a sexpot! *Raaah!*) but instead I'm feeling a bit rattled. The thing is, I don't think I *want* Flora to find me sexy. We have a deep, almost spiritual connection, and that sort of talk – well, quite frankly, it cheapens it. I actually begin to feel quite indignant.

'Well, thank you again,' I say primly, taking off the cap and smoothing my hair. 'I'm sure I'll get a lot of use out of it.'

Thankfully the first course then arrives – a single scallop nestling amidst some leafy stuff – and any awkwardness is brushed aside as we try to work out what the sweetish orange goo is on top of the scallop. Butternut squash? Carrot? Angel Delight . . . ?

One thing's for certain: I can talk to Flora like nobody else. Our conversation flows back and forth with a delightful ease. We're like the Murray and Djokovic of chat. Flora gives me the low-down on the project she's been working on in Boston, which will see her relocating to New York for a few months later this year ('Perhaps you could come out to visit?' she asks, to which I only just stop myself screeching 'YESSSS!' and punching the air), while I tell her about my work on the conference, pleased that for once I actually have something interesting to talk about. The food is delicious, but I'm so engrossed in our conversation that after the scallop with Angel Delight I barely notice what we're eating. At times like this when we're chatting away – making each other laugh, finishing each other's sentences, just totally *getting* each other – I'm convinced that EROS Tech has got it right and Flora and I *are* the most compatible people in the world. Funny thing is, though, I keep forgetting that we're meant to be on a date: it feels much more like I'm hanging out with an old friend. Any moments of intimacy during our meal, such as when Flora touches my hand or offers to feed me a bite of her food, come as a shock every time, and I have to keep reminding myself that we are potential lovers, not just BFFs. And much as I am having a brilliant evening, there's this vague sense of unease nagging at the back of my mind and getting more insistent with each course, which is odd because now the pressure is off in terms of coming clean I haven't really got anything to worry about. It isn't until pudding arrives that I work out what's wrong. It's the fact that tonight, for the first time since Flora and I met, we will be sleeping in the same town, which means that there is a strong possibility that our date will continue *after* dinner, which means that if we wanted to take things up a gear, we could do. Because that's what people do after they've had a few brilliant dates, isn't it? They do sex – and if they don't, well, they do everything but. The idea of getting intimate with Flora has been scaring me since we met, but it looks like I won't be able put it off any longer. In short: shit just got real. But, you know, maybe that's a good thing. What was Milo's motto? 'Always do what you're afraid to do.' And this is probably going to be *way* easier than ice-climbing – and certainly at least as enjoyable.

But by the time we've eaten ourselves silly and I've paid the bill (after much quibbling from Flora) there's still been no mention of post-dinner activities, and as we leave the restaurant together I'm wondering whether maybe I've been presumptuous and Flora is actually just intending to head back to her hotel, when she turns to me and says: 'Shall we go for a walk? It's such a lovely night. You can give me a tour of the city.'

Yes, a walk is good. Walks require participants to be fully clothed at all times. Most of them do, anyway. Certainly ones in Norwich.

'Excellent idea,' I say. 'I'll take you to see the Cathedral, it looks quite impressive all lit up at night.' I indicate the way with a flourish. 'Walk this way, madam . . .'

The restaurant is just a few minutes from the centre of town, so I lead Flora along the main road, past City Hall, pointing out noteworthy landmarks as we go – although as my knowledge of local history is a bit hazy my noteworthy landmarks tend to be things like: 'That cafe does a lovely Bakewell tart,' and: 'This is where I fell off my bike and broke my arm when I was nine.' We walk through streets of deserted shops, past Jarrold's – 'the Harrods of Norwich,' I tell Flora – and then past the bars and clubs of Tombland, which reminds me of our Old-School Girls' Night Out at Club Xtreem when Jaye got busted for being off her chops on MSG, which of course was also the night I asked my friends' advice about SoulDate. Christ, so much has happened since then it feels like a zillion years ago . . . I wonder if I would have still gone on that first date had I known what I know now? I glance over at Flora, whose hair has turned a blazing red under the glow of the garishly lit club facades, and despite all the craziness that's gone on since then, despite the confusion and soul-searching, I smile to myself as I realise yes, I probably would.

We're getting near the Cathedral now, and as we approach the walls enclosing the historic buildings I feel Flora's hand wrap around mine and, without either of us acknowledging this significant new development, we walk on holding hands. I'd like to say it feels like the most natural thing in the world, but I'd be lying. Within a few steps my palms are sweaty and I'm feeling all weird and jittery. Can your hands suffer from claustrophobia? I wonder whether it would be rude to remove my hand from hers and decide that it would be. Jesus, what the hell is wrong with me? I swerve erratically between being desperate for Flora's attention – over here! Look at me! *Woooo!* – and running screaming the other way when I get it, like a hysterical, hyperactive toddler.

Obviously, though, I say none of this to Flora, and we stroll onwards, hand in clammy hand, until we're in front of the Cathedral. It really is an awesome sight by night, lit from beneath in such a way that the whole building glows as if made out of gold.

'Beautiful,' murmurs Flora, as she stops to gaze up at the spire. 'Any idea how old it is?'

'Nearly a thousand years, I think,' I say, racking my brain for more information. 'It's the most complete Norman cathedral in England and is one of the finest example of Romanesque architecture in Europe. Here, for instance, you can see a wonderful example of a Gothic, um, arch thingy, and a very impressive . . . uh' – I wave vaguely at the nearby bricks – 'wall.'

I look at Flora with an apologetic grimace and we both start to snigger.

'Sorry,' I say. 'I'm a rubbish tour guide.'

We're still grinning at each other and during the pause in our conversation I'm suddenly aware how quiet it is here. I glance over my shoulder to see if there's anybody else around and through the trees spot the moon, which is so perfectly full and bright that it looks like a prop in a school play. I've no idea how I haven't noticed it before now, because for some reason tonight it seems extraordinarily huge, as if it's been creeping closer to earth without any of us realising – the winner in a game of interplanetary Grandmother's Footsteps. I turn back to Flora to say something about it and in that instant the moonlight, the Cathedral's golden glow and the soft warmth of the night air magically combine to create the most ridiculously romantic moment imaginable: a backdrop that's just begging for a kiss. Flora clearly thinks so too, as before I can speak she reaches up to touch my cheek.

'Beautiful Percy,' she says softly. 'I missed you when I was in Boston.'

'Me too,' I say, telling myself to ignore the butterflies that have just started stirring up my insides and go with the flow.

Flora smiles, tracing a path down my arm with her fingers. 'I'm so glad I met you.'

'Me too,' I say again, more nervously. The butterflies have now transformed into a flock of highly aggressive geese. I need a distraction, something to move us on from this dangerous moment. *Think*, Percy . . . 'Hey, I've got an idea!' My voice is wincingly loud in the silence. 'Would you like to see the cloister? It's where all the monks used to live. Really fascinating and quite a spectacular sight.' I know I'm babbling, but if I'm talking I can't kiss. 'Do you know, I think it might be the largest cloister in England? Or maybe it's the second largest, but still, definitely worth a look . . .'

But Flora reaches for me, wrapping her arms around me, and I catch the scent of her hypnotic perfume. 'The monks can wait,' she says, and even now, in the midst of going to pieces, I think how beautiful she is. And yet . . . I don't want to have sex with her. There: I've said it. As lovely as it was when we kissed before, it doesn't feel right to do it again. I'm drawn to her just as strongly as ever, but while I want us to be more than friends, I don't want to be her lover. Is there such a thing as platonic soulmates?

I'm overwhelmed by panic yet frozen to the spot. I've been deceiving myself all this time, haven't I? I've been desperate for Flora to like me because she's cooler, funnier and more successful than I could ever hope to be, but I'm not gay. That much at least now seems crystal clear.

But despite the adrenalin coursing through me I still seem unable to move and Flora is pulling me closer, a sexy half-smile playing on her lips, and unless I do something drastic kissing looks set to happen in five, four, three, two . . .

'Flora, wait, I need to talk to you.'

I've pulled away from her with an abruptness that takes her by surprise. A look of concern glances across her face, but she's still smiling. 'What is it, Percy? Is something wrong?'

'Can we sit down for a moment?'

She nods, but looks puzzled. 'Sure.'

We go to sit on a nearby bench, the only sound our feet crunching across the gravel. I feel like a condemned woman walking to her doom.

'So – what's up?' asks Flora.

Oh God, where to begin? I shuffle round in my seat so I'm facing her. 'Flora, I feel terrible about this, but I've not been completely honest with you.' I take a deep breath. 'My mum has never had malaria.'

'Okaaaaay,' she says, with a slight frown. 'So why tell me that she did?'

'I just panicked and it came out. I was trying to come up with an excuse so I could leave without being rude, but it was crass and stupid and I'm really ever so sorry.'

'Wait – you're talking about when we first met at the Savoy?'

I nod.

'So why did you want to leave? I thought we had a good time.'

'We did! I loved meeting you. But it's just . . . I was a bit, uh, uncomfortable.'

'Well, it wasn't the most relaxing of circumstances, was it? I mean, blind dates are never easy and that one was more blind than most. But you could have just told me you were finding it weird. I would have understood.' She puts a reassuring hand on my knee. 'I was nervous too, you know, Percy.'

'The thing is, there was a bit more to it than just nerves. Meeting you came as rather a shock.'

'A shock? I'm not that repulsive, am I?'

'No! God no, you're beautiful. It's just . . . I wasn't expecting . . . someone like you.'

'Who were you expecting, then?'

I take a deep breath. Jesus, Percy, just spit it out! 'I was expecting a man.'

Flora stares at me so intently that I can almost visualise her chain of thought and although I can see from her face that she's pretty sure what's coming next, she asks: 'And that was because . . . ?'

'Because Theresa Lefevre knew that I was already in a relationship with a man.'

There is a horrible silence.

'Ah. So Adam's not a dog,' says Flora – a statement, not a question.

'No, Adam's my ex-boyfriend.'

'Hmmm. I did have my doubts. And Amy?'

I just shake my head.

Flora lets out a long exhalation. 'Well, I'll give you this – that was quite a story you came up with . . . So you're bisexual, then?'

I'm about to agree, but I need to be completely honest with her. 'You're the first woman I've ever kissed.'

She nods slowly, but then closes her eyes and rubs her face, as if exhausted. 'That's an awful lot of lies, Percy.'

I just stare at my hands in my lap, too ashamed to speak.

'I can see, in the circumstances, that it must have been a shock meeting me for the first time,' she goes on, her voice icily calm, 'but what I don't understand is why you didn't say something to me. I would have understood. In fact, I would have probably found it funny – at that point, anyway. Now – not so much.'

'But I *was* going to say something! I was too embarrassed to tell you on our first date, but when I spoke to Theresa I asked her to explain to you that there'd been a mix-up, but she just went on and on about how a women's sexuality is fluid and how gender doesn't matter and, as you know, she can be *very* persuasive, and she convinced me to meet you one more time, and then I got your invitation to the party and assumed, because you told me to bring someone with me, that you just wanted to be friends—'

Flora gives a snort of sarcastic laughter. 'I don't kiss my friends like that, Percy.'

'No, no, of course I realise that, but that was what I had assumed *before* the party, and then we had such an amazing evening together and there was this incredible spark between us, wasn't there? And I was – *am* – so attracted to you, that I felt perhaps Theresa was right and we did have a future together after all. And I was hoping that if I saw you again things would be clear, but I'm still so confused . . .'

'That's because you're not gay, Percy,' she says, bluntly.

'But I'm definitely attracted to you! It's deeper than friendship, I'm sure. I love spending time with you and I think about you the whole time, but I'm struggling with the idea of . . . taking things further . . .'

'You mean sex?'

I nod miserably. 'And I've been tying myself in knots trying to work out what our relationship can be, because I think you're amazing and I desperately want you in my life.'

There is a flash of anger in Flora's eyes, but that's quickly replaced by something worse: disappointment. 'Am I supposed to be feeling sorry for you right now, Percy? Because all I'm hearing is how *you* feel and how confused *you* are and how, if you saw me enough times, you might suddenly decide you're a lesbian.' She shakes her head incredulously. 'What about how *I'm* feeling,

Percy? Up until about five minutes ago I presumed I was in a relationship with you, but now it seems I was just part of an experiment to test how gay you were.'

'It's not like that!' I say passionately. 'I haven't been stringing you along, I promise. I genuinely thought we might have a future together.'

'But that was all based on lies.'

God, this is horrible. I know I deserve it, but I can't bear how cold Flora's being with me. If I could only make her see how much she means to me . . . I try to take her hands in mine, but she twists away. I plough on, desperate to make things right. 'Flora, I know I've been stupid, but the last thing I wanted to do is hurt you. You're the most amazing woman I've ever met. And now you know the truth and everything's out there, can't we just . . . start again?'

'Start again as *what* exactly?' She's losing patience with me now. 'Friends? Lovers? What is it that you think we can be?'

I shrug helplessly. God only knows. I just know that I don't want to lose her.

Flora stands up. 'Percy, I wish you every happiness and I hope you find what you're looking for, but I can assure you that I am not it.'

She looks at me for a moment and then turns and walks away.

'Please, wait!' I say, my throat getting tight with panic. 'Flora, don't go!'

She hesitates, as if trying to come to a decision, then by some miracle turns and walks back to me. Oh, thank God! If we can just sit and talk for a while I'm sure I can get her to understand.

'Could you please tell me where I can get a taxi?'

My heart plummets, but I can see there's no point me trying to beg her to stay and so I give her directions to the nearest cab rank.

'Thank you,' she says, setting off again. But after a few steps she pauses and turns back slightly, just enough for me to see the sadness in her face. 'Why didn't you talk to me about this sooner, Percy?'

And then she strides off across the green, the moonlight turning her silver, making her seem more like some other-worldly creature than ever, and it takes every ounce of willpower not to run after her as she reaches the gate and disappears from view.

27

My home phone is ringing – well, I say 'ringing', but a nice 'brrrrring' would be far preferable to my current ringtone. The jarring electronic melody is far too loud and a bit sinister, like a creepy dancing clown, but as the only people who ever call me on my home phone are my mother, Adam and cold-callers wanting to know if I've been mis-sold a PPI I've never got round to changing it. I push myself up on my elbows and check the time: 7.42 a.m., which means I have had a grand total of three hours' sleep. Far from adequate, especially because today I was hoping to spend the whole day under the duvet to avoid the emotional fallout from last night's conversation with Flora. I get a sudden flashback to her face, her eyes filled with hurt and disappointment. *Don't even go there, Percy* . . . I flop back onto the mattress, willing myself back to sleep. Whoever it is can leave me a message.

A split second after it stops, however, the dancing clown starts up again. My eyes flick open. Two calls in a row would suggest that it's fairly urgent – either that or it's my mother. But what if it really is something important? Hang on a sec, did I ever give my home number to Flora? I struggle upright. I don't think I did, but if that *is* her calling, perhaps to say she wants to meet for breakfast, then I should definitely answer it. It's a long shot, I know, but I can't risk missing the chance to speak to her. Scrambling out of bed I throw myself across the room, stubbing my toe in the process, and manage to get to the phone just before the machine kicks in.

'Hello?' I pant, furiously rubbing at my injured toe.

'Morning, darling. Have you just come in from a jog?'

Shit. It *is* my mother. Before I have a chance to reply, she goes on: 'I'm just calling to check what time we're meeting this morning. I think we agreed eleven o'clock in Jarrold's?'

What's she talking about? Then I remember: we arranged to go shopping together today to look for outfits for Maggie's wedding. Oh God. It's not something I'd usually agree to, as I try to avoid giving my mother opportunities to pass comment on my appearance/taste/thighs, but I'd gone to Sunday lunch at my parents' house shortly after Mum's spa mini-break – or rather mini-breakdown – to recover from the shock of me breaking up with Adam, and although she managed not to mention our split throughout the whole of lunch I could tell that the effort of not mentioning how I had RUINED MY LIFE was taking every last ounce of her energy, so when she suggested we go shopping together I went along with it out of guilt over depriving her of a son-in-law. Today, however, it's no exaggeration to say that it's the last thing I feel like doing.

'Don't you even think about cancelling, madam,' says my mother smartly, as if reading my mind. 'I'll see you there at eleven. Bye, darling.'

And she's gone. Apart from 'hello', I don't think I managed to get another word in.

I arrive in Jarrold's formal-wear department to find my mother standing in front of a mirror, holding a pale-pink suit up in front of her, turning her head from side to side as if posing for a photographer.

'Ah, Percy, perfect timing.' She kisses me on each cheek, barely making contact, then gestures to the outfit. 'Thoughts?'

'Beautiful,' I say, with as much enthusiasm as I can muster. The quicker she finds an outfit, the sooner I can get back to bed. 'Exactly like something Carole Middleton would wear.'

Mum sparkles with pleasure. 'Well, I have a few other options in the fitting room, so let's keep this one as a possible for now, shall we? Now, what about *your* outfit, darling? I saw a lovely lilac dress and coordinating bolero that I thought would be very flattering on you.' She peers at me, narrowing her eyes in scrutiny, and then breaks into a delighted smile. 'Percy, have you lost weight? Well *done*, darling! So we'll need a size ten then? Wonderful!'

I'm about to explain about the recent craziness at work, which has necessitated the occasional missing of meals, which therefore *may* have had the side effect of shedding a few pounds (although I wouldn't know because I've been far too busy to weigh myself), but she's already shot off across the shop floor. I am not feeling at all confident about Mum's taste: alarm bells started to ring at 'lilac dress' and became deafening at 'bolero'. Perhaps I should tell her I've already found something to wear? No, I'm bound to get the third degree about *exactly* what it looks like and, quite frankly, I'm all lied out.

'Ah, here we are!' She holds the outfit up with a flourish, smoothing down the material. 'Now, isn't that smart?' Her eyes flick over me again. 'On second thoughts, let's start you off with the size twelve. We can always go smaller, but it can be rather demoralising to have to ask the assistant to fetch a larger size, don't you think, darling?'

A few minutes later I am in a changing-room cubicle staring miserably at the mirror. A dumpy, middle-aged mum who is trying on something 'jazzy' for a 'fancy do' stares miserably back.

'Are you ready in there?' comes my mother's voice. 'Can I come in?'

Reluctantly, I unlock the door.

'Right now, let's have a look at you,' she says, putting her hands on my shoulders and turning me to face the mirror again. 'So – what do you think?'

'I'm not sure . . .'

'Well, I think you look absolutely lovely!' she trills. She is fizzing with even more manic energy than usual, which is a worry. 'And look, here's the matching fascinator! Isn't it gorgeous? Just look at the beading detail on the butterflies!'

I get a sinking feeling of Titanic proportions. 'It *is* very nice, but perhaps I should have a look round to see what else there is before making a decision?'

'Of course, of course. We want to make sure we get it right for Maggie's special day, don't we? By the way, darling, I keep meaning to ask – will you be bringing a guest to the wedding?'

Ah, so that's what's on her mind. 'No, it'll be just me,' I say with deliberate cheeriness.

'I see.' She looks at me in the mirror, her eyes taking on a steely glint of determination. Here it comes . . . 'Percy, your father made me promise I wouldn't say anything to you about this, but as your mother I feel it is my duty to tell you when you're making a mistake.'

'Mum, please, don't . . .'

She holds up her hand to stop me speaking. 'You need to hear this, Percy. You may not want to, but it's for your own good.' She is keeping her voice steady – just – but her manic twisting of her necklace hints at an inner torment. 'I didn't say a word when you suddenly ended your relationship with Adam, even though it came as the most terrible shock. To be quite honest, I don't think I will ever understand *why* you did it because I can't imagine you will find a better boyfriend than the one you just threw away on . . . on . . . a *whim*.' She has been getting increasingly agitated, but now she stops, takes a breath to compose herself, and continues serenely. 'My point is that I spoke to Adam at your father's office last week and it's clear to me that he still thinks very highly of you, and I'm sure that if you went to see him and explained the situation, he might well look favourably on the idea of rekindling your relationship.'

She is beaming at me and is looking so hopeful that I feel terrible about having to disappoint her.

'I'm sorry, Mum, I don't want to rekindle our relationship.'

'BUT WHY NOT?' She shuts her eyes and takes another deep breath. 'I'm sorry, I didn't mean to raise my voice. I'm just a little upset.'

'Mum, I know you've always been very fond of Adam and I do appreciate that you're finding it difficult to understand why I ended things, but I need you to take my word for the fact that we're not right for each other.'

'But how on earth can Adam be NOT RIGHT FOR YOU?' She's so tense the sinews in her neck are standing out like wires. 'Are you looking for a man who's a little less charming, perhaps? Someone who doesn't have a fantastic career and his own house?' She is almost shouting now. 'Or was it that Adam was just too *handsome* and *successful* for you? Is that it? Because frankly, darling, the whole thing is a complete mystery to me!' Her voice disappears into a hysterical squeak.

'Mum,' I say, with forced calm, 'I know that Adam's a lovely guy, but our personalities just didn't work together and we would have ended up making each other miserable in the long run.'

She is looking at me with complete incomprehension. 'Darling, I love you,' she says, slowly. 'You're my daughter and I think you're wonderful in every single way. But you are in your thirties now and you need to face up to the fact that the number of eligible men is shrinking with every passing year. Soon, all that's going to be left are divorcees and homosexuals. Don't you want to get married and have a family?'

I sigh. This is hopeless. 'Even if I do, surely that's not a reason to stay with someone when I know it's not right?'

'It wasn't that wrong though, was it?' she asks frantically. 'Please, Percy, just speak to Adam. Give it another chance.'

'Did he ask you to talk to me about this?'

For the first time Mum's resolve appears to waver slightly. 'Not as such, no.'

'Then I'm sure you'll find that he has no interest in speaking to me, let alone rekindling anything.'

Mum throws up her hands with a huff of frustration. 'Oh, I give up, Percy! It's almost as if you want to be single and childless forever.'

'And would that really be so bad?' I'm trying to stay in control, but given my lack of sleep and emotional fragility after last night I can feel myself getting wound up. 'Given the choice between being happy on my own or unhappy in a relationship then I know which I'd prefer. Besides, just because it didn't work out with Adam it doesn't mean I'm going to be on my own for the rest of my life. And I would have hoped, as my mother, that you would be a little more supportive and trust me to know what's best for myself.'

But Mum ignores me. 'Well, at least I know exactly where I stand,' she says, with a sniff of martyrdom. 'I'll give up on my dream of grandchildren, then. I suppose you'll be one of these women who's happy with cats.'

She says 'cats' in the same tone as she would 'herpes', and something inside me snaps.

'Fine!' I yell. 'You want to know exactly where you stand? Well, here you go. I would rather *eat* this fascinator than wear it out in public. This dress makes me look like a fat air hostess. And yes, before you say anything, I probably could do with losing a few more pounds, but the only person who seems to have a problem with the fact that I'm not a size six is *you*. Oh, and by the way – ' here comes the killer blow – 'Adam voted Labour at the last election.'

Mum's hand flies to her mouth in horror. 'That's not true!' she gasps.

'I'm afraid it is.' I give her a coldly triumphant look. 'And now, if you'll excuse me, I need to get changed. Us spinsters like to spend Sunday sobbing into our single duvets and googling pictures of cats. Goodbye, Mother.'

By the time I get home I have calmed down enough to wonder whether I should phone Mum to apologise, as deep down I know that in her own weird way she does have my best interests at heart, but I just don't have the energy. Instead, I pick up the phone to Charlie, because if I don't talk to someone about what happened last night with Flora I'll keep rerunning our conversation obses-sively in my head and will probably drive myself loopy with all the 'if only's and 'what if's – either that or I'll drive myself to the bottle of tequila that I've been eyeing up in the kitchen. Thankfully Charlie saves me from both insanity and alcohol poisoning by patiently listening to my rambling account of the disastrous night, and even manages not to say 'I told you so' when I get to the part about realising that I'm not gay after all.

'Percy, you need to get some sleep,' says Charlie gently, once I've finally run out of words.

'But shouldn't I phone Flora to clear the air?'

'No. Well, not today, at least. Give it a few days for the dust to settle and for you to get your thoughts in order, then phone or write her an email.'

'But that might be too late! She might have written me off as a lying nutter and refuse to have anything to do with me!'

'Flora sounds like a very reasonable person to me, I'm sure she'll listen to you once you've both had a chance to think things through calmly.'

'I'm not sure, Chaz . . . I mean, I realise that Flora and I don't have a future romantically, but I'm desperate not to lose her as a friend, so don't you think I need to speak to her sooner rather than later?'

Charlie sighs. 'Do you know what you need, Percy? You need to have *fun*. You went straight from the trauma of the split with Adam to this emotional rollercoaster with Flora. The best thing for you would be to forget about all the soulmate crap and just go out and dance and drink and get off with someone unsuitable. Join Tinder! Have a one-night stand! Just stop stressing about your love life, okay? Things will fall into place in their own time, I promise you.'

She's right, of course. I've been far too tied up in various emotional wranglings of late. Despite my gloom over how I handled things with Flora, I become aware of a tiny green shoot of positivity sprouting somewhere deep inside me, which brings with it a vision of a man who looks quite a lot like Ryan Gosling, standing by a moonlit fountain in the grounds of a mid-priced country house hotel. I feel some of the tension inside me start to fade a little, and my mouth relaxes into a smile.

'Thank you, my love,' I say to Charlie. 'I needed to hear that. I've got my work conference next weekend, which means I can get started on the drinking and dancing at the very least.'

'Excellent. Roll on next weekend and some outrageous behaviour. But right now, chick, you need to go to bed.'

Which would be the logical thing to do, but unfortunately I'm not in a logical sort of mood and as soon as I put the phone down to Charlie I dial Flora's number. I know: *idiot*. But I can't bear the idea of her thinking that I deceived her. We're not going to be lovers, I get that, but I'm still convinced we have a deep connection and I need to make things right between us. Unsurprisingly, Flora doesn't pick up, but instead of putting the phone down and leaving it a few days before I try again like a sensible person, I leave her a horrifically long-winded message, blathering on and on about how we *are* soulmates – 'but spiritual, not sexual ones' – until even her voicemail gets bored with me and cuts me off.

And *then* I go to bed.

28

After weeks of unbroken sunshine, the following morning dawns grey and chilly, as if the weather has suddenly remembered we're in East Anglia, not the Algarve, and promptly rectified its error. In the office the dreariness of the day taints everyone's mood, with an air of gloom hanging over the fifth floor.

'Typical, the week of the conference and the sun goes in,' sighs Kerry, as I pass her desk on the way to the kitchen to make tea.

'I'm sure it'll perk up by the weekend,' I say, although I'm far from confident. When I checked the forecast on my phone this morning there was a depressing column of little grey clouds all the way into next week.

'Well, it better,' says Kerry, with a look implying that as chair of the conference organising committee I am to blame for the area of low pressure currently settled over East Anglia. She goes on, huffily: 'I've bought a strappy dress from Marks & Sparks specially to wear on the Saturday night, and it looks all wrong with a cardi.'

'Pashmina?' I offer, with a sympathetic face, before escaping into the kitchen. I don't mean to be dismissive, but of far greater concern than Kerry's fashion dilemma is the fate of the team games on Sunday, which are currently scheduled to take place outdoors. If the weather doesn't improve we'll have to swap them for Scrabble and charades – and I can imagine how well that will go down; some people have already told me they're only coming for the inflatable sumo wrestling.

Even more important than the weather for the conference, however, is the forecast for Maggie's wedding the following weekend – and that's looking worryingly iffy, too. They're having an outdoor ceremony and it would be such a shame if we had to huddle under umbrellas during the vows. I once read that rain on your wedding day is considered lucky because a wet knot is much harder to untie than a dry one, but that sounds a lot like something a quick-thinking bridesmaid came up with to console a hysterical bride with a drenched updo: 'Don't worry about a bit of frizz, Kel – this is a *good* thing! Honest, babes, in the long run you'll be *glad* it rained today!'

I wonder if I should ask one of my friends to Maggie's wedding as my plus-one? Much as I'd have loved to take

Flora, clearly that's not going to happen. She hasn't called me back and I cringe every time I remember the rambling message I left on her voicemail; after listening to it she's probably feeling like she had a lucky escape. Anyway, Jaye and Charlie both love Maggie (as does Lou, but she's still giving me the silent treatment) and it would be great to share the day with one of them. But then another idea hits me, so brilliant that I can't believe I didn't think of it before. Why don't I ask Milo? I owe him after the ice-climbing date, after all, and he'd be a wonderfully charming guest, and while Mum would have no hesitation in berating me about my man-repelling abilities in front of Jaye or Charlie, she's bound to be on her best behaviour around Milo. Plus – and here's the clincher – I'd really like to see him again. I quickly bash out an email:

Morning! My granny is getting married to a darts player a week on Saturday and, as a thank-you for the ice-climbing, I wondered if you would like to come as my guest? I know that darts isn't necessarily classed as an extreme sport, but if you fancy getting beaten by a girl again then it would be a pleasure to oblige. Percy.

PS It should be a fun day, and there will be free vol-au-vents at the very least.

I hit Send; a few minutes later I notice that I've already received a reply:

Thank you for your email. I'm currently on a work trip abroad and will only be checking email intermittently, but will get back to you as soon as possible, broken limbs and concussion permitting.
Milo

Bugger. Well, hopefully he'll see my message sooner rather than later. I reread my original email to him, as I sent it off in haste, and it occurs to me that he might take it the wrong way – like I'm asking him to come as my date. Before I can stop to think, I write another and hit Send:

Just to clarify, I'm asking you as a friend, obviously. Martha is unavoidably detained that weekend.

Oh bloody hell, that sounds a bit po-faced, doesn't it? I was so keen for him not to get the wrong idea that I've made it sound like he was my absolute last resort. Oh well, too late to worry about it now . . .

That afternoon, as well as more clouds and rain, the wind blows in another unwelcome guest. I'm at my desk doing Susannah's expenses when the phone starts to ring.

'Susannah White's office.'

'Perseus, it's Theresa LeFevre.'

My immediate instinct is to put the phone straight down again. Bloody, effing Theresa LeFevre. This whole mess with Flora is entirely her fault. Okay, perhaps not *all* of it, but at least 99.9 per cent of it; I will take responsibility for the 0.1 per cent that constitutes the minor fibs about my mother's malaria and Adam being a dog. Nevertheless, I resist the urge to hang up, partly because I want to know if Theresa has spoken to Flora – and if so what she said – and partly because I am above that sort of childish behaviour.

'Hello, Theresa,' I say, flicking V-signs at the phone. 'How are you?'

'Very well, thank you. I spoke to Flora this morning and I understand that the two of you had a difficult conversation at the weekend. Such a shame things didn't work out, you had so much potential as a couple.'

I grit my teeth. 'Theresa, I told you after my first meeting with her that I wasn't sexually attracted to women, so I don't think this should come as a huge surprise. If you remember, it was you who persuaded me to see her again.'

'Yes, I did, because as I said at the time I felt it was important that you put aside any preconceptions to give your relationship with Flora a chance to flourish. All the data pointed towards you being a perfect match, and our computer system does not make errors. Unfortunately the same cannot be said for human nature.' Jesus, she is unbelievable. Perhaps she's actually a robot? 'However, I do admit that the channels of communication might have been clearer in this instance,' she goes on. 'For

example, Flora pointed out that it would have been bene-
ficial if she'd been given more information about your
personal circumstances prior to the first date . . .'

'You mean the fact that I had a boyfriend and wasn't gay?'

There is a slight pause, as if her circuit boards are
struggling to compute sarcasm. 'That's correct, yes. The
SoulDate system is truly revolutionary and a powerful
tool, but my colleagues and I are still learning the best
way to handle the data it produces.'

'Pesky human error, eh?'

Theresa gives the briefest of laughs. 'Indeed. Anyway,
Perseus, on behalf of EROS Technologies I am phoning to
apologise for any dissatisfaction you may have experi-
enced and to compensate for your inconvenience I would
like to offer you a complimentary SoulDate match.'

'No, thank you,' I reply instantly. I just want to put this
whole fiasco behind me.

'Are you sure? Flora was your Ultimate Compatibility
Match, but as I explained to you before, even the tenth
match on your list would be many millions of times more
compatible with you than someone you meet at random.
Our clients pay a great deal of money for such an incredible opportunity, but you would be getting it for free.
Really, what's the worst that can happen?'

'You set me up with another woman.'

'Touché,' says Theresa, with something approaching
warmth. 'Only men this time, Perseus, I promise you.'

And I want to stick to my guns, I really do. The thought of having any further dealings with Ms LeFevre sets my teeth on edge. Besides, there's Dan to consider. If he happens to make a move at the conference this weekend – far from certain, I know, but it *is* a possibility – then there's nothing to stop us taking things further. I'm single, he's single – and as Charlie says, a meaningless snog could be just what I need. (Well, maybe it wouldn't have to be entirely meaningless; Dan's a nice bloke, it wouldn't be fair just to *use* him like that. The snog could perhaps lead to dinner next week – on Friday, for instance. Just in theory, obviously . . .) Anyway, the point is that I'm supposed to be having fun and not getting bogged down in any more intense, emotional stuff, which means I definitely shouldn't be having anything more to do with SoulDate.

But then again . . . It's not like I have to marry whoever I get matched with, is it? Take away all the soulmate bollocks and it's basically a blind date – and that falls into the category of 'fun', surely? And while Theresa LeFevre did screw up one very significant aspect of my match with Flora, I can't deny she got the compatibility part bang on.

'If I meet this person – this *man* – and I'm not interested in taking things any further, you won't try to persuade me to see him again?'

'Absolutely not. I give you my word.'

'And there aren't any other conditions that I should know about? I won't need to give an interview to your marketing team or anything?'

'No strings attached, I assure you, Perseus.'

I mull it over for a few seconds more. What *is* the worst that can happen? I have a crap evening, which I could quickly put behind me and move on with my life, armed with a funny story with which to entertain my mates. But I'm afraid to admit that the deciding factor in all this, the reason I think I will take Theresa up on her offer after all, is that for the past twenty-four hours my mother's voice has been playing in a loop in my head: 'Single and childless forever . . . Single and childless forever . . .'

'Perseus?' asks Theresa. 'What do you think?'

I take a deep breath. 'On second thoughts, Theresa, yes, I'd like to accept your offer, thank you very much.'

'Wonderful. I'll fast-track your match and will be in touch with details of your date as soon as possible. Goodbye, Perseus.'

29

So this is it: the weekend of our annual conference. The culmination of all the weeks of hard work, food deprivation and bitching from Mr Hedley, who by some miracle has decided to boycott the conference in protest at – well, too many things to list, really. But the point is that Chief Inspector Hedley of the Norwich Fun Police won't be on duty this weekend, and partly because of that and partly because of the aforementioned hard work, so far things are going rather well. TOUCH WOOD.

Susannah kicked things off this morning with an inspirational welcome speech in which she outlined her five-year plan for the company, and then our Financial Director, Gary Dobson, gave a lengthy presentation about, um, financial things, which no doubt the relevant people found useful. Lunch was a cold fork buffet: arguably a little heavy on the pork products (sausages, sausage rolls, ham, Parma ham, Scotch eggs, pork pies, salami, pork terrine), but it was all perfectly nice, and I'm sure the vegetarians enjoyed the generous selection of breads. And the sun is shining! So Kerry will be able to wear her new dress without a cardi tonight, and tomorrow's inflatable sumo is ON, thank God.

Best of all, in a last-minute coup we've secured the manager of Norwich City Football Club to be tonight's after-dinner speaker! Just to put this feat into context, at last year's conference the celebrity guest was the bloke who reads the travel news on Radio Norwich, so this is an out-and-out triumph. I'm afraid I can't take any credit, though, as it's all down to my fellow committee member Jane Townsend (the gossipy one from Claims) who has a friend whose cousin's stepbrother's uncle has done some business with the Norwich City manager. Jane spoke to the uncle last week, who asked the manager yesterday, and we've just heard that he'll definitely be joining us this evening. Word of this is only now getting out and during the coffee break there was a stream of people (mainly men, admittedly) rushing up to me, eyes shining, asking: 'Is it true, Percy? Is he coming here tonight?' I feel like a parent on Christmas Eve telling an overexcited five-year-old that yes, Santa really *is* on his way.

But first things first. We are currently in the conference suite listening to the afternoon's guest speaker, the American motivational guru Troy Salazar. Troy is wearing a black polo neck and Simon Cowell's jeans and is delivering a blisteringly upbeat presentation based on his self-help book, *Who the Heck is Driving this Thing? Harnessing the Power of the Subconscious Mind for Superconscious Success.* I get the impression that Troy has delivered this same speech many, many times before, simply inserting the words 'East Anglia's insurance experts' where he's previously used 'Oldham's premier nail technicians' or 'North Devon's pig-farming professionals'; still, people seem to be enjoying it, and Troy is certainly working the crowd, striding back and forth across the podium in his Britney-style head mic like he's headlining at Wembley.

'Did you know, in just one second the conscious mind is processing with two thousand neurons?' he asks us. 'So right now, your conscious mind might be thinking, "Hey, this is interesting stuff", or "Man, this dude looks *exactly* like Tom Cruise." ' He pauses for laughter, a wry smile on his face. 'But in the same second the subconscious mind is processing with four billion neurons. Two thousand compared to four billion.' He stops again, this time for dramatic effect. 'Now, just who the heck is driving this thing? The conscious or the subconscious?'

Mel, who is sitting to my right, leans over to me and whispers: 'Where did you find this wanker?'

'Oh come on, he's not that bad. Apparently Oprah's a fan.'

She gives a derisive snort. 'Yeah, that bloody figures.'

The truth is, though, that I've not really been listening to Troy, because sitting on the other side of me is Dan, and for the past ten minutes, since Troy made his entrance to a burst of Bon Jovi's 'It's My Life', Dan's leg has been pressed up against mine – and both my conscious and subconscious have been struggling to focus on anything else. My heart is pounding and every one of my billions of neurons is so intensely focused on the point of contact just above our knees that my skin feels like it's burning. Surely Dan must be able to feel this too? I take a quick look at him, but he's fiddling with his phone and certainly doesn't appear to be helpless with lust. On second thoughts, perhaps I'm reading too much into this; in fact, perhaps he doesn't even realise that his leg is touching mine. We are all quite squashed up in here, so I suppose it could well be down to a lack of legroom rather than anything more deliberate? I subtly shift in my seat to break the contact and then wait to see if his leg finds its way back to mine, but a few minutes later I'm still waiting. I swallow my disappointment and tell my subconscious to bloody well pull itself together.

But then there's a tap on my arm and I look down to see Dan holding out a piece of folded paper to me. Intrigued, I take it, then glance at Mel to see if she's noticed, but her eyes are closed – and was that a snore? The coast is clear. With a shiver of anticipation I unfold the paper to find a drawing of a noughts and crosses frame, empty apart from a cross in the top left square, and I look up to find Dan's eyes locked onto mine.

'It's your move,' he mouths.

But is he talking about the game – or something else?

Someone on the conference committee came up with the bright idea of seating people from different departments next to each other at dinner, the aim being to encourage new friendships, improve interdepartmental relation-ships and so forth. And it *is* a nice idea in theory, but after a long day of presentations and seminars I can't be the only one who just wants to have a drink and a laugh with my mates, rather than make polite small talk with Craig, the new guy from IT. On my other side I have Alan who is something senior in Legal, but he has the new receptionist sitting to his right and her boobs are prov-ing far more interesting than anything I can come up with. I shoot an envious glance over to where Mel and Dan have been seated together at what is obviously the Fun Table, judging by its raucousness and the number of empty wine bottles they've already accumulated. Never mind, it's probably best if I stay sober until after dinner, as I've still got a few COC responsibilities to fulfil – most importantly, of course, assisting in the safe delivery of our special guest speaker. On that note, shouldn't he be here by now? We've already got our start-ers and he's due to speak between the mains and dessert. I feel a twinge of anxiety in my stomach. I'm quite sure Jane's got it all in hand, but it's probably worth double-checking, so I wave an arm in her direction until she looks over.

'Where is he?' I mouth at her.

'Here in five minutes,' she replies.

Sure enough, a little while later she leaves her table, giving me an enthusiastic thumbs-up as she goes. Thank God, he must be here. I'll just finish my prawn cocktail then go and introduce myself and check he has everything that he needs. This is so exciting! I'm not a huge football fan, but a premiership manager is definitely a big deal.

'It looks like our guest speaker has just arrived,' I say to IT Craig, keen to share the good news.

'I'm not really into football myself,' he says. 'I'm a gamer.'

'Really? I love a bit of Candy Crush. What are you into?'

He gives me a withering look. 'Multiplayer fantasy, mainly. The Elder Scrolls. Skyrim. Runescape.'

'Interesting . . . So is that, um' – I'm choosing my words very carefully here to avoid a gaming faux pas – 'a Dungeons and Dragons type of thing?'

Craig snorts like an angry barbarian troll. 'Dungeons and Dragons is for losers and babies,' he spits.

'Oh, right. I see.'

Feeling way out of my depth, chat-wise, I let my eyes wander around the room, searching for an escape, and with perfect timing I spot Jane beckoning to me from the doorway.

'Ah, sorry, Craig, duty calls. Back shortly.'

As I make my way across the dining room, passing by the tables of smiling faces and empty plates, I feel a flush of pleasure. You helped to achieve this, Percy; this is the direct result of *your* hard work. Give yourself a pat on the back.

Jane beams at me as I approach.

'Everything okay?' I ask happily.

'Absolutely fine. Really great. Except . . .' Her smile wavers a little. 'Did you know that he doesn't speak English?'

'Who?'

'The manager of Norwich City.'

I consider this for a moment. 'I'm no expert, Jane, but isn't the manager of Norwich City from England?'

'Well, the only word he's said to me that I've understood is "translator".' Her brow furrows in confusion. 'And I might be wrong, but he seemed to say it as if he was asking a question. You know, like – "translator, question mark"?'

Trying to ignore a twinge of unease, I follow Jane through to the lounge, which is empty apart from a handsome, dark-haired man in a shell suit, who is currently getting stuck into a bottle of red wine. Probably one of the manager's entourage.

'So where is he?' I ask her, hovering in the doorway.

She nods at the man in the shell suit. 'There.'

'Jane,' I say, doing my best to stay calm, 'that is not the manager of Norwich City.'

'Yes, it is.'

'No, it's very definitely *not*.'

She looks at him through narrowed eyes for a moment. 'Who is it, then?'

'I. Don't. Know,' I reply through gritted teeth. Oh Christ, this is bad.

The man sees us and raises his hand in greeting; plastering on a smile, I cross over to where he's sitting.

'Hello,' I say, slowly and clearly, 'my name is Percy James. *Percy James*.'

He beams at me. 'Translator?'

'No.' I shake my head. 'Me no translator.'

The man frowns.

'What is *your* name?' I ask. 'Your NAME?'

He looks blank.

'Try it in Spanish, Perce,' whispers Jane. 'He looks Spanish.'

'I don't know any fucking Spanish,' I hiss. Honestly, this is bloody hopeless. We need to find a translator – there *must* be someone at Eagle who can speak Spanish. And then I remember: Dan's recent surfing holiday was to Spain. Surely he must have picked up a few words of the language?

'Just hold on,' I tell Jane. 'Keep him busy. Get him some Pringles.'

I rush back into the dining room, where they're now serving the main course, and work my way across the room to the Fun Table.

'Shithead!' slurs Mel, lovingly. 'Pull up a chair, mate!' She's clearly responsible for a large proportion of the empties on the table.

'We've missed you, James!' Dan gives me a woozy, sleepy-eyed grin. Ah, on second thoughts perhaps Mel doesn't deserve *all* the blame. 'Come and sit here, have a drink,' he says, patting his lap then holding out his arms.

'Sorry, this isn't a social visit. Dan, do you speak Spanish?'

'*Si, un poco,*' he says, with a boyish swagger, which makes Sheila from the post room who's sitting to his left collapse into coy giggles.

'Oh, thank God,' I say. 'Could I please borrow you for a sec?'

'Sure.' He pushes back his chair and follows me back through the dining room. 'What's up?'

By now we have got to the entrance to the lounge. 'Could you please find out what that man's name is? I'm not sure he's Spanish, but it's worth a try.'

'Who is he?'

'Well, that's the problem – we don't know. He's meant to be the manager of Norwich City FC.'

Dan shakes his head with drunken emphasis. 'Nah, that's not him.'

'Yes, I realise that,' I say, with as much patience as I can muster. 'So can you ask him? Please?'

Thanks to Dan, we discover that our friend in the shell suit is called Luka Popovic and after some swift googling we discover that he is currently the caretaker manager of the Norwich City under-sixteens and is from Serbia (he played briefly in Madrid, hence the few words of Spanish), so, interesting as his speech may well be, it's highly unlikely that either Dan or anyone else in the company will be able to translate it for him. Serbian isn't one of those languages you remember a bit of from GCSE.

I turn to Jane, who has been looking increasingly horrified. 'You'll just have to go and make an announcement explaining what's happened.'

Her eyes widen in terror. 'I can't do that, Perce, I'll have a panic attack. Please don't make me do it.' She grabs her chest and starts wheezing. 'Oh my God, I think I'm hyperventilating. Has anyone got a paper bag I can breathe into?'

Oh bloody hell. 'I'll do it, then,' I mutter.

I walk back through the dining room to my table and tap on my wine glass.

'Everyone? Could I please have your attention for a moment?'

There's a ripple of cheers and some banging on the tables. At least everyone's drunk – or maybe that's not a good thing.

'I'm afraid I've got some bad news. Norwich City's manager won't be able to make it tonight after all.'

The room erupts into booing. Someone even chucks a bread roll, although it misses me and hits Alan from Legal, briefly interrupting his leering at the receptionist.

'I know, it's a shame and we're all disappointed. But the good news is that the caretaker manager of Norwich's youth team, the former Serbian midfielder Luka Popovic, has kindly stepped in to take his place!'

Unbelievably, this is met with an enormous cheer. Perhaps he's actually famous . . . ? Nah, it's probably just because everyone's pissed.

'Anyway, I'm sure Luka will be happy to, um, pose for selfies. And if anyone here speaks Serbian, he's probably got some terrific stories.'

As it happens, the mix-up isn't such a disaster after all. Within minutes of making his entrance into the dining room Luka is leading a conga between the tables, swigging from a bottle of Prosecco. Someone produces a football and he bounces it on his head like a performing seal then does what Dan assures me is a brilliant display of 'keepy-uppy'. It turns out that our guest of honour is quite the all-rounder: as well as football, his talents include downing shots, singing Serbian folk songs (at least I assume that's what they are), excelling at the Gangnam Style dance and seducing Eagle's womenfolk.

The general consensus seems to be that Luka Popovic is

far more entertaining than the real manager of Norwich City FC could have ever been. He is last seen disappearing off into the grounds with Sadie and Anne-Marie from Accounts.

Later in the evening I'm on the dance floor with Mel when Susannah comes over and throws her arms around me. 'Percy, you are *brilliant*,' she says. 'Today has been a triumph. I am the luckiest boss ever, thank you for everything.'

We dance around the floor together, locked in a drunken hug, and I feel giddy with pure joy. I'm on such a high right now, buzzing from all the love in the room and my delight at how well things have gone today. I might be crap at relationships, but I can certainly organise the *shit* out of a conference! And just as I'm thinking that actually I don't need a man, because I'm a powerful, successful woman with a great life and wonderful friends, and I'm more than strong enough to be on my own, I feel a pair of hands snake around my waist and I spin round, giggling, to come face to face with Dan, and in that instant all my thoughts and everything else in the room disappear and there's just me and him, looking into each other's eyes.

'The woman of the hour,' he says, pushing a strand of hair out of my face and tucking it behind my ear. 'Want to get some fresh air?'

I nod, as fireworks of excitement explode inside me. *Whoosh!* There's a Roman candle of joy! *Zoom!* There's a Catherine wheel of desire! I thought this evening couldn't get any better, but it looks like it might just be about to.

30

I follow Dan down the stairs from the terrace and across the lawn, my ears still ringing from the music, the evening air deliciously cool against my hot cheeks. There are little groups of people dotted around, drinking and smoking, and we stop to chat, but my mind is elsewhere and after a few minutes, without either of us needing to say a word, Dan and I start walking away from the hotel as if we've made the decision via telepathy. Now we're outside I realise that I'm actually quite drunk: I've worn my strappy sandals tonight (having their first outing since my Cinderella moment on the night of Flora's party) and am having to focus intently on putting one foot in front of the other so as not to stumble. I'm focusing so hard on this, in fact, that I walk straight into a low-hanging branch.

'Careful!' Dan grabs my arm to stop me hitting the deck.

I giggle, tipsily. 'Thank you, kind sir,' I say, attempting a wobbly curtsy.

Dan grins. 'You did a really top job today, James.'

'It went okay, didn't it?'

'It certainly did. You should be very proud of yourself.'

We wander on for a while and find ourselves on a path leading along a walled garden. It's far quieter here, and now that we're some distance from the hotel's terrace lights I'm increasingly aware of the brightness of the moon. It suddenly occurs to me that this is the second time in as many weeks that I've been in the moonlight, waiting for a kiss.

'You know, James,' says Dan, as we walk, 'I'm glad I've got you on your own because there's something I've been meaning to talk to you about. For quite a while, actually.'

'Mmmm?' I say casually, although my insides are giddy with anticipation.

'It's just never seemed the right time,' Dan goes on. 'Too many people around.'

Incredibly, we're now approaching the fountain that I noticed from the terrace when I was here the other day. This scene is playing out *exactly* like in my vision!

'Well, we're alone now,' I say. 'So ask away.'

'Okay, so the thing is . . .' He tails off, rubbing his stubbly jaw. 'God, this is hard.'

We're standing by the fountain and the moonlight is turning the water into showers of silver sparks.

'Don't worry,' I tell him. 'I think I know what you're trying to say.'

'You do?'

'Mmm-hmm,' I murmur, giving him a bold, knowing look. Then I bite my lip, sexily. Men *love* that kind of thing; it drives them wild.

Dan frowns ever so slightly. 'Uh, okaaaaay. Right, well, do you remember a couple of months ago I bumped into you and your mate Jaye outside the office?'

Huh? What's that got to do with anything?

'Well, since then – God, this is embarrassing – since then I haven't been able to stop thinking about her. Jaye, that is. I had a massive crush on her when she was in that TV series years ago, and then when I saw her with you the other day . . . well, I was gone.' He shakes his head, lost in the memory. 'I wouldn't admit this to anyone else, but when Jaye looked at me that day it felt like there was this *connection* between us, you know? It's ridiculous, I barely know her, but I think . . . well, maybe it's the beer talking, but I feel like we might be soulmates.'

I hold up my hand to stop him, my sozzled brain cells struggling to piece together what he's saying. 'Wait a minute, are you telling me you fancy *Jaye*?'

He nods sheepishly.

'And that is the important thing that you've been meaning to tell me? This is what you were going to talk to me about that evening in the pub?' *This is what I've been daydreaming about all these past months?*

'Told you it was embarrassing,' he grimaces.

I open my mouth to speak then shut it again because I'm afraid the words will come out as a howl. I feel crushed, literally. No, I feel destroyed. I got it right the first time: Dan doesn't fancy me. To him I'm just the fat, funny friend: the one who's a laugh and worth a harmless flirt, but fancy her? You've *got* to be joking. I feel a hot, prickling sensation behind my eyes. Oh, don't cry, Percy, for God's sake . . .

Blissfully unaware of my imminent breakdown, Dan presses on. 'Anyway, I was wondering if there was a chance, because we're mates, that you might be able to put in a good word for me? Maybe pass on my number? Unless, of course, she's already seeing somebody else. Girls like that aren't usually single for long.'

'No,' I say, turning away to hide the tears that I haven't managed to stop from falling, 'girls like that usually aren't.'

It's taking every ounce of my self-control to hold myself together right now. I'm *this close* to throwing myself to the ground in a wailing, sobbing, teeth-gnashing heap; I even find myself glancing downwards to check whether I'd have a soft landing. All I can say is it's a good thing we're standing on gravel rather than grass, or the next few moments would be playing out very differently. How can I have got this so horribly, humiliatingly wrong? Were all those little moments of intimacy that Dan and I shared really just in my head? The only tiny shred of comfort in all this is that Dan seems to have no idea that I've been conducting an imaginary love affair with him. If he found out – well, not to be melodramatic, but I'd have to emigrate. So I remain upright, my jaw rigid with the effort of keeping my emotional explosion safely contained.

'James? What do you think? I know I can be a bit of a flirt, but I promise you I'll be a complete gentleman.'

'Of course, I'll . . . I'll talk to Jaye. Leave it with me.'

'You're a legend.' Dan claps his hand chummily on my back. 'Right, shall we get back to the party? 'Scuse my language, but I'm desperate for a piss.'

The short walk back to the hotel feels like a punishing ten-mile hike. Dan whistles happily, clearly relieved to have finally broached the subject of his 'soulmate', while I try to keep a step or two behind to hide my snivels from him. It doesn't work.

'You okay, James?' he asks, as we cross the lawn.

'Hayfever,' I mutter.

At last we reach the terrace and before Dan can get a proper look at me I mumble, 'Just got to get something for the hayfever,' and make a beeline for the stairs, keeping my head down to avoid making eye contact with anyone. It's only once I have got to my room, double-locked the door and turned up the volume on the TV that I finally open the floodgates.

*

A little while later I'm lying on the bed, still fully dressed, watching a seventies disaster movie on TV and working my way through the complimentary shortbread fingers. I'm dizzy with tiredness but too wound up to sleep. It's terrible what a fragile thing confidence is – well, my confidence anyway. In a matter of seconds out there in the garden I went from ass-kicking superwoman to snivelling loser, just because I discovered that a bloke didn't fancy me. It's pathetic really. I'm trying to find a silver lining to this particular cloud, telling myself that a no-strings fling with Dan would be just the thing to help Jaye move on from her arsehole ex, but I'm ashamed to say that self-pity is currently beating the shit out of self-lessness. Seriously, I had no idea how much I'd been banking on things working out with Dan – although my subconscious has clearly had him pegged as the fallback plan for some time, which must be why I managed to bounce back relatively unscathed from the split with Adam and the whole Flora saga: I believed I had Dan on the back burner. I'm not saying that I knew he was a dead cert, but I got so wrapped up in the fantasy of us getting together that I hadn't even considered Option B – and now here we are at Option B, and having never really given it a moment's thought I'm utterly at a loss at how to deal with it. Alcohol would help, naturally, but there's no minibar in the room and I can't go back downstairs because my face is so blotchy and puffy it looks like I've suffered an allergic reaction, so rather than whisky I'm drowning my sorrows in English Breakfast tea, although as a final kick in the nuts I spilt the one and only plastic tublet of milk so I'm having to drink it black – and I *hate* black tea.

On the television I watch impassively as a woman with a flicky mullet wearing a mustard-coloured dress dangles one-handed from the top of a burning building, screaming hysterically. *I know exactly how you feel, love.* I reach for another shortbread finger only to discover that I've eaten them all, which nearly sets me off crying again. This was *so* not the way tonight was supposed to play out. I should be rolling around the bed with Dan right now, not lying on it alone, covered in crumbs, drinking evil tea. Why am I such a disaster when it comes to love? On screen the woman in the mustard dress is now in a passionate clinch with Burt Reynolds. Jesus, even with terrible seventies styling, covered in soot and probably suffering from post-traumatic shock she is *still* better at pulling than I am. My mother is right: I'm going to be single and childless forever.

With another wave of tears threatening to break over me, I bury my face in the pillow and try to get a grip. This is as bad as it's going to get, I reassure myself through gritted teeth. You have lost Adam, buggered things up with Flora and Dan is in love with your best friend: when it comes to matters of the heart, Percy, *this* is your rock bottom. From here the only way is up.

Then from somewhere near the bed I hear a muffled beep – the sound of an email arriving on my mobile. I look at the bedside clock radio: who's emailing me at nearly 1 a.m.? Grateful for the distraction, I grab my phone from my bag and my heart soars when I see that the message is from Milo. What perfect timing! This is *exactly* what I need right now: one of Milo's funny, chatty emails to remind me that I'm not a total emotional dead-beat after all. With any luck he's getting in touch to say he can come to Maggie's wedding. With a surge of hope, I open his message.

Thank you very much for asking me to your grandmother's wedding but I'm afraid I have plans for that day. Milo.

Wait, that's it? I stare at it in dismay – surely there must be more to his email than just that? I close the email and open it again, to make sure that the rest of it hadn't . . . oh, I don't know . . . got lost in the ether or something, but that's all there is to it. No explanation, none of Milo's usual jokes, no suggestion that we meet another time: not the slightest hint of what I thought was our blossoming friendship. Nothing apart from that one line, which to me, in my already fragile, drunken state, feels like a painfully polite 'fuck you'.

And that's the moment I *really* hit rock bottom.

31

The setting for Maggie and Derek's wedding is a wild-flower garden just outside Norwich, where chairs are laid out in a sun-dappled glade and the bride and groom will say their vows underneath an arch of woven willow. Despite the forecast, the day is beautifully warm with a few wispy clouds providing occasional shade, and the scent of fresh-cut grass, wild herbs and hairspray mingle to make the air smell like Pimm's. Just taking a deep breath makes you feel woozily happy. It's a perfect English June day – and Maggie is the perfect bride in a daffodil-yellow trouser suit, chunky turquoise necklace and a pair of vintage platform sandals, with a new fringe cut into her sharply bobbed hair. The navy-and-white stripy dress that I eventually bought for today makes me look like a school-run mum in comparison; it comes to something when your seventy-something grandmother is more stylish than you are.

The ceremony was due to start at 3 p.m. but it's now ten minutes past, and inside the fairy-light-draped yurt that the bohemian woman in tie-dye who owns this garden calls 'the bridal bower', the bride is over halfway down a bottle of champagne with the father of the bride – well, the father of the bride's stand-in, at least. As Maggie's dad Jack died over twenty years ago she has asked if I will be the one to give her away. ('Not that I've ever been keen on the idea of being "given away",' as she said to me. 'I've always thought it makes the bride sound like a bag of old socks.')

For the past half hour Maggie and I have been sitting here in the bridal bower getting gigglier and sillier, peeking through a crack in the yurt and providing a running commentary on the wedding guests as they arrive.

'Here come Roger and Iris,' says Maggie. 'Hmmm, not sure about that hat, Iris. It's a bit "fruit bowl", isn't it? And ooh, look, here's my husband-to-be! Goodness, doesn't he look handsome in that suit? I *told* him pale blue was his colour. Brings out the colour of his eyes . . . Ah, now here come your mother and father, finally. Cutting it a bit fine, aren't they? Well, better late than never, Anthea . . .' I peer over Maggie's shoulder as Mum takes up her position on the front row in a cream coatdress and matching wide-brimmed hat, a pained smile on her face as she takes in the wind chimes tinkling in a nearby tree.

'She looks like Camilla Parker-Bowles at Glastonbury,'

mutters Maggie, which makes me snort champagne out of my nose.

'To Camilla Parker-Bowles!' I say, raising my glass.

'And all who sail in her!' cries Maggie.

Clearly any hope that the solemnity of the occasion might be observed has long gone.

You know, despite all my stressing I think it's actually a *good* thing that I haven't been able to bring a guest with me today, as it's meant that I've been able to spend this precious time with Maggie without having to worry about a plus-one. The most important thing today is supporting my beloved granny and, as I'm here on my own, I'll be able to spend more time being sociable and getting to know her and Derek's friends, which will be a far more valuable contribution than just hanging out with Milo.

Milo. The thought of him sweeps me up on a wave of happiness, which then a moment later dumps me on the shore leaving me with a bruised arse and sand in my bikini bottoms. We were getting on so brilliantly that I can't for the life of me work out why he so abruptly changed his mind about being friends. I reread his last email countless times, trying to decipher what those few brief words meant, and the only explanation I could come up with is that despite my lesbian facade he somehow got wind of the fact that I find him mildly attractive – okay, *very* attractive – and ran a mile, straight back to the safety of Luiza's glossy hair and nutcracker thighs. That email was so out of character that I've been half expecting him to get in touch this week, perhaps to tell me that he was rushing for a flight when he wrote it, but I haven't heard from him. It's such a shame, as he would have been a brilliant plus-one: I can picture him out there now amongst the other guests, dressed in some typically flamboyant outfit, charming my mum and chatting to the ukelele trio who will accompany Maggie up the aisle. I wish I could talk to him, try to smooth things over . . . Well, there's no point crying about it now: he clearly doesn't want to be in contact so that's that.

There's still no word from Flora either, although I guess that shouldn't be surprising after our last conversation and that lunatic voicemail I left her. Perhaps I was naïve to think we could be friends after what happened, but I'm convinced there's a bond between us, something that runs deeper than silly arguments, and I figured that would bring us back together in the end. I miss her so much that in my darker moments I wonder if perhaps I've got it wrong, and we *are* supposed to be a couple after all. I've been meaning to send her an email, to try to make things right, but every time I sit down to write it I remember that look she gave me before she disappeared off into the night, like she thought I was this pathetic loser. I always felt like she brought out the best in me when we were together, but I guess in that moment she saw me for who I really am.

On the bright side, at least I've managed to put the

whole Dan fiasco behind me. It only took a couple of days of moping for me to realise that I could never truly love a man who wears skinny jeans, and while a one-night stand might have been exciting in theory it would have been highly inconvenient to spend the rest of my working life at Eagle trying to avoid him. Perhaps I should have known he wasn't right for me by the hours I wasted trying to figure out whether he *was* right for me. What was it that Maggie said? When you meet your soulmate it will be simple, you'll just think: 'Oh, so there you are. What took you so long?' It certainly wasn't that straightforward with Dan, not by a long shot. Besides, my loss will be Jaye's gain. I phoned her last Wednesday, three days after the conference, by which time I was confident I could impart news of Dan's mega-crush without getting all weepy and woe-is-me – although she didn't call me back until the following day because she'd been in London, having her second audition with the Shoptabulous TV channel.

'I had to pretend to sell all these different things on camera, from beauty products to this *amazing* Spin 'n' Go Pro Mop,' she told me, her voice sparkling with excitement. 'It's not easy talking about cellulite cream for a solid ten minutes, I can tell you – although to be honest that mop would sell itself. Seriously, Perce, the Spin 'n' Go's sensational cleaning results on wood, stone *and* lino have to be seen to be believed. You can even use it on carpets!'

I eventually manage to get a word in about Dan, although compared to Jaye's excitement about Shoptabulous – 'And my agent reckons the job's in the bag!' – the news that she has a not-so-secret admirer causes a mere ripple of interest.

'How weird, I barely know the guy,' she muses. 'I've never even spoken to him.'

'Well, he's very keen. Get this – he thinks you might be soulmates.'

Jaye gives a honk of laughter, and I'm so glad to see she isn't taking this too seriously. The last thing she needs right now is to fall in love again – especially with Dan, whose intentions are, despite his protestations, questionable.

'So what do you think I should do, Perce?'

'Do you fancy him, from what you can remember?'

She thinks for a moment. 'Well he *is* hot. A bit on the short side, but hot.'

'Well, then I think you should meet him for a drink. It'll be good for you to be put on a pedestal and worshipped for an evening.'

'Okay then, I'll go for it,' she says after a bit more deliberation. 'But are you sure you're cool with this? Didn't you have a bit of a soft spot for him?'

'Yeah, he's cute, but not really my type,' I say quickly. 'I'll give him your number.'

They have arranged to meet tomorrow afternoon and I have been left with a warm glow of satisfaction from playing Cupid – although a tiny, evil part of me is secretly hoping that Jaye will ditch Dan after one date, leaving him heartbroken. No, that's unfair, he might have been a bit flirty, but it's not Dan's fault that I'm so rubbish at relationships. Other people make it look easy: they meet somebody, fall in love and get married, but I'm still struggling to get off the starting blocks. As far as I can tell the only other unattached people here today are Maggie's gay manager from Gap (who according to Maggie has a different boyfriend every week, so he doesn't count) and a couple of older widowed ladies, and as I watch the guests filing into the glade two by two, like animals into the ark, I can't help feeling like I've failed at one of the most basic purposes of life. Ridiculous, I know, but there's nothing like a wedding to make you feel conscious of your single status.

I take another peek outside the yurt and see Derek, who has been patiently chatting to the registrar, glancing at his watch. I think fifteen minutes is probably nudging the boundaries of fashionably late.

'Time to go,' I say to Maggie. 'Are you ready?'

She takes a final glance at her make-up and snaps her compact shut with a brisk nod.

'Ready,' she says, standing up with a smile. 'I love you, Percy.'

'I love you too.'

She looks at me for a moment, as if weighing something up. 'It will happen, you know,' she says.

'What will?'

'You'll meet a wonderful man and it will all fall into place, I promise you. You've just got to stop worrying about it and let it happen in its own time.'

Trust Maggie to know exactly how I'm feeling. Out of nowhere I feel a lump appear in my throat: don't cry, Percy, for God's sake! Thankfully I manage to hold it together, although clearly not convincingly enough to fool my granny.

'It's all right, my darling,' she says, putting an arm around me. 'I just wish I could give you the benefit of all my many years of experience and let you know that it's going to be okay. Because it really is, you know.'

I swipe at an escaped tear. 'As the father of the bride, isn't it supposed to be me offering you the wise, worldly advice?'

She pulls me a little closer. 'My sweet, beautiful Percy. I can't think of anyone I'd rather have here with me now.' She gives me another squeeze and then takes a final sip of champagne. 'And darling, the only advice a woman needs on her wedding day is never to iron a shirt. Once he knows you can iron – you're doomed.'

The ceremony passes in a beautiful blur. During their vows Derek cries, Maggie gets the giggles and everybody cheers when the registrar pronounces them man and wife and the ukelele trio strikes up Stevie Wonder's

'Signed, Sealed, Delivered'. After champagne and canapés in the garden, a double-decker bus whisks the guests to a nearby pub for the reception, where we dine on fish and chips and Maggie and Derek make a joint speech that produces more tears and laughter. It's a wonderful day filled with joy and happiness, yet I can't seem to shake the gloom that's settled over me. It feels like I have a tattoo on my forehead reading SINGLE AND CHILDLESS FOREVER, decorated with a small picture of a cat and a ready-meal lasagne for one. It doesn't help that at dinner I'm seated next to Clive, one of Derek's darts buddies, who is currently going through a divorce from his wife Judith, which he talks me through with forensic relish.

'So, are you married, Percy?' he asks, once he's finally finished slagging off Judith's cooking skills.

'Nope,' I reply.

'Really?' Clive regards me with interest. 'Boyfriend?'

'No, just . . . single.'

His eyes light up. 'So you're footloose and fancy-free then? Hot to trot?'

'I suppose so,' I say, draining my wine glass; Clive quickly refills it. 'Not that I ever do that much trotting.'

'I bet you have some fun though, don't you, Percy?' He raises his eyebrows and grins at me. 'You single career girls are *wild*.'

'Oh yeah, non-stop partying, that's me,' I mutter, stabbing at my chips.

With an enthusiastic leer, Clive shuffles his chair a little closer. 'I'm staying here tonight,' he says, lowering his voice. 'And I've got a very nice room upstairs. Queen-size bed, flat-screen telly, tea- and coffee-making facilities. How about the two of us get together later? We could have a party of our own, if you get my drift . . .'

I turn to look at him and he gives me a roguish wink, just in case I had any confusion about his drift. Now, Clive is probably in his early fifties with what I'd describe as a darts player's physique, but for a fleeting moment I'm ashamed to admit that I consider taking him up on his offer, my reasoning being that at least then I couldn't be considered a total flop with men.

Thankfully, however, I still have an iota of self-respect.

'Sorry, Clive,' I say, 'that would have been lovely, but I have a prior engagement.'

He grins, shaking his head. 'I knew it,' he mutters admiringly. '*Wild*.'

Thankfully, at that moment there is an announcement that the first dance is about to begin and I jump up, relieved to have an excuse to escape.

I get to the dance floor just in time to hear the opening notes of Nat King Cole's 'L-O-V-E' and see Derek lead Maggie out onto the floor. I watch as they dance together, lost in each other's eyes: Maggie looking not a day over fifty in her sunshine-coloured suit and Derek grinning like he's won the Lottery. It would be obvious even to a complete stranger that these are two people who are madly in love, yet never in a million years would you have put them together. Even Maggie didn't think they were right for each other when they first met. I remember her telling me the story of how Derek came into Gap and approached her to help him choose some socks. 'You could have knocked me sideways when he asked me out for a drink,' recalled Maggie. 'I thought he was rather handsome, but he was so much younger than me, plus of course he had that godawful tattoo. I mean, Kim Wilde, I ask you . . . So I turned him down, obviously.'

But then Derek came back the next day to exchange the socks for a different colour and asked Maggie out again, and when she said no again, he came back the following day on further sock-related business. A week and eight pairs of socks later, Maggie finally agreed to meet him for a quick drink, 'just to get him off my back,' but it took another six months for them to start properly dating. When I asked Maggie why it took her so long to make up her mind about him she said with a shrug: 'I was busy.'

There's a valuable lesson in that, I think, as I watch Derek dip Maggie backwards and lean down for a kiss. For as long as I can remember I've been scurrying blindly around like an ant without a single thought in my tiny ant-brain beyond MUST FIND A PARTNER, and anyone who's had the misfortune to cross my path has been pounced upon and dragged back to my ant-hole, whether or not they've actually even been an ant. It's almost as if I've been trying to *make* myself fall in love with people, no matter how unsuitable they might be, rather than getting on with doing something more useful – like, I don't know, maybe having a life? – and letting love happen in its own time.

As the next song begins and everyone surges past me onto the dance floor the swirling fog of thoughts in my mind begins to clear and I find myself wondering why I've been so obsessed with the idea of finding my perfect match. What's so great about being in a relationship anyway? Maggie and Derek might have struck gold, but it's far from a guarantee of happiness: I mean, look at Clive and Judith, or indeed Jaye and Stewie or Lou and Phil. Instead of spending all my time trying to fix my love life – something that is completely out of my control – I should be pouring that energy into aspects of my life that I *can* control. As I watch my fellow guests throwing themselves drunkenly around under the flashing lights of Dave's Mobile Disco I get a flashback to my moment of triumph on the dance floor during the conference weekend, when I was on such a high from the satisfaction of a job well done. I felt strong and powerful, as if I had achieved something really worthwhile, like, for example, Kofi Annan, or whoever it was who invented the Cronut. How amazing would it be if I had a job where I could do that sort of thing full-time? *That's* what I should be focusing on – developing my career – not moping over whether or not some bloke fancies me!

The opening notes of Beyoncé's 'All The Single Ladies' blast over the speakers and it feels like a sign, sending positivity shooting through me like electricity. Right, that's it. I'm not going to waste another moment stressing about my love life. I am going to embrace being single and concentrate on making myself happy, rather than waiting for somebody else to do it for me.

'How about a dance, sexy?' I look round to see Clive's belly jiggling in front of me. He looks nine months pregnant.

'Absolutely!' I say happily.

Clive is a terrible dancer and keeps trying to touch my bum, but I don't care. From now on, I vow to myself, as I nimbly shimmy out of the way of Clive's octopus arms, things are going to be different. I am going to be too busy becoming a kick-ass events-planning professional to have any time to think about love!

I can't put it off any longer: on Monday I'm going to bite the bullet and talk to Susannah about my job. There's no way I can go back to ordering paperclips and doing expenses, it's time for a new challenge – and if there isn't an opportunity to expand my career at Eagle . . . well, I'm just going to have to look elsewhere.

Then I feel a hand on my shoulder and spin round to see my mum.

'Sorry to cut in,' she says, eyeing Clive disdainfully, 'but could I have a quick word, darling?'

Apart from a brief hello Mum and I have barely spoken today – in fact, we haven't had a proper talk since that falling-out in Jarrold's fitting rooms – and as I follow her through to the quiet of the dining room, pursued by Clive's shouts of 'I'll be waiting here for you, hot stuff!', my euphoria of a few moments ago dissolves into nervous jitters. I really hope she's not going to give me another lecture about my love life, as I doubt she'll be thrilled to hear that Project Husband has been put on hold for the foreseeable future.

'I've been meaning to phone you,' she says, as we take a seat at one of the deserted tables, 'to apologise for what I said to you at Jarrold's the other day. I was wrong, and I want you to know that I fully respect your decision about Adam. I can't deny that I thought the two you made a wonderful couple, but, as your father reminded me, the only people who really know what goes on in a relationship are the two people inside it.'

Well, that's a pleasant surprise. 'Mum, it's okay, really,' I say. 'I shouldn't have shouted at you.'

'No, it was my fault and I'm sorry.' She glances quickly around as if to check we're not being overheard, then lowers her voice. 'Your father was furious with me when I told him about our conversation. *Furious*. I don't think I've ever seen him so angry. He told me that your love life was none of my business, and that I should support you in whatever you decide and however you choose to live your life, whether that involves having children *or* cats. And he's right, of course, I know he is, and I shouldn't have got involved, but I promise you that I've always had your best interests at heart.'

'I know, Mum.'

'I just want you to be happy, Percy,' she says earnestly, reaching for my hand. 'You're a wonderful girl and I just know there's a wonderful man out there for you – if that's what you want, of course,' she adds quickly, patting my hand. 'Now, on a different subject entirely, I read something the other day about this wonderful clinic in London, where all these busy career ladies go to get their eggs frozen, then simply . . . defrost them when they want to get pregnant, like a sort of wonderful fertility fridge!' She beams, her eyes bright. 'Imagine that, darling!'

'Amazing,' I say. She's trying her hardest, bless her.

'Anyway, I've kept a note of the address and contact details,' she goes on. 'You know, *just in case*. You never know when something like that might come in useful.'

She gives me a very deliberate look, and after a moment I break into delighted grin.

'But this is wonderful news! I had no idea that you and Dad were thinking about another baby. How exciting, I've always wanted a younger brother or sister!'

Her face crumples in panic and confusion. 'Um, no, that wasn't *quite* what I had in mind, darling. You see, I'm not sure that I'm still . . .' The penny drops. 'Oh yes, very funny, Perseus. Ha ha.'

We smile at each other and I feel a big soppy wave of love for her. I'm so glad we've made up. Mum's methods might be questionable at times (and at other times infuriating), but her heart is undeniably in the right place.

'Well, I suppose we ought to rejoin the throng, I promised your father a dance,' says Mum. 'Although quite how one's supposed to dance to *this* I'm not entirely sure . . .'

32

The next morning I wake early, still bubbling with optimism from the previous night, and jump as joyfully out of bed as if I'm starring in a Bodyform advert. I'm in such high spirits that I actually sing in the shower, something I thought people only did in bad eighties movies. Once dressed, I make myself scrambled eggs and a pot of proper grown-up coffee, then I get out my laptop and open a new Word document and save it under the heading 'Percy new CV'. If I'm going to have a meeting with Susannah about my career I need to be fully prepared.

As I gaze at the blank screen, my fingers flexing with anticipation over the keys, it occurs to me that I actually updated my CV not so long ago, when I applied for that job at Saboteur. Rather than starting from scratch, surely it would be easier just to polish that one up a bit? Yes, that makes far more sense; after all, apart from my conference-organising glory I haven't had many other CV-worthy achievements since then. Ice-climbing, of course, but that's about it.

I find the document and click it open; a moment later I recoil as my name appears written in 26 pt copperplate Gothic caps – PERSEUS ANDROMEDA JAMES – huge and menacing, taking up most of the screen. Wow, that's a rather bold statement. I remember thinking at the time that as Saboteur is such a cool company I should sex up my CV with some daring font choices and an edgy design. Well, I have no need for such flashy, attention-grabbing tactics now: my achievements will speak for themselves. I'll go for something capable and businesslike: Helvetica, perhaps, or good old Lucida Sans.

The first section of my CV is 'Education'. I skim through my academic achievements: 'A Level results . . . blah blah blah . . . Middlesex University . . .' That all seems fine: I actually look quite well qualified on paper.

Next up is 'Skills', which is where I need to slot in my events-planning experience alongside the 60 wpm touch-typing, proficiency on Microsoft Office Suite, excellent communication skills, clean driving licence and conversational Italian. (Well, if *'ciao'*, *'si'* and *'grazie'* aren't conversational, then I don't know what is.)

Finally we have 'Hobbies and Interests'. Now, from memory I might have exaggerated things a teensy bit here, but then who doesn't? Otherwise this part of everyone's

CV would just read: 'watching telly'. Right, let's have a look . . .

- Kite-surfing
- Krav Maga
- Banjo lessons
- Travel (particular interest in high-altitude trekking)
- Vintage cinema
- Cookery (specialising in the cuisine of Scandinavia)

Oh. My. God. What a catalogue of bullshit. The only vaguely truthful part is the bit about cinema – and I'm not even sure *Ferris Bueller's Day Off* falls into the vintage category. Staring at my list of imaginary hobbies, I don't know whether to laugh or cry; and then I think about that disastrous interview at Saboteur when I boasted about my crazy weekends clubbing, the trek I had planned to Tibet and my idea for a Scandinavian pop-up restaurant, and crying seems like the only option. What was I thinking? I seem to remember reading somewhere that it's illegal to lie on your CV – shit, I could have ended up with a criminal record!

On the bright side, perhaps I should give myself credit for making me sound so interesting. Imagine if I actually did all those things, rather than just pretending to? I'd be *fascinating*. People would be desperate to talk to me at parties. I'd probably have a blog and an Instagram account to document my amazing lifestyle, and I'd *definitely* have more than thirty-two followers on Twitter . . .

Then, with the force of a speeding truck, it hits me: what's stopping me? It's not like I've got a husband or kids to worry about. If I'd like to be the sort of person who has interesting hobbies and wild adventures then why the hell don't I just get on and *do* it?

Excitement bubbling up inside me, I take another look at the fantasy Percy's list of hobbies – and my heart promptly plummets again. Exactly where do I think I'm going to go kite-surfing in the city of Norwich? And Krav Maga just isn't one of those things you find being taught down your local leisure centre alongside Legs, Bums and Tums, is it? *Is* it . . . ?

With a flicker of hope, I type 'Krav Maga Norwich' into Google. At the top of the list of results is something called the Norwich School of Combat, whose website is illustrated with photos of black-clad ninjas knocking the crap out of each other. Further investigation reveals that by coincidence it is located a short walk from my flat – and they have Krav Maga beginner classes every Thursday night. Bingo! Before I can have second thoughts, I fill out the online enquiry form and hit Send. I'm still not sure *exactly* what Krav Maga involves, but it looks a lot more fun – and certainly far more useful – than Bikram Yoga. Could you fight off a hostile attacker using the half-lotus pose? No, you could not! Then I remember, with a pang of some emotion that I'd rather not analyse too closely, that Flora does Krav Maga too. She keeps popping into my mind and I keep having to shoo her away again, as it's too painful to dwell on our ruined relationship. Come on, Percy, pull yourself together . . .

Right, next on the list: banjo lessons. Well, first of all I'll need to get a banjo, obviously. After further googling I discover that you're looking at north of £150 for a decent banjo and there's a choice of four-, five- or six-string models. Hmmm, perhaps it's not such a good idea to jump straight in and commit to buying one without learning a little more about the instrument first. It's not like a banjo can be easily transformed into a coffee table, is it? Ooh, it looks like there's a banjo society that meets at a pub near my parents' house once a month. The web page features a picture of the society's chairman, a smiley man with a beard, and announces in large letters: 'From beginners to advanced, all levels will receive a ban-jovial welcome!' With a rush of enthusiasm I take down the details and make a note of the date of the next meeting in my diary, underlining it twice. Two weeks on Tuesday I shall be there, my beardy, waistcoat-wearing friend!

What's next? Ah yes, the high-altitude trek to Tibet. To be honest, my perfect break would involve little more than lying on a sunlounger, floating in the sea and drinking cocktails. The idea of a high-altitude trek to Tibet would register quite low on my fantasy holiday scale; in fact I have serious doubts over whether it could even be classed as a holiday. But it was as if I were guided by some invisible hand to include this on the fantasy Percy's CV – and if some higher power reckons that I should go on a high-altitude trek in Tibet, then who am I to argue?

I find a company that does three-week guided walks at prices that are more than a week in Spain but a lot less than two weeks all-inclusive in the Maldives, and click through the photos of Gore-Tex-wearing trekkers with flushed faces and broad smiles standing amidst some of the most jaw-dropping scenery I've seen outside a David Attenborough documentary: snowy mountain ranges, endless dusty plains, a lake of the most vivid emerald imaginable. It looks so exhilarating that I immediately fire off an email asking for the dates of their next trek. After all, one beach is much like another – but this place looks like it's on an entirely different planet!

Finally, I go onto Amazon and buy a selection of classic black-and-white movies on DVD and a Scandinavian recipe book, ticking off the last two hobbies on the list, then I sit back in my chair with a real sense of accomplishment. It might not seem like much of an achievement, just sending off a few emails, but it feels like I've taken the first steps on the road to a more exciting life. Who knows where these adventures will lead – and who I'll meet along the way? I've got that same giddy feeling that I used to have as a child before birthdays or Christmas, when you know something wonderful is just around the corner and the sense of anticipation is almost as thrilling as the event itself.

I reach for the coffee pot to top up my mug and realise it's empty. Hmmm, perhaps some of that giddy feeling is down to the five cups of coffee I've just drunk . . . Still, while I'm in this invincible mood there's something else I need to do.

I open a blank email, then begin: *Dear Flora* . . .

Before I can get any further, however, my doorbell rings. That's odd, I'm not expecting any visitors, and you don't usually get deliveries at eleven o'clock on a Sunday morning. I hesitate for a moment, wondering whether to ignore it, but then it rings again, for longer this time. Frowning, I cross over to the window and when I peek out I'm shocked to discover that my surprise caller is Lou. I pull my head in before she sees me; much as I'm glad she's here, the last time we met up she made it quite clear that she thought I was an idiot for splitting up with Adam, and since then she's blanked every attempt I've made to contact her. I've been trying to give her the benefit of the doubt, telling myself that there's bound to be a reason for her coldness – perhaps I'm about to find out what that is?

When I open the front door Lou greets me with the face of someone who fears she's about to get shouted at.

'Percy, hi.'

'Hey, how are you?'

'Oh, fine, fine . . .' She shrugs, giving the impression she's anything but. 'Is this a bad time?'

'Not at all. Would you like to come up?'

'Is that okay? I'd completely understand if you didn't want to have anything to do with me.'

'Don't be silly,' I say, ushering her in. 'Would you like a cup of tea?'

'That would be lovely, thank you,' she says, as we walk into the flat.

Usually Lou would throw herself on the sofa and start rifling through my pile of magazines, but instead she hovers awkwardly by the front door.

'Take a seat and I'll get the kettle on,' I say.

'Thank you,' she says, perching on the edge of the sofa. 'So, how have you been?'

'Good. Busy at work.'

Lou nods, glancing apprehensively around the room as I whip round the kitchen getting out teabags and mugs. She really does look very nervy, like she's going to make a bolt for the door at any moment.

'Right, the tea won't be long,' I say, sitting next to her and giving her a reassuring smile.

But she can't meet my eyes and instead looks down at her fingers, which are twisting at her wedding ring, and then she takes a deep breath as if getting up the nerve for a difficult task.

'Percy,' she begins, 'I have so much to tell you about

what's been going on that I don't know where to start, but first of all I need to apologise to you for being a total fucking bitch.'

I start to speak, but she holds up her hand. Her eyes look strangely bright, as if she's about to cry.

'Please, let me finish. I'm so ashamed of the way I've behaved towards you and hopefully once I've explained what's been going on you'll understand a little of why I've been so distant, but it's no excuse for treating my best friend like shit.' She brushes away a tear. 'I feel so terrible that I wasn't there for you when you were going through the break-up with Adam, I just hope that you can forgive me.'

'Shhh, it's okay, love,' I say, putting my arms around her. 'I've just been concerned about you, that's all.'

'Oh God, please don't be nice to me,' she howls, burying her head in my shoulder. 'That'll just make me cry even more . . .'

We stay like that for a while, until her sobs turns to sniffles, and by the time I've been to get the tea and come back again Lou has dried her face and is sitting cross-legged on the sofa, thankfully looking a little happier and more relaxed.

'Sorry about that,' she says, grimacing. 'I don't know what's wrong with me. I think I must be turning into Jaye.'

I grin, relieved to see a glimpse of the old Lou. 'Do you feel up to talking about what's been going on?'

She nods, pushing her hair behind her ears. 'So Phil and I have been having a few problems.'

'Yes, things did seem a little frosty between you during that Sunday lunch at Adam's.'

She cringes at the reminder. 'I'm sorry, it must have been so awkward – and you had your own issues with Adam to deal with as well.'

'It's fine, but I was worried about you. And then when you stopped replying to messages . . .'

Another grimace. 'You must have thought I was so bloody rude. I just didn't know how to cope with . . . Well, let me start from the beginning. I guess the problems really began two years ago, just after Alfie was born. I didn't tell you at the time but I really struggled with becoming a mum. The whole thing was such a shock: the sleep deprivation, leaky boobs, crazy hormones, the relentlessness of looking after this tiny, demanding baby . . .' She shakes her head sadly. 'I loved Alfie more than anything, but I was knackered, confused and, as time went on, I hate to admit it, but I was bored. It seemed to me like everyone else instantly loved being a mother, whereas I didn't love it at all – in fact at times I hated it so much that I felt like having Alfie was a terrible mistake.' She flinches, as if in pain. 'Isn't that an awful thing to say?'

I'm stunned; I always thought Lou had taken to motherhood as effortlessly as she appeared to achieve most things in her life. Sure, she grumbled occasionally about the dirty nappies and lack of sleep, but I had no idea she was so unhappy.

'Why didn't you say anything to us? We would have completely understood – Charlie complained non-stop when the twins were little, don't you remember? I wish you'd told us you were struggling, we could have helped.'

'Not my style,' she says regretfully. 'I was sure I could cope with it on my own. Anyway, I was worried that people would think I was an ungrateful cow, because really, what did I have to complain about? I had a gorgeous baby, a supportive husband, a beautiful home and enough money not to need to return to work. It's not exactly *a Greek tragedy*, is it? No, I assumed the negative feelings would pass in time, so I just got on with it.' She takes a sip of her tea. 'And the feelings did pass – or I learnt to live with them – but I think I was left with a kind of identity crisis. My job had defined me: I'd been successful in my career and people had respected me for it, but now that I was a stay-at-home mum – well, I know this is ridiculous, but I didn't feel valuable or important any more. And I felt *so* unattractive. When I looked in the mirror it was like my head was stuck on someone else's body – and whoever it actually belonged to had *really* let themselves go.' She widens her eyes for emphasis. 'My boobs looked like deflated balloons, I was literally covered with stretch-marks and as for . . . downstairs . . .' Lou drops her voice.

'In hospital they'd told me I'd had a second-degree tear, but nothing – and I mean nothing – could have prepared me for what it looked like afterwards. Honestly, Perce, it was like a fucking *bomb* had gone off down there . . .' We're both silent for a moment, as if out of respect for Lou's poor, ruined vagina. 'Anyway, Phil was supportive and said all the right things, but we were so busy with Alfie that we gradually became more like mates or co-workers. On the rare times we had sex we were just going through the motions: there was no spark, no romance – and that made me feel even more shit about myself. I was desperate to feel attractive and desired again, to feel like a woman rather than a mother.' She swallows uneasily. 'So I did something really stupid.'

'What did you do?'

She chews her lip, looking anxious. 'I joined Tinder.'

'Ah. Right, I see.' *Oh shit.*

'I would never actually have met up with anyone, honest, Perce, I just wanted to see if men still found me attractive. I figured I'd be on there for a week or so, just to get a bit of an ego boost, and then delete my profile, but right away I started getting all these flirty messages and it was so addictive, that buzz of discovering someone fancies you, that three months later I was still on there.'

'So what happened?'

Lou takes a breath and then slowly exhales. 'One of Phil's workmates saw my profile.' She shakes her head, as if marvelling at her own stupidity. 'What was I thinking? It was obvious I was going to get caught. Maybe, deep down, I actually *wanted* to. Anyway, this guy told Phil that he'd seen his wife on Tinder.'

I wince. 'And how did Phil take it?'

'About as well as you'd expect. He was devastated. He told me I'd betrayed him, destroyed our marriage and ruined our family. He kept going on and on about how we were meant to be a team, and asking how I could do this to Alfie.' She starts to cry again, softly. 'Anyway, all this came out the week before that lunch at Adam's, so you can understand why things were a little tense. Phil wanted to cancel, but I thought it would be better to try and carry on our life as normal. As you saw, it wasn't working.'

God, poor Phil – and poor Lou. What a mess.

'Phil's still struggling to deal with it,' she says, wiping her nose. 'We're going to a marriage counsellor, which has definitely helped, and we're getting there, slowly. I think at least he now understands why I did it, but it's going to take a long time for him to trust me again. Anyway, all this was going on, and then you finished with Adam.' She sighs heavily. 'I hate myself for being so unsupportive to you, but I think it was down to a combination of guilt over what I'd done to Phil and jealousy over the fact that you were now single.'

I gawk at her. 'You were *jealous* of me being single?'

She nods. 'It seemed to me that you had everything that I felt like I'd lost – a great job, a busy social life, the freedom to do exactly what you wanted without having to worry about a husband or a baby. It's no excuse for how I behaved, but deep down I think I felt it was unfair that you could just simply . . . step out of a relationship that wasn't making you happy, whereas I was, well, trapped.'

'But you wouldn't want to leave Phil. Would you?'

'No, not at all. But sometimes I'd really like *not* to be a wife and mother. Sometimes I'm so desperate to have my old life back again, and to be free to do exactly what I want when I want, that I feel like throwing a chair at the wall.'

I obviously look alarmed, because Lou gives a grim smile.

'I don't actually do that, Percy,' she says. 'I've started going running instead. It helps work out some of my frustrations, plus it might help with my bomb site of a body.'

We both sit for a moment, absorbed in our own thoughts, and then suddenly an idea of devastating brilliance pops into my mind.

'I know what you need,' I say.

'A brain transplant?' deadpans Lou.

'A girls' holiday! A few weeks away from your everyday life to remind you who you actually are. Your mum would be able to help Phil with Alfie while you were away, wouldn't she? I think a bit of space might be helpful for both of you.'

Lou nods slowly. 'Yes, that might be a good idea.' Then she looks at me, registering my state of about-to-burst excitement. 'Percy?' she says, narrowing her eyes. 'What exactly do you have in mind?'

I wait a few moments, eking out the suspense like they do on *Strictly* and *The X Factor*, and then I say in a dramatic voice: 'How would you feel about . . . a three-week trip to Tibet?'

33

EAT ME

by Melanie Martin

Oh delicious Michael Bublé
You make my heart rise like a soufflé,
You satisfy my soul
Like an all-you-can-eat buffet.

Oh gorgeous Michael Bublé
Your voice is sweet like sorbet,
It intoxicates my spirit
Like a glass of vintage Cabernet.

Oh sexy Michael Bublé
Bubblier than Perrier,
I want to smear you on my toast
Like chicken liver parfait.

'So what do you think?' Mel is perched on the edge of my desk, brows raised in expectation. 'Awesome, right?'

'Brilliant,' I say. 'Profound, yet punchy.'

'Yeah, well the competition's judges obviously thought so, because I only bloody won!'

'What? You're kidding me!'

'Nope.' She pumps her fist in triumph. 'In a month's time Michael and I will be getting married.'

'Um, wasn't the prize just to spend a day backstage with him? I don't think there was any *specific* mention of marriage, was there?'

She looks at me like I'm a lunatic. 'Of course there bloody wasn't, any nutter could have won it. As if they're going to offer the chance to be Michael's wife as a competition prize!' She shakes her head incredulously. 'But Michael and I are soulmates, so we'll obviously end up together. It's called *fate*, shithead.'

'Of course, but . . .' I hesitate, unsure whether I should mention the enormous tutu-wearing elephant dancing about the room. 'I don't want to put a dampener on things, but isn't he already married?'

Mel shrugs. 'We've all got baggage, right . . . ? Well, I can't waste my morning sitting here gassing with you,' she goes on. 'I've got a wedding dress to buy, and maybe one of those sexy negligee things for our wedding night. Laters, fucker.'

I watch Mel sauntering over to the lift, singing Bruno Mars' 'Marry You'. Actually, is Mel's relationship with Michael any more ludicrous than the imaginary romance I had with Dan? And if the idea of being soulmates with him makes Mel happy, then who am I to burst her Bublé? In fact, who's to say that they *aren't* actually soulmates . . . ?

'Morning, Percy, how was your weekend?'

I look round to see Susannah standing by my desk, newly arrived at work, and anxiety immediately starts to bubble away in the pit of my stomach. We chat about Maggie's wedding, but my mind is elsewhere: specifically, it's trying to work out how and when to broach the subject of my need for a new challenge in my career. It's not going to be the easiest conversation as I'm effectively saying that I'm bored of being her PA – although hopefully I'll be able to put it in slightly more positive terms than that. But just as I'm getting up the courage to mention that there's something I've been meaning to talk to her about and could we get together in her office later, Susannah says: 'Percy, there's something I've been meaning to talk to you about. Shall we get together in my office later – say, in half an hour?'

'Absolutely,' I say, masking my surprise by shuffling the papers on my desk in a businesslike fashion. 'Let's do that.'

'In summary,' I say with a smile, 'while I can't thank you enough for all the opportunities you've given me over the past few years, I hope you understand that I'm now ready for a fresh challenge. After my work on the conference I'm keen to gain more experience in events-planning, and I very much hope that there may be scope for me to achieve this while continuing my career at Eagle, where I've been so happy for so many years.'

Silence.

'Well, what do you think?' I ask.

More silence.

Then my reflection slumps its shoulders and I rest my hands on the sink, regarding myself unhappily in the mirror of the ladies' toilets. I thought that having a last-minute run-through of what I plan to say in the meeting with Susannah would be helpful, but instead I'm beginning to think that this whole career-change chat might be a terrible idea. No, perhaps I should just sit tight, shut up and count my blessings . . .

Then from somewhere inside me I hear a familiar little voice.

If moping was an Olympic sport, Perseus James, you would undoubtedly win gold.

Oh, hey, Brenda. Long time no hear.

Honest to God, woman, I am so sick and tired of your moaning! Just talk to Susannah, will you?

But what if she says there aren't any opportunities for me at Eagle? I can't very well go back to my old job after telling her I need a new challenge. I'll have to leave the company. It's a massive, scary gamble.

Always do what you're afraid to do.

That sounds familiar . . .

It's Milo's motto. You remember Milo, don't you, Percy? Handsome chap. Questionable taste in clothes. You have an almighty crush on him.

I do *not* have a crush on him!

You don't? Sorry, my mistake. Seeing as how you think about him the whole time I assumed you had the hots for him.

Well, you're wrong.

Clearly. But his motto stands. So stop fretting and talk to Susannah. Oh, and Percy, one more thing. I'm all for the trek and banjo lessons, but Krav Maga? Really . . . ?

A few minutes later I'm sitting in Susannah's office, settled in my usual spot on the sofa by the window, my CV cunningly concealed between the pages of my notepad, ready for The Chat.

'HobNob?' Susannah holds out a packet and I take two for pre-Chat fortification. 'How long have we been working together now, Percy?'

'Over four years, I think.'

She nods. 'It's a long time. And I couldn't have asked for a better PA.' A pause – and then her smile seems to waver slightly. 'Which is why what I've got to say to you next is so difficult.'

Huh? That sounds a bit ominous.

'There's something I need to tell you,' Susannah continues, 'and for the past couple of weeks I've been agonising over whether it's the right thing to do because it will mean losing you as my PA, and I can't imagine what I'll do without you. But as much as that prospect pains me, I don't think I have a choice.'

She shifts uneasily in her seat, much as you would do if you were the bearer of bad employment-related news, and I feel my insides lurch and heave as if I've just stepped off a rollercoaster. Bloody hell, she's going to fire me! I reach for my coffee, but my hand is shaking so much I abort before the cup even reaches my lips. Christ on a bike, why am I getting fired?

'Over the past year the board and I have been discussing various ways to improve client relations and something that has come up repeatedly is the need to have more corporate events, be that roadshows, seminars or client dinners. To that end, we've decided it is necessary to create a new role for someone to be responsible for developing this side of the business and, as much as I'm desperate to hang on to you as my assistant, I can't think of anyone in the company who'd be better suited to the position of Eagle's new Events and Marketing Manager than you, Percy.'

In my mind Susannah has been gradually morphing into Lord Sugar on *The Apprentice*, but the beardy frown and pointy finger promptly vanish.

'So . . . I'm not getting fired?' I say, before I can stop myself.

'What? God, no! You're a real asset to Eagle, why on earth would we get rid of you?' She smiles at me. 'So, in theory, would you be interested?'

Interested? I am so interested that it's taking quite a lot of self-control not to start jumping up and down on the sofa, Tom-Cruise-on-*Oprah* style.

'I'd need a little time to consider my options,' I say, trying my hardest to remain professional despite my euphoria.

'Of course,' says Susannah.

'But my initial thoughts are that it sounds very interesting indeed.' I break into an unprofessionally goofy grin. 'Thank you so much, Susannah, I really appreciate you giving me this chance.'

'You deserve it, Percy, you more than proved yourself with your work on the conference. We'd have to go through the formalities, of course, but the job's yours if you want it.'

Honest to God, pinch me! This meeting is turning out even better than I could have hoped in my wildest dreams.

'Oh,' she goes on, 'I'll need an updated copy of your CV, just to keep things official.'

I rummage between my papers and pull out a document, which I hold out to Susannah with a smile.

'Well, it just so happens . . .'

When she came over yesterday Lou and I decided to celebrate our renewed friendship by going out for dinner tonight – and Jaye and Charlie didn't need much persuading to come along too. It's been ages since the four of us went out together (I don't count that uncomfortable evening at the Wig and Pen shortly after I'd split with Adam) and when I arrive to find the three of them already sitting at a corner table, cracking up about something or other – Charlie, back to brunette again, her hair piled on her head and pinned with a silk peony, Jaye looking like an off-duty Victoria's Secret Angel, and Lou, her dark hair scraped back into a ponytail and pale skin flushed from laughing – I feel such an overwhelming rush of love for them that I have to stop myself breaking into the theme tune from *Friends*. *I'll be there for you . . . Cos you're there for me tooooo . . .*

The four of us have a lot of news to catch up on, what with Lou's Tinder scandal and my lesbian dalliance, and it isn't until after we've finished our starters that I get a chance to tell them about my new job.

'Ooh, don't tell us,' gasps Charlie, after I announce that I have exciting news. 'You're planning to have a sex change and want us to call you Bruce.'

'Yes, ho ho, very funny. No, you'll be pleased to hear that this is work-related news.' I sit up a little straighter. 'You, ladies, are looking at Eagle Insurance's new Events and Marketing Manager.'

'Oh, congratulations, babe!' Jaye leans over to kiss me, leaving a smudge of lip gloss on my cheek.

'Well done, Perce, that's fantastic,' says Lou, pecking the other side. 'And richly deserved.'

'A toast!' Charlie holds her beer bottle aloft. 'To Bruce's amazing new job!'

Then I notice Jaye's expression, which is one of barely contained excitement. 'On the subject of new jobs,' she says coyly, 'I have some news too.'

'Shoptabulous?'

She nods, eyes gleaming. 'My agent called me this afternoon to tell me they've offered me a twelve-month contract – I start on air next month!' She makes a '*scream!*' face.

After more hugs and kisses Jaye turns to me, clasping my hands in hers, her expression suddenly serious. 'Percy, I have so much to thank you for. If it wasn't for that pep talk you gave me I'd probably still be sitting in my bedroom watching old episodes of *Too Much, Too Young*, eating Haribo and pining for Stewie.' She gasps in delight. 'See, I can even say his name now without crying! STEWIE! StewieStewieStewie! My ex-husband Stewie, who's giving me a very generous divorce settlement!'

'Ooh, how much are you getting?' asks Charlie.

'Chaz, you can't ask that,' mutters Lou.

Jaye smiles serenely. 'Enough for me to feel able to wish him and the lovely Cliché every happiness together.' She turns to me again. 'Honest, babe, you really helped me to move on with my life. This amazing mantra I learnt at my

Buddhist prayer circle in LA to encourage blessings obviously played a part, but it was you that suggested I should contact my agent, so thank you.'

'My absolute pleasure,' I say – and then something occurs to me. 'Hey, how did the date with Dan go yesterday?'

'Ooh, I'd almost forgotten about that! It was . . . nice. We went for a couple of drinks and then he asked if I wanted to go for dinner, but I told him I already had plans.'

'Excellent work,' says Charlie, impressed. 'Keep him on his toes.'

'He's a sweet guy,' Jaye goes on. 'And I do fancy him. But he's very keen. I mean, like, slightly *too* keen. He sent me a WhatsApp before I'd even got home saying how much he enjoyed our date and asking if we could meet up again this week.'

'What did you say?'

'Nothing.' She looks rather pleased with herself. 'I haven't replied yet.'

'Way to go, Jaye!'

'I think I *will* see him again,' she muses, 'but I definitely want to keep it casual. Occasional sex might be nice, but I'll be far too busy with my career for a serious relationship.'

Just then our main courses arrive and I feel like a proud mum watching Jaye get stuck into her falafel wrap and chips (chips!); after all, this is the girl who just a few weeks ago wouldn't have eaten anything that wasn't essentially an organic, fair-trade lentil.

'Oh, Perce, I forgot to tell you,' says Charlie, wiping a smudge of ketchup from her chin. 'I was in Boots the other day and I bumped into Adam.'

The unexpected mention of my ex-boyfriend's name brings me up short.

'Oh yes? How was he?'

'He seemed really well. One of the first things he did was to ask how you were. I get the feeling he'd really like to hear from you.'

I just nod, unsure of how to react to this information.

'There's something else,' says Charlie, now looking a little uncertain. 'The thing is, he wasn't on his own. He was with a girl. Her name's Anna. I get the impression they're, um, seeing each other.'

Well, I wasn't expecting *that*. 'Ah,' I say. 'Right.'

I realise that all three of my friends are now staring at me, clearly concerned about how I'll take this bomb-shell.

'Guys, seriously, I'm *fine* with this.' At least, I *think* I am . . . 'So, what's she like?'

'She seems nice. Not half as gorgeous as you, obviously, but quite pretty, quiet, smiley. Just the sort of girl that you'd imagine Adam might go for.'

'Well, that's great,' I say brightly. 'I'm really pleased for him.'

And although I only said that because it was the sort of thing I thought I should say, I realise that I actually mean it. I *am* pleased for him: Adam's a lovely guy and he deserves happiness. Perhaps I'll drop him an email later in the week, just to say hello . . . Then I look around the table at the others, who are still watching me in a caring, sisterly fashion, and I'm engulfed by another wave of love for them.

'Aw, isn't this lovely, all of us here together?' I say. 'Makes me feel quite emotional.'

Jaye leans over and puts her head on my shoulder and I rest mine on top of hers, while Charlie blows me a kiss.

'Soppy sod,' Lou smiles at me. 'Actually, while we're having a warm and fuzzy moment, it might be a good time to mention a proposition that Percy and I have for you both.'

Jaye and Charlie look between us quizzically.

'How would you feel about a girls' holiday later this year? Specifically, what do you think about the idea of a trip to Tibet?'

Jaye gasps, her hands flying to her mouth. 'You are kidding me!'

'Nope,' I say. 'We're thinking about a high-altitude trek.'

'Oh my God, this is karma!' gushes Jaye. 'You know I mentioned that Buddhist mantra I've been chanting that helped me get the Shoptabulous gig? Well, Tibet is like the *birthplace* of Buddhism. I can go there and give thanks to the Buddha directly for his blessing!'

'It won't be very luxurious,' I tell her warily. (I know from experience that Jaye doesn't travel with a toiletry bag: she has a whole toiletry suitcase, plus another one for make-up.) 'We'll be camping, and you'll have to carry your own equipment. There'll be a certain amount of roughing it.'

Jaye looks at me like I'm an idiot. 'Uh, hello? That's *exactly* what Buddhism's about, dummy! Letting go of worldly possessions, freeing yourself of attachments and all that.'

'Yeah, which would obviously explain why the Buddha helped you get a job on a shopping channel,' mutters Lou. 'So are you in?'

'I am *so* in,' squeals Jaye.

'Excellent. Chaz?'

'Hell yeah. I'm always up for an adventure. I'm sure I can rope in my sister to help Jake with the twins.'

'Well, okay then. Tibet it is.' I look around the table, taking in my friends' eager faces. Who would have thought that a blatant lie in a disastrous job interview would set us all on the road to adventure? It just goes to show: very occasionally honesty *isn't* the best policy.

We talk late into that evening, making plans and googling pictures of Tibet, and it isn't until I'm walking home after saying goodbye to the others that I notice I have a missed call on my phone and a new voicemail. As I turn into my street, I listen to the message.

'*Good evening, Perseus, it's Theresa LeFevre here. I'm sorry to call you so late, but I couldn't wait to let you know the good news. We have found a delightful SoulDate match for you, and he – yes, as promised it is a he! – is keen to meet up as soon as possible. Would this Saturday afternoon in central London be convenient? If you could let me know I will make the necessary arrangements.*'

34

The bar is in Soho, hidden amongst the network of narrow streets between Oxford Circus and Piccadilly Circus. During the last quarter of an hour I have walked past three times, trying to make up my mind whether or not to go through with this, on each occasion hurrying by on the opposite side of the street with barely a glance into its darkened windows in case he's already inside. Seeing as I'm now ten minutes late, he probably is.

From the little I've seen, the bar (it's too trendy to have a name, just a door number) couldn't be more different to the American Bar of the Savoy Hotel where my first Soul-Date date took place. The peeling paint and exposed brickwork frontage give it a seedy, run-down air, although the shabbiness is clearly the result of a designer's artistic vision rather than years of neglect. It looks like the sort of establishment that serves cocktails in jam jars and employs staff purely on the basis of their tattoos. I feel way too old and untrendy for such a place – and I'm worried that means I'm too old and untrendy for who-ever's probably waiting for me inside, too.

There is a men's underwear shop next door to the bar and this time, rather than walk straight past again, I hover outside, pretending to browse in its window. The door to the bar is now just a few feet away from where I'm standing and, as I peer at the display of mannequins, my hand involuntarily slips into my bag and brushes the pale-grey folder that's inside, sending a shiver of nerves through me. My eyes flick towards the bar's entrance again. Come on, Percy, decision time: are you going to do this or not?

There's been so much going on over the last couple of weeks that I'd all but forgotten about the promise of my new SoulDate match, and when I listened to Theresa's voicemail on Monday night my immediate impulse was to phone her straight back and tell her that I'd changed my mind and wasn't interested in taking things further. No bloody way. For starters, the prospect of going on another date and then dealing with the fallout, good or bad, felt exhausting. Then there's the fact that I don't actually want a boyfriend – well, I certainly don't *need* one, anyway. With all the other exciting things happen-ing in my life there isn't room for a relationship: I really am too busy for love, just as I hoped to be. So after listen-ing to Theresa's message I went to bed convinced that I would call her first thing the next morning and say thanks but no thanks.

But then the next morning came and I began to feel a little less certain because really, what did I have to lose by agreeing to the date? A little self-respect, perhaps, if it was a total tits-up disaster, but apart from that there didn't seem any convincing reasons *not* to go, whereas the pro-date arguments included:

- It's free (Theresa agreed to pay my travel expenses)
- I don't have any other plans for the weekend
- In life you should always take the more interesting of two options
- Bradley Cooper???

So that's why I find myself here, standing in front of the windows of International Adonis checking out the, um, buckled leather jockstraps and the . . . Good God, what *is* that? It looks like a sort of gold lamé 'pouch', but what the hell do you do with those straps . . . ? I peer at it more closely, trying to work out exactly what goes where, then realise that there's a shop assistant standing on the other side of the window, watching me.

'Just shopping for my boyfriend!' I mouth with a grin.

He raises his eyebrows archly and it occurs to me that any potential boyfriend of mine probably would be unlikely to be International Adonis's target customer, unless I was a dating a gay stripper. So in the end it's actually embarrassment that makes up my mind for me and sends me scurrying into the bar.

Thanks to the moody lighting it's quite dark inside, but even though it's only mid afternoon it looks full: all the tables seem to be occupied and there are no free stools around the bar. I decide that I'll order a drink, identify my target and only then will I take out my folder: after being so wrong-footed on the first date with Flora I want to make sure I get the opportunity to check out my 'soul-mate' before he sees me, just in case there are any surprises. Be prepared, as the Scouts wisely say. I order an Aperol Spritz and while I'm waiting I scan the room, starting with the immediate bar area, and within a matter of seconds I see it: a grey folder, lying on the bar, just a couple of stools away from where I'm standing.

I look away again in shock. Oh my God, he's right here. Like, just a few feet away! After taking a few moments to compose myself I look back again – yup, that's unmistakably a SoulDate folder – and then, my heart hammering in my chest, I glance round to locate the folder's owner and find . . . nobody. In the place where a person should be there's just a jacket on top of an empty bar stool and a half-finished glass of red wine.

My brain immediately switches to Miss Marple mode. The jacket is made of brown leather: classic, inoffensive, expensive-ish. This tells me that he's probably not *very* young – it looks more like something a trendy dad would wear – and that he's either naturally cautious or else extremely thin, because it must be nearly eighty degrees out today. He's drinking wine, rather than beer or spirits, which suggests: 'man of distinction' and 'not a cheap-skate' – unless of course it's house red, which any idiot can order.

Right, so what does that give me? Mid-to-late thirties, not vegan, prone to feeling the cold, not completely skint. Hmmm. It doesn't exactly narrow things down, does it?

Just then my drink arrives and I refocus my attention on working out how much to tip the barman, and then examining the barman's extensive selection of tattoos, and by the time I've settled the bill with what I immedi-ately realise is a stupidly over-generous tip (maths has never been a strong point) I look round and realise with a jolt that the empty stool is now occupied.

First impressions: he's actually quite handsome – and I'm using the word 'handsome' deliberately here, rather than fit or hot, because this guy has the classic square jaw and Roman nose of an old-fashioned movie star. His col-ouring is Mediterranean – dark hair, dark eyes, olive skin – which might explain his choice of drink, and also his choice of jacket: if he's from somewhere hot it might feel quite chilly to him outside. I'm pleasantly surprised by how attractive he is, although this is quickly followed by a wave of anxiety that he's going to think I'm not attractive *enough*. He takes a sip of wine and then runs a hand through his hair, revealing a small hoop earring. Ah. I'm a bit 'bleugh' about men with earrings, but hey, it's hardly a deal-breaker; you can take out earrings, right? And I'm sure it doesn't take *that* long for the hole to grow over . . .

I'm jumpy with nerves, but force myself to reach into my bag and take out my folder and in that moment he looks in my direction, notices what I'm holding and his eyes seem to light up, which I guess is encouraging; he doesn't look actively repulsed, at least. As my nerves increase from a vigorous simmer to boiling point, he gets up from his stool and walk over to me and now here he is, standing in front of me: tallish, definitely dark and rather handsome. I smile, and from behind his back he produces a single red rose, which he holds out with a flourish.

'Is for you,' he says, in a deep, heavily accented voice, then grasps my shoulders and kisses me on both cheeks.

'Oh, thank you!' I say, flustered. 'How lovely. Gosh.'

We smile at each other for a moment.

'I'm Percy.'

He holds a hand to his chest. 'Enzo.'

There's another pause.

'Did you have far to come today?' I ask.

He frowns slightly. 'Sorry?'

English clearly isn't his first language.

'Where are you from?' I ask slowly.

'Roma.'

Ah, so he's Italian. That makes sense.

'I'm from Norwich.'

'Nohhrrreech?'

'*Si*,' I say, smiling.

'*Parli Italiano? Ah, che piacere! Siamo veramente anime gemelle!*'

I freeze for a moment and then shake my head. 'I don't understand, sorry.'

I shrug, Enzo shrugs and we smile at each other some more; hmmm, I can see this is going to be tricky. Then I notice a nearby table has just become free and gesture towards it, eyebrows raised, in the international sign for, 'Shall we go and sit over there?'

Thanks to the fact that Enzo's English is only slightly better than my Italian our conversation is faltering at best, but over the course of two Aperol Spritzes I learn that he is thirty-six and lives in Rome where he runs the family restaurant alongside his father, who is also called Enzo – at least, I think he is, but I might have got my wires crossed. Enzo Jr likes football, Formula One and Liam Neeson action films. He was once engaged, but has never been married, and hopes to have five – *five!!* – children, as he comes from a large family. Or perhaps he comes from a fat family – it's difficult to be certain from his hand gestures. This is Enzo's first time in London and he thinks it's a great city, but the coffee is '*disgustoso*'. He has come over for the weekend with his brother, whose name also seems to be Enzo – although *surely* one of us has got confused here – and they have been out sightseeing this morning, visiting Buckingham Palace and Niketown, which both Enzos enjoyed.

Despite the language barrier I get the impression that Enzo likes me: he's certainly very flirty, constantly touching my arm or leg and calling me *'Bella'*. He is intensely emotional, one moment talking softly about his deep love for the football team A.S. Roma and the next rocking back in his chair in hysterical laughter about . . . well, I'm not actually sure. But the point is, his manner is very un-English and very attractive. I find myself staring at his mouth, which is full-lipped and cartoonishly expressive, and wonder what it would be like to kiss it.

We're just comparing the merits of the films *Taken 1* and *Taken 3* when Enzo's phone starts to ring.

'Scusi, amore mio,' he says to me, and picks it up. *'Pronto?'*

I'm not sure who is on the other end of the line, but Enzo is talking very rapidly and animatedly, and listening to him sends delightful shivers down my spine that quickly find their way into my groin: he could be discussing tax planning or a violent bout of food poisoning and it would still sound sexy. But the conversation is going on a bit, so after a few minutes I slip off to the loo.

As I reapply my make-up in the mirror I lapse into a wonderful daydream. In it I am strolling through the sun-drenched streets of Rome, looking tanned and curvy, a dark-eyed baby balanced on each hip. I stop at a charming outdoor market to buy tomatoes and wild mushrooms, where I chat to the stallholders in fluent Italian. '*Ciao, Percy!*' they cry, as I sashay past the stalls like Sophia Loren. The scene then shifts to a restaurant garden at night-time where I am sitting beneath a vine-clad trellis drinking Limoncello with my handsome husband, who takes my hand and showers my fingers with kisses. 'I love you,' he murmurs, having learnt fluent English during our incredibly romantic long-distance courtship. 'You truly are my soulmate, *amore mio . . .*'

When I get back to the table Enzo tells me it was his mother on the phone and that she was asking all about me; from what I can understand he described me as beautiful and intelligent, which is nice. Then he says: 'Mama, she ask, "*Lei puo cucinare?*"'

I look blank and he pretends to chop, stir and taste.

'Cooking?' I ask, mirroring his gestures.

'*Si!*' Then he points at me. 'You, cooking?'

The penny drops. 'Ah, your mother wants to know if I can cook?' Enzo nods enthusiastically and I start to laugh. 'Very funny,' I say. 'Ha ha!'

But his smile falters slightly and he asks again, more seriously this time: 'You cook?'

Christ, he's not joking.

'Um, yes – *si* – I can cook.'

'*Molto bene*,' he beams, looking so relieved that I decide not to mention that my speciality is Hummus Surprise.

The delightful *Dolce Vita* fantasy that I've had in my mind is abruptly shoved aside by a vision of me sweating over a stove alongside a fat, frowning *mamma*, while waiters yell orders and five wailing children tug at my apron.

We get another round of drinks but the conversation is starting to flag – it's difficult to have much of a discussion when communicating mostly through sign language – and although alcohol would usually help things along, in this case it's just making us more confused. I certainly fancy Enzo, but I can't help thinking how much more of a connection I felt with Flora on our first date. Yes, there were some mortifyingly embarrassing moments, but in between the cringy bits the conversation flowed with an effortless ease, whereas with Enzo I almost feel like I'm playing a role: the bashful English rose to his Italian stallion.

The problem is that Enzo and I might well be soulmates, but it's impossible to tell because we don't speak each other's language. Ronan Keating might have thought that you say it best when you say nothing at all, but he's clearly never had to explain that he works in insurance and has just received an exciting promotion to the position of Events and Marketing Manager purely through the medium of mime. And okay, I love Italian food and I do think that Liam Neeson was brilliant in *Love Actually*, but it's not exactly overwhelming proof of our compatibility, is it?

While all this is going through my mind, however, something altogether less complicated is apparently going through Enzo's. His touches are becoming more lingering, his gaze more intense, and after draining the last of his wine he reaches for his jacket.

'We go now, Percy?' he asks, as he offers me his hand. 'To my hotel, yes?'

I hesitate for a moment. The idea of having sex with Enzo – because that's clearly what is on the cards – is very appealing, and I'm quite sure if I was in a different place in my life I'd be biting his hand off, not to mention other bits of him, but right now I just feel like I don't need the extra admin. I haven't got any clean clothes or a toothbrush with me, for starters, and what would we do after it was over? Sleep? My train ticket is a day return and I'd rather not have to shell out for another one tomorrow; Anglia's weekend prices are ridiculous. Eat? I don't have enough energy left to mime conversation all the way through dinner, let alone after vigorous sex.

To be perfectly honest, it all feels like a bit of a hassle. As for where the sex might lead, I realistically can't imagine having a long-distance relationship with Enzo. We could Skype, but the phone calls would be excruciating – and as soon as he discovered exactly how well I cook it would probably all be over anyway. No, I think it's probably sensible to part now with our dreams and dignity intact.

'I'm sorry, I have to get home,' I tell him. 'I've got to get the train to Norwich.'

He gives a shrug, as if to say, 'Fair enough,' and kisses me on each cheek.

'You come to Roma?' he asks, eyes smouldering, and he looks so gorgeous that I wonder if I'm being a total idiot turning him down.

'Yes, please,' I say – although I think we both know that's not going to happen.

As I walk along Oxford Street on the way back to the Tube I catch sight of my reflection in the window of Topshop and hold myself a little straighter. You are a strong, independent woman, I think. You don't need a man. I've said these words to myself before, but this time I really believe it. My reflection smiles back at me and I feel wonderfully light and happy. Life is good, Percy.

What I do next is almost involuntary – it certainly isn't something I do consciously, otherwise I wouldn't have the guts go through with it – but it is something I feel I must do, as natural as walking or breathing. As if on autopilot, I take out my phone and dial a number. It rings for a while and just as I think it's going to go to voicemail, it's picked up.

'Hi, it's Percy.'

There's a pause. 'I know. Your name comes up, obviously.'

'Oh right! Of course, silly me. So how have you been?'

'Fine. I've been travelling a lot.'

'Great! Anywhere interesting?'

'Um, what's this about, Percy?'

'Well, I've been thinking about you and there are some things I need to say to you, but I'd much prefer to do it face to face. I know this is probably a long shot, but how would you feel about meeting up?'

There's a long pause, so long that I begin to think we've been cut off, and then just as I'm about to give up and end the call I hear: 'Okay, then. How about next Sunday?'

35

'Are you sure this is the right address?' I peer doubtfully out of the taxi window. I wasn't expecting something so grand. Or so enormous.

'This is the address you gave me, love,' says the driver, stretching his arm back out of the window to open my door, in a gesture that clearly implies, 'Get out of my cab now.'

'Okay, well, thanks very much.'

As soon as I slam the door the taxi speeds off, leaving me stranded on the pavement like a lowly country mouse who's ventured up to the Big Smoke to visit his wealthy relatives. All that's needed to complete the picture is for me to be carrying one of those spotty handkerchiefs on a stick.

I'm standing outside a house in a secluded, cobbled mews, a couple of blocks to the north of Hyde Park. There is a selection of very expensive-looking cars parked along the street, plus a beaten-up Mini, which looks as out of place as a Shetland pony in a field of racehorses.

I double-check the address on my phone one more time – yes, this is definitely right – and then wonder whether I should have a last-minute make-up check, but this looks like the sort of place that has multiple cameras trained on the entrance monitoring for undesirables; I'm probably being watched by a roomful of black-clad security personnel right this second. So instead I stride up to the glossy black door, outwardly breezily confident, and press the bell.

Nothing happens for quite a long while, but then this house looks so large it probably takes ages to get from one wing to another – either that, or the security guards are busy scanning my retinas or something – and I'm just wondering whether I should ring it again when the door swings open.

'Hello,' I manage after a few moments, my heart hammering away in my chest. 'Thank you so much for agreeing to see me.'

With frosty composure Flora folds her arms and gives me the briefest of smiles. 'Well, Percy, if you want to talk you'd better come in.'

Struggling to keep my nerves in check, I follow Flora down a corridor and into a wood-panelled living room decorated with oil paintings, tartan sofas and a coffee table covered in stacks of leather-bound books. There's even a set of antlers hanging over the fireplace, from the tip of which is dangling a fragment of tinsel: it looks like the inside of a Scottish castle as recreated by a Hollywood set designer. When I imagined where Flora lived it was somewhere modern and minimalist, not Hogwarts.

'Make yourself comfortable,' she says, gesturing to one of the huge sofas. 'Coffee?'

'Yes, please.' I take a seat, sinking so far into the bosomy cushions my feet are dangling off the floor. 'Quite a place you have here.'

'It's not actually mine,' says Flora, pouring out cups from a cafetière that's waiting for us on the table. 'Well, it belongs to my family. Our main home is in Scotland, but my parents moved to London after I'd left for university and my younger brother and sister grew up down here. Mum and Dad are now back in Perthshire, but they kept hold of this place and we all use it whenever we're in town.'

She says 'this place' as if it's some cramped bedsit, but the house must be worth several million at the very least. I had no idea Flora was from such a wealthy family; it doesn't make me feel any more relaxed.

'So is this where you stay when you're working in London?' I ask.

She nods. 'Although it looks like I might be spending less time here now, because I've just been offered a job in San Francisco.'

'Oh, congratulations,' I say, my heart sinking at the thought of her moving to the other side of the world.

'I'm still trying to decide whether to take it. It would be a big move.'

Please don't go, I want to say – but instead I ask about the new job, keeping the conversation skimming over the surface to avoid tackling the challenging depths beneath. After a few minutes of polite chit-chat, however, I realise we're running out of things to say to each other. Flora obviously notices it too, as she abruptly asks: 'So, Percy, what was so important that you needed to speak to me in person?'

Right, here we go: crunch time. I try to reposition myself on the sofa, as it's hard to have a dignified conversation when you look like a pixie perched on top of a toadstool, but I'm just swallowed up further by the cushions.

'Well, first of all I need to tell you how sorry I am about the way I handled our relationship. I know I screwed up badly, but I swear I never set out to deliberately deceive you.'

'Including the time you told me your mother was in hospital with malaria?'

My cheeks feel uncomfortably hot. 'Yes, that was extremely stupid, but I was so thrown by the fact that you were a woman that I panicked and the malaria thing just sort of . . . popped out. And then as I got to know you I started to have strong feelings for you, and I wasn't sure whether that those feelings meant I actually *was* gay. I mean, Theresa LeFevre certainly seemed to think I was, and then we had that kiss at your party . . .' I tail off, remembering my hurricane of feelings on that fateful night. 'Anyway, by that point I liked you so much that I was worried that if I *did* tell you the truth about me you'd either run a mile or think I was a nutter, and to be honest neither option seemed particularly attractive.' I shrug hopelessly, struggling to find the right words. 'Honestly, Flora, throughout all of this my intentions have been honourable, even if my actions have been . . . um . . .'

'Dishonourable?'

I cringe. 'Yes, but please don't think I'm a terrible person, in spite of that.'

Until now Flora has been listening to me with a neutral expression, so I have no idea how she's taking any of what I'm saying, but now the ghost of a smile appears on her lips.

'It's okay, Percy, I don't think you're a terrible person. And perhaps I shouldn't have stormed off like that in Norwich, but I genuinely thought we had a shot at a future together. Sure, I got the impression you were a little uncertain, but I put that down to the fact that you'd just come out of a long-term relationship. The news that you were straight came as a bolt from the blue, to put it mildly.'

'I know, I'm so sorry.' I feel a prickle of shame and stare at my feet.

'But I don't actually blame you for what happened between us.'

I look up at her with a start. 'You don't?'

'No. Well, not entirely. In my opinion SoulDate are the guilty party for creating such wildly unrealistic expectations. In fact, I've been tempted to report them for false advertising. Claiming they can find your soulmate' – she gives a cynical snort – 'what a load of nonsense.'

I frown. 'You think so?'

'Well, don't you?'

This has completely thrown me. It's fair to say that I've had my doubts about SoulDate, but I've been convinced that the way I feel about Flora proves that we have a deeper connection than just friendship, which would suggest that there's something to Theresa LeFevre's algorithms after all. But if Flora thinks it's all bollocks – well, that must mean she doesn't think there's any special bond between us at all. Perhaps, in her eyes, I'm just some loony she once dated and now wants nothing more to do with! Suddenly, the importance of remaining dignified and finding exactly the right words flies out of the window, and the only thing that matters is making Flora understand how I feel.

'All I know,' I say fervently, 'is that I think you're amazing. You're funny and clever and brilliant and I love spending time with you; in fact I've sometimes wondered why somebody as incredible as you would want to hang out with me, but we just seem to click – well, I thought we did, anyway. And this might sound crazy, but I think that on some level we're meant to be together and although I know we can't be *together* together, I'm sure there's something between us – some sort of connection – and it would be like defying nature if we weren't part of each other's lives. Don't you think so? Because I really do.'

I'm aware that I'm babbling and Flora is looking at me like I'm foaming at the mouth, but I don't care, I just need to get the words out.

'It's like you're Ferris Bueller and I'm Cameron Frye,' I say, warming to my theme. 'Ferris might be dating Sloane Peterson, but who's the first person he calls in the film? Who's his go-to pal? Cameron.' I slap my thigh for emphasis. 'So yes, maybe SoulDate *is* a load of shite and perhaps we aren't the most compatible people in the world, but whether or not that's true I can honestly say you make me want to be a better person, to live a more exciting life, to climb mountains – quite literally, as it happens, because it's largely thanks to you that I'm going on a trek to Tibet later this year, but that's another story . . . Anyway, the reason I came here today was to apologise but also to tell you that I think we actually could be soulmates, just with the emphasis on *mates*, and it would be a terrible, terrible shame if we never saw each other again. And that's, um, it.'

I come to a wild-eyed, shuddering halt; for a moment neither of us speaks, and in the silence I think I can hear a door shut upstairs (butler?), then Flora takes a deep breath and slowly exhales. I'm half expecting her to tell me to get the hell out of her gigantic tartan house, but instead she says: 'That was quite a speech.'

'I meant every word,' I say stoutly.

Flora leans towards me, an earnest look on her face. 'Percy, just because I'm not sure whether SoulDate does what it claims, it doesn't mean I'm questioning *our* compatibility. I do actually agree with you on that issue, as it happens, and once I calmed down after Norwich and had a chance to think things through I could see that although we weren't necessarily meant to be lovers, we did have the makings of a very special relationship.'

'So . . . does that mean we can be friends?'

She breaks into a smile. 'I hope so. I've missed you these past few weeks.'

'And you think you can forgive me?'

'Consider yourself forgiven.' Then Flora comes over to where I'm sitting and wraps her arms around me in a hug. 'You are a righteous dude, Percy James,' she says, and with that line from *Ferris Bueller's Day Off* – *our* film, as I've begun to think of it – relief floods over me like warm syrup on ice cream, melting away the tension between us, and I realise that I haven't lost her after all.

We stay like that for a few moments, locked in a hug, then Flora sits next to me on the sofa, sensibly tucking her legs beneath her to avoid the pixie-on-a-toadstool effect, and the atmosphere between us is transformed, like when the sun comes out after a storm. Flora tells me more about San Francisco – it turns out she's flying there later today for further discussions – and then shyly reveals that since we last spoke she's been on a couple of dates with a woman she met through work. Apparently the fact that this woman, Jessica, lives in a place called Palo Alto just outside San Francisco has nothing to do with Flora's interest in taking a job there. Absolutely nothing at all, Flora insists – although the way she keeps dropping Jessica's name into our conversation tells a different story. Yet I'm relieved to discover that I don't feel even the slightest flicker of jealousy, just excitement about their budding romance.

From somewhere in the room an unseen clock chimes midday.

'I should get going,' I say. 'You'll need to get ready for your flight.'

'Let's have another coffee first,' says Flora. 'I want to hear your news.'

I smile. 'Okay, then.'

Flora gets up from the sofa, picks up the empty cafetière and starts for the door, but before she gets there I hear it click open and a man's voice says: 'I'm just heading out, Flo – oh, sorry, I didn't realise you had company . . .'

Then I look round to greet the surprise newcomer and the world turns upside down as I find myself face to face with Milo.

36

'Percy?' Milo is frozen to the spot, staring at me in open-mouthed shock. He looks different: more tanned than when I last saw him and his hair's been neatened up a bit, but the biggest surprise is how ordinary he's look-ing. There's no fancy dress costume, no extreme sports gear, just a plain white T-shirt and jeans – and I've got to say, ordinariness really suits him. Without any sartorial distractions you can focus on his broad shoul-ders, the perfectly symmetrical 'T' shape formed by his brows and nose, the gold flecks in the stubble across his jaw . . .

'You two know each other?' Flora asks incredulously, as I drag my eyes away from the glorious, shocking vision that is Milo.

'*You* two know each other?' I ask, glancing between them as my brain races around frantically trying to pro-cess this bombshell.

'Flora's my sister,' says Milo. And now I can see a resemblance: the same wide-apart eyes, similar colouring (although his hair is much lighter) and that open, easy smile.

'But you're Scottish,' I say to Flora, then turn to Milo, 'and you're . . .'

'Scottish too,' he says.

'You don't sound it.'

'No, I grew up in London. Flora had left home by the time we moved down here, but I was still at school so I lost my accent pretty quickly.'

'And you . . . you have different surnames.'

'Apparently "Milo MacDonald" doesn't say "extreme sports journalist",' says Flora, rolling her eyes, and I get a glimpse of their relationship: the big sister teasing her little brother.

'It just sounds a bit posh,' says Milo defensively. 'Turnbull is our mother's maiden name,' he explains to me. 'But how do you and Flora . . . ?'

I presume I must look embarrassed at the mention of our relationship, because his eyes slowly widen as the realisation dawns.

'Good God, Flora's not *Martha*, is she . . . ?'

'Who the hell's Martha?' asks Flora. 'And will somebody please tell me how *you* two know each other?'

'Milo helped me when I got mugged outside your party.'

'You got mugged?' Flora looks alarmed, and I realise that I never mentioned to her what happened. So much else was going on, what with my split from Adam and the subsequent emotional uproar, that it got forgotten.

'I was getting out of a taxi on the way to your do,' explains Milo, 'and came across Percy lying on the pavement while some arsehole made off with her bag.'

'Jesus, were you hurt?' asks Flora.

'Oh no, just a bit shaken. Milo was brilliant, taking me back to the station and lending me money to get home.'

'Ah, so *that's* why you never made it to the party.' Flora raises her eyebrows at her brother. 'Luiza was furious.'

'Yes, I know,' mutters Milo.

'Oh God, I'm sorry,' I say. 'I hope I didn't cause too much trouble . . .'

'Don't be silly,' says Milo. 'I wasn't really dressed for black-tie and anyway, I wanted to help you.'

'This is unbelievable,' marvels Flora, shaking her head. 'So the two of you kept in touch, then?'

Milo and I look at each other, then he turns to his sister and says, almost under his breath, 'Flo, Percy is the mystery girl I mentioned to you the other day.'

She looks blank for a few seconds and then her eyes grow enormous. Oh God, what's he been telling her about me? That I've been hassling him to meet up? That I've been *stalking* him? Shit, what if Flora thinks I was hitting on Milo while she and I were seeing each other – or worse, that I 'dumped' her because I fancied him? I'm desperate to put the record straight, to reassure both of them that

I've only ever thought of Milo as a friend, but judging by the meaningful glances shooting between them they seem to be having some sort of unspoken conversation, in the way that siblings often can, and it would be rude to interrupt. (Besides, I think, as I catch myself admiring the curve of Milo's biceps under his T-shirt, strictly speaking it would be a lie to say I've only ever thought of him as a friend.)

'Well, well, well, this *is* an interesting situation,' says Flora, turning to me with a smile. Now the initial shock has subsided, she looks far more relaxed than both Milo and me; in fact, her tone suggests that she's finding this whole thing quite funny. I'm just relieved that she doesn't seem to think I've been stalking her brother.

'Right, I'm going to make that coffee,' she goes on, giving Milo, who is still frozen by the door, another significant look. She is clearly communicating something of great importance with that single raised eyebrow. 'You two have things to discuss,' she adds pointedly.

I watch as Flora leaves the room, desperately wishing she would stay. Christ, this is such an awkward situation. The clear subtext of Milo's last email was that he didn't want to see me again, yet now here I am sitting in his parents' living room and he has no means of escape. Surely he must be feeling uncomfortable too? As he hovers by the door, running a hand nervously through his shaggy hair, he certainly looks it.

'I'm so sorry about this,' I say. 'I had no idea, obviously. Would you like me to leave?'

'You have nothing to apologise for, Percy,' he says quietly – although I notice that he doesn't answer my question.

Milo hesitates by the door a little while longer and then he starts walking towards where I'm sitting and for a crazy, wondrous moment I think he might be about to take me in his arms, and I imagine pressing my face into the warmth of his neck, drinking in his scent and feeling his hands on me, but instead he takes a seat at the opposite end of the enormous sofa as far away from me as possible, like he's afraid he might catch something. We sit in silence for a little while, both of us looking anywhere but at each other – and for the first time I notice the array of silver-framed family photos, many of which feature a gangly teenage Flora with two white-blonde children, obviously Milo and their little sister – but then he turns to me and I'm relieved to see he's smiling.

'So you're the crazy fake lesbian, then?'

I bury my face in my hands, mortified. 'Did Flora mention me?'

'Don't worry, only in passing. I don't see Flo that often and when we do get together she gets so tired of hearing about my disastrous relationships that we have an unspoken vow never to discuss our love lives in any detail. She didn't even tell me your name – obviously – otherwise

I'm sure I would have twigged it was you.' Milo shoots me a grin. 'I don't know that many sexually confused Percys.'

I feel my cheeks flush, partly because I'm ashamed of how I behaved, but also because when Milo said the word 'sexually' I'm afraid to admit that my insides quivered like a very horny jelly.

Thankfully, he moves the conversation on before I say or do something stupid, like take a lunge at him.

'So what happened between you two?'

Christ, this is embarrassing . . . 'Well, basically I met your sister and we hit it off, but Flora assumed I was gay and I was too embarrassed to tell her that I wasn't, and then I started to think that perhaps I *might* be gay – because you do hear about women falling for other women after only being with men, don't you? – and by the time I realised that I definitely wasn't we'd already been on a couple of dates.' I pull a face. 'I'm afraid I didn't handle things very well.'

Thankfully Milo doesn't look too disapproving. 'Well, at least it's nice to talk to someone whose love life is even more complicated than mine.'

'How *is* the Brazilian supermodel?'

'We split up a few weeks ago.'

'Oh, I'm sorry . . .'

'Don't be. It was for the best, we were never a long-term prospect.'

'Was it your decision?'

Milo looks away, fiddling with his watch strap, clearly uneasy at the way the conversation is heading.

'Sorry, it's none of my business,' I say quickly.

'No, it's okay . . . I think I might have mentioned to you that when it comes to women I've always had a type?'

I nod. Leggy, dark-haired, a bit unbalanced: I clearly remember because his type was nothing like me – not physically, anyway.

'Well, out of the blue I found myself attracted to some-one who wasn't anything like that.' More watch-fiddling. 'Nobody was more surprised than I was. *This is it!* I thought. *This is where I've been going wrong all these years!* So I decided to finish things with Luiza, because our relation-ship had virtually been hanging by a thread anyway, and planned to make a move. But then this amazing woman who I felt might be the answer to everything told me that she was in love with another woman, so it looked as if I'd swapped one unsuitable type for an even less suitable one.'

I frown, trying to take all of this in. Surely he can't mean . . . ? No, I must have the wrong end of the stick.

'When I first met you, Percy,' Milo goes on, 'I thought, "Hey, isn't this great, being mates with a girl without sex getting in the way." We got on really well, didn't we?'

I flinch at his use of the past tense. 'Yes. Yes, we . . . did.'

'But then the next time I saw you – when we met up in

Norwich – I realised that perhaps I didn't want to be mates with you after all. Not *just* mates, anyway.'

Milo looks up at me through his floppy fringe, his eyes wide and filled with meaning, and something inside me turns cartwheels.

'Are you saying . . . you were attracted to me?' I stammer, not quite believing what I'm hearing.

Milo breaks into a grin. 'Do keep up, Percy. I was all set to ask you out for dinner after the ice-climbing, but then you told me you were swearing off men, so . . .' He tails off, ending in a shrug.

'But I only said that because I didn't want you to think I was hitting on you!'

'But you weren't hitting on me,' says Milo, furrowing his brow. 'Were you?'

I need to change the subject. 'That last email you sent me, after I invited you to my granny's wedding . . .'

'Was unforgivably abrupt, yes, and I apologise for that. But – God, this sounds corny – I didn't want to be just friends with you. I thought that if there wasn't a chance we could be together, because you were with a woman, it would be better not to see you at all. Less painful.'

'But I wasn't with a woman,' I say quietly. 'I'm not with anyone.'

'So it would seem,' murmurs Milo, his eyes fixed on mine.

I'm in a daze, my head spinning as I try to take all of

this in. Milo fancies me! Or, at least, he *fancied* me: after discovering how I lied and mucked his sister around it's highly unlikely that he'll want anything more to do with me. Christ, I'm an idiot. All that time I was frantically trying to hide the fact that I was attracted to him, *he* was summoning the courage to ask me out for dinner! Unsure whether I'll ever be this close to him again, I take the opportunity to drink in every detail of his appearance: the freckles sprinkled over his cheekbones, a tiny scar on his left cheek, his pale-blue eyes, which are usually filled with laughter but are now fixed on me, steady and intense. Perhaps he thinks I'm staring, but I don't care: I have to commit every bit of him to memory. Now the floodgates have opened, I want him so much I can barely breathe.

Milo opens his mouth to say something and my heart leaps, desperately hoping he's going to tell me that he still feels the same way, but at that moment the door opens and Flora breezes in, making us both jump.

'Right then, kids, what have I missed?' she says, looking between us with a smile.

For a moment during the conversation with Milo I got the impression that something magical, possibly life-changing, might be on the cards, but as soon as Flora arrives the atmosphere instantly lightens and it's as if our heart-to-heart never even happened. I'm still reeling from the earth-shattering discovery that once upon a time Milo fancied me (seriously, how *did* I miss that?) but he already seems to have put the whole thing behind him and is now laughing with Flora about one of the mugs that she's brought in with the coffee, which was apparently given to him by some elderly great-aunt who . . . Oh, I don't know, I'm so floored by what's just happened that I'm struggling to follow the story.

Milo and Flora. Flora and Milo. Emotional turmoil aside, I'm entranced by how similar they are; in fact it now seems bizarre that I never noticed it before. They have the same laugh, an identical way of widening their eyes when they're making a point, the same fluttery hand gestures. Sporty, posh and ginger: they're like the Spice Girls, minus Baby and Scary (although Flora *was* quite intimidating earlier). It's as if Milo is the male version of Flora and vice versa . . . Hang on a sec, if that's the case, and Flora is indeed my soulmate, then shouldn't it follow that Milo is as well? To a degree, anyway. I'm not sure about the exact statistics, but surely siblings must share a lot of DNA, especially peas in a pod like these two. No wonder Milo and I got on so well – we're bloody soulmates! Soulmates-in-law, at the very least . . .

I look at him again, his eyes crinkling with laughter, and feel an actual twist of pain. Didn't Maggie tell me I'd meet a wonderful man and it would all fall into place?

Well, it turns out she was absolutely right. It's just a shame that the wonderful man in question thinks I'm a – what was it he called me earlier? – a crazy fake lesbian. Yes, it's a terrible, heartbreaking shame.

Then Flora gives a catlike stretch and glances at her watch. 'Shit, sorry to break up the party, folks, but I need to finish packing.'

'Of course,' I say, struggling to get up from the quicksand of the sofa. 'I should get going anyway.'

Milo stands too, as polite as ever. 'Are you sure? You're welcome to stay a while longer.'

'Thanks, but I better get home.'

He and Flora glance at each other, clearly having another of their secret sibling chats.

'Well, I'll see you out, Percy,' says Flora, heading for the door.

Milo and I briefly lock eyes; he looks as embarrassed as I feel.

'It was great to see you, Percy,' he says.

'You too.' I hesitate for a moment longer and then give an awkward wave and scuttle out of the room. Not to be melodramatic, but as I follow Flora back down the long corridor past more family photos and an enormous oil painting of a hunting scene I feel like I'm walking away from my future. *Run after me, Milo!* I urge him via telepathy. *Don't let me go!* Unsurprisingly, however, by the time we get to the front door he's yet to appear.

'Well, that was all rather unexpected,' says Flora, opening the door.

'It certainly was.'

She smiles. 'I'm so glad you got in touch again.' Then she puts her hands on my shoulders and says: 'Listen, Percy, whatever happens I'm fine with it, okay?'

I look at her quizzically, and she gathers me to her for a hug. 'You have my blessing,' she whispers into my ear, then kisses my cheek and pulls away. 'I'll call you when I get back. Let's go for dinner.'

'I'd like that,' I say, smiling, but all I can think is: her blessing for *what*?

I start walking along the cobbles towards the main road, glancing back for a final wave to Flora before she shuts the door and I'm left alone with my thoughts, the row of supercars and several doves that are pecking at something on the cobbles. Even the pigeons round here are upmarket. I half-heartedly attempt to will one of them to poo on the tank-like black Bentley I've just passed, which I know is childish, but in my defence my heart feels like it's just been through the spin cycle on a washing machine. On the one hand I'm thrilled that Flora is back in my life, on the other there's Milo and the thought of what could have been. The last thing I need right now is a relationship, but I don't ever remember feeling so sure about someone, so convinced that we would be right together. Well, that ship has sailed, I think miserably as I reach the main road and glance around for the nearest bus stop.

'Percy, wait!'

I spin round and see Milo jogging towards me, sending the doves scattering up into the air, like a scene from a movie. Somewhere inside me a tiny flame of hope flickers into life.

'This might be completely inappropriate in the circumstances,' he says. 'Actually I think it *is* completely inappropriate in the circumstances, but to be quite honest they're fucked-up circumstances . . . Anyway, I was wondering, and I completely understand if you'd rather not, but would you like to go for dinner with me on Thursday?'

My heart soars like the doves, circling high in the clouds and turning loop-the-loops. I'm going for dinner with Milo! On Thursday! Then I remember what's happening on Thursday and my heart plummets back to earth.

'I'm so sorry, I can't do Thursday,' I say, reluctantly. 'I've got a Krav Maga lesson.'

'Okay, how about the following Tuesday?'

I wince. 'No, sorry. Banjo society.'

Milo's hopeful expression wavers. 'Uh, Friday, then?'

'I've arranged to have dinner with my friends. We're going on a trek in Tibet and that's the night we earmarked for making a list of things to pack. Sorry.'

By now Milo is clearly thinking I'm making all of this

up, but before I can reassure him he shoots me a resigned smile and says, 'Oh well, can't blame a guy for trying. Take care, Percy,' and starts to walk away.

For a moment I'm struck dumb with panic. Christ, he's surprisingly fast – in just a few moments he'll be back at the front door and then . . . *Quick, Percy, do something!*

'I'm free a week on Wednesday, if you are?' I virtually scream.

Milo stops in his tracks. 'Are you absolutely sure? Not abseiling down the Shard? Rowing solo across the Pacific? Doing a spot of lion-taming, perhaps?'

I shake my head.

'Dinner with me, then?'

'I would love that,' I say, happiness bursting over me like a shower of confetti.

Then I hold my breath, waiting for the usual torrent of debate and doubt to flood my mind about whether this is really, truly right, but as Milo starts walking back towards me and breaks into a smile, sending my insides tumbling helplessly with desire, I realise that there is nothing in my mind apart from one simple thought.

So there you are. I've been waiting for you.

ACKNOWLEDGEMENTS

Like Gwyneth Paltrow at the Oscars – but without the pink ballgown and sobbing – this is where I get to say a huge, heartfelt THANK-YOU to the following wonderful people:

Rowan Lawton of Furniss Lawton and Kathryn Taussig and her team at Quercus, for believing in the book (and me), supporting me throughout the writing process and giving me all the best ideas.

Freya Williams, Kirsty Tyler, Charlotte Hardman and Haydee 'Yaya' Dullas, for reasons they will hopefully know.

All my friends whose names/appearances I shamelessly stole for my characters, especially the real-life Charlie.

Sunni, David and Anna of the Camden Coffee House – aka the best coffee in London – for the daily caffeine and chat.

Michael Bublé, for letting me borrow his song title. At least, I assume he's okay with me borrowing it . . .

Dad, for generating the spark of the idea that became EROS Tech while we were walking Bonnie and Lara.

Daisy and Bear, my beloved *raisons d'être*, without whose input this book would have been finished a year earlier.

Above all to OJP – the one in seven billion – without whom none of the magic would ever happen.

And finally, thank YOU for reading this book, I really hope you've enjoyed it. If you fancy a chat you can find me at www.catewoods.com.

THAT TIME I GOT DUMPED BY A VERY FAMOUS SINGER

Being a ghostwriter is a bit like being an actor – without the fame or money – in that before you get the job you usually have to go for an 'audition'. This involves meeting the subject of the book (i.e. the person whose name will be on the cover) so they can check you're not a stalker. And, like an actor, you need a thick-ish skin for the occasional rejection.

Over the years I'm proud to admit that I've been turned down by some very famous names. Reasons for not hiring me have included 'not funny enough', 'too old' and 'not Northern'. You can't take it personally – I've had the chance to meet some very interesting people and besides, if you're going to write your memoirs at nineteen then it's no wonder you consider anyone over twenty-five to be ancient. Good luck with finding a teenage ghostwriter, love.

Yet there *is* one huge star who turned me down for a job – and it's been bugging me ever since – because IT SHOULD HAVE BEEN MEEEE!

What happened was this. I got a call from my agent who told me that an A-list celebrity was going to write her autobiography and, by some miracle, I was on the list of ten ghostwriters who were being considered. So far, so routine.

The weird thing was, however, my agent had no idea who the celebrity was. Not a clue. Her identity was being kept a secret because she was so famous that if we knew who it was our tiny muggle brains might explode – either that, or they wanted to keep news of her autobiography out of the papers at this early stage. Anyway, the star's PA was going to meet the ten candidates on her behalf, and would then select the final two who would be granted an audience with her majesty, which effectively meant that the ten of us would be in the strange situation of going for an interview for a job that we knew absolutely nothing about.

HOWEVER. The star's people hadn't banked on the fact that I used to be a celebrity journalist and as soon as I heard the name of the star's PA – let's call her Daisy – I knew beyond a doubt the identity of the woman in question. Let's just say she was a Very Famous Singer (VFS).

Well, I was literally giddy with excitement. Not only was I up for this amazing job, I had an immediate advantage over all the other candidates because *I knew who she was!*

Armed with this covert intel, my meeting with Daisy went brilliantly. I mentioned how much I loved dogs (knowing the VFS owned one herself) and I geared our conversation towards subjects that I knew the VFS would find interesting, all without letting on that I had any idea who she actually was. Two days later my agent called to tell me I was down to the final two. This was *so* in the bag . . .

And so it came to pass that a week later I arrived at an office in central London, breezily confident that I would ace this interview as I had the one with Daisy. And there she was: a titchy, tiny, perfectly symmetrical, pocket-sized package of hair and teeth. Smiley and radiant. Heart-meltingly beautiful, obviously. But with a look in her eyes that said, *I will SLAY YOU if you cross me.*

Suddenly, I was horrifically nervous.

'Ooh, I love your cardi,' she said softly, still smiling.

'It's from Monsoon, but it's last year's I'm afraid.' Then I remembered who I was talking to. 'Although you could probably just phone up and they'd make you one for free. In fact, they'd probably pay you to wear it! Or you can have mine – but it'll cost you! HAH!'

She continued to smile, icily polite. My nerves kicked up a gear.

'So, what sort of books do you like to read?' she asked.

My mind instantly went blank. I love reading, I am a bloody *writer* for goodness sake, but I couldn't think of anything at all, except . . .

'*Beowulf*,' I said, remembering a book I had skimmed at university, fifteen years ago. 'The epic Anglo Saxon poem. Have you, um, read it? It's really quite good.'

'No, I haven't.' *Of course she hasn't, you div. It's an epic Anglo Saxon poem.*

'And I believe you used to work for *Closer* magazine?' she went on.

I flinched, vividly remembering the time her publicist had phoned me in the office and screamed at me for five minutes because of a story I'd written about the VFS's love life.

'Yes, but only doing the interviews, I didn't write the gossip stories,' I said quickly. 'That was . . . someone else. Not my sort of thing *at all*. I just did the chats. Nice, friendly, PR-approved stuff, you know? Besides, that was ages ago . . .' And then, that was it. By some invisible sign the VFS instructed her people that I was to be dismissed. I hadn't even had a chance to tell her how much I loved dogs.

She said that it was lovely to meet me, but her eyes were telling a different story. They were telling me she wouldn't work with me if I were the last person on earth.

Sure enough, I didn't get the job. To be fair, it would have been a tough gig: the publisher wanted the book finished quickly, and access to the VFS sounded horrifically limited. I don't even like her music that much. And yet . . .

Why didn't you like me, Very Famous Singer? What on earth is wrong with me? We could have been *friends*. YOU COULD HAVE BORROWED MY CARDI!